THE MISSING WITNESS

TAM MAY

For my dearest friend, Becky (1960 - 2025), whose warmth, encouragement and support lingers on in my heart and inspires me.

CHAPTER 1

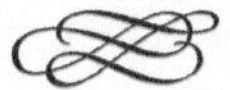

It was an unusually hot summer in Gyver that August of 1921. All the windows were open in the Grave house. Every so often, Agnes, the housekeeper, regarded the ornate fireplace with a loathsome stare as if its menacing grate was trying to devour what little air there was.

Eve, the eldest of the Grave sisters, was in her usual place on the sofa, the *Gyver Bee* in her lap. Helena, the middle sister, had her nose buried in one of her journals. Violet, the youngest, was, as usual, out for the evening, although her older sisters had the satisfaction of knowing she was not tearing up the town in Joe Reid's beat-up Ford but safely behind the Rooty Toot Drugstore's soda fountain with Kitty Markie, serving sandwiches and sundaes and gossiping with her friends.

Felix, Helena's husband, had stayed home for dinner instead of his usual meal "out with friends." He sipped Agnes's excellent coffee, patting his stomach with satisfaction. "Maybe I should have dinner at home more often, my love," he threw out to his wife.

"Maybe you should." Helena did not look up from her journal.

He leaned forward, peering at the title. "*Police Science Chroni-*

cles." He made a face. "Good Lord, I thought you were through with that nonsense."

"I've always been interested in crime science, Felix," she said. "You know that."

"And *you* know I don't like my wife filling her head with gory details," he snapped. "I thought I made my position clear when you and Eve got involved with the Libby Cinder case."

Eve remained silent, straightening the edge of the newspaper.

Helena, as always, remained calm. "As a matter of fact, I'm reading a fascinating article on Mrs. Glessner Lee's Nutshell Studies of Unexplained Deaths."

"Who's what?" he asked.

Helena finally looked up, taking off her reading glasses and rubbing her nose with a little smile. "Mrs. Frances Glessner Lee. She's experimenting with crime scene dioramas."

"You're speaking Greek, my love," Felix said. "We weren't all fortunate enough to indulge our intellects with college learning and eye-opening revelations from rich spinsters like Zadie Hummer who can afford to stick their noses into police business!"

"Helena worked hard for her education, Felix," Eve snapped.

"And *I* worked hard to put bread and milk on the table for my brothers and sisters!" he snapped back.

Eve's voice softened. "I wasn't dismissing that."

Felix put another lump of sugar in his coffee and stirred it. "I'm simply trying to understand."

"Mrs. Glessner Lee is making miniature crime scene reenactments in order to teach detectives how to look for evidence," Helena said patiently.

"Perhaps she ought to come here and teach Oliver Clarke a thing or two."

"Oliver is the county district attorney, not a police detective," Eve reminded him.

"I'm not likely to forget that," Felix snapped. "I expect him to come through the door any minute, flailing his arms helplessly and begging for assistance. And you'd give it to him, wouldn't you?" He eyed her.

Helena dropped her glasses on the rug and picked them up, cleaning them with her napkin. Eve felt a pain in her heart at her younger sister's discomfort. She cleared her throat. "It looks like the veterans are finally going to get the help they need."

"Oh?" Felix inquired.

"'Veterans will be able to cut through all the red tape, as three government agencies —the Bureau of War Risk Insurance, the U.S. Public Health Service, and the Federal Board for Vocational Training— will merge into one place. President Harding signed a bill today to establish the Veterans Bureau,'" Eve read.

"Good for Harding," Helena said.

"It's about damn time," Felix growled.

"Disgraceful how those poor boys have had to suffer, bad economy or no bad economy," Eve said with a sigh. "All that waiting and paperwork to get what they need and deserve."

"It's almost as bad as the injuries they suffered in battle," Felix agreed as he rose. "They get blasted in the trenches and then come home to what? Unemployment is on the rise, and they have to tear their hair out getting acclimated into society and vocational training."

"You talk like you were fighting right there with them," Agnes mumbled, collecting the coffee cups.

Felix glared at her. "I may not have been on the Western Front, but I had friends who were." In a softer tone, he added, "For some of them, their letters are the only thing I have left."

"I didn't mean nothing," the woman murmured as she went out.

"Does the article say anything about the men with shell shock and war neurosis?" Helena asked.

"Not specifically," Eve said. "I imagine the bill covers them all."

"I imagine not," Helena grumbled.

There was a clamor in the hallway and Agnes's voice rose. "Don't you go trailing dirt on my floor, missy!"

Violet rushed in with Kitty and Jimmy, Kitty's beau, in tow. "Eve, you've got to talk to Oliver!"

"Steady there, young man." Felix caught Jimmy by the shoulders. It was clear from the young man's swaying figure that he was not entirely sober. "Some bad whiskey on your breath."

"Nonsense. Best money can buy." Jimmy's words came out slightly slurred.

"Agnes, get Jimmy a strong cup of coffee. Very strong," Eve emphasized.

"Who's at the drugstore now?" Helena looked at Kitty with suspicion.

"Never mind that." Violet waved her away. "They've arrested Hank Convoy!"

"Who's he, Jimmy's bootlegger?" Felix asked, amused.

"Don't be a sap," Kitty snapped. For once, she had a somber look on her face instead of her usual petulant pout. "He's a friend of ours from school."

"He's the one who used to come around and fix the hearse when it was acting up, remember?" Violet asked, a little breathless. "He was two years ahead of me in school."

"I remember." Eve nodded.

"He went off to war and came back last year."

"One of the lucky ones," Felix remarked. "He'll benefit from the Veterans Bureau all right."

"Oh, why don't you blow?" Violet snapped.

"As you wish, madame." He saluted her, and, giving Helena a peck on the cheek, sauntered out.

"Calm down, honey." Eve put her arm around her sister. "Kitty, you and Jimmy sit."

Both obeyed like little children.

"Hank's in jail, and it's all a mistake," Violet insisted.

"Maybe it isn't a mistake," Jimmy said. "Maybe he really did it."

"Oh, shut up!" Kitty barked.

"Did what?" Helena asked. "Vi, make sense."

"Joe Savage came down to the drugstore tonight and was shooting his mouth off about how the sheriff's arrested Hank," said her sister.

"It's probably nothing more than drunk and disorderly," Helena said. "Lots of soldiers have been letting loose since they got back."

"Joe said Hank murdered someone!"

"Murdered!" Eve stared. "That nice kid?"

"He's not a kid anymore," Kitty insisted. "He was old enough to get his brains blown out in the trenches."

"Only he didn't," Jimmy added.

"Maybe Joe's just trying to impress you," Helena suggested. "He's always flirting with you."

"That's what I said," Jimmy insisted. "Nobody believes me."

"Agnes, take Jimmy and Kitty to the kitchen and get them the coffee," Eve ordered.

"I didn't touch a drop of that firewater!" Kitty insisted.

"Nevertheless." Helena rose and pushed both of them at the sour-faced Agnes.

"Eve says coffee, and coffee you'll get!" Agnes growled as she seized both of them by the arm.

Violet breathed a little easier when they were gone. "I didn't ask them to come. Honest."

"Now tell us what happened slowly," Eve commanded.

"Joe came in for a sandwich about a half hour ago," Violet said. "He was being his usual pesky self, and I was ignoring him of course."

"Of course," Helena mumbled.

Glaring at her, Violet continued, "Then I heard him say, 'That friend of yours from the Mold District just got hauled to the station, and Sheriff's got the handcuffs on him.' I said, 'Who in

Sam Hill are you talking about?' and he said, 'How many friends you got from the Mold District?'"

"Get on with it, Vi," Helena snapped.

"He said, 'The Convoy kid. Sheriff says he's going to fry in the electric chair for murder.' Kitty told him he was crazy since there's no electric chair in California." She looked satisfied. "I told her that."

"Brilliant deduction," Helena said dryly. "Now go on."

"Joe said, 'Well, the noose then, and serves him right.' I said, 'And who is Hank supposed to have killed?' Joe said, 'Old army pal of his, I think. And he *did* kill him. He said so to the sheriff and the district attorney.'"

"I think he was just telling you a story, Vi." Helena pressed her hand.

"But it's not just a story," Violet insisted. "We went down to the police station ourselves."

"Who's 'we'?" Eve asked.

"Kitty and me, of course!"

"And Jimmy?" Helena raised an eyebrow.

"Are you kidding?" Violet stared at her. "In his soused state?"

"And the sheriff told you he's arrested Hank for murder?" Eve asked.

"Of course not," said her youngest sister. "He still resents us for solving the Libby Cinder murder instead of him."

"We didn't solve the murder," Helena corrected. "Oliver did. We just helped."

"Oh, applesauce, we solved it and you know it," Violet growled. "Anyway, that old boar of a sheriff wouldn't tell us a thing, but Deputy Elwood hinted Hank was there. He wouldn't tell us anything else."

"Joe Savage could still be wrong," Eve offered.

"That's what we've got to find out." Violet grasped both her sisters' hands.

"We're not policewomen, Vi," Eve protested.

"We're the three Sherlockas, remember?" Violet asked.

"That's your game," Helena said. "I prefer not to think of myself as Sherlock Holmes' sister."

"It's ridiculous for us to go storming into his house and demanding he present the case," Eve added.

"I'm not suggesting that," Violet said. "I'm only saying if we went there and you used a little sweet talk, he'd cough up the whole story."

"Just because he asked for our help once doesn't mean he plans on doing it again," Helena pointed out.

Violet looked from one sister to the other. "All I'm asking for is information about a friend who's been arrested, Eve," she appealed to her sister, her foxlike features melting into a little girl's plea. "I know you don't like going to Oliver's house now."

Eve stiffened. "I don't know what you mean, Vi."

"I know Ellen's been a big snob lately, soft-soaping the Brenas people," Violet continued. "I know she's been treating everyone in town as if they're no better than fruit flies, including Mrs. Beaton and her bunch. But she'll probably be in bed already, and we'll have Oliver all to ourselves. If you asked him, he would tell you anything you wanted to know."

"You talk as if I'm one of those vamps from the moving pictures," Eve said warily.

"Well, if Oliver weren't married —"

"Vi!" Eve's voice shook. "I don't want to hear you talk like that!"

Her youngest sister heaved a sigh and turned to her other sister. "Helena, make her go."

"I think we should all go," Helena said simply. "He can't put us all off."

"He'll think we're all pouncing on him at once," Eve objected.

Violet rose. "If neither of you will go, I'll go myself! Me and Kitty."

"Lord," Helena mumbled.

Eve put her hands on her sister's shoulders. "If it means that much to you, darling, we'll go. But we'll be making fools of ourselves."

"Hot dog!" Violet hugged her. "I'll get Kitty and Jimmy out of here." She straightened her skirt. "We've got Sherlocka business to attend to."

"Heaven knows it won't be the first time we've made fools of ourselves for that girl," Helena remarked as her sister scurried out of the room.

"We might do someone else some good, though," Eve said softly as she thought about Hank Convoy, the kind young man who had willingly fixed their hearse.

~~~~~

The warm breeze filtered through the open windows as they sped in the Model T Ford, Violet lavishing her usual complaints about the car and the usual hints that five years was far too old for an automobile in this modern age. Her praise of the new Ford models fell, as usual, on deaf ears since Eve considered older cars to be safer and Helena didn't care what they drove as long as all four wheels turned.

The lights were on downstairs in the gray house with the blue trim where Oliver lived. Jennie, the Clarke maid, answered the door with her usual grumpy expression. "The lady of the house does not wish to see callers after dinner," she said in a haughty tone and proceeded to close the door.

Violet pushed it back, nearly hitting the girl in the face. "Isn't it lucky we're not here to see the lady of the house, then? We've come to see the man of the house. Oliver!" Her screech echoed through the doorway.

"Vi!" Eve scolded her. "You needn't yell like a market woman."

"Oh, Mr. District Attorney!" Violet sang out, ignoring her sister as she walked down the hallway.

Eve and Helena followed her, and all three sisters found the Clarkes in the living room. Eve couldn't help but marvel at how,
~~~~~

even with its pale tones, it was as stuffy as a Victorian parlor. Oliver, his handsome and lively face a little pinched, was pressing tobacco into the cup of a pipe. Ellen sat across from him, her legs crossed, filing her nails. She did not even look up to greet the sisters. Eve felt at once as if a layer of fog had filled the room with a thick tension, but she realized the fog had been there before they entered.

"We're sorry to disturb you, Oliver," she began.

"I'm always glad to see the Grave sisters," he said. "What's with you, youngster?" He grinned at Violet. "I thought you were perfecting the cream on top of your chocolate sundaes."

"We have something important to discuss with you, Oliver." Violet plunked herself down on the sofa beside him. "It's police business." She looked pointedly at Ellen.

"Indeed?" Ellen said in a chilly tone.

"Why did you have Hank Convoy arrested?" Violet asked.

"Vi, maybe you'd better explain your interest in Hank," Helena said as she leaned against the back of an empty chair. "Otherwise, Oliver might think it's just idle curiosity."

"I don't mind a little idle curiosity," he said.

"I should say you wouldn't!" Violet put her hand on her hips. "After we helped you solve that case this winter —"

"Really!" Ellen put down her nail file.

"Really!" Violet shot back.

"Ellen, I think we can get the ladies some coffee, don't you?" He glanced at Jennie waiting in the corner. Her sour expression was more pronounced as she looked to her mistress for instructions.

Eve said quickly, "We've had our coffee, thank you, Ellen."

The woman sank back into the seat.

"Hank and I went to school together," Violet explained. "We're still friends. I see him all the time in the drugstore, so I know he's no criminal."

"See him all the time, eh?" He raised his eyebrow.

"Don't be a goop!" she snapped. "We were two years apart but he never treated me like a kid. And now Joe Savage said he's been arrested for murder!"

Oliver's eyes rolled. "I'll never get used to how people gossip in a small town!"

"Not in all small towns, dear," Ellen said quietly. "Some towns are very discreet."

The glare she received from her husband made Eve think this was part of an argument they were having before the sisters arrived. "It does take some getting used to," she said meekly.

"And you want to know if it's true?" Oliver guessed.

"I know it's true," she declared. "Kitty and I went down to the jail and saw for ourselves. What I want to know is the details."

"Details?"

"The lowdown," she said. "What have you got on him?"

"Don't sound like the gangsters, Vi," Helena snapped. In a more polite tone, she said, "As he's a friend, we wanted to see if we could help."

"It's none of their business, don't you think, dear?" Ellen asked. "They're not working for the police, after all."

"The headlines will be in the newspaper tomorrow anyway," Oliver said with a sigh. "I couldn't keep Jack Shane out of it this time."

"I'm not surprised," Helena snorted. "In school we used to call him Bloodhound Jack."

"How terribly quaint the way you all have nicknames for one another," Ellen said icily.

"Would you like to know what yours is?" Violet growled.

Eve put her hand on her sister's shoulder. "We realize we have no right to know as citizens, Oliver. But as friends of the boy —"

"I understand, Eve," he said. "I can't tell you everything, of course."

"Just the juicy details," Violet said as she settled onto the couch.

"Tell us what you can," Helena said.

Oliver glanced at his wife. "Ellen, maybe you prefer to go to bed."

It seemed like every feature in his wife's face stiffened. "I suppose I have a right to hear the 'juicy details,' as Violet insists on referring to them, even more than they do." She threw her head back. "Jennifer, you may retire."

The sulky look on the maid's face told Eve she would have loved to stay and listen.

CHAPTER 2

*I*t began very early, about five o'clock that morning. The phone rang, waking up both of them, even though Oliver had tiptoed to the hallway, closing the bedroom door behind him so as not to wake up Ellen. He knew it was for him.

"Peterson here." The county coroner's voice was stoic. "We found a body you should come and take a look at."

"Where?" Oliver asked.

"Down in Marlestra. It's in the alleyway off of Dean Street near what used to be the artillery factory building."

As Oliver drove through the twilight, he thought about why Mr. Peterson had sounded so exacting. The Mold District, as the locals called the neighborhood, housed most of the crime in Gyver and although murder was usually not among them, it seemed to Oliver a little out-of-the-way for Mr. Peterson to be taking such precautions.

He parked on Dean Street next to the office building Mr. Peterson mentioned. Though he didn't know the area well, there was no mistaking the place. A large garbage truck was parked right at the entrance to the alleyway, blocking it from view of onlookers. Surprisingly, there were a handful of them, mostly men with early shifts at the lumber company. Oliver nodded at one of Sheriff Warner's assistant deputies as he let him through the blockade they had created out of crates.

Oliver walked down the alleyway which was lit up like a Fourth of July parade. He commended Sheriff Warner and his men for being prepared with lanterns and candles to light the sidewalk and the beacon lights that were directed at the far corner where the alleyway almost met with Wadding Street.

The sheriff and Deputy Elwood were there, their uniforms a little haphazardly put on. Mr. Peterson greeted him, and he was glad to see Dr. Myers was already examining the body. George Parks, the town photographer engaged to take pictures of crime scenes, was already at work, as was Franki Dencker, an art teacher, who was doing sketches. He was even surprised to see Daniel Frazer standing behind Mr. Peterson, his hands in his pockets, staring down at the stretched dark figure on the ground.

Sheriff Warner came forward and said in a soft tone, "Dan was having dinner with Mr. Peterson so he came along. I told him this ain't his jurisdiction, but he says he wants to help."

Oliver held out his hand to Daniel. "Morning, Dan, Mr. Peterson. What have we got here?"

"The man's name is William Hicks," Mr. Peterson said. "People around here call him 'Wild Bill.'"

"Wild Bill, eh?" Oliver cocked his head. "I don't think he's one I've met."

"You wouldn't, Mr. Clarke," said the sheriff. "He's one of the boys who came home from the war only last year."

"He's not much of a boy," Daniel remarked. "He's in his mid-thirties if he's a day."

"Who found him?" Oliver asked.

"Henderson brothers." Sheriff Warner jerked his head toward the garbage truck where Oliver saw two young men in white uniforms standing with their arms folded, peering into the dark alleyway.

"Anybody talk to them?"

"I did," Daniel said. "They came here on their usual rounds. They moved the garbage cans, found Wild Bill lying there and immediately called the police."

"They said they didn't touch nothing," Sheriff Warner said. "Guess only the doc can say for sure if that's true."

Oliver glanced at the sheriff. "I take it Wild Bill wasn't exactly a stranger to you."

"You mean, had he been in trouble with the law?" The sheriff shrugged. "We hauled him in for a drunk and disorderly charge a couple of times, but that's it. He had a reputation for being a little too fond of a private poker game. You know how these ex-soldiers are."

"He's not an ex-soldier, Sheriff," Daniel said in a stiff tone. "He's a veteran with several medals to his name. Mr. Peterson told me he was just awarded a medal and some prize money from the Legion of Valor."

"Legion of Valor." Sheriff Warner sniffed. "I ain't knocking those guys, you understand, but if you want to talk valor, you look at every man on every police force these days. We win wars every single day."

"No one is disputing that, Sheriff." Oliver patted him on the back. Then, he eyed Mr. Peterson. "That's what this is all about, isn't it?"

The sheriff stared. "I don't get you. What's what all about?"

"This urgency," Oliver said. "Because he was a veteran."

Mr. Peterson was quiet for a moment. "As you know, Oliver, this country hasn't done so well by the ex-soldiers these past few years —"

"That ain't up to us," Sheriff Warner insisted. "That's up to the government."

"A lot of people aren't happy about the bread lines and the soup kitchens," Mr. Peterson continued. "Especially for the decorated soldiers. So when a veteran is killed, it doesn't make us look good."

Oliver glared at Mr. Peterson, feeling his temper rise. "I make every murder in my jurisdiction a top priority, whether it's a veteran or somebody's grandma."

"Of course you do, Oliver," Daniel said kindly. "It's my priority too."

"This ain't your case, Mr. Frazer," the sheriff insisted.

"Mr. Peterson asked me to come," Daniel said in a stiff tone. "When he or Oliver tells me to leave, I'll go."

"Thanks, Dan." Oliver pressed his arm. "Who called the photographer and sketch artist?"

"That was Dan's idea," said the coroner. "I think it's too early, but —"

"The crime scene's probably already been trampled on by those people." Oliver shot a glance at the small crowd still beyond the garbage truck. "You can't keep the people back, Mr. Clarke," Deputy Elwood chimed in. "Or the press."

"Press?" Oliver shot a look around.

"I thought I saw Jack Shane around here a minute ago."

"Well, somebody find him," Oliver barked. "I don't want this getting into the *Gyver Bee* before we've had a chance to figure out what's going on."

"I'll tell you what's going on." This came from Dr. Myers who had now joined them, straightening his coat over his small frame.

"Glad you could be here, Doctor." Oliver couldn't keep the sarcasm out of his voice. He recalled the long wait for the doctor to show up when they had found Libby Cinder by the side of the river earlier that year.

"As it happens, Mr. Clarke, I was just getting back from a patient visit when the sheriff called, so I was already dressed and with my bag." Dr. Myers gave him a pointed look.

"Well, out with it," Oliver said in a gruff tone.

"The man died from a bullet wound to the stomach."

"When?"

"Last night sometime," said Dr. Myers. "Between ten and midnight, I'd say. Probably closer to ten or eleven."

"Well after dinner, then," Daniel remarked.

"What's it matter?" The sheriff glanced at him.

"It might matter a great deal," the young Moody district attorney snapped.

"We'll only know that after the autopsy," said Dr. Myers. "I can't get the bullet out just yet, so you'll have that in the morning too."

"Bullet to the stomach." Mr. Peterson flinched a little. "Pretty bad way to go."

"Any way's a bad way to go," Dr. Myers remarked. "He probably died within five minutes, if that eases your mind."

"Just isn't right," Deputy Elwood lamented. "Man fights for his country, manages to survive battle, and then comes home just to get shot and dumped in an alleyway."

"It ain't like we haven't seen it before," his superior reminded him. "Only this killer was a little cleverer than most. He hid the body behind the trash cans."

"And they happened to send the garbage trucks out this morning," Mr. Peterson added.

"Our killer couldn't have known that," Sheriff Warner said.

"Maybe he wasn't as clever as you think," Dr. Myers said. "He moved the man after he shot him."

"How can you tell?" Oliver asked.

"The blood went out of the internal organs," the doctor said. "There's some on his shirt and coat. If he'd been shot here, he would have bled internally with hardly anything to show for it on his clothes."

"Anything else?" Oliver asked.

"The position of the body isn't consistent with the way a man would have fallen after being shot to the chest."

"George!" Oliver's deep voice filled the alleyway with a

pleasant growl. The photographer appeared. "Take some photos of the body and the surrounding area. Use all the lights you need."

"Right away, Mr. Clarke," the young man said.

"Miss Decker!"

"Yes, Mr. Clarke?" The woman appeared in the circle of light, her short hair framing her face.

"We need a sketch of the body quickly. Every last detail, including the position of the arms and legs."

"You'll get it." She saluted him and joined George.

Oliver turned to the doctor again. "You think the body was dragged and left here. From where to where?"

Dr. Myers shrugged, rolling down his sleeves. "That's your headache, Mr. Clarke, not mine."

"You mean our headache," grumbled Sheriff Warner.

"I can tell you more about the bullet and the wound when you get the body to me for the autopsy," said Dr. Myers.

"How about the Grave Funeral Home mortuary?" Oliver suggested.

The doctor looked annoyed. "I have my own equipment, as I told you the last time."

"And we established the last time that Mrs. Wright's equipment is much more advanced than yours," Oliver barked back.

"Well, naturally, that's her job," he said. "But we don't need anything fancy, Mr. Clarke. I've extracted many bullets in my time."

"I'm sure Helena wouldn't dream of interfering, Dr. Myers," Daniel chimed in. "She respects other people's work."

"She respects my work so much that she took it upon herself to examine Miss Cinder's body before I could even get to it," the doctor sneered. "Don't think I didn't know about that!"

"I agree with Dr. Myers," said the sheriff. "We got no use for those Grave girls in this."

"What about the hospital?" Daniel suggested. "They're well equipped."

"Good idea," Mr. Peterson said with a nod. "I'll drive you down and get the paperwork started for this crime so we can get to it."

"I'll bring in Mrs. Hicks to identify the body as soon as I can," said Oliver. "If Jack's around, I don't want her finding out about it in the morning paper before we've had a chance to tell her."

The coroner glanced at Oliver. "I leave it in your hands."

A sharp, warm breeze blew in just as the men headed toward Wadding Street. The scent of hot tar and decaying vegetables made Oliver think of the city streets of San Francisco on a warm night where anything, including murder, could happen.

"Somebody bring a flashlight!" he barked.

Deputy Elwood appeared, holding one in his hand.

"Shine it down on the street," Oliver commanded.

As the lawman did so, Oliver saw immediately the wet streak that, even with the dim gray sky, bore a red glare. "Let's see where it begins, shall we?"

With the sheriff's and deputy's help, he found the beginning of the trail which started about two thirds of the way across the alley and ended where Wild Bill lay sprawled in the corner near the wall of the office building.

"Just a few feet from that door." Sheriff Warner pointed to the house across the way.

"Who lives there?" Oliver asked.

"I don't know these people, Mr. Clarke," said Sheriff Warner.

"Looks like you'll need to find out," he said.

"I got in my head to talk to all the neighbors here," said the sheriff. "Somebody might've heard something."

"They wouldn't talk if they did," his deputy advised.

"This ain't Falcon Hill," the sheriff agreed. "But people are always on the lookout for somebody with a gun or knife." He glanced at the body. "Maybe he should've been a little less careless, eh?"

Oliver shone the light on Wild Bill. He was a tall, lanky sort of man who, as Daniel said, was no longer a boy and hadn't been for some time. Oliver guessed him to be in his late thirties. The narrow face was long and rough with stubble, but the suit and coat he wore showed a preference for style. The legs were thrust out straight and one arm was by his side. The other was bent a little.

"Certainly was a sharp dresser," Sheriff Warner remarked.

"That jacket's a little heavy for this weather," Oliver said. "Do you notice something about that hand, Sheriff?"

Sheriff Warner nodded. "Bent like he was holding something."

Oliver grinned. "Can't say you don't know your business."

"Might've been a wallet," the sheriff offered. "We didn't find nothing on him when we searched him."

"Too bad we haven't the fingerprint expert," Deputy Elwood remarked. "If he was robbed, somebody might have left fingerprints."

"I'm still trying to get the expert approved," Oliver said. "But I don't think whoever it was would have left a mark."

"Nah, too smart," Sheriff Warner said. "Only by chance we found him this fast because of the trash."

"Here, son, hold this." Oliver handed the flashlight to Deputy Elwood. "Keep it shined on him. I'm going through his pockets."

"We've already done that, Mr. Clarke," the sheriff said.

"Maybe you missed something." Oliver glanced at him. "I used to do this kind of work too, you know."

"Used to," Sheriff Warner mumbled.

Oliver carefully dug into the outside pockets of the trench coat and the pants pockets, careful not to touch the bloody areas. He unbuttoned the coat and laid the sides open. "He must have had half his belongings on him."

"Why do you say that, sir?" Deputy Elwood asked.

"He's got more pockets on that coat than a woodpecker has homes," Sheriff Warner agreed. "Ain't none of them filled, though."

"They may have been filled," Oliver said. "A man doesn't wear a jacket with that many pockets unless he plans on taking things with him."

"Too bad whatever he had on him didn't keep him from danger," the sheriff remarked.

CHAPTER 3

One of the junior assistant deputies who had been sent by the sheriff to scout around the alley appeared and handed the sheriff a small box. Inside, there were a few cigar butts and cigar ash.

"That might have been left here ages ago," Oliver said.

"Not that brand," Sheriff Warner said. "Cuban cigars are hard to get, especially for these people."

"Maybe it was from one of the executives in the old factory building," Deputy Elwood offered. "They've been renting out office space since the end of the war."

"McCay!" the sheriff called over his shoulder, and the assistant deputy who had handed him the box appeared. "Where'd you find this?"

"Over there, Sheriff." The young man pointed a boney finger at the house closest to Wadding Street.

"Right outside the door?" Oliver asked.

"Nearby, sir."

"Didn't I tell you to always label evidence as soon as you find it?" Sheriff Warner scolded.

The young man fidgeted. "Miss Decker drew a picture of it, Sheriff."

"Get Miss Decker over here," Oliver ordered.

The young woman stepped gingerly around the wavy line of dried blood. "You asked for me, Mr. Clarke?"

"I'd like to see those sketches."

"I'm not through yet." The young lady was firm.

"Show us what you got so far," Sheriff Warner snapped. "This ain't no time for artistic temperament."

She continued to frown as she handed Oliver the sketch pad.

He flipped through the pages until he found what he was looking for. The sketch of the corner where Wadding met the alleyway was neatly done, and the detail of the small strip of grass growing along the side of the house led to three steps before the door and a small patch of ground with the cigar butts and ash.

He showed it to the sheriff. "Might be Wild Bill was visiting someone in the neighborhood, and they went out to smoke a cigar after dinner."

"And then he got shot," Sheriff Warner agreed as he motioned toward his deputy. "Time to question everybody."

"I'll stick around here." Oliver handed the sketch pad back to Franki.

"You might want to have a word with the gentleman of the press." She threw a glance toward Dean Street. Standing in the light was Jack Shane.

"You want me to chase him out of here, Mr. Clarke?" Sheriff Warner looked as if he relished the idea.

"No, I'll talk to him." Oliver sighed. "We can't keep the press away forever."

Jack always reminded Oliver of a skunk with his large nose and beady eyes and in the way he slunk around. His smile showed too many teeth as he said, "Morning, Mr. Clarke. Any statement to give to the press about this shooting?"

"Nobody said it was a shooting," Oliver said sharply.

"Dr. Myers did," said the young man. "Wild Bill Hicks was shot in the stomach, died from internal bleeding. You know why they called him 'Wild' Bill, don't you?"

"No." Oliver crossed his arms. "But I'm sure you do."

"He was quick on the draw," said the young man, ignoring the district attorney's sarcasm. "He could get mad quicker than a grizzly bear."

"I'll keep that in mind, Jack," said Oliver. "Now, get out of here!"

But Jack seemed unperturbed. He moved a lantern that one of the assistant deputies had left lying on the ground a little sideways with his foot. The light shone on the line of blood leading toward the trash cans. "Looks like someone tried to hide him, eh?"

"Listen, Jack," Oliver's voice was harsh, "I'm asking you to keep the story out of your paper for twenty-four hours. Give me a chance to break the news to his relations."

"You mean his mother," Jack said. "That's who he's been living with."

"All right, his mother," Oliver corrected. "I don't want her knowing about it from the newspaper."

"It's not against the law to print a story, Mr. Clarke." The man sniffed.

"No, it's just against all decent human instinct to print one before the mother of the victim has a chance to identify the body," Oliver snarled. "Now get out of here! And don't mention the body was moved either."

The young man grinned, showing even more teeth. "I didn't say the body was moved. I just said it looked like someone tried to hide him."

"The sheriff's just itching to arrest you, you know," Oliver said. "I might even let him."

"Freedom of the press, sir," the young man reminded him with a salute as he slunk off.

"Young punk," Oliver growled. He watched as Jack sidled up to Franki, whose head was bent down to the sketch pad. "Miss Decker!" he shouted. "Don't let that reporter see anything!"

Franki turned over the pad and glared at Jack.

"George!" Oliver motioned toward him. "I think we got all we needed here, so go home now, and get those photographs to me as soon as you can."

"Yes, sir!" George grinned, collapsing his camera.

"And don't let Jack Shane have even a peek at them." Oliver shook a finger at him. "If I find even a thumbprint smear in the morning paper —"

"Don't you worry, Mr. Clarke," the young man promised. "I kept him away from the Libby Cinder photographs, didn't I?"

"Good man." Oliver patted his cheek. "Miss Decker," he addressed Franki, who was lingering behind George, "the same goes for you. Bring those sketches to my office as soon as you can and under no circumstances allow Jack or his brother Abe to get even a peek at them."

"I'd just as soon cuff them on the ear," Frankie said with certainty. "Just like when we were kids."

Oliver roared with laughter and waved at them as they made their way to Dean Street.

Waldo Henderson, his puffed face looking tired, approached Oliver. "Mr. Clarke, can we go now? We've got to continue our rounds, you know. The garbage ain't going to get dumped by itself."

"Sure thing," Oliver said. "Thanks for helping keep the crowd at bay."

"They're mostly gone now," he said with a grin. "The workmen, that is. Now it's the housewives with nothing better to do."

Sheriff Warner and Deputy Elwood came back to the alleyway. By this time, a pale light had broken the dawn. The sheriff's face was grim.

"Sheriff, can't you send some men to get those people out of here?" Oliver indicated the edge of the alley where the garbage truck had now pulled out, exposing a gathering of about ten people, most of them women with bandanas on their heads and apron dresses.

"We'd better," the sheriff agreed. "Or Jack'll start getting to them too, and there'll be a lot of fanciful stories in the papers." He dispatched two of the assistant deputies to deal with the crowd. "Jack already talked to the neighbors before we did."

"Beat us to everyone," the deputy said with a nod. "Can't say Jack lets the grass grow under his feet."

"You say the word, and I'll arrest him for obstruction," Sheriff Warner said.

"Let him go," Oliver said. "Did you get anything from the neighbors?"

"Plenty." The sheriff nodded. "Plenty of nothing, that is."

Oliver chuckled. "The working neighborhoods aren't as friendly to the police as the upper classes, eh?"

"We've gotten opposition from the Falcon Hill bunch too," Deputy Elwood said.

"We got some names at any rate." The sheriff nodded at his deputy, who took out his pad. "The Kramers—theirs is the house over here on Dean Street—heard nothing, saw nothing." He grimaced. "I ain't exactly their favorite citizen in Gyver, though. Their kid was involved in some petty crime in high school."

"That their back door?" Oliver indicated a worn entrance further away.

Sheriff Warner nodded. "They did tell us the house behind theirs that enters from Wadding Street belongs to Annie Convoy. We tried knocking on her door but there was no answer."

"At six-thirty in the morning?" Oliver glanced at his watch.

"The Kramers told us she was talking about some woman's

baby being due any day," the sheriff said. "She might have had to go out."

"She's a midwife, Mr. Clarke," Deputy Elwood chimed in.

"The Convoy back door's the closest to where we found the cigar butts, isn't it?" Oliver glanced at it.

"Seems like it," said the sheriff.

"Who else did you talk to?"

"Henry and Selma Blake," Sheriff Warner continued. "Theirs is the house right next to the Convoys on Wadding."

"They saw something?" Oliver's eyes were alert.

"Just Wild Bill knocking on the front door of the Convoy house," said the sheriff. "They happened to be out on the front porch."

"When was this?" Oliver asked.

"They say about seven or seven-fifteen last night."

"Around dinnertime, then." Oliver pressed his fist into his hand. "So he came to have dinner with the Convoys."

"That's what they think," said Sheriff Warner. "And by Hank Convoy's invitation, most likely."

"They were together in the army," Deputy Elwood supplied.

His superior glared at him. "Why didn't you tell us that before?"

The young deputy sheriff didn't flinch at the severe tone. "I heard they had some kind of falling out, so I didn't think it was important."

"Everything is important in a crime, Deputy!" the sheriff said. "You oughta know that by now."

"Don't be hard on the man, Sheriff," Oliver said.

"They must have patched things up," the deputy offered. "Mr. Blake said everything seemed friendly-like."

"There's friendly and then there's friendly," his superior said with a knowing look. "Don't always trust what witnesses say at face value, Deputy."

The young man nodded.

"The Anthonys were the last," said Sheriff Warner. "They live in back of the Blakes on Dean Street. Frank Anthony says he thinks he might have heard a car backfiring but that ain't unusual for this neighborhood."

"Did he say when?"

The sheriff snorted. "He's not the type to look at a clock."

"He did say it was sometime after dinner," Deputy Elwood said.

"Car backfiring, eh?" Oliver leaned his head back. "Or a gun, maybe?"

"I thought of that," said Sheriff Warner. "I asked him how far away it sounded. He said it was a little muffed."

"That's not surprising," Oliver said. "Their house is pretty far away from the alleyway." He rubbed his chin. "Anything else?"

Sheriff Warner threw his head toward the alleyway. "The office people get out at five-thirty. Somebody might have been working late, though."

"I doubt any of the offices are on the first floor," Oliver said. "And no windows on this side for anybody to see anything." He glanced up at the three-story building. "I think our best bet would be to find Hank Convoy and talk to him."

"I'm with you, Mr. Clarke," Sheriff Warner said. "I think the guy did it. Can't tell what these doughboys will do. Life ain't so grand for them since they came back from the war."

"I'm not ready to make a commitment to the guilty party yet, Sheriff." Oliver gave him a sharp look. "There's still too much we don't know. But if Wild Bill came to see the Convoys last night, it's a good place to start."

~~~~~

Oliver would have preferred breaking the news of Wild Bill's death to his mother alone, but as the sheriff had left the police car with the assistant deputies at the scene to maintain the blockade, he had no choice but to take him and Deputy Elwood along in his Dodge. It was daylight by then, and the streets of the Marlestra
~~~~~

District were now filled with men and women, all in working clothes, on their way to the warehouses and offices along the block.

"Mrs. Hicks might not even be home," Sheriff Warner remarked as he glanced out the car window.

"What's she do?" Oliver asked.

"Waitress at the steakhouse," said the sheriff.

"Pretty posh place," Oliver said with a whistle.

"She's been there for a while," said Deputy Elwood.

"They only open in the afternoon," Oliver pointed out. "I'm guessing she doesn't start her shift until later in the morning."

He was right, as Mrs. Hicks opened the door right away. She was a thin woman, her face strained and bony like a skeleton. Her small figure was wrapped in an oversized dressing gown even though the August heat had already begun to penetrate the air.

Oliver wiped his face with his handkerchief. "Mrs. Hicks?"

"Yes?" Her eyes were on the sheriff and his deputy, their badges gleaming. "Has something happened to my son?"

"May we come in?" he asked gently.

Mrs. Hicks led them to the living room filled with shabby furniture. "Well?" Her tone was expectant.

"Ma'am." Oliver leaned forward, his hands pressed together. "There's been an accident involving your son." He ignored the sheriff's look.

"Accident?" The woman's eyes were now watchful. "With the truck?"

"No, ma'am," said Sheriff Warner. "Your son was found in an alleyway. Shot."

"Shot?" Her voice broke. "Oh, no! No!" She covered her eyes.

"I'm afraid he's dead," Oliver said.

There was a long stretch of silence as Mrs. Hicks sobbed. But she recovered quickly, and when she uncovered her face, it was still. "He was killed, you mean."

"It's not suicide, if that's what you're thinking," Sheriff Warner said.

"I hate to ask you this, ma'am, but we need you to come down to the hospital with us," Oliver said.

"You mean identify the body?" The woman rose, giving a few sniffs. "Just give me ten minutes to get dressed."

"I'm sorry we have to —"

"I'm all right," she said in a resolved tone. "I've seen my share of tragedy in this life, Mr. Clarke. My husband died when Bill was ten, and we had to scrape by. Then Bill went to war, and it was worrying about him every day."

"It's hard on the mothers," Sheriff Warner agreed.

It was a few hours later when Oliver, the sheriff, and Deputy Elwood drove down to the police station. Mrs. Hicks had kept her composure until Dr. Myers wheeled the body out, and she saw her son's gray but peaceful face.

Oliver decided he would hold off questioning her until the next day and called George Griffin, the owner of the Buckeye Steakhouse, who sent another waitress to the hospital to take Mrs. Hicks home and stay with her. There was still the tenseness in the pit of his stomach, a feeling that stayed with him whenever he had to speak with a victim's relatives.

At the station, Sheriff Warner dispatched Deputy Elwood to gather all the assistant deputies with orders to "Pull them out of bed if you have to" and scour the town looking for Hank Convoy.

"Do they know him?" Oliver sipped at the flat coffee one of the assistant deputies had given him.

"More or less," Sheriff Warner said. "Some of them even went to the same boot camp."

Oliver was thoughtful for a moment. "You notice something about the blood on the street, Sheriff?"

"Eh?"

"It wasn't just the trail."

"I don't get you, Mr. Clarke."

Oliver leaned back in the hard wooden chair. "I was looking at those sketches Miss Decker made of the blood. There were some splatters outside the trail."

"Well, there would be with the impact of the bullet to the stomach," the sheriff said.

"I'm not so sure," Oliver murmured.

Sheriff Warner eyed him. "What are you driving at?"

"You think someone like Wild Bill who's won medals for battle and trained in combat would let someone draw a gun on him without fighting back?" Oliver asked.

"A gun's a gun," the sheriff insisted. "Don't matter if it's an assassin or your Aunt Minnie who pulls it on you."

"If Hank did shoot him," Oliver said slowly, "Wild Bill wouldn't have gone down without a fight. And if there was a fight, some of that blood might have been Hank's."

"I still don't get you." Sheriff Warner shook his head.

"I think Mr. Clarke is trying to say that Wild Bill would have fought Hank off, and Hank might have gotten injured," Deputy Elwood ventured.

"Good man." Oliver pounded him on the back. "I think we should call the Veterans Hospital in Moody and ask them if they treated Hank for an injury early this morning."

The sheriff squinted. "He'd be stupid to go there. That's the first place we'd look."

"If he was injured badly enough, he might have had no choice," Oliver said.

Sheriff Warner picked up the phone. "Well, since it's the first place we planned on looking anyway —"

A few moments later, he hung up with a grin. "Your hunch was right, Mr. Clarke. Doc on duty says Hank's there all right. Got some kind of deep cut on his arm. I told him to hold Hank until we got there."

Oliver jumped up. "Call off your men and let's go!"

CHAPTER 4

As they drove across the bridge to Moody, the sun was now in its full glory, beating down on the roof of the car. Oliver was vaguely aware they had had no breakfast, but the attention to duty always made his stomach feel like iron.

"Too bad we couldn't get something out of Mrs. Hicks about Wild Bill and Hank today," the sheriff remarked. "Might have given us somewhere to start."

"Considering the state she's in now, I thought it would be better to talk to her tomorrow," said Oliver.

The sheriff glanced at him after a few moments of silence. "You and who else?"

"That's my business."

"You ain't planning on getting the Grave sisters involved with this one, are you?" Sheriff Warner grumbled.

Oliver grinned. "They didn't do too badly by us the last time."

"Women involved in murder!" the sheriff sneered.

Oliver slid down the street past the *Welcome to Moody, Nevada* sign. "If Wild Bill came to the Convoys for dinner, who else would be there other than Hank?"

"His grandmother for sure," said Deputy Elwood. "Probably his sister too."

"She's just a kid," the sheriff said.

"Nevertheless, I'll interview them too," said Oliver.

"The deputy and I could go —"

"I'll interview them," Oliver said firmly. "This is a delicate matter, Sheriff. Her grandson might be involved."

The hospital, though small, had an impressive structure complete with a long stairway between pillars and three floors, all with balcony rooms.

The young doctor the sheriff had spoken to met them at the door. "He's in here." He walked quickly down the hallway.

"When did he get here?" Oliver asked.

"I'd say about seven this morning."

"He's injured pretty bad, then?" Oliver glanced at Sheriff Warner.

The young man threw his head back. "A gash on his right forearm but not as bad as it could have been."

"Did he say anything about it?"

The doctor shrugged. "He said he'd been in a fight. That's all."

Oliver stopped him. "Is that what it looked like to you?"

"It looked like a serious knife wound to me," said the doctor as he threw open a polished white door. "We tried giving him some food with the morphine injection but he wouldn't take anything."

"Morphine?" Oliver frowned. "We need to question him."

"I can't help that." The doctor shrugged. "He's lucid, though a little drowsy and confused."

"Swell!" the sheriff grumbled. "We find our man, and you have to get him hopped up on morpho."

"Hardly 'hopped up.'" The doctor sounded offended.

They entered a small room. A young man was sitting on an examination table.

"Hank Convoy?" Oliver asked.

The young man shot him a look. Like many ex-soldiers, he

had let his hair grow in from the short cut required by military regulations, and the wheat-colored waves sat in disheveled layers on top of his head. His clothes were scruffy with streaks of dry mud, and the right sleeve was torn to the elbow, replaced by a heavy bandage. His blue eyes fell immediately on Sheriff Warner whose uniform lay crisp against his semi-portly form, his badge glaring under the hospital lights. Oliver recognized the dubious glance of the wounded, watchful soldier.

The sheriff stood tall with his hands on his belt where the holster hung on one side and the handcuffs on the other. "You know why we're here, don't you, Hank?"

The young man began to tremble, and bewilderment replaced the suspicious look.

Oliver approached him, and Hank flinched. The nurse attending his arm jerked back. "You ought to get some breakfast, son."

"You mean lunch," Deputy Elwood said softly.

"Hurt your arm, I see," the district attorney continued, ignoring this.

"Yes, sir." Hank's voice was thin and quiet.

"How did it happen?"

"I don't recall, really," the young man said.

"You recall!" Sheriff Warner shot out.

The suspicious look came back. "What's he doing here? Who are you?"

Oliver put out his hand. "I'm Oliver Clarke. I was appointed district attorney of Gyver County earlier this year."

The young man stared at him. "I remember you." He looked down at the bandaged arm. "District attorney." He glared at the sheriff. "And him?"

"You know me, Hank," Sheriff Warner said.

"I was never arrested," Hank snarled, raising his uninjured arm.

"Not yet," the sheriff mumbled.

"We came to tell you that your friend Wild Bill Hicks has been found dead in an alleyway," Oliver said.

"He's not my friend," the young man said, his tone wistful. "We were friends."

"That's what we heard," Sheriff Warner said.

"I haven't seen him for weeks." Hank was a little calmer now, though still slightly trembling.

The nurse finished with the hypodermic needle, and Hank looked down at it as if it were a snake. His head suddenly dropped, and he began to sob. Oliver handed him his handkerchief, letting him cry for a few minutes.

The sheriff was a little moved, as his voice softened. "That won't bring him back, son."

Hank's head shot up. "I told you, I haven't seen him! Can I smoke, Nurse?"

"Shouldn't smoke," the woman said as she held the cart in front of her with both hands. "Bad for you."

"Come on, son." Oliver held out his arm but the young man flinched. "We'll go outside, and I'll give you a cigarette. Get some sun on you."

They found a grassy area on the hospital lawn with some benches. Oliver, who didn't smoke cigarettes but always carried some with him, put a few in Hank's hand. The young man's suspicion eased.

Oliver signaled the sheriff to remain silent. "Let's take things one at a time. We're just looking for information."

"I haven't seen Wild Bill for weeks," the young man said.

"You told us that already," Sheriff Warner said.

"The neighbors saw him ringing your doorbell yesterday evening around dinnertime," said Oliver.

"They're lying!" the young man barked.

"Suppose you tell us what you were doing last night, then," said Oliver.

The young man pressed his hand to his head. "My head hurts."

"I could get some aspirin, Mr. Clarke," the deputy volunteered

"He just got a shot of morpho," Sheriff Warner grumbled.

"Get it anyway, Hugh." The district attorney nodded. "I'm sure that efficient nurse can find some. You go with him, Sheriff. Assert your authority." He gave him a meaningful look.

The two lawmen retreated into the hospital, the sheriff glaring back over his shoulder.

"I don't think he likes me much," Hank remarked. "He's like a lieutenant I had in the army."

Oliver couldn't help smiling. "He doesn't much like anybody, so don't let it worry you." He leaned forward. "Can you take me through your movements last night? We'll take it one step at a time."

"We had dinner," Hank began.

"Who's 'we'?"

"Granny and Ellie and I," he said.

"Who's Ellie?"

"My sister." He looked down at the grass. "I can't remember what we ate."

"That's all right," Oliver assured him just as the lawmen came back with the aspirin and a glass of water. "Here, this will kick your headache right out." As Hank took it, Oliver said in a low tone, "Hank's just telling me about last night."

"Go on, then." Sheriff Warner sat at the edge of the bench. The young man cowered, his eyes wide.

"What did you do after dinner?" Oliver asked.

There were a few moments of silence. "I went out."

"Where?"

"Just walking," said the young man. "It was a nice night."

"It was sweltering," the sheriff growled.

"When you're stuck in those stifling trenches, any wind is good wind!" Hank snapped.

"Of course it is," said Oliver. "How long did you walk?"

"I don't remember."

"You don't remember nothing, do you?" Sheriff Warner asked.

The young man's determination came back. "I went to Litt."

"Why all the way to Nevada?" asked Oliver.

"You can have some fun there." Hank's face reddened a little.

"They got some speakeasies and bawdy houses there, don't they?" The sheriff eyed him. "Is that what you mean?"

"Yes, sir."

"They're not as clean-living as we are on this side of the state line," Deputy Elwood said in an ironic tone.

"How did you get there?" Oliver asked.

The young man stared at the grass without saying anything for a time. Oliver realized his eyes were on a single wild violet that had sprouted past the dull green blades. The sheriff opened his mouth, but Oliver pressed his arm to signal silence. The young man's trance remained for a time. When it broke, he looked at Oliver. "What were you saying?"

"He asked you how you got to Nevada," the sheriff said.

"Nevada?"

"You were telling us you went into Litt last night after dinner to have fun," Oliver prompted.

"Oh, yes, yes," the young man said. "I must have hitched a ride, I guess."

"You guess?" Sheriff Warner asked.

"I do that all the time," said the young man. "I'm not afraid!" Then, he added in a softer tone, "Not anymore."

"Go on," Oliver said. "Where'd you go?"

Again, the lingering silence. "Gus's Place."

"Make a note of that, Deputy." Oliver glanced at the young man, who had his pencil and pad out.

"What for?" Hank's suspicious look returned.

"So we can check it, of course," Sheriff Warner said. "If that's your alibi, son."

"Alibi!" Hank looked from one to the other. "Alibi for what?"

"For murder," the sheriff snarled. "What you think we've been talking about all this time?"

"Murder — murder — " The young man's tremor became more violent.

Oliver touched him lightly on the shoulders. "We're just getting information, son. You had dinner and hitched a ride to Litt where you went to Gus's Place. Is that right?"

"Yes, yes!" Hank pushed his hair out of his face. Oliver saw the sweat running down it.

"When did you get to Gus's Place?"

"I don't know."

"He's got a big clock on the wall just above the bar," Sheriff Warner said. "It's staring you in the face when you walk in."

"Ten, maybe," he said. "I got into a fight there."

"You remember that, eh?" The sheriff eyed him.

"Some guy was bothering one of the girls, and I told him to back off." Hank's voice was steadier. "He pulled a knife on me. That's how I got this." He raised his bandaged arm.

"That was noble of you," Oliver said.

His eyes narrowed. "You're mocking me."

"Not at all," Oliver said in a calm tone. "I would have done the same thing. When did you leave Gus's Place?"

"I don't remember."

"You're beginning to sound like a parrot," Sheriff Warner remarked.

"Look, my memory isn't too good since I got back from France," the young man said.

"Some of the doughboys have bad memories since they got back, Sheriff," Deputy Elwood said quietly.

"Is a bad memory a crime all of a sudden?" Hank snarled.

"Depends on what you did in that lost time," the sheriff said. "If that includes shooting your friend in the stomach, it's a crime people get hanged for."

"He wasn't my friend. I told you that." Hank grasped the edge of the bench with his left hand.

"He wasn't your friend but he came for dinner?" Sheriff Warner looked at him.

"I never said he did!"

"How did you get to the hospital?" Oliver asked.

"I — I don't remember!"

"You didn't go to the hospital in Litt," Oliver said. "Why not?"

"It wasn't that bad," said Hank. "It only got bad later. Please, Mr. Clarke. I have to get some sleep."

"You'll get sleep when we finish," Sheriff Warner snapped.

Oliver looked up at the young man for a long time. Hank squirmed a little under the silent study as the birds from a nest above cried for food. His knees shook from side to side, and his head flicked back and forth.

Oliver said in a quiet voice, "I'm sorry, son, but I don't believe you."

Hank looked at him with wide eyes.

"I don't believe you were in Litt last night either," Sheriff Warner said. "We can check it, you know, and we will."

Hank's gaze transferred to the grass.

Oliver's voice was hard. "Once we talk to Gus, he'll tell us you were never there last night. Isn't that right?"

Now the young man gazed at the sky.

"Tell us the truth, son," he said quietly.

Hank finally looked at him. "Wild Bill did have dinner with us last night."

"We heard you and him were on the outs," the sheriff said. "Why so chummy all of a sudden?"

"We were friends," Hank said.

"You told us you hadn't seen him in a long time," Oliver said.

"Did I?" Hank stared.

"You said so fifteen minutes ago," Sheriff Warner said. "Said it three or four times."

"I couldn't have said that."

"Well, you did!" The sheriff was clearly becoming impatient.

Hank was quiet for a moment. "Maybe I did say I hadn't seen him in a long time." He startled. "But I didn't say we were on the outs, did I?"

"How come you hadn't seen him in a while?" Oliver asked.

"He was busy with his work," Hank said. "He drives his own truck, you know."

"Drove his own truck," the deputy corrected.

"We didn't know that," said Oliver.

"He hauls lumber, produce, anything you can think of." Hank smiled a little. "He used to say you have to be creative in the trucking business."

"You mean he *used to* haul that stuff," Sheriff Warner said. "You killed him, remember?"

"Who says I did?" Hank asked. "He was my friend."

"At least you're talking in the right terms now," the sheriff said warily.

"So he came to dinner," Oliver said. "What happened after that?"

"Nothing."

"What do you mean, son?"

"He had dinner and then he left."

"Right after dinner?" Sheriff Warner asked.

"I guess so." The young man shrugged, pressing his hand to his head again.

"I guess you're going to tell us you don't remember killing Wild Bill with a gun, is that it?" Sheriff Warner frowned.

"Gun?"

"Yeah, gun." The lawman leaned forward. "Lots of veterans brought back souvenirs from the war. Including guns."

"Did you bring back any souvenirs?" Oliver asked.

"A German flag and an aluminum ring," the young man said. "And a Picklehaube. Got that off of a German soldier."

"Proud of killing them, eh?" The sheriff eyed him.

"Yes. No!" The young man looked wild. "I was just doing my duty, Sheriff."

"That's enough of that, Sheriff!" Oliver barked. "And you didn't bring back a gun?"

"Why would I?" Hank challenged.

"Pretty rough neighborhood you live in," Oliver remarked.

"Neighbors said they heard a shot," Sheriff Warner said. "Right in the alleyway just in back of your house

"They're lying!" Hank lashed out. "They all lie!"

Just then, the nurse who had given the painkiller approached. "Here are your discharge papers, Mr. Convoy."

"Like in the army," Hank murmured.

"The doctor included the prescription here." She pointed to a section of the form. "The druggist will explain to you how much to use and when." She gave him a kind smile. "How's the pain now?"

"Not too bad," Hank said. "I just feel sleepy."

"I don't think you'll have much trouble with it," said the nurse. "Just make sure to come back a week from today so we can take a look at it." She glanced at the two lawmen but, as if deciding it wasn't her business, retreated into the hospital.

"We'll make sure to bring you back here in a week," Sheriff Warner assured him.

"What do you mean?" Hank grasped his knee.

"I mean you're coming down to the police station," said the sheriff.

"Sheriff —" Oliver began.

"Well, he's got to know, Mr. Clarke." The lawman looked at the young man. "You might be there for a while."

"I need to sleep!"

"You'll have plenty of time to sleep," Sheriff Warner said. "We just replaced the cots in all the cells, so you'll be nice and comfortable."

"Cells!" Hank looked at Oliver, his eyes ferocious. "He's lying, isn't he? He's trying to scare me."

"We do need to take you down to the station for questioning, Hank," Oliver said. "We'll just go from there."

"But why? Why are you arresting me?"

"Nobody said you were being arrested."

"Ain't it obvious?" the sheriff cut in. "What we been talking about all this time? You killed Wild Bill, and that's a crime."

Oliver stiffened. "Sheriff, that's enough."

Hank was shaking his head, his eyes so wide, they looked ready to jump out of the sockets. Now, he broke into a run down the narrow street that led to the hospital entrance.All three men — Oliver, Sheriff Warner, and Deputy Elwood — ran after him, but they didn't have to go very far. Hank stumbled over a thin branch and fell. It wasn't a hard fall, and the young man knew how to land without injuring either his head or his bandaged arm, which, Oliver guessed, he had learned in the army. Hank screeched, his legs kicking up in the air, and his good arm punching upward.

"Acting crazy won't help," Sheriff Warner said. "That won't work with a judge."

"Sheriff, please!" His deputy looked alarmed.

Oliver bent down and spoke to the young man in a soft tone. Gradually, Hank calmed down and lay on his side, his legs curled toward his stomach and his arms folded into his chest.

"I've heard of men coming back from the war like this," Deputy Elwood said in a low tone.

"No!" Hank's voice was composed. He slowly unfolded himself and, grasping Oliver's shoulder, sat up. "I'm all right now."

Oliver helped him stand. "Might be better if you spent a night in the hospital, son. We can talk later."

"Only if I can send one of my men to watch him," Sheriff Warner insisted.

"No, sir." The young man was completely self-possessed now. "I want to go down to the police station. I want to explain what happened."

"About time," the sheriff said.

"It's not what you think," Hank said as Deputy Elwood gently led him to the car.

"It never is," said Sheriff Warner.

CHAPTER 5

Oliver persuaded Sheriff Warner to go down to Browly's Diner for some sandwiches and coffee. He then coaxed Hank into eating. The food and coffee revived the young man a little.

But in spite of the district attorney's compassion for the distraught young man, he didn't forget he had an obligation to the county to do his duty. He felt the search for Wild Bill's killer was over. And he was right.

When he and Sheriff Warner had settled into the room the police used for questioning suspects, the first words out of Hank's mouth were, "I killed Wild Bill."

"God Almighty, we figured that out a long time ago," scoffed the sheriff.

"I'll take over the questioning, Sheriff," Oliver said in a rough tone. "Get your notebook ready, as we want to take all of this down."

"Yes, sir," The sheriff pulled out his notepad and pencil and straddled a chair across from Hank. "I'll take it down myself."

"You can take this down, Sheriff," Hank said in a firm tone. "I had to kill Wild Bill to defend myself."

Oliver heard the lawman mumble, "They all say that."

"So you weren't in Litt last night," Oliver said. "And you didn't get that wound from a bar fight."

"I shouldn't have lied," said Hank. "I panicked."

Oliver patted the young man's arm. "Listen, son, do you want someone here with you?"

"I can't afford a lawyer." Hank suddenly broke down, hiding his face with both hands.

"I didn't mean a lawyer," Oliver said gently. "I meant a family member."

"No one was home when we knocked on the door earlier this morning," Sheriff Warner reminded him.

Hank stared at him. "What do you mean, no one was home?"

"No one answered," he said.

The young man blinked. "Ellie's always home unless she's with Sarah Anthony."

"She wasn't with the Anthonys," the sheriff said.

"You don't understand." He turned to Oliver. "Ellie's blind, and she can't walk well. Even if Granny was out, she wouldn't leave her alone."

"If she was home, she wasn't answering the door," Sheriff Warner said.

"Maybe Granny came back from the Solarises' and took Ellie somewhere when she saw I wasn't there," Hank lamented.

"We can send someone to the Solarises' to get them," Oliver offered.

"It's just as well they aren't here." Hank shook his head. "It would only upset Ellie." He took a deep breath. "I don't need anyone here. I want to tell what happened. It's eating me up inside."

"Start from the beginning," Oliver said.

"Wild Bill came for dinner last night," the young man began.

"You were on the outs, weren't you?" Sheriff Warner asked.

"We weren't on the outs!" Hank snapped.

"All right, you were great buddies," the sheriff scoffed.

"You just write things down, eh?" Oliver glared at him. "Whose idea was it for him to come to dinner?"

"Mine," Hank said. "We hadn't seen one another for a while. I told you, we were both busy."

"When did he arrive?"

"Didn't the neighbors tell you that?" the young man asked. "You said they told you they saw him ringing the doorbell."

"When did he come?" Oliver repeated.

"I told him to come around seven o'clock," said Hank. "Granny likes dinner early."

"And how did he behave?" Oliver asked. "Was he agitated, upset, anything?"

"He wasn't anything," said Hank.

"What do you mean, anything?" Oliver looked at him intently.

"I don't know." The young man closed his eyes. "I'm tired, Mr. Clarke. Give me a chance to think."

"Take all the time you need," Oliver said kindly.

"You don't even know what mood your buddy was in when he came to dinner?" Sheriff Warner asked.

This seemed to spur Hank out of his wariness. "He was at ease. He always was when he came to our house for dinner."

"So he'd been there before?" Oliver asked.

"Of course he had!" Hank glared at him. "He was my section leader in the army, and we saw a lot of each other when we came home."

"What did you do in the army?" Oliver asked.

"Automatic rifle squad." Hank smiled. "We were the backbone of the entire platoon."

"You know how to shoot a gun pretty well, eh?" the sheriff asked.

"What does that have to do with anything?" Hank gave him a skittish look.

"Let's just keep to the story, Sheriff," the district attorney said.

"Were your grandmother and sister as happy to see him as you were?"

"Sure they were." Here, the young man gave a faint smile. "He taught Ellie how to play baccarat with her deck of cards. Granny wasn't too happy about a fifteen-year-old knowing how to play a card game like that, of course, but it was just for fun."

"I thought you said your sister was blind," Sheriff Warner intervened. "How could she play cards?

"Her hearing is perfectly fine, Sheriff," said Hank stiffly. "We call out each card as it's dealt to her."

Oliver grinned. "Rather ingenious. Go on."

"Ellie told him she was going to see our aunt in Carson City in a week," Hank said. "Wild Bill wasn't too keen on that."

"Why?"

"She was going on the train by herself," he said. "He was worried about her."

"Because of her blindness?" Oliver guessed.

Hank nodded. "But Granny told him she already spoke with one of the porters who serves that train, and he promised to look out for Ellie. He was a friend of my father's."

"What happened after that?"

"Wild Bill coaxed Ellie into playing her violin for us," said Hank. "We were just settling down when Charley Solaris came running into the house."

"Who's Charley Solaris?"

"Fred and Mary's boy, isn't he?" Sheriff Warner asked.

Hank nodded. "He told Granny his ma was having her baby, and Dr. Lloyd sent him to get her."

"So, she did go out, but last night, not this morning." The sheriff glanced at Oliver.

"At about what time did your grandmother leave the house?" asked the district attorney.

"Around eight, I guess."

"You guess!" the sheriff scoffed.

"I didn't look at the clock!" Hank snapped. "But we usually finish dinner around that time."

"And you three were left alone," Oliver said. "What then?"

"Granny took out the bottle of bourbon that belonged to Pa." Here, the young man grinned. "She keeps it locked up."

"Pre-Prohibition bourbon?" Sheriff Warner sneered.

Hank looked offended. "Of course it is!"

"Go on." Oliver patted the young man's arm.

"Wild Bill and I had bourbon and coffee, and we all talked a bit after Granny left," said Hank. "We were feeling pretty festive. I figured if Granny already gave him Pa's bourbon, then it wouldn't hurt to offer him one of Pa's special cigars."

"A Cuban cigar?" Oliver glanced at the sheriff.

"Yes, sir," said the young man. "Wild Bill liked a good cigar."

"So you had coffee, bourbon, and a cigar," the sheriff said. "All friendly-like."

"Yes!" Hank gazed at him with narrow eyes. "I mean, no!"

"No?" Oliver asked.

"I mean, we had the bourbon and coffee, but when Wild Bill accepted the cigar, he and I went outside to smoke. Granny doesn't allow anyone to smoke in the house."

"And where did Ellie go?" Oliver asked.

"Upstairs to bed."

"About what time was that?" asked Oliver.

"It was around nine." With a determined glance, Hank added, "I looked at the clock because I knew it was getting close to her bedtime."

"So Ellie went upstairs, and you and Wild Bill were left alone to smoke," Oliver concluded.

"That's right, Mr. Clarke."

"Then what?"

"Wild Bill put on his coat."

"His coat?" Sheriff Warner stared. "It was hot as blazes yesterday night."

"That's what I told him, but he insisted." Hank shrugged. "When you're in the trenches, hot and cold get kind of skewed."

"You weren't far from the back door, were you?" Oliver asked.

"How did you know that?" Hank blinked.

"We found the cigar butts and the ash."

"That's right." Hank's hands tightened on the chair. "You would find them, wouldn't you?"

"They were at the scene of the crime," Sheriff Warner said.

"The scene —"

"The alleyway." The sheriff's tone was again impatient. "Stick with the subject, boy!"

"My head's not so clear," Hank growled.

"Take your time." Oliver motioned to the water pitcher on the table. Sheriff Warner rose and poured a glass of water, handing it to Hank. "Did you have the gun with you when you went out?"

"Gun?"

"The gun you shot Wild Bill with," the sheriff said in a rough tone.

"Of course not!" The young man looked horrified.

"You must have had it on you at some point," Sheriff Warner persisted.

"That was after?"

"After what?"

Oliver pressed the sheriff's arm. "Let the boy tell it in his own way."

"We went out to the alleyway," said the young man. "It was a fine night. Just the right breeze to blow away the stink from the garbage cans, you know."

"I know," Oliver said with a smile. "I used to live near an alleyway too."

"We smoked and talked."

"Talked about old times?" Sheriff Warner raised his eyebrows.

"Yes, as a matter of fact." Hank glared at him. "Anything wrong with that?"

"Then what?" Oliver asked.

"I told him Granny found a doctor in New York who was willing to operate on Ellie's leg," he said. "Make it almost like she could walk regular."

"And what did he say?" Oliver asked.

"Nothing," Hank said. "He was just really quiet. Then I told him I saw this truck in the junkyard in Litt. I said if I had the money to buy it, I could fix it up and go on the road. Lots of routes around Carson City need hauling."

"You ever done that kind of work before?" Oliver cocked his head.

"Sure," said Hank. "I was doing that for a while, sharing Wild Bill's truck when he wasn't using it."Truck driving's a hard life," the district attorney remarked.

"It's freedom," Hank said. "It's the open road and seeing new things." He gave a small smile. "Granny wouldn't understand that. She wants me to bury myself in some factory or warehouse like my father and die of a heart attack." In a stronger voice, he added, "But if I could take care of her and Ellie like she wants, I don't think she would mind."

"So you asked him for his prize money." Sheriff Warner glanced meaningfully at Oliver.

There was a pause as a horn sounded from the far-away street. The young man squirmed and placed his hands on the table. "I read in the paper he'd won it. I wasn't asking for all of it. But I swore I'd pay him back as soon as I could."

Oliver flinched a little as he saw Hank had been grasping the ends of the chair so hard that they made indentations in his palms. "Then what happened?"

"He went kind of loony," said Hank. "He said that money was for his ma in her old age, and he wasn't giving it to anyone."

"And what did you say?"

"I couldn't say anything." Hank's head went down. "I felt like a heel. A thief for wanting to take his mother's old age money."

"A thief, eh?" the sheriff asked, and Oliver knew he was thinking, *a murdering thief would be just about right.*

"Then what happened?" Oliver asked.

"I offered him another cigar," said Hank. "Just to show there were no hard feelings. I hadn't brought anymore out with me, so I had to go back into the house to get it."

"But there were hard feelings, weren't there, Hank?" The district attorney watched the young man's face. It had suddenly grown as sharp as a fox's, a soldier ready for battle.

"Yes." Hank's voice was steady. "That money was my whole life, and Ellie's. Granny's too."

"So you decided to take your gun out and kill him for it," the sheriff said.

"No!" Hank gave him a vicious look. "It wasn't like that at all!"

"Then what was it like?" Oliver asked.

"I went back in, and Ellie was there at the bottom of the stairs," he said. "She asked if everything was all right. I told her to go to bed. It was almost nine-thirty by then."

"You're clock-happy all of a sudden?" Sheriff Warner snorted.

"I knew Ellie would stay up for a little bit," he said. "She always did when Granny was out. I didn't want her going to bed too late."

"She went upstairs, and you got the cigars," Oliver concluded.

"And the gun," the sheriff added.

"That's right." Suddenly, he grabbed Oliver's wrist. "I wasn't going to use it, Mr. Clarke, I swear! I was just going to scare him a little."

"All right, son, all right," Oliver calmed him. "You went back out and then what?"

"It's all so hazy." Hank pressed his forehead. "I don't remember much."

"What do you remember?"

"I had the gun in my hand," he began.

"Was that before or after you smoked the second cigar?" Oliver asked.

Hank stared at him. "What?"

"The cigars," Sheriff Warner said. "Wild Bill asked for another cigar."

"After — maybe before — I don't know!"

Oliver glanced at the sheriff. "How many cigar stubs did we find?"

"I gotta look it up," said Sheriff Warner. "I think it was more than two, though."

"What does it matter how many cigars we smoked?" Hank asked.

The sheriff gave him an even look. "In a murder investigation, every little detail matters."

"It wasn't murder!" Hank screeched.

"All right, just tell us what you remember," Oliver said.

"I had the gun in my hand," he said. "I remember feeling the trigger against my finger. I told him I needed that money, and he was going to give it to me."

"And what did Wild Bill say?"

"He said he would."

"Just like that, eh? Handing over two hundred dollars at gunpoint," Sheriff Warner said.

"I didn't ask for the whole two hundred!"

"What was that you said earlier about feeling like a thief?"

"But I never intended to steal it," Hank insisted. "I was going to pay back every cent with interest, if that's what he wanted."

"You put the gun away then?" asked Oliver.

"I don't know," Hank admitted. "I don't remember much until he said he'd kill me."

"He threatened to kill you?" Oliver glanced at the sheriff.

"Yes, sir," said Hank. "He went crazy!"

Sheriff Warner narrowed his eyes. "What do you mean, crazy?"

"Just that," said Hank. "There was a knife in his hand."

"And you shot him?" Sheriff Warner asked.

The young man was quiet at first, pressing his fingers to his forehead. He stared at the sheriff. "What did you say?"

"Wild Bill came at you with a knife, and you shot him," Oliver repeated. "How did you get the cut on your arm?"

"I guess he must have stabbed me or something," Hank lamented. "That's when it happened. He stabbed me, and I pulled the trigger and shot him."

"Is that what happened, Hank?" Oliver asked.

"I suppose so," the young man murmured.

"You suppose!" the sheriff snarled. "You gotta be surer than that if you don't want to be tried for murder, son."

"Murder?" Hank blinked. Then, he jumped up. "You think I would murder my best friend like that? I was sobbing the whole time."

"I'll bet you were," the sheriff said.

Oliver calmed the young man. "What did you do then, Hank?"

"Do?"

"After you shot him," said the district attorney. "You must have seen him lying on the ground."

"I couldn't believe it." Hank's eyes were so glassy and wide that Oliver felt uneasy. "It was like — like —"

"Like the battlefield?" Oliver asked softly.

"Like a potato field," said Hank.

"What potato field?" Sheriff Warner squinted.

"My uncle had a potato field back in Idaho," Hank said. "I went to visit one summer when I was a kid. I helped pick the potatoes. We did it by hand because he couldn't afford one of those machines." His eyes grew dreamy. "We dug them out of the ground with shovels for my aunt and cousins to pick up later." He looked at Oliver. "Potatoes aren't round, you know. They're shaped like people with curves and bumps."

"Maybe they are," said Oliver with a little smile. "I never noticed."

"I thought they looked like little people sleeping in the soft dirt," said the young man.

"And that's what you thought about your friend," Sheriff Warner said. "Sleeping on the dirt of the alleyway. Only he wasn't sleeping. He was dead."

Hank's face twisted with rage and then despair. "I didn't mean to! He had the knife going for my chest, and the gun just went off."

"So now it was an accident," Sheriff Warner said. "Accident or self-defense, make up your mind!"

Hank buried his head in his hands, sobbing.

CHAPTER 6

Oliver let the young man alone for a few moments until the sobs subsided. "What happened after you shot him?"

"I ran." The young man was trembling.

"Where did you run?"

"I just ran."

"Mr. Clarke asked you where," Sheriff Warner said in a harsh tone. "Come on, come on!"

"To the woods."

"You mean Rosser Woods?" Oliver asked.

Hank nodded. "We used to play there all the time when we were kids."

"Where in the woods?"

"Where?" the young man asked in a vague tone.

"There ain't no markers there, Mr. Clarke," Sheriff Warner supplied. "I'll bet Hank's going to say he doesn't know."

"I *don't* know!" Hank shrieked. "We played all over the place."

"You just hid out in the woods, eh?" Oliver eyed him.

"A brave soldier like you hiding out!" scoffed the sheriff.

Hank stiffened. "Sometimes hiding out is the best way to live to fight another day, Sheriff."

"Why didn't you call the police?" Oliver asked.

Hank looked squarely at him. "I knew you would do just what you're doing now. Accusing me of murder!"

"If the shoe fits —"

"Sheriff!" Oliver growled at him. "That's enough!" Then, in a calmer tone, he turned to Hank again. "What about that arm of yours? The doctor said it was bleeding pretty badly."

"It wasn't at first," said the young man. "I wrapped my handkerchief around it, and that seemed to stop the bleeding. I went to sleep, although it hurt like — it hurt bad." He looked down at the bandage. "When I woke up, it was worse."

"And that was about what time?"

"I don't know," Hank snapped. "There are no clocks in the woods."

"Was the sun out when you woke up?" Oliver asked patiently.

"It was, but it was sort of pale."

"Then about six or seven in the morning." Oliver glanced at the sheriff. "After the police discovered the body."

Hank began to tremble so violently that his teeth chattered. Oliver took gentle hold of his shoulders, and the young man eventually calmed down. "Is that when you went to the veterans hospital?"

"Yes, sir."

"How'd you get there?" asked the sheriff.

"I walked," said the young man. "I didn't want to hitch a ride when I was bleeding."

"Thoughtful of you," said Sheriff Warner dryly.

"It must have taken some time," Oliver remarked.

"Yes, sir," said Hank. "The sun was bright by the time I got to the hospital."

"The doctor said you'd been there since seven."

"If you know already, why ask me?" Hank scowled

"We're trying to corroborate your story with what others have told us," Oliver said. "It's for your benefit, son."

The young man sagged in his chair. "You've been decent to me, Mr. Clarke. Everybody says you're a decent guy."

Oliver couldn't help but grin. "Thanks." Then, in a more serious tone, he asked, "Why did you try to hide the body, Hank?"

"What?" The young man's head shot up.

"Why did you drag Wild Bill's body behind the trash cans?"

The young man blinked as if absorbing the words. Then, the wild look came back. "I didn't!"

"Sure you did," Sheriff Warner said. "Bad idea, son. The garbage men were the ones who called the police."

"I didn't touch him." Hank swallowed. "He was just lying there, just —"

"Just like a potato," the sheriff said in a scornful tone.

Hank grabbed Oliver's wrist. "Maybe I didn't kill him. Maybe I just wounded him or something. And someone else came and killed him."

"And hid the body behind the garbage cans?" Oliver raised his eyebrows. "It's highly unlikely, son."

"We'll know once we get the ballistics expert in," said Sheriff Warner. "Where'd you put the gun?"

"The gun?"

"The gun you shot your friend with!" the sheriff growled.

Hank's head tilted a little during a prolonged silence.

"Well?" the lawman prodded.

"I think I threw it in the trash can."

"That's a lie!"

"Sheriff!" Oliver glared at him.

"Mr. Clarke, my men searched every inch of those cans, inside and out," he insisted. "There was no gun."

Oliver's legal mind clicked into place. "What's your explanation for that, Hank?"

"They must be wrong," the young man said.

"You said you think you threw it in one of the trash cans." Oliver leaned forward. "Which one?"

"What?"

"There are three cans in the alleyway," he said. "Which one has the gun?"

The young man's breath was coming out in small gasps. "The — the middle one."

"So you remember there were three garbage cans?" Oliver asked.

"Yes. It was the middle one. It had to be."

"Why did it have to be?" the sheriff asked.

"Because I always use that one when Granny sends me to throw out the trash."

They were all silent for a moment. Oliver could tell Sheriff Warner didn't believe one word of what Hank said, and now he wasn't sure he did either.

"Most men would remember where they threw a gun they just used to shoot someone," Oliver said quietly.

"I'm not most men!" Hank pressed his hands hard against his forehead. "I told you my memory isn't too good since I came back from the war."

"Even for something that happened less than twenty-four hours ago?" Oliver eyed him. "Your story doesn't hold up, son."

Oliver didn't like the look on the young man's face. "I've told you the truth, Mr. Clarke."

"Doesn't matter whether we find the gun," Sheriff Warner said in a hard voice. "We got a confession now, and that's good enough."

"You didn't get anything," Hank mumbled.

Oliver realized the young man was right. They had a confession of self-defense, not murder.

He knew Sheriff Warner realized this too, as he suddenly changed his tone to one of almost fatherly concern. "Listen, Hank. We know you've lied to us already. So why don't you make it easy on yourself?"

"What do you mean?" Hank blinked.

"Tell us what really happened between you and Wild Bill," he said. "You invited him for dinner that night, sure. Then you had some kind of falling out, and you lost your head and killed him."

The young man took this in. "Are you saying —"

"We'll talk to the judge and get you an involuntary manslaughter defense."

"You're crazy!" Hank jumped up so violently that the chair he was sitting in fell backward, making a loud bang on the floor.

Deputy Elwood was at the doorway, his hand on his holster, but his superior gave him a sign that everything was fine.

"You're crazy." Hank's voice was more normal now.

"Is he?" Oliver raised an eyebrow.

"I told you what happened." The young man leaned over the table and shook the bandaged arm in Oliver's face. "Where do you think I got this?"

Sheriff Warner stared at the young man's arm. "Doctor said it was a cut on the forearm."

"Not a cut. A gash," said the young man.

"You said he went for you," said Oliver. "A cut on the arm wouldn't have killed you."

"He wasn't aiming for my arm," said Hank. "He was aiming for my heart. Don't you think Wild Bill knew the difference?"

"So how did your arm get slashed?" the sheriff asked.

"I held it up to my chest to defend myself," said Hank. "Like this." He demonstrated by raising both arms with the forearm facing outward toward the left side of his chest and the right forearm on top.

"And his knife got your arm instead of your heart?" Oliver asked.

"Yes."

"Then you aimed the gun at his chest and fired, only you got him in the stomach," the sheriff guessed.

Hank dropped in the chair, staring down at the floor. "I guess that's how it was. It all happened so fast."

"And where is the knife?" Oliver asked.

"I don't know," said Hank. "Everything is foggy. I heard a champagne cork popping, and then everything went foggy, and when the fog cleared, he was lying there."

"Champagne cork!" Sheriff Warner scoffed.

"Some guns sound like champagne corks when they go off," Oliver said quietly. "Especially smaller guns. Was the knife still in Wild Bill's hand when you saw him on the ground?"

"I don't know."

"Seems like you don't know nothing, boy," Sheriff Warner growled.

"I don't remember!" Hank said. "I'm feeling kind of sick, Mr. Clarke. Can't I go to my cell now?"

"You'll go to your cell when we're finished with you," the sheriff said. "Suppose you were the one who did it?"

"Did what?"

"You were the one who inflicted that gash, as you call it, on your own arm," said the sheriff. "The knife was yours, not his. You went to get it at the same time you went to get the gun."

"It was Wild Bill's knife. He always carried a knife with him for protection." With a narrow look at the sheriff, he added, "Don't tell me even *you* hadn't heard that, Sheriff."

"You cut yourself on the arm to make it look like it was self-defense, and then you hid the knife along with the gun," the sheriff said. "I reckon we'll find one when we find the other."

"You're looney if you think I gave myself this." Hank indicated the bandaged arm.

"Hank." Oliver reached out and patted the man's shoulder. "We didn't find any knife on Wild Bill."

"What?"

"There wasn't any knife at the scene of the crime," Oliver repeated.

There was a deadly silence as Hank looked from one man to the other. He was out of his seat again, bouncing back and forth, trembling and shouting, "This is a frame-up, isn't it? A frame-up, frame-up, frame-up!"

It took a half hour for Dr. Myers to arrive and give Hank a sedative, and the young man fell right to sleep after that. Oliver tried to persuade Sheriff Warner to allow Hank to return to the veterans hospital in Moody, but the sheriff refused.

"He already tried to escape once," Sheriff Warner reminded him. "I reckon it won't do him any harm to stay in a jail cell, Mr. Clarke. At least he won't be hurting anyone if he's behind bars."

"Order the young man some dinner," advised Dr. Myers as he left. "He's going to be hungry when he gets up."

"He'll get his victuals," Sheriff Warner snapped. "We don't starve our prisoners, Doc."

"Keep on hand, Doctor," Oliver said.

"Certainly," said Dr. Myers as he put on his hat. "We don't want his lawyer to claim he was mistreated by the county, do we?"

"If he gets a lawyer," the sheriff remarked as the doctor left.

"He'll get one," Oliver said. "I'll talk to Joe Curry once we figure out what's what."

"I know what's what," the sheriff said. "This ain't no self-defense. The kid killed Wild Bill when he wouldn't give him the money, cut himself to make it look like he was attacked, and then ran and hid the gun."

"All we've got is circumstantial evidence so far," Oliver reminded him.

"And a confession," Sheriff Warner insisted. "The two together have sent more than one criminal to the gallows."

"Not in my jurisdiction," Oliver growled. "I don't play that way, and you know it."

"Look, Mr. Clarke." The lawman glanced at him. "I know what you're thinking. I feel sorry for these fellows who come back from the war too. It ain't easy for them, forgetting what happened, trying to get back into civilian life with no jobs around. But I've seen too often how some of them turn to crime. And that ain't right. We're here to fight crime, remember?"

Oliver glared at him. "I haven't forgotten, Sheriff. But fighting crime doesn't mean we can't feel compassion for the criminal now and then, especially the criminal of circumstance."

"He killed his buddy," Sheriff Warner insisted. "He admitted it. Whether it was murder or self-defense, he killed him."

"Yes," Oliver mumbled. "He did."

"And we got to take action," the sheriff said. "We got the community to think of, not to mention our jobs."

Oliver grimaced. "Sheriff, you have more logic than I gave you credit for."

"I'll round up my men and a few volunteers to scour Rosser Woods for the gun and the knife," the sheriff said. "Probably hid them there somewhere."

"It won't be an easy job," Oliver warned.

Sheriff Warner grinned. "I ain't never told you this before, Mr. Clarke, but when I was a kid living on the farm, I used to spend my time looking for needles in haystacks."

Oliver laughed and patted him on the back. "I guess if anyone can find that needle, you can, Sheriff." He sighed as he put his hat on. "My job now is as thankless as yours."

"Talking to Mrs. Hicks?" the sheriff guessed.

"And Annie and Ellie Convoy." Oliver nodded. "I think I'd rather be looking for needles in haystacks."

"Annie must have read about it in the paper by now," said Sheriff Warner. "I'll bet Jack made a dash for the *Gyver Bee* offices the minute you threw him out of the crime scene."

"I asked him to hold off publishing the story until we told Mrs. Hicks," Oliver said.

The sheriff snorted. "I wouldn't bet on it, Mr. Clarke."

"We might get some information out of Annie," Oliver said.

"She'd know if Wild Bill and Hank had a falling out, that's for sure."

"I suppose you're going to take the Grave sisters with you?" The sheriff eyed him. "Or shouldn't I ask?"

"I'll ask Eve," said Oliver. "I don't want to do this alone."

The sheriff gritted his teeth but said nothing.

CHAPTER 7

The clock in the hallway of the Clarke house, a rather ornate silver one with Swiss trim, struck eleven o'clock. Oliver had smoked two pipes by the time his story was over, and he now sat tapping the edge of the empty wooden tube against his hand. Small pigments of ash and powder fell into his palm.

Ellen had, Eve noted, gone to bed sometime after Oliver reached the part in his story about finding Hank at the veterans hospital. The curtains on the windows were billowing softly from the breeze outside, now stronger and cooler than when they arrived.

Helena's knees were drawn tightly together, her arms resting on the chair, staring at the empty fireplace. Her forehead was wrinkled like when she was a child thinking hard about something.

Violet was the only one who had reacted to the narrative. She held her handkerchief to her face as the tears fell, the white linen stained severely with the red, peach, and black shades of her makeup. Now the tears had stopped, and she looked at Oliver with determined eyes. "I knew there had to be a mistake."

"Mistake?" Eve echoed.

"Hank admitted he shot Wild Bill, Vi," Helena said gently but firmly. "There's no mistake in a confession."

"But he did it in self-defense." Violet leaned toward Oliver, covering his hand. "You believe him, don't you, Oliver?"

"You've no right to put Oliver on the spot like that, Vi," Eve said sharply.

"Oh, applesauce!" Violet's solemn mood was gone as she stuffed the stained handkerchief in her purse. "If Hank said Wild Bill attacked him, then he attacked him."

"We're still gathering evidence," Oliver said.

"What you're saying is you make no promises." Violet eyed him.

"That's right, youngster," he said in a serious tone. "There are parts of your friend's story that don't add up."

"You're a district attorney, not an adding machine!" Violet snapped.

"That's right." His voice was sharp. "I'm the district attorney of this county, and it's my job to investigate crimes, whatever their nature."

"Oliver," Eve ventured, "if you do prove Hank killed Wild Bill out of self-defense —"

"If!" Violet glared at her sister. "Of course he did!"

"But they've got to prove it," Helena objected.

"If it was self-defense, what will happen to him?" Eve asked.

"The crime would be justifiable homicide," Oliver said.

"Then he wouldn't go to jail or —" Violet swallowed, "get the death penalty."

"He would probably be acquitted," Oliver said quietly.

"But you don't believe it was justifiable homicide!" Violet snarled. "You or that goof of a sheriff."

"Oliver never said that, Vi," Eve objected.

"But that's what he's thinking." Violet looked intently at the district attorney. "Isn't that right, Oliver?"

He filled the pipe again and lit it. "I said there were a few things that don't add up."

"Such as?"

"Why did he suddenly invite Wild Bill to dinner if they hadn't seen one another in weeks?"

"He explained that," Violet said. "They were both busy."

"Was he busy?" He eyed Violet. "You said he came into the drugstore all the time."

"Lots of people who are busy come into the drugstore all the time," Violet snapped. "You make your fair share of visits, don't you?"

"Vi, Oliver is trying to help," Eve said.

"No he's not," said her sister. "He's trying to get a conviction. Hank's right. It's a frame-up."

"Don't be a goose," Helena snapped. "Would he have told us the whole story if he intended to incriminate Hank?"

Violet pouted for a moment. Then her face softened. "I'm sorry, Oliver."

He patted her arm. "It's all right. I realize he's a friend of yours."

"I know what you're getting at," Violet said. "He asked Wild Bill to dinner so he could hit him up for money. Well, maybe he did, but that doesn't mean he deliberately killed him."

"He threatened Wild Bill with a gun," said Helena quietly. "You can't ignore that."

"He was desperate!" Violet insisted. "He said so himself. He wanted to prove to his grandmother he could make good like she wanted him to." A few tears sprang up in her eyes.

"What about the missing gun?" Eve asked.

"He explained everything," Violet said. "He threw it in the trash can. Would he have been so exact about which one if he was lying?"

"Probably not," Oliver admitted. "But the sheriff keeps insisting he didn't find it."

"I wouldn't be at all surprised if he hid it somewhere."

"Really, Vi," Eve said. "Now you're being ridiculous."

"Hank isn't a criminal," Violet said with a sob.

"What else would you call a man who killed another man?" Helena's tone was more factual than vicious.

"Stop it, Helena." Eve put her arm around her youngest sister's shoulders.

"I'm not saying it's one or the other," Oliver objected. "I'm saying we have to investigate to find out what happened."

"You don't believe Hank did it because he was attacked." Violet glared at him.

"Now, wait a minute, Junior." Oliver held up his hand. "I have to go where the evidence points. Our only witness to the crime wasn't exactly reliable."

"What do you mean?" Eve asked.

"Hank. He contradicted himself more than once, and he did a lot of guessing," said the district attorney. "Not to mention he was shaking like a leaf the whole time."

"Poor Hank!" Violet sobbed.

"I'm not saying he was shamming," Oliver insisted. "Not on purpose anyway. But I just don't know."

"He wasn't shamming," Violet said. "Of course he was upset with you and the sheriff pointing the finger at him for murder!"

"I think Vi's right," Helena said slowly. "He wasn't playacting. It was shell shock."

"Shell shock?" Oliver took the pipe out of his mouth.

"Also known as war neurosis," she said. "It's been in all the medical journals I've been reading lately."

"In the papers too," Eve said. "Westley was talking about it last week when I went to order that headstone for Aaron Wagner's mother."

"Constant shaking, erratic behavior, bad memory, and that outburst he had," Helena said. "It all fits."

"Like a key in a lock, eh?" Oliver eyed her.

"If Hank was shell-shocked, he might have believed Wild Bill was going to attack him even if he didn't," Helena ventured.

"Maybe Wild Bill didn't even have a knife," Eve offered. "Maybe it was something else he took out, totally innocent, like a lighter to light the cigar."

"And Hank mistook that for a knife and killed him?" Oliver shook his head. "I don't think any judge or jury would believe that."

"They don't know how delusional these young men can be," Helena argued. "I've read about cases —"

"Including cases where veterans killed someone because of shell shock?" Oliver intervened.

Helena looked down at her lap. "I'm sure there are such cases."

"Maybe Hank did go a little crazy," Violet said. "But who wouldn't, with Sheriff Warner coming at you like a wild boar?"

"You seem to forget that wild boar has a job to do." Oliver puffed on his pipe. "So do I." He regarded Helena with a nod. "I'm sure Hank's lawyer is going to think of that. He's bound to get him checked out by several doctors."

"Well, that's something, anyway." Eve pressed her knees with her hands. "If he is sick, he'll at least get help."

"Provided his lawyer is up on the latest medical research on veterans," Helena pointed out.

"I'm sure you'll enlighten him," Oliver said ruefully. "A nice case for your clinical study."

Helena looked hurt. "I'm interested in science and medicine, Oliver, but I don't use people as my guinea pigs!"

"That's *if* he can get a lawyer and a good one," Violet said. "He hasn't the money and neither does Annie." She grasped her older sister's hand. "Eve, can't we get him one?"

"And where do *we* get the money?" Helena snapped.

"From the trust Mother and Dad left us," her younger sister snapped back.

"We want to help Hank as much as we can, of course," Eve said. "But that money is for your college, honey."

"Oh, applesauce, who cares about college?" Violet shrugged. "This is more important."

Oliver took her hand in both of his. "You've got a heart of gold, Violet, just like your sisters." He glanced at Eve and Helena, both of whom blushed. "But that won't be necessary. I've already contacted Joe Curry."

"The lawyer you told Sheriff Warner about?" Eve inquired.

"He's a friend of mine," said Oliver. "He's in charge of the Legal Aid Society in Moody. He'll find Hank legal help. He might even take the case himself."

"So you don't believe Hank murdered Wild Bill after all." Violet looked at him shrewdly. "Otherwise, you wouldn't be trying to help him."

"I feel sorry for him," the district attorney admitted. "I had friends in the war too. The only thing the government really gave those who weren't injured when they came back was a lecture on how to behave. They didn't get much else."

"They'll get more now with the Veterans Bureau," Helena said.

"That might help Hank, but not his family." Eve sighed. "When are you going to tell Annie and Ellie?"

"In the morning," he said.

"Poor Annie." Eve shook her head.

"Poor Annie nothing." Violet sniffed. "She's like one of those trees out there, going around with an iron face while Hank gets in trouble. Poor Ellie, though." Her eyes grew sad. "First the accident and now this."

"What accident?" Oliver asked.

"Didn't anybody tell you?"

He shook his head. "I just assumed she was born blind."

"A careless accident," Helena said.

"Hank admitted he was wrong," Violet insisted.

"Hank caused the accident?" Oliver looked from one sister to another. "I think you'd better tell me."

"It happened a year ago," said Eve. "Hank was driving a truck —"

"Probably Wild Bill's," Helena intervened.

"You mean this has to do with the dead man?" Oliver sat up, his eyes alert.

"Only indirectly," Eve said.

"Let me tell it," Violet insisted. "Hank's my friend, and he told me the whole thing."

"All right, Junior, spill it," Oliver said.

"Hank couldn't get work, so Wild Bill offered to let him take his truck on weekends for hauls," Violet explained. "Hank couldn't find clients around here, so he had to go to San Francisco."

"That's a long way off," Oliver remarked.

"He was driving at night to get to the city in the early morning. Then he'd wait around until it got dark for them to give him hauls in the city, and he'd drive back to Gyver," Violet said. "All weekend like that."

"Grueling work," Helena remarked, not without a little sympathy. "Like the hospital shifts we did in Santa Barbara."

"He was drinking too." Violet paused for a moment and then, with more defiance, "Well, how else was he going to stay awake?"

"Go on," Oliver said.

"One night, he drank a little more than he should have and got into a fight with one of the company overseers. The guy cheated him out of ten bucks!"

"All right, the guy cheated him," Oliver said. "Well?"

"He drove all the way home from San Francisco mad and drinking. But he wasn't drunk! He swears he wasn't drunk."

"Drinking too much while driving is as bad as being drunk," Helena said.

"Oh, what do you know about it? You've never done either," Violet said.

"Finish the story, Vi," Eve commanded. "We're all tired, and we want to go home."

"Hank pulled the truck into the alleyway where he always parked it," said Violet. "Only it was dark, and his eyes were a little cloudy, so he didn't see Ellie standing there."

"He ran her over?" Oliver flinched.

"He hit her," said Violet.

"Thank God he wasn't going fast," Eve said.

"He didn't mean it!" Violet screeched. "He knocked her down."

"And as a result, she's now blind and walks with a limp," Helena finished.

"Poor girl." Eve's face sagged.

"It's a miracle she doesn't hate him," Helena said.

"Ellie's not that kind," Violet said. "She's always been a sweet girl."

Oliver rose and stretched. "I imagine Hank's hated himself enough for both of them."

"It's about time we go, isn't it?" Eve asked with a small smile.

"We all need some sleep," Helena agreed, shaking herself out of the chair.

Eve gathered her bag, playing with the clasp for a moment. "Oliver, would it help if Helena and I came with you to talk to Annie and Ellie?"

"It would help a great deal," Oliver said. "And Mrs. Hicks too. We've got to find out what happened between Wild Bill and Hank."

"I agree," Helena said. "Start with the relationships."

"I thought you would be more interested in the autopsy report," Oliver said dryly.

"I will be when Dr. Myers gets it to you," Helena said. "If you'll tell me about it, that is."

"I have no objections, though I'm sure Dr. Myers would." Oliver chuckled. "Fortunately, it's not his call."

"I'll come with you tomorrow too," Violet said.

"Oh, no, you won't, Junior." Oliver's face was stormy as he opened the front door for them. "You're far too involved with this case as it is. I want you out of it."

"I won't say anything," Violet insisted. "I'll just be there for moral support."

"You have a job now, remember, Vi?" Eve said firmly as Oliver opened the car door for them. "You can't just take a day off when you feel like it."

"You've already abandoned your post tonight," Helena reminded her.

"You talk like we're in the army," Violet grumbled.

"You concentrate on your job, and I'll concentrate on mine." Oliver shut the car door and saluted them as Helena drove off.

"He'll concentrate on his job all right!" Violet snarled as she slouched in the back seat. "Snooty Ellen wants him to rack up convictions so she can brag about it to the Brenas crowd."

"That's not true, and you know it, Vi," Eve snapped. "Oliver only seeks the truth."

"He wouldn't even let the sheriff do what he wanted with the Libby Cinder case," Helena pointed out as she took the hairpin curve a little too quickly.

"Well, he's not going to make me give up my part as the third Sherlocka," Violet insisted. "I know Hank better than anybody."

"He's two years older than you are," Helena said.

"We're pretty close, though," Violet said. "He knows what it's like to lose your parents." She looked out the window, her lips turned down. "No one around here really knows what it's like."

"No, they don't," Eve said softly.

Helena steely eyes remained on the road.

CHAPTER 8

Eve's heart pinched as they drove in silence. The memory of her younger sisters' devastation when she had to tell them their parents had died would always remain embossed in her mind. The many nights of tears and empty looks, the bewilderment, the sadness.

She heard Helena's voice within the fog of her thoughts. "Didn't Hank's father die from some work-related accident?"

"He was seventeen," Violet said with a nod. "That's when Annie started in on him."

"Started in?" Eve asked.

"She expected him to take care of her and Ellie," Violet said.

"That's a big burden to put on the shoulders of a seventeen-year-old," Helena remarked.

"Annie's that kind," said Violet. "I met her once. She doesn't say much, but she scares the hell out of me."

"Vi, watch your language," said Eve warily.

"But Hank's not the kind to be stuck in a boring job." Violet made a face. "He likes adventure. He was almost glad to go to war."

"I shouldn't wonder," Helena said.

"Hank says the war wasn't so bad at first," said Violet. "They didn't send him to the front right away. That was only the last six months." She shivered. "That's where all the horror happened."

"What's he been doing since he got back?" Helena asked as she swerved to miss an empty box in the road. "Other than drive Wild Bill's truck, that is."

"Odd jobs, mostly," Violet said.

"Lots of those veterans can't get steady work even now," her sister said with sympathy.

"Is that why he's been drinking?" Eve asked softly.

"He's not a boozer, Eve." Her youngest sister gave her a meaningful look. "His grandmother would kick him out if he were."

Helena pulled the car up behind the hearse. "Is that all he's been doing, Vi? Odd jobs and drinking?"

"He's playing cards too." Violet linked her arm with Eve's as they started toward the house. "Not a lot, though. Not as much as Wild Bill."

"How do you know that?" Eve asked.

"He told me," her sister said. "Hank's a good card player, better than Wild Bill was. He said some nights he can make more at cards than he did in a month of doing work."

"It's a chancy way to earn a living," Eve remarked.

"You talk as if he's a professional gambler!" her sister snarled. "He wins fair and square. And he always gives some of the money to his grandmother."

"That doesn't make it right." Helena opened the door with her key.

Violet burst into tears. "How can you be so hard-hearted!"

Eve hugged her younger sister. "You know Helena didn't mean it that way, honey."

"Of course I didn't." Helena's tone melted as she took over the embrace. "You know me, Vi. I always look for rational explanations."

"And what did Hank say about Wild Bill?" asked Eve.

"He didn't have to say anything," Violet said. "Wild Bill came into the drugstore too."

"So what do *you* have to say about Wild Bill?" asked Helena.

"I didn't like him," said her sister. "He treated us like kids."

"Well, aren't you?" Eve hid a smile.

Violet shot her a look. "Some of us were old enough to get killed in the war, Eve."

"I know, honey." She put her arm around her shoulders. "I'm sorry."

"He treated Hank that way sometimes too," said Violet. "And he was scary."

"In what way?"

"Once he came into the drugstore and some guy — a little soused on bathtub gin, I guess — started digging into the veterans and how they get all the jobs, and the citizens who supported them get nothing."

"And Wild Bill didn't like that," Eve guessed.

"That's putting it mildly," Violet said. "He started razzing him and wouldn't leave when Sudie insisted on it. Then, he suddenly went nutty and grabbed a razor, holding it to the guy's neck like he was going to slash his throat." She shivered. "Sudie had to call in Paulie and a couple of his friends to get him out of there."

"Why didn't she call the police?" Helena asked.

Violet grinned. "You've never seen Paulie's friends, have you? They could take on Sheriff Warner and the rest of them like they were mice."

"I'm not surprised." Helena's glance slid toward Eve. Rumors were going around town for years that Paul Fiske, Sudie's "friend" was a bootlegger and had connections.

"Is that why he and Hank had a fight?" Eve asked. "Wild Bill threatened him too?"

Violet picked at the beads on the edge of her bag. "Who said they had a fight?"

"Oliver didn't believe Hank's story about their being buddies who hadn't seen one another for a while," Helena reminded her. "Come on, Vi, spill the beans."

"I don't know the whole story," Violet admitted. "Only from bits and pieces he told me."

"So they did have a fight!" Eve glanced at Helena.

"Not exactly." Violet squirmed. "Wild Bill got in trouble with the trucking company when Hank had that accident. So they fired him."

"I don't blame them," Helena said. "They can't afford a risk like that."

"It all turned out for the best because Hank said that's what made Wild Bill decide to drive his truck," Violet defended. "He said Wild Bill was making more money hauling on his own than he would have if he'd stayed with the trucking company."

Agnes came into the hallway in a dressing gown, her hair in curlers. "Land sakes, do you all know what time it is?"

"Too late to see a vision like you in that robe." Violet wiped her eyes. "Now I'll have nightmares."

"Don't you sass at me, missy," Agnes barked. "You got to get your sleep now that you got a job."

"If I have to get my sleep, how come you wake me up early every morning?" Violet barked back.

"Because I ain't having your lazy bones in bed interfering with my work!"

Eve laughed. "Did Kitty and Joe get home all right, Agnes?"

"I called a cab for 'em." Agnes nodded. "Joe kept hollering about that wreck of his." She sniffed in the direction of the street where Joe usually parked his old Ford. "I told him he'd better come for it tomorrow, or I'd call Rapp to haul it to the junkyard."

Violet gave her a quick hug, laughing. "You're terrible, Agnes."

Agnes waved her away "Now, you three get to bed. I ain't so old I can't paddle you if the lights ain't out in ten minutes."

"But we're old enough to paddle you back," Violet threw over her shoulder as the sisters moved upstairs.

Just as Eve was brushing her hair, Violet appeared at the doorway. With her kimono robe and her face cleared of all lipstick and rouge, she looked like a child again.

Eve turned around. "Vi, honey, what is it?"

Her younger sister toddled into the room. "Eve, promise me we'll get Hank out of this."

"We?"

"The Sherlockas," she said. "Oh, I know Oliver doesn't want me involved, but he didn't say anything about you and Helena."

Helena came into the room. "Why don't you just leave the police to do their job?"

"Their job is hanging people," Violet insisted. "You saw Oliver tonight. He doesn't believe Hank killed Wild Bill in self-defense."

"He didn't say that," Eve reminded her. "He said it was too soon to know anything."

"He's being cautious," Violet said stubbornly. "But he thinks Hank planned everything. He thinks Hank wanted Wild Bill's money and took the gun out into the alley to kill him if he didn't get it."

"It's a plausible theory," Helena said quietly.

"So is self-defense!" Violet snapped. "Especially with that gash on his arm to prove it."

"If it was self-defense, Oliver will find out," Eve promised.

"Not if he's not looking for it." Violet looked from one sister to the other. "That's why you and Helena have to be involved. So you can steer him in the right direction."

"What an idea!" Eve laughed. "Two women who run a funeral parlor steering the county district attorney in the right direction."

"Oliver promised to help Hank get a lawyer, Vi," Helena reminded her. "If Hank is tried for murder —"

"He can't be!"

"I said *if.*" Her sister was emphatic. "*If* he does, his lawyer will probably bring in experts to show Hank is suffering from shell shock and wasn't responsible for his actions. They'll put him in a hospital and give him the help he needs."

"They'll put him in a hospital for the criminally insane," Violet shrieked. "Hank's no criminal!"

Her sister's voice was quiet as she said, "He killed a man, Vi. According to the law, he has to answer for that."

"He is," Violet insisted. "He killed in self-defense, and you and Eve are going to prove it."

"As the two Sherlockas, you mean?" Helena asked dryly.

"As two citizens of this town trying to help another citizen," Violet said. "As two sisters trying to help their younger sister's friend." She burst into tears and collapsed on the floor, burying her face in Eve's lap.

Eve petted her head, trying to keep her own tears back. It was always despair that overtook her younger sister when someone she cared for was in trouble. Even Helena was touched as she bent down and laid her hands on her sister's shoulders.

"Oliver may not want our help," Eve said quietly.

Violet's head shot up. "You helped him with Libby Cinder. She was an innocent victim. Hank is an innocent victim too."

"Not quite," Helena mumbled.

Violet rose. "Promise you'll show Oliver and Sheriff Warner that Hank is telling the truth?"

Eve looked at Helena, whose lovely blue-violet eyes were almost wistful as she studied her younger sister. She nodded.

"We'll do all we can, honey," Eve promised.

"We'll do all we can to find out the *truth*," Helena chimed in. "But if the truth points to anything other than self-defense, you've got to accept it, Vi."

"It won't." She kissed each sister in turn and ran out of the room.

CHAPTER 9

Although it was usually only Violet and Felix who slept in until lunchtime, the older Grave sisters were so tired from the events of the night before that they got up late. Agnes moaned about the breakfast being spoiled with no one there to eat it, but ended up giving it away to the church. As a result, everyone was more focused on their food than on conversation. Felix, whose job as a watchman on the night shift at the Gyver Bank and Trust kept him in bed until nearly dinnertime, did not join them.

Eve was, as usual, the first to read the *Gyver Bee*. "It looks like Oliver got his wish."

Helena glanced at her as she put a dab of applesauce on her pork chops. "I gather you mean the story of Wild Bill's death is in the paper."

Violet grabbed it out of her eldest sister's hands. Her eyes grew hard as she read the headline. "Why those miserable —"

"Jack even had a chance to interview Hank," said Eve. "At least he mentions the idea of self-defense."

"He also mentions the body was moved, which Oliver told him not to," Violet said. "Listen to this: 'A trail of blood led from the dirty trash cans where the killer had hidden the body in an attempt to conceal his crime right up to the doorstep of the Convoy house. One wonders what might have gone on between Hank Convoy and Wild Bill Hicks, once comrades in arms and brothers.'"

"One wonders," Helena repeated dryly.

"Hank said, 'Wild Bill came at me with a knife. I had to defend myself.' One wonders about that too, especially when, in the words of Sheriff Arthur Warner, 'You can never be certain what happens in cases like this until all the evidence is in.'" Violet slammed the paper on the table. "I hope Oliver let both Jack and that sheriff have it. Serves them right!"

"You go spilling that applesauce on the table with your slamming things around, missy, you're gonna be doing the cleaning up before you even get to the drugstore," Agnes snapped as she took the paper away. "Never did like the paper at the table. Spoils the appetite."

"My appetite was spoiled the minute I sat down," Violet said.

Eve saw the tears standing in her eyes and pressed her sister's hand. "Don't worry, honey. Even the sheriff said all the evidence isn't in yet."

"He can't say anything else," Helena said in a matter-of-fact tone. "Hank could sue him for slander." She closed the paper and dropped it on the empty chair usually occupied by her husband, far away from her younger sister. "No more reading about it now. I read a study some time ago that bad news makes the blood slow down which slows the digestion."

"Ain't that what I said?" Agnes put down a plate of honey buns in front of Violet.

"In a layman's way." Helena smiled.

"Karl sent those over?" Eve eyed the pastries. The Gohls, who owned the bakery in town, had a son who had made his intentions toward Violet known and sent treats over most mornings.

Agnes nodded. "They're a soggy, greasy mess now, of course.

Should've had 'em this morning." She gave them all a meaningful look

"I thought you promised to tell him to stop," Helena said.

"I did, but he's stubborn." Violet broke a bun apart. "Don't worry. I'll stop by the bakery and pay for them."

"And tell him if he sends something over one more time, I'm giving them to Bobbie Price's dog!" Agnes snapped.

"Don't you dare!" Violet hollered just as Oliver breezed in, dressed in his hat and coat.

"How'd you get in here?" Agnes glared at him.

"You left the back door open." Oliver shook a playful finger at her. "Shouldn't do that, Agnes. Very dangerous nowadays."

"Fiddlesticks," the woman mumbled. "This ain't San Francisco."

"Ah, but we've had two murders so far this year," Oliver said in a light tone. "One can never be too careful."

"Agnes would just go after anyone who tried to come in with a meat cleaver," Helena said.

"There's a reason I'm so good at cutting up chickens and turkeys, honey," Agnes declared. "You'll want coffee, Mr. Clarke?"

"Agnes." Oliver took her by the shoulders. "Isn't it time you called me Oliver?"

"I'd just as soon call you Mr. Clarke," she said. "I ain't getting friendly with the district attorney, like *some* people." She eyed Eve as she waved out of the dining room and Eve blushed.

Oliver didn't seem to notice, as he let out one of his deep loud laughs and called after her, "Don't worry, Agnes, if you take up that meat cleaver, I'll make sure you get off with self-defense!" He looked around the table. "Well, looks like everybody slept in after pestering me late into the night about Hank, eh?"

Violet grabbed his hand and pulled him down on the chair beside her. "We just saw the morning paper, Oliver."

The joviality in his face disappeared, and he said in a snarling tone, "When I get my hands on those Shane boys —"

"I'm glad to see you don't approve of their kind of journalism," Eve remarked.

"And the sheriff too," Helena chimed in. "He only added fuel to the fire."

Oliver's temper dissipated as Agnes put the coffee in front of him. "Well, I guess I can't be surprised at either of them. Jack's always on the hunt for a sensational story, and the sheriff's got to tell them something."

"At least George and Frankie kept their word," Eve offered. "There aren't any photos or sketches in the paper."

"Not yet," he corrected her. "Sheriff Warner called me this morning. Abe's been on the phone with him, asking for the photographs and sketches to the press."

"I hope you told the sheriff to tell Abe to go fly a kite!" Violet said.

He picked up a soggy bun and examined it. "Sheriff Warner thinks we should. There may have been someone passing by the alley that night who might have seen something."

"Oliver, maybe you shouldn't antagonize the Shane brothers," Eve ventured. "They're the only paper in town, you know."

"The power of the press?" He eyed her.

"They could do you a lot of damage," she pointed out. "They were behind you during the elections last year, but that doesn't mean they can't turn people's minds around."

"The power of the press won't be for long," Helena declared. "Wait until we get a radio station here. Then people won't be buying the papers so much."

"Why don't you ask Hank if there was anyone around that night?" Violet asked.

"Maybe I will when I see him," Oliver said.

"You mean you haven't been down to the jail yet?" Her tone was clearly disappointed.

He patted her hand. "Sheriff Warner is taking very good care of him."

"Sheriff Warner couldn't take care of a mutt!" she snorted.

"I'll go down later," he promised. "I had to see Dr. Myers and Glenn MacDonald this morning."

"Who's Glenn MacDonald?" Eve asked.

"Old friend of mine from the city." He smiled. "He's a ballistics expert who just happened to retire to Pilead."

"You have the autopsy report, then." Helena leaned forward.

Oliver nodded. "Pretty much confirms what we suspected. Hank shot Wild Bill at close range in the stomach. The bullet hit the aorta."

"Hank had good aim," Helena remarked.

"He'll be happy to know you said that." Violet glared at her sister.

"He was taught how to shoot in the army," Eve said quietly.

"It's horrible!" Violet hid her face in her napkin.

"He would have died in a few minutes, Vi." Helena placed a comforting hand on her sister's arm. "Five minutes at the most."

"Blood everywhere." Violet sobbed.

"Not really," Helena said in her methodical tone. "He bled mostly internally."

"Except for what was on the street when Hank moved him," Oliver added.

"Hank said he didn't touch him!"

"All right, Junior, all right." Oliver patted Violet's arm.

"Any other injuries?" Helena asked.

"Scrapings on the back of his hands," said Oliver. "That's consistent with the body being dragged behind the trash cans."

"I was wondering about the hands," she murmured. "Was one of them clenched or bent in any way?"

"What are you driving at?" Eve stared at her.

"Hank said Wild Bill attacked him with a knife —" Helena began.

"And if he died with the knife in his hand, it would have been clenched." Violet squeezed her sister's shoulders. "It would prove Hank was telling the truth."

"It wouldn't prove anything," Helena reminded her. "Just a theory of mine."

"You might be right," Oliver said. "I looked at the sketches Miss Decker made of the body. The arms were stretched out, but both hands were clenched. That's how the back of his hands got scratched up."

"If there was a knife —" Helena began.

"Of course there was!" Violet snapped. "Hank said so, didn't he?"

"If there was a knife," her sister continued, "and someone took it, they must have taken it before rigor mortis set in. Otherwise, they wouldn't have been able to pry it loose from his fingers, if he were clutching it like this." She gave a demonstration.

Eve shuddered. "How could the neighbors not have heard anything?"

"The doctor said Hank couldn't have been more than a foot or so away from Wild Bill," said the district attorney. "And since it was a small gun, the sound would have been muffled a little, like a car backfiring."

"Exactly what Frank Anthony said." Helena nodded. "Did Dr. Myers say anything else?"

"The contents of Wild Bill's stomach were consistent with having had a big meal an hour or so before he was shot."

Helena snorted. "He would waste time analyzing something that confirms what we already knew!"

"It confirms the timeline anyway," Eve pointed out.

"Did the doctor get the bullet out?" asked Helena as Agnes came in to take the plate of honey buns away.

"Got it out nice and clean," said the district attorney.

"Land sakes!" Agnes growled. "Ain't you got better things to do than talk about dissecting a dead man at the table?"

"Don't be mean, Agnes," Violet scolded.

"We talk about dead people at the table all the time in this house," Helena snapped. "It's our business, remember?"

"That's different," she said. "They're your dead people, not the district attorney's."

Oliver laughed, grabbed Agnes hand, and kissed it. "I'll try to bring in my dead people when the ladies are not at the table in the future, Miss Bishop."

"Hmmm!" She left the room.

"Good thing I had a ballistics expert at hand." Oliver poured himself another cup of coffee. "The county approved that test, at least."

Helena smiled. "Still trying to get the forensic expert here?"

"Fingerprints are no joke," he insisted. "The sooner we start a local file on every person we take in, the easier it's going to be to track criminals down."

"Only you don't really need it in this case," Eve said. "Hank admitted to the killing."

"He admitted to self-defense," Violet reminded her.

"I assume Mr. MacDonald identified the gun that matched the bullet?" Helena asked.

Oliver nodded. "A 1908 Colt Vest Pocket Pistol."

"What's that?" Violet asked.

"A very small weapon," he said. "The theory is a man can conceal it in his vest pocket and pull it out whenever needed. Lots of gamblers use it."

"I thought they used the Tommy gun," Violet said.

He chuckled. "Only in the motion pictures."

Helena turned to her sister. "Vi, did you ever see such a thing on Hank?"

"Of course I never saw it!" Her sister was indignant. "Hank would never walk into the drugstore waving something like that around. I don't even think it was his."

"You might be right, youngster," Oliver said.

"What do you mean?" Eve asked.

"We checked with the army records. Hank turned in all army-issued equipment after the war, including a handgun." He leaned over the table. "And it was a 1911 Colt .45, not a Colt Pocket Pistol."

"What's the difference?" Violet asked.

He grimaced. "According to McDonald, about four inches, twenty-six ounces and two inches on the barrel."

"So, there's no chance one could be mistaken for the other, even when the bullet is extracted from a dead man," Helena said.

"Hank may have bought the Colt after the war," Eve offered. "They say a lot of veterans have guns now."

"We checked the sheriff's files for gun permits, and there's no record of Hank having been issued one," said Oliver. "The sheriff doesn't remember it either."

"Is that unusual?" Helena asked.

"Not really," he admitted. "We try to encourage people to get permits, of course, but it's not a required state law."

"It should be," Eve said savagely. "If it were, maybe Hank wouldn't have been able to get one so easily."

"Don't blame Hank!" Violet jumped in. "If he has a gun, it's to protect his grandmother and sister."

Eve took her sister's hand. "Of course, honey." She glanced at the clock on the wall. "Are you going down to the drugstore early?"

"You should, after you ran out on Sudie yesterday," Helena remarked.

"I didn't run out on her," Violet said. "We had important business to attend to."

"Still, don't you think you ought to go down there, Vi?" Eve peered at her.

"Oh, all right." The young woman sighed.

Eve followed her and watched as Violet adjusted her hat. "Vi, don't tell anyone about what Oliver just told us. He's telling us all of this in confidence, you know."

"What do you take me for, a fink?" Violet wrinkled her nose. "You just give me the lowdown when I come home for my dinner break tonight."

"What lowdown?" Eve asked.

"You're going with Oliver, aren't you?" Her sister's face grew somber. "Remember your promise, Eve."

Eve petted her cheek. "I haven't forgotten and neither has Helena."

"And don't let her ask too many of those searching questions of hers." Violet lowered her voice. "She'll shut Mrs. Hicks and Annie up like clams if she does. They're working-class people, not scientists."

Eve laughed. "I'll give her a subtle reminder."

Satisfied, Violet bounded out of the house just as Joe Reid, looking as if he had just rescued a drowned cat from the river, dragged himself to his car still parked outside the house.

CHAPTER 10

As they drove to the Marlestra part of town, or, as the townspeople called it, the Mold District, Eve filled Oliver in on what Violet told them about Hank.

"A transient, eh?" Oliver asked.

"No different than a lot of ex-servicemen," Helena argued.

"Except that he started well before the war," he reminded her. "Drinking and card playing doesn't bode well for respectable living."

"But it doesn't point to a cold-blooded killer, either," Eve snapped.

He grinned. "Now you sound like that young sister of yours."

"Violet insisted he isn't a drunk," Eve said.

"That I believe," said Oliver. "He seemed sober when we picked him up, although now that I look back, he might have had a hangover. That would account for some of his confusion and head pain."

"So would shell shock," Helena said. "Someone with a hangover wouldn't be kicking and beating his fists in the air."

"I'll leave that to his lawyer." Oliver swerved into the narrow, dirty streets of the Marlestra District. "You didn't happen to ask Violet about Wild Bill, did you?"

"As a matter of fact, we did," Helena said.

"She and her friends don't seem to have had a very high opinion of him," Eve admitted.

"You know Vi hates to be treated like a kid," Helena said.

"He looked like the type who would treat youngsters like your sister that way," Oliver said. "Of course, you can't always tell a man's personality after he's dead."

Eve shuddered, though the idea of looking into a dead person's face was hardly new to her.

"It sounds like he had a violent temper too," Helena said.

"I got that from Jack's remarks about him." Oliver nodded. "That's one thing in Hank's favor, of course." He stopped for a moment to let two mothers with baby carriages cross the street.

"Your hunch was right about Hank and Wild Bill," Eve said. "Vi admitted they had a fight." Eve related what they knew. By the time she finished, they had pulled into a vacant patch of ground across from a row of small houses.

Oliver turned off the ignition. "We're still looking into his background, of course. But I'll tell the sheriff to check with Jesse at the trucking company."

"He'll have a field day, won't he?" Helena eyed him.

"I don't know about that," mumbled Oliver.

"Of course he will," she said. "You both suspected Hank wasn't telling the whole truth about his relationship with Wild Bill."

"Sheriff Warner was saying all along that they had a falling out," Eve agreed.

"And a big one," Oliver remarked. "In these times, losing a job is a serious thing. Especially for veterans."

"If he was letting Hank use the company truck, it was probably without authorization," Helena agreed.

"He was trying to help a friend," Eve insisted as she got out of the car.

"A friend he knew was drinking more than was good for him," Helena fired back. "He may even have known Hank had shell shock but chose to ignore it."

"He's no doctor, Helena," Eve said.

"I wouldn't call that very responsible, Eve."

"Let's argue about it once we get the whole story." Oliver took each one's arm.

The moment Mrs. Hicks opened the door, Eve could see she was in the darker stages of grief. She was a thin woman already, but her face was now so tight with desolation that it looked like a skeleton. She was fully dressed in a Buckeye Steakhouse uniform even though the August heat had already begun to penetrate the walls of the ill-furnished house. Oliver wiped his face with his handkerchief from the stifling air.

"How are you today, Mrs. Hicks?" Oliver asked in a soft tone.

She answered in a raspy voice, "I'm all right now, Mr. Clarke."

"I brought a few friends with me." He glanced at the sisters.

She nodded. "I know Eve and Helena."

"If we're intruding on your grief —" Eve began.

The woman frowned. "Who knows more about grief than you do?" She opened the door all the way for them to enter.

The living room made Eve's heart sink, as it was filled with shabby, dusty furniture.

"I don't get as much time to clean around here as I would like," Mrs. Hicks said apologetically, brushing some of the dust from a chair. "Bill always said we ought to get Mrs. Bright in once a week. She does cleaning around town."

"You're just on your way to work?" Helena glanced at the uniform.

The woman nodded. "George wants me to take the week off, but I can't afford to."

Oliver said in a soothing, gentle tone, "If you'd like us to come back later, Mrs. Hicks —"

"No, no." The woman's voice was firm. "I'm all right." She took a gaping breath. "Life is about living through the tragedies."

"Yes, it is." Eve thought about the death of her own parents before she was even twenty.

The woman looked at Oliver. "The paper says Hank Convoy admitted to killing my son."

"Yes, he did," Oliver said. "Does that surprise you, Mrs. Hicks?"

The woman shrugged her sagging shoulders. "It must have been a terrible accident."

"According to what Hank said, it was," Eve said softly.

"I knew they weren't on good terms, but I didn't think it was so bad, especially after last week," the woman lamented.

"What happened last week?" asked the district attorney.

"Hank came over with a bouquet of roses for me." There was a shadow of a smile on her face. "He always knew I loved them. Then he asked Bill to dinner."

"For Wednesday evening?" Helena questioned.

"That's right." The woman nodded.

"And Wild Bill accepted even though they were on the outs?" Oliver asked

"Hank said he wanted to make amends," said Mrs. Hicks. "You didn't know Bill. He was always giving people second chances." Her lip quivered for a moment, but she controlled it. "I was always telling him he'd run into trouble if he didn't watch out."

Helena glanced at her sister, and Mrs. Hicks did not miss the look. "I'm sure you've heard he was wild in his youth," she said. "I don't deny he made a lot of mistakes. But the war changed him."

"It did most men," Oliver said softly.

"He was disgusted watching how some of the boys he led into battle were behaving." The woman's voice heightened with graveness. "Running around, whiling away their time in the speakeasies, getting into debts with gamblers, getting girls in trouble. He wanted to show them how to lead a better, cleaner life."

"He wanted to be a role model for them in civilian life as he had been in army life," Eve guessed.

"That's why he did all those things for Hank," she said. "He wanted to help Hank make a new start."

"So he was glad when Hank asked him to dinner?" the district attorney asked.

"He was glad," said Mrs. Hicks. But there was a catch in her voice.

"But not entirely?" Eve guessed.

Mrs. Hicks patted her hand. "I see why Mr. Clarke brings you with him, Eve.

"He was cautious," Helena guessed. "Like many of the soldiers who came home."

Mrs. Hicks gave her a stony look. "I know you're a doctor, Helena. I know what you're thinking. Bill wasn't one of those crazy ones."

"You mean the ill ones," Helena corrected with an equally stony look. "It was hardly their fault they were subjected to bombs going off alongside them and walking through fields of dead bodies!"

"Helena, dear." Eve pressed her sister's hand.

The woman looked tired. "You're right, of course. All the same, Bill wasn't like that. He was just a little apprehensive."

"He didn't believe Hank was sincere?" Oliver asked.

"It wasn't that," she said. "But he said he felt in his bones Hank was going to ask him for something."

"Did he say what?"

"He thought maybe Hank wanted to use the truck," she said. "For weekend hauls, you know, to make a little extra money."

"And Wild Bill didn't want that." Helena nodded. "I can under-stand him."

Eve noticed Oliver was studying Mrs. Hicks with the concentrated gaze she had seen him use on people they questioned in the Libby Cinder case. The dark eyebrows evened over the dark eyes, and the intensity of the stare was something no one could escape.

"And what do *you* believe, Mrs. Hicks?" he asked.

"I don't understand." The woman blinked.

"Do you think Hank wanted to borrow the truck for weekend hauls?"

The woman clenched and unclenched her hand. "To be frank with you, Mr. Clarke, no."

"You thought he was after the prize money Wild Bill won," Oliver said.

She glanced at him. "You know about that?"

"Yes, ma'am," he said. "Hank told us himself. He didn't tell us how much it was, though."

"Two hundred dollars."

"A nice sum," Oliver remarked.

"Hank admitted to the police he was after that money," Helena said.

"Everyone was after that money," Mrs. Hicks said in a harsh tone. "Two veterans who served with Bill in the war had already asked him for a loan."

"And he didn't give it to them in spite of giving people second chances?" Helena asked.

The woman smiled. "My son was forgiving, not reckless."

"I'm sure he wasn't," Helena mumbled, and Eve knew she was thinking about the incident at the drugstore Violet had related to them.

"He had plans for that money," said Mrs. Hicks.

"Can you tell us what they were?" Oliver asked. "I don't mean to be nosy, but we need all the information we can get."

"He wanted it for me." The woman looked a little embarrassed. "He even said he might put it in the bank." She gave a little chuckle. "Bill was like that. He believed in taking care of his own."

Oliver patted her arm. "Is that where the medal and the money are now?"

"I don't think so," she said. "Like his father, Bill didn't trust banks."

"Are they somewhere in the house?" Oliver threw a glance around the living room.

She stiffened. "My son was a grown man. I didn't pry into his life."

"Is that why you weren't concerned when he didn't come home last night?" Oliver asked.

"Bill kept his own hours," she said. "He told me he was trying to negotiate with a private company for a big haul. I thought he might have gone to see that man after his dinner with Hank."

Oliver took both her hands. "Mrs. Hicks, this isn't easy for me to say —"

"Don't hedge, Mr. Clarke," the woman said sharply. "I told you, I've seen a lot of tragedy in my life."

"Hank claims Wild Bill attacked him with a knife."

The crisp uniform folded around her gaunt figure. "I don't believe it!"

"He has a bad cut on his arm," Helena said. "Doctors at the veterans hospital in Moody treated him."

The woman stared at the floor. "My son wasn't a violent man by nature, Mr. Clarke, in spite of having been in the war. He hoped to never use a gun again."

"There were rumors he carried a knife," Oliver said.

"Yes, he did," she admitted. "But he would never have used it. He just took it — well, to feel safe."

Oliver looked down a moment, then patted her hand. "When a man is in the army, he feels safer if he has a knife in one pocket and a pistol in the other."

"I'm glad you understand." Mrs. Hicks looked relieved. "He was on the road a lot. You never can tell what might happen."

"Can you tell us what the knife looked like?" the district attorney asked. "We're trying to find it."

She shook her head. "I only saw it once, and it was folded up."

"You said he was on the road a lot," Helena said. "It might be in his truck."

"Where is his truck now?" Oliver jerked his head toward the alleyway to the left of the house. "Parked over there?"

She grimaced. "Bill didn't feel safe keeping it in this neighborhood."

"Where then?"

"He's got a friend who lives on the outskirts of Gyver," said Mrs. Hicks. "George Pugg. He was his corporal in the army. He's got a nice open field right in back of his house, and he let Bill keep it there."

"Corporal, eh?" Oliver eyed her. "He knew Hank too, then."

"Yes, sir," she said.

"Could it have also been in Wild Bill's coat pocket?" Eve asked. Oliver glanced at her.

"His coat?" The woman blinked.

"He was wearing a coat with a lot of pockets when he was found," Helena said.

"Oh, yes." The woman sighed. "He took his coat with him, didn't he?"

"Don't you find that odd, Mrs. Hicks?" Oliver asked. "It was a hot night on Wednesday. Most men were in their shirtsleeves."

Mrs. Hicks stared at a frayed edge on the carpet. "He always took his coat with him."

Oliver signaled the sisters and rose. "Thank you, Mrs. Hicks. I'm sorry to have distressed you."

"Just a minute." She looked at Eve and Helena. "You own the funeral home on Euclid Street, don't you?" Eve nodded. "I'd like to come see you about Bill." There was a pause.

Eve glanced at Helena. "Well, you're certainly welcome, Mrs. Hicks, but —"

"There's the Chester Funeral Parlor, Mrs. Hicks," Helena interrupted. "They might suit your needs better."

The woman's eyes narrowed. "Because they're inexpensive?"

"I didn't mean —" Helena looked alarmed.

"I know you do fancy funerals and such," the woman continued. "I can pay for my boy's burial. I don't want Bill buried in a rough box wrapped in a linen sheet."

"We'll do the best we can for you," Eve promised.

"A woman with a lot of fierce pride," Helena remarked as they settled back in the car with George Pugg's address scribbled on a piece of paper.

"She hasn't anything else left now but her pride," Eve said sadly.

CHAPTER 11

They drove to the very outskirts of Gyver. Apple and cherry orchards separated houses on either side. The street name that Mrs. Hicks gave them was really no more than a private road that led into the thicket with tall trees and a house that looked surprisingly new and spruced for such a deserted area.

"A nice place for a veteran to settle," Eve said with a smile.

"Mr. Pugg must have used the money he received when he was demobilized for materials to build," Helena agreed.

Oliver grinned. "I imagine he needed a lot more than what the army gave him. He must have gotten some kind of loan."

A woman with rich blond hair and a cheerful smile let them in, introducing herself as Rachel Pugg, George's wife. "George is out back with the chickens," she said. "We're trying to gather the rest of the eggs for the farmers market tomorrow."

"You look like you've done mighty well for yourselves," Oliver complimented.

"We were lucky," she said. "My father works as head accountant for the Chester Furniture Factory, and he was able to get George a job as his assistant when he came back from the war."

In a modest tone, she added, "George was getting his certification before he got called."

"I'm glad of your luck," Eve said with a smile.

"You're the Grave sisters, aren't you?" The woman threw her head back to look at them as they followed her through the house. "You'll help Mrs. Hicks, won't you? She takes too much upon herself."

"We'll do what we can," Helena promised.

George was a stout, fresh-faced young man about Hank's age whose infectious smile immediately put Eve at her ease.

"Here about the murder, I take it," he said as soon as he saw Oliver. "Terrible thing."

"I'm sorry you had to read about it in the papers," Oliver said.

George laughed. "You can't beat the power of the press, Mr. Clarke."

"We'd like to start by taking a look at Wild Bill's truck."

"Sure thing," George said. "Over here." He led them to a shed where a Ford Model T truck was parked. It had a rough wood box for the driver's side with windows and a long bed in the back.

"Not a bad rig," Oliver said with a whistle.

"When Wild Bill did something, Mr. Clarke, he did it all the way," George said in a stiff tone. "Whether it was an ambush or a job."

"I don't doubt it, son," Oliver said. "You have the key?"

The young man shook his head. "He never kept it locked."

"That doesn't fit what we were told about him being the cautious type," Helena remarked.

"He didn't think he had anything to fear out here," said George. "Ain't nobody come to see us unless they're invited or they're the police." The last he said with a meaningful glance at Oliver. "I'll get back to the chickens, if you don't mind."

"Just stick around," Oliver said in a firm tone. "We may have questions for you."

The young man raised his eyebrow a little but retreated to the yard.

"I don't think he appreciates you very much, Oliver," Eve said.

Oliver chuckled. "Too many ex-servicemen still see us as the enemy." He opened the door to the front seat and hauled himself up, bending and fumbling.

"What are you looking for?" Helena shielded her eyes.

"Anything," Oliver said. "The knife, for one."

"How could it be here if Hank was injured with it?" Eve asked.

He stuck his head out the door. "That's the question, Eve. Was Hank injured with Wild Bill's knife?"

"You can't believe Sheriff Warner's theory about the wound being self-inflicted." Eve stared at him.

"Men who kill from panic sometimes come up with wild ideas," he said. "It's not uncommon for a criminal to feign a burglary to cover up the fact that he killed his wife, for example."

"But that's only in the detective novels," Helena snorted.

"Maybe it is and maybe it isn't," he argued. "But if the knife's here, that means Hank's story doesn't fly. Gives us something to think about."

"Maybe Vi was right, dear," Eve said in a low voice. "Oliver is going on the assumption that it was murder."

"The police always have to look for a crime first," her sister assured her. "It's their duty, Eve."

Oliver jumped out the front, brushing the dust off his coat.

"Did you find anything?" Eve asked.

He produced an envelope from his jacket pocket and slipped out a photograph. They peered at the group of soldiers, all looking at the camera, grave and unsmiling.

"From Wild Bill's platoon, I guess," Oliver remarked.

Eve recognized the man standing to the far left as Wild Bill. Unlike Violet's description, this man had no beard and his rugged handsomeness struck her. His face was very different from the smooth-faced boys that made up the rest of the group. His was wiser, older, and more experienced.

She also recognized Hank sitting on what looked like an outdoor table with Wild Bill standing behind him, his hand on his shoulder. The expression on his face was of one determined to do his duty. There was something of a father and son in their pose.

"They were once very close," she said in a soft tone.

"Men in battle have to be," Helena said. "Their lives depended on it."

"I think it was more enduring than that, Helena," her sister chided.

Helena smiled. "You're as bad as the romance novels sometimes, Eve."

"I think Eve is right," Oliver said. "I saw the boy's face when we interviewed him. His remorse at what he did was genuine."

"But that doesn't mean he isn't a cold-blooded killer?" Helena raised her eyebrows.

"That doesn't mean he didn't kill out of rage or desperation," Oliver corrected. "Not every man who kills does so in cold blood"

"You didn't find the knife, did you?" Eve challenged.

"I haven't examined the entire truck yet, Eve," he pointed out.

"Surely, there can't be anything back there." She glanced at the long truck bed which looked more like a coarse wooden coffin for a giant.

"I won't know until I check it," he said.

They moved to the back of the truck, Oliver scrambling around the truck bed. "Looks like Wild Bill made some adjustments here."

"I've never seen a truck like that," Eve said.

"He must have rebuilt this one." Oliver jumped off. He took his handkerchief out of his pocket and cleaned himself off. "No knife there either."

"Now do you believe Wild Bill had it with him the night he went to the Convoys for dinner?" Eve inquired.

"You'd make a very poor prosecuting attorney, Eve," he remarked.

"Wild Bill had no reason to bring a knife to a friendly dinner," Helena agreed. "He might have put it somewhere else."

"I'm sending the sheriff and his men to search the Hicks house for the prize money," Oliver said. "There's no harm in them searching for the knife as well."

"You really think Hank cut himself on the arm so badly he needed to go to the emergency room to have it mended?" Eve asked. "I don't think any prosecuting attorney would try to argue that."

Oliver burst out laughing.

"Eve's right, Oliver." Helena looked at him, "I don't profess to be an expert in mental illnesses, but I can tell you the confused mind of a shell-shocked victim would hardly have the foresight to give himself a motive for murder by finding a knife, figuring out what kind of cut an attacker would make, and then performing the deed well enough to need medical attention."

Oliver smiled. "I don't doubt you know more than you claim, Helena."

She looked mildly gratified, and Eve remembered how disappointed her sister was when Fieldstone College, while allowing her to take courses, had denied her a degree because, "It might be fitting for a woman to learn about mortuary science but hardly fitting for her to practice it."

George approached them, wiping his hands on an old rag. "Find what you're looking for, Mr. Clarke?"

"Yes and no." Oliver held up the picture. "I guess every soldier in the platoon has one of these, eh?"

"Why, I haven't seen that for two years!" George's eyes were wide. "I sent mine to the missus, of course. Hey, honey!"

Rachel came out with a tray of lemonade. "Just made it fresh from the lemons on our tree," she said with a smile. "Now what are you yelling about, George?"

"The picture I sent you from the front." He waved the photograph Oliver had given him. "The one with all of us. Where'd you put it?"

Her face was a little grave. "Where I put all the things you sent me—in the back of the closet. When we're well past the war years, I'll take them out again."

He put his arm around her and kissed her. "I didn't want to upset you, honey."

"It's my fault," Oliver apologized. To George, he said, "You all look pretty close here."

"We were a close-knit group," George said.

"Then you knew both Wild Bill and Hank Convoy pretty well."

"Sure," he said. "You know how Wild Bill got his name?"

"Because he's quick on the draw," Oliver said dryly. "Jack Shane told me."

"I don't know about that," George said. "But we called him Wild Bill because he used to get all keyed up before a raid. It was like some demon got hold of him. Oh, he wasn't mean or anything," he added quickly when he saw the look on Eve's face. "He'd just be talking loud, running up and down the trenches, putting cigarettes behind guys' ears when they weren't looking. Just — well, wild."

"I imagine he was always level-headed when it came time for the raid," Helena said quietly.

"Yes, ma'am," said George. "When it came to his men, Wild Bill had only one thing in mind — get as many back alive as possible, preferably unwounded."

"Wasn't the doctor concerned about his behavior?" she asked.

"You mean did they think he was crazy?" George glanced at her.

"I didn't say crazy," she said in a sharp tone.

"I know they call it shell shock now," he said. "But it's the same thing."

"Were they concerned?" Oliver asked.

"No, sir. Nothing wrong with Wild Bill's head."

"But Hank's?" Helena asked, her eyes keen.

"Well, ma'am, I don't like to say —"

"Say it, George," Oliver ordered.

"He hasn't been quite right in the head since he got back." George flinched a little. "Like a lot of guys."

"How so?" Eve asked.

"Always confused and forgetting things," said the young man. "We make a date to meet, or Rachel invites him to dinner and he never comes. Then when we call him, he says he forgot, or he was looking at the stars or something like that."

"It hasn't been easy for any of you," Eve said softly.

"I expect the veterans will get what they need now," Rachel said. "George's brother is looking into it for us."

"I'm glad." Eve smiled.

"Let's all go into the house where it's cooler." She took Eve's arm. "You know, your parents buried my grandparents."

"I didn't know," Eve said softly, glancing at Helena. "I'm glad they were able to help."

Settled into the pleasant living room with the windows open to let in the quiet breeze, Oliver leaned forward, his lemonade glass in both hands. "We're looking for a few things, George. Maybe you could help us."

"If you're looking for a reason to hang Hank for murder, like the paper says, you won't get it from me," said the young man in a fierce tone. "The Fifth takes care of its own."

Oliver chuckled. "We're not looking to pin anything on Hank he hasn't already confessed to."

"That's right, he did confess, didn't he?" George blinked. "I can't understand it, Mr. Clarke. Hank isn't the kind to take a gun to a man unless he's ordered to."

"We're trying to find out what happened," said Oliver.

"The paper said it was self-defense," Rachel said.

"Not the paper, Mrs. Pugg," Oliver said. "Hank."

"If Hank says that, he's telling the truth," George declared. "I've never known him to lie."

"But he might have been confused," said Oliver. "That's what we're trying to find out." He leaned forward. "What was it like being in the Fifth? I mean, the camaraderie?"

George stiffened. "Just the same as any other section, I reckon."

"That photo makes Wild Bill and Hank look mighty chummy," the district attorney said.

"They were." George jiggled the ice in his glass.

"You didn't approve, did you?" Helena eyed him.

"We were all chums," the young man insisted.

"But Hank was different," Helena said. "Hank was Wild Bill's pet."

"You're an astute observer, Helena," Mrs. Pugg said with a smile. "I told George that myself."

"That does seem a little out of line for a sergeant," Oliver remarked.

"It's a dangerous thing when a leader picks favorites," George said in a rough tone. "He's supposed to watch out for all his men." His tone softened. "And Wild Bill did. The Fifth only lost two men throughout the entire war."

"A shame things went sour between them," Oliver said.

"It's a different world in the trenches, Mr. Clarke," George mumbled. "A different world."

Eve's heart sagged. His wife reached out and covered his hand.

CHAPTER 12

The district attorney allowed for a few silent moments before he went on. "Hank says he was attacked with a knife. Mrs. Hicks couldn't tell us what Wild Bill's knife looked like, so we were hoping you could help."

"It was a pocketknife, most likely," said George. "We all carried one in the army. I guess it might have been the trench knife too, but that one's pretty big."

"I thought soldiers had to give back their equipment when they were released from the army," Eve said.

George grinned. "Some of them found ways of keeping things, Eve."

"Wild Bill should have given it back." Rachel frowned.

"So he may have had two knives," Oliver said. "You think he expected to run into trouble when he got out of the army?"

"He counted on it," George said.

"How so?"

"Wild Bill said he was going back into the trucking business," said the young man. "His father and grandfather drove trucks, and that's what he was doing before he got drafted. He said those night hauls could get pretty dangerous."

"It makes sense he would keep at least one knife in his truck for protection," Helena said with a nod. "Probably both."

Eve noted Oliver giving George one of his magnetic, intense looks as his deep voice flowed out like honey. "Is that what you meant, son?"

"Sure it's what I meant." George gave him a meaningful look. "You can't fault a man for wanting to protect himself, can you?"

"Can you describe both knives for us?" asked Oliver.

"The pocketknife's a Damascus with a rose wood handle and pretty slick," George said. "The trench knife is double-edged with a spiked handle and spiked finger grips. I didn't keep mine, or I'd show you."

"So you not only could stab someone with it but also bludgeon them with the spikes," Helena concluded.

Rachel flinched. "How awful!"

"Helena has a candid way of putting things sometimes," Eve said sheepishly.

"It's about right, though," George said. "It could turn into a savage fight if you encountered an enemy soldier."

"Both knives would make a pretty serious cut on a man's arm, wouldn't they?" Oliver asked.

"Yes, sir, they sure can," said George

"What about Hank?" asked the district attorney. "Did Hank have a pocketknife or keep his trench knife?"

George grinned. "He was never good at using knives. He couldn't even cut an apple in half."

"And his pistol?" Oliver asked. "You did carry pistols, I take it."

"We were the rifle section, Mr. Clarke, remember?" George said with some amusement.

The district attorney smiled. "So he would have had, what, an automatic and a pistol with him at all times?"

"He was the first private," said George with a nod.

"He didn't keep his pistol, did he?"

George was quiet for a moment. "Hank shot Wild Bill, didn't he? That's what the paper said?"

"Yes, he did," Oliver said. "But not with that gun."

George stared. "How do you know?"

"They have experts now, honey," said Mrs. Pugg.

"That's right, ma'am," said the district attorney. "The bullet in Wild Bill's stomach matched a 1908 Pocket Pistol."

George nodded. "I was with him when he bought it. I kind of laughed at him for buying a woman's gun."

Helena glared at him. "Even a woman's gun can be lethal, George."

"Oh, I didn't mean anything by it." He bowed his head. "It's just that they're so small. He said he wanted something he could easily hide in his pocket."

"He certainly did that," Oliver remarked. "I imagine Wild Bill didn't see it coming."

"But if Wild Bill's life was threatened, Mr. Clarke, why wouldn't he go for him?" George defended. "Anyone would, especially a man who's been in the trenches."

"It wasn't as if Wild Bill wasn't capable of killing someone," Rachel said.

"His mother didn't think so," Eve argued.

"No, she wouldn't," the woman said. "She thinks Wild Bill was the biggest hero in the war, save Sergeant York." She sighed. "I suppose I can't really blame her. A mother with an only son —"

"— is delusional," Helena declared. "Her equilibrium is gone."

"I think you're being a little too harsh, Helena," Eve chided.

"Wild Bill was a good guy," George said. "He kept us alive during the war."

Oliver accepted a refill as Rachel passed around the lemonade pitcher. "Hank told us he invited Wild Bill to dinner that night because of the money he just won."

George stared. "You mean the prize money?"

"You sound surprised," Eve said.

"I never thought Hank would do something like that," George said.

"You have a reason for saying that?" Oliver asked.

The young man and his wife exchanged a glance.

"I suppose you know about Hank's sister and the accident," Rachel said. Oliver nodded. "George and I decided to offer Hank what little money we had."

"We were saving up to build this house," George interjected.

"The bills were piling up, and we knew he didn't have much money," said the woman. "Neither did Annie." With a twisted smile, she added, "Annie's the old-fashioned type who thinks the men in the family should support the women."

"A rather outdated family model," Helena remarked.

"That was a very decent thing to do, son." Oliver patted George's arm. "Army buddy or no army buddy, it was a big sacrifice."

"Did Hank take it?" Eve watched the young man's face.

"He refused," he said. "He told us he still had his discharge money."

"How much did you fellows get, if you don't mind my asking?" Oliver took out his pad. "Sorry to be so nosy but it might prove important."

"Sixty dollars." George's mouth set in a line. "If you came out alive, that is."

"A paltry sum." Helena's eyes were like stones. "Shameful!"

"That's what I thought too, but I guess we're grateful to get anything," Rachel said.

"Did you believe him?" Oliver gave the young man a pointed look.

"Frankly, no, sir," said George. "The accident happened about six months or so after Hank got home. A fellow like Hank doesn't hold on to money for that long."

"We think he refused because he knew we wanted this house so badly," Rachel said. "He didn't want to take away our dream. He's not a bad man, Mr. Clarke!" She looked at the district attorney. "That's why you must believe him when he says he shot Wild Bill in self-defense."

Oliver looked at George. "But that was a year ago. What about now?"

"I still say the same," George said.

"Even if he was determined to take care of his family?" Oliver eyed him.

"I don't get you, Mr. Clarke," said the young man.

"Hank told us he wanted to buy an old truck and fix it up," said the district attorney. "He wanted to take care of his grandmother and sister. That's a pretty strong motive for theft."

"We were all hopeful when we got out," George said slowly. "Since then, we got hit in the face with how things really are. When you're at war, you forget about the rest of the world."

"What's your point, George?" Helena leaned forward.

"I've seen lots of guys I knew in the army who, well, do things I wouldn't have thought them capable of doing during the war." His hands tightened into fists. "Good things and bad things."

Oliver was silent for a moment, regarding him with dark solemn eyes. "I know what you mean, son. When a man's desperate to survive, he either rises like a phoenix or falls from grace."

"I didn't mean that!" George looked at him.

Oliver patted the young man's shoulder. "I know, son." After a few silent moments, he continued, "We can't locate the money Wild Bill won. His mother doesn't seem to know. Do you have any idea what he might have done with it?"

George laughed. "He didn't put it in the bank, that's for sure!"

"Wild Bill didn't trust banks," said Rachel.

"His mother told us as much," Eve said.

"So you think he might have hidden it." Oliver studied the young man. "Come on, son, you have some idea, don't you?"

"Hank didn't steal it," George insisted. "I know he didn't."

"Then he has nothing to worry about," Oliver said in a harsh tone.

"Some of the boys used to go into the woods when the enemy was down and bury their precious belongings near trees and rocks and things," said the young man. "I know it sounds silly, but —"

"I understand." Oliver nodded. "They intended to find them again after the war."

"And if they buried them, they wouldn't be confiscated by the enemy," Helena concluded. "A clever idea."

George clearly appreciated her remark as he saluted her. "You would have been a good sergeant, Mrs. Wright."

Eve hid a smile, thinking what Felix would say if he heard this.

"You think Wild Bill could have buried his treasure, then?" Oliver asked.

"It's possible," George said. "He'd trust a hole in the ground more than he'd trust a bank vault."

Oliver made a note of this in his pad, and Eve imagined he would pass it on to the sheriff and his men when they went to search the Hicks house.

"One last question," said the district attorney. "If we're talking about hiding places, what about Hank? Any places he's likely to hide something?"

"What would he have to hide?" George blinked.

"Just answer the question," Oliver said.

"Not that I know of."

But the response sounded too abrupt to Eve's ears.

She realized Oliver noticed it too, as he cocked his head. "You sure about that? No special place around here? For example, Rosser Woods?"

"Why there?" George asked abruptly.

To Eve's surprise, Oliver seemed content to let this go. "No special reason." He closed his leather pad and put it in his pocket. George breathed a sigh of relief.

A persistent clock that had been ticking loudly in the hallway suddenly rang. Rachel jumped. "Goodness, honey, I've got to get lunch ready." She turned to Oliver and offered in a polite tone, "You're welcome to stay for dinner, Mr. Clarke. And you too." She smiled at Eve and Helena.

"That's mighty kind of you, Mrs. Pugg," Oliver said, "but we have a few other visits to make."

"Including to Annie?" She threaded her arm through Eve's. "Has anyone told her Hank is in jail?"

"I expect she's read it in the paper by now," Helena said.

"She might not have," said Rachel. "She's often out all night because of her midwifery duties, and she doesn't come home until the late morning. Hank says she goes straight to bed without even having breakfast." She was quiet for a moment as she stood at the doorway. "I don't think you'll have much trouble with her."

"What do you mean?" Oliver held his hat in his hand.

"Annie's not the hysterical kind," she said. "She takes things as they come."

"I reckon she's seen her share of tragedy in life at her age," George remarked.

"Just like Mrs. Hicks," Eve murmured.

Oliver pressed George's shoulder. "Thanks, son. You've been a big help."

George followed them to the car. When they were settled, he leaned over and knocked on the window. Oliver rolled it down.

"Mr. Clarke, can I ask a favor of you?"

"Sure, son."

"If it's true Hank's sick, just like Mrs. Wright said," he glanced at Helena, "will you make sure he gets to a doctor?"

"His lawyer will probably see to that," said Oliver.

"I mean for treatment," he said. "I've heard there are things doctors can do about that now."

Oliver patted his hand. "I'll see to it."

As they drove away, Eve knew he was telling the truth.

CHAPTER 13

As they drove back into town, the dusk stood over the far away hills, creating a victoriously red and purple sky. Eve saw her sister was contemplative, remaining silent while she and Oliver chatted about last Sunday's church potluck.

It wasn't until they turned into the road with the *Welcome to Gyver, CA, Population 1,827,* that her sister spoke. "If it's true Wild Bill didn't trust banks and buried his money somewhere," she said, "maybe Hank knew where it was."

"What do you mean, dear?" Eve asked.

"They were close until a few weeks ago," said her sister. "They may have talked about such things. Maybe Hank wasn't very trusting of banks either."

"What's your point, Helena?" Oliver asked.

"If Hank knew, or suspected, where Wild Bill hid the prize money, he wouldn't have a reason to kill him, would he?"

"In other words, it would prove he killed Wild Bill in self-defense and not murder," Oliver said.

"It wouldn't prove anything," she protested. "You need much more conclusive evidence to make that call, Oliver."

"I'm glad you think so." He chuckled. "Because Hank may still have shot his friend out of anger."

"Because he wouldn't give him the money he asked for?" Eve asked.

"He did go back into the house to get the gun, Eve," her sister pointed out.

"To scare him," Eve insisted. "Not to shoot him."

"All too often, someone who doesn't intend to use a gun ends up using it," Oliver said as he turned into the Mold District. "Things go terribly wrong."

"Only if the person has no conception of what the gun can do, even as a threat," Eve said. "Hank knew exactly what a gun could do. He was trained to use them, remember?"

Oliver let out a roar and stopped the car on Dean Street. "When you're stubborn about a point, there's no getting around you, Eve." But there was a note of warm admiration in his tone, and Eve blushed.

"You're both forgetting one important thing," she said. "Hank wouldn't accept the money George offered him for Ellie's hospital bills. Does that sound like the soul of a man who would kill for a few dollars?"

"Two hundred isn't a few," Helena objected. "It's a lot of money. And survival overrides the soul every time."

"Meaning?" Eve eyed her.

"We don't know what kind of financial straits Hank is in right now," she said. "Hank said he wanted to get a truck and fix it up so he could start working again. He had something to prove to his grandmother, and he could have been so determined to prove it that he would steal someone else's money to do it."

"That sounds more like an emotional argument than a logical one," Oliver observed.

"I'm not a machine, Oliver," Helena said. "We have human motives for what we do."

"If Hank was so desperate to please his grandmother, he

would have taken the job she got him at the lumber company," Eve pointed out.

"There's a difference between working in a mill and being out on the open road," Helena retorted. "Hank said himself that he wanted freedom. Men with shell shock often suffer from headaches, and the noise from the saws would make them much worse. We already know Hank has tremors. That would have been dangerous for a sawer."

Oliver took each woman's arm. "I'll bet when you two got into a real squabble as girls, your mother had a time separating you."

Eve smiled with affection at her younger sister. "We don't fight much. We just have to air out our differences once in a while."

A few wooden barriers had been haphazardly constructed at the entrance to the alleyway. Assistant Deputy Joe Savage stood near the barrier, clearly unhappy to be hampered by his full uniform in the heat. He was a gangly young man with large teeth, all of which gleamed when he grinned at the sisters.

"Violet said you'd be on the case," he said in a thin tone of voice.

"Thanks to you, I hear," Oliver growled, though Eve suspected he only half meant it. "You'd better learn to keep your mouth shut about police business in the future, Assistant Deputy. You might find yourself buried in the file room."

"Oh, yes, sir!" The young man's eyes shone like his teeth, though he wasn't smiling now.

"Anything happening here?"

"Only the neighborhood kids asking to see my gun." He grinned again. "I won't let 'em, of course."

"You'd better not," the district attorney snarled. "I don't want to hear about the police being called in because someone heard shots around here. They've had about all the shots they can take for now."

"Yes, sir."

They passed the barrier and walked through the alleyway. As they neared the trash cans, Eve averted her eyes, thinking of the trail of blood left by Wild Bill's dragged body.

"There's nothing there, dear," her sister assured her, as if sensing her reaction.

At the other end of the alleyway on Wadding Street, there was another wooden barrier with Assistant Deputy Steven Lamb standing guard. He had only been on the job for six months, and his uniform shone crisp in the sunlight. He stood with a stoic expression, his hands behind his back, cocking his hat to Oliver.

"Everything all right here, Steve?" asked the district attorney.

"No one's been near the alleyway, sir." Steve saluted him.

"Not even the kids wanting to play?" Oliver asked.

"No, sir," said the young man. "Not on my watch."

Oliver patted his arm. "Good man. Did you see Mrs. Convoy come in?"

"Assistant Deputy Ford said she came in around ten this morning," he said. "Made him a pot of coffee too. Mighty nice of her."

"Did she ask what the barriers were about?"

The young man shook his head. "She didn't have to, sir. Tom said she had the morning paper under her arm."

Oliver sighed. "I was hoping we would get to her before Jack Shane and his muckraking did. Well, carry on."

Annie Convoy looked as if she had just woken up from a long sleep when she opened the door to their knock. She was orderly in her appearance, with vigilant eyes and gray-streaked hair in a chignon. The house dress was loose as if she had lost weight recently.

"I was expecting you, Mr. Clarke," she said.

"You've read the paper, I understand?" Oliver glanced at her.

She nodded. Then, her eyes moved from one sister to the other.

"I'm sure you know the Grave sisters," Oliver said, nodding at them.

"Everyone in town knows Eve Grave and Helena Wright."

"We're helping Oliver," Eve chimed in, feeling like a school girl having to explain her presence at a speakeasy.

"I gathered," said the woman in a dry tone as she led them to the living room. The house was small and compact, but not as shabbily furnished as Mrs. Hicks'. "Ellie knew Libby Cinder from the school. She liked her."

"Yes, it was a tragedy," Oliver agreed.

"It was nice of you to help catch her killer," Annie said. "Nice for the Cinders."

"The papers made a bigger thing of it than it really was," Helena said. "We helped identify who Libby Cinder was, that's all."

Annie smiled, her abrasiveness lightening. "I think Mr. Clarke would say it was more than that." She sat on what looked like the most uncomfortable chair in the room. "Have you come down to tell me about Hank?"

"I'm afraid the morning paper got here ahead of me," said the district attorney.

"No matter," she said. Then, in a quieter tone, she added, "Meg Hicks knows?"

"Yes," Oliver said. "She identified the body."

"Poor woman!" The vigorous countenance broke, and Annie's upright features gave way to the sagging skin of her advanced age. "Losing a son is about the worst thing a mother could endure."

"Losing a loved one is the worst thing anybody could endure," Eve said in a vague tone.

Annie patted her hand. "You know what that feels like, Eve. Losing your parents like you did."

"We both know what that feels like," Helena said in a soft tone.

"Oh, but you were only a child, dear," said the woman. "And your sister was just a baby."

"That's not true!" The passion in Helena's tone startled even Oliver, who stared at her. "I was sixteen, and Violet was four."

"It's difficult having to care for children all on your own." She sighed. "I tried my best with Hank and Ellie after their father died. Heaven knows it wasn't easy, especially after Ellie's accident." The vigorous features returned.

"Violet is very fond of Hank," Eve offered. "We like him too."

"I'm glad to hear that," said the woman.

"Oliver will do all he can for him," Eve promised.

"I know how upsetting it is when someone in the family is in jail —" Oliver began.

"I'm not upset," Annie interrupted. "I realize your position. The paper said Hank told you he killed Wild Bill."

"Yes, he did," said Oliver.

"You couldn't do much else but arrest him under the circumstances, could you?" She smiled a little. "A boy admits to killing someone, and you have to put him in jail so he doesn't kill anyone else."

Eve felt as if ants were crawling up her arm at the woman's sensible tone. She realized Helena felt it too, as her sister mumbled, "Good of you to take it so well."

"We're trying to piece together the story of what happened," Oliver said. "We're hoping you can help us."

"Didn't Hank tell you everything?"

"I prefer not to build a case based just on a confession," he said in a discreet way.

"Hank has many faults, to be sure," said Annie. "But my grandson isn't a liar. I'm sure whatever he told you is the truth."

"One good word in his favor," Eve heard Helena mumble.

"Well, you see, ma'am, he seems to be a little hazy on the details about that night," said Oliver.

"I don't see how I can help," she said.

"You and your granddaughter had dinner with Wild Bill too," he said.

"That's right."

"I'd like to get a statement from both of you about what you know regarding the events leading up to the — the tragedy."

"I don't want Ellie upset by all this."

"She has to know, Annie," Helena said. "Hank's her brother."

"She doesn't need to know anything!"

"Won't someone eventually mention it?" Eve stopped.

"No one will mention it," the woman said fiercely.

Helena rose. "Someone is bound to. It's better she hear it from us. I'd be happy to bring her down for you."

Eve felt an alarm go off in her chest. Since their parents' death, Helena had an aversion to hiding tragedy. She never stood for clients begging to withhold something from a family member about the death of a loved one, and Eve couldn't help but admire her bold way of always facing the truth, even if it meant little regard for those who couldn't.

"Ellie isn't here," said the woman. "I put her on the milk train to Carson City early yesterday morning."

Helena sat down slowly, glancing at Oliver.

"To visit her aunt?" Eve questioned. At the woman's inquiring look, she added, "Hank told the police that's all Ellie could talk about at dinner."

"Yes," said Annie.

"That was rather sudden, wasn't it?" Oliver asked.

She smiled. "We've been planning this for some time. I'm thankful she went now, so she doesn't have to endure any of this."

"You can't hide it from her forever." Helena gave her an incredulous look.

"My granddaughter suffered a great tragedy last year." Annie voice shook. "Her broken leg never mended properly, and she has trouble walking. She lost her sight." Each word dropped like a stone. "I have no intention of making her suffer more in this life than she already has."

"Your devotion to your granddaughter is touching," Helena said in a dry tone.

The woman's lips curved with condescension . "When you have grandchildren, my dear, you'll know what it means to be devoted to them."

"I'm sorry, Mrs. Convoy," Oliver intervened, "but we may need to call your granddaughter back if the case goes to trial, since she was one of the last people who saw Wild Bill."

The woman stared. "But you just said you had a confession."

"A confession of self-defense," he said.

The woman was quiet for a moment. "I think I see. You're not sure if it was self-defense."

"We need to gather all the evidence to present to the judge," Oliver explained.

She laid the paper on her lap. "Ellie can't give you any evidence, Mr. Clarke. She told me she was up in her room reading. She wouldn't know anything."

"Nevertheless," Oliver said. "I might need a statement from her just for verification —"

"I won't allow it!" the woman snarled.

"I'm afraid you may have no choice," he said quietly. "And it might help your grandson."

"I tell you, there's nothing she can help with," said Annie.

"You let us be the judge of that, ma'am," said Oliver in a firm tone. "Now, I'd like you to tell us exactly what happened that night."

"But I know nothing," she insisted. "I wasn't even here most of the night."

"You were here when Wild Bill came to dinner?"

"Naturally," she said.

"When did he arrive?"

"A little after seven," said Annie. "He was always very punctual."

"Then you've had him to dinner before," Helena said.

"Once or twice," said the woman. "I think he tried not to come see us at mealtimes because he knew what a strain it was on our food budget." She said this without any shame, which Eve admired.

"He must have been a very thoughtful man," Eve murmured.

Annie looked distant. "Yes, he was. He reminded me of my son."

"Didn't you find it odd that Hank invited Wild Bill to dinner that night?" Oliver asked.

"They've been friends for a long time," she said simply.

"Not for the last few weeks," Helena said. "Several people told us they had a falling out."

"I didn't realize," said Annie. "I knew Wild Bill wasn't coming around the house as much, but I didn't know why."

"So, you didn't find it odd when he showed up for dinner," Oliver hinted.

"Not really," she said. "Hank had been talking a lot about the war the last few weeks."

"I thought most of the veterans are trying to forget the war," Eve remarked.

A grim expression appeared on Annie's face. "For some of them, Eve, the war was a way to escape their responsibilities."

"They did have a duty to their country," Helena said in a sharp tone.

The woman looked at her, then replied in a wary tone, "Yes, as you say."

"What kind of a meal was it?" asked Oliver.

"Meat loaf, scalloped potatoes —"

"No, ma'am," Oliver interrupted gently. "I meant the company. Did you sense any tension between your grandson and Wild Bill?"

"None at all," she said. "Wild Bill was very friendly. I always appreciated how he made Ellie feel comfortable. She's a shy child, but she can chatter on with the right person." A small smile appeared on her face.

"And Wild Bill was one of those right people," Eve said.

"She told him all about going to her aunt's in Carson City," said Annie. "She was so excited about it. He told her stories of his own visits there before the war. I imagine he left out some of the more colorful anecdotes." She looked amused.

"I'm sure he would," Eve said.

"He was worried, of course."

"Worried?" Oliver leaned forward.

"About Ellie," she said. "She was telling him all about going on the train alone to Carson City, and he didn't think that was such a good idea. On account of her — handicaps." Her lip tightened. "He saw how hard it's been for the injured veterans, and he was worried she'd have trouble."

"It does seem like a heavy load for a fifteen-year-old to carry," Helena remarked.

"I wouldn't be sending her alone if I hadn't thought of that," snapped the woman. "I asked Louis Durham, who works that line to take care of her for me."

"He's a porter, I take it?" Oliver asked.

Annie nodded. "He was a good friend of my son's. He took care of her as if she were his own. And Paula met her at the station, of course. Paula is my daughter and Ellie's aunt."

"You've already heard from her?" Helena asked.

"Of course I've heard from her." The woman looked almost offended. "I take care of my grandchildren, Helena."

"What about after dinner?" the district attorney asked.

We came in here, of course," she said. "I went to get the coffee ready, and Ellie went upstairs to get her violin. Wild Bill asked her to play." Her tone was wistful. "She was going to be a great violinist."

"You mean before the accident," Helena prompted.

"Yes." The wistfulness disappeared. "She can still play from memory, and she plays beautifully."

"Tom Wiggins was blind," Helena offered.

"Who?" Annie had been staring down at her hands, and her head jerked up.

"Tom Wiggins," Helena repeated. "He was a pianist and composer of the last century."

Annie's face softened. "Thank you for saying that."

Eve pressed her sister's hand. In spite of Helena's sometimes factual approach to life, she was not without compassion.

"I would have liked to have heard her play," Oliver said with a smile.

"I didn't get a chance to either," Annie said ruefully. "Just as I was bringing the coffee in, Charley Solaris nearly crashed through the door and said I was called."

"Who's Charley Solaris?"

"Mary Solarises' boy," said Annie. "She had her baby yesterday."

"We heard you work as a midwife in the neighborhood." Oliver nodded.

"I may not have a fancy medical degree, Mr. Clarke, but I know how to bring babies into the world," Annie said.

"So that's why you weren't here when we knocked on your door early this morning," the district attorney said.

"I had a duty to perform," she said. "And we need the money, of course."

"When did you leave?"

"The clock over there said just past eight," she answered. "I looked at it because Charley said his mother had just started feeling pains."

"In order to know how far along she was in labor," Helena finished.

Annie looked at her. "Yes."

"So you left here at eight the night Wild Bill was killed and didn't come back until the next morning?" Oliver asked.

The woman grasped the arms of the chair. "I didn't say that."

"Then you did come back earlier?" Eve asked.

"In a manner of speaking," said the woman.

"Please be clear, ma'am," Oliver said.

"I'm sorry." The woman brushed her forehead. "I just meant I came back in the early morning hours to help Ellie get ready for the train," she said. "But it was still pitch-black outside."

"Hank told us Ellie was going to see her aunt in a week or so," Oliver said.

The woman gave a small smile. "She was so excited about it when she spoke with Wild Bill, I started thinking when I was at the Solaris house. I thought, why make her wait a week? There was no reason really."

"When did you come home to get her ready?" asked Oliver.

"Two-thirty or so."

"Two-thirty in the morning?" Eve stared.

"The milk train leaves at three," Annie defended.

"Isn't it a little brutal to ask a fifteen-year-old girl to take the milk train?" Helena eyed her.

The woman glanced at her. "Tickets are cheaper than the day train, Helena. People like me have to think about those things."

Helena kept her steady gaze on the woman, refusing to be humiliated by the insinuation. Eve knew how many early morning trains her sister had taken back and forth to the college in Santa Barbara when she went to study.

"When did you get back to the Solaris house?" Oliver asked.

"I watched the train pull out and then rushed right back to the Solarises'. I don't know what time it was when I got there. Maybe someone in the house could tell you if you really want to know."

"Do you usually stay all night with the mother and child?" Helena asked.

"Not usually," Annie admitted. "But Frank, Mary's husband,

works the early morning shift at the lumber company, and he has to be out of the house by five. And the Solarises have eight children."

"Eight!" Eve couldn't keep the alarm out of her voice.

Annie smiled. "They all start school around nine."

"You stayed to help get the children to school, so Mary wouldn't have to," Helena said with admiration.

"We help one another in this neighborhood, my dear," she said mildly.

"In ours too," Helena said in an almost defiant tone.

"I came home after I saw them off and went straight to bed," Annie finished.

Oliver fixed his eyes on her. "All the time you were here getting Ellie packed and off on the train, you had no idea Wild Bill was lying in the alleyway dead?"

Eve had to admire the woman's unflinching response. "I never went near the alleyway."

"Was Hank home when you came back?" asked Oliver.

She shook her head. "Only Ellie."

"And that didn't worry you?"

The woman gave him a wary look. "It's happened before." There was a silent moment, and then suddenly, her straight features broke, and she let out a whimper. "Poor Mrs. Hicks!"

Eve looked at her sister. She knew what Helena was thinking — how strange it was that the pitying tone was directed at Mrs. Hicks and not at her grandson.

CHAPTER 14

Oliver walked to the windows facing Dean Street, looking out of the lace curtains. Eve noticed the windows looked out into the neighbor's, as the houses were almost back-to-back.

"You mentioned Hank has been out at such a later hour before," he said.

"He's been doing it more often lately." A grittiness appeared in her tone.

"Did he give any reason?"

"He didn't have to!"

The sharpness of the retort made Eve and Helena exchange a glance.

"You know where he goes, then?" Oliver's dark eyes regarded her with concentration.

Annie proved a worthy opponent. "I can guess," she said curtly.

"Would you mind enlightening us, then?" Oliver asked. "It might be important."

The woman picked at some loose threads on the seat cushion. Then, as if realizing she was drawing attention to the age of the furniture, she quickly smoothed it down. "He's been coming home in the late morning looking like — well, frankly, like a dog that's been fished out of the river."

"Not very complimentary," Helena mumbled.

The woman glared at her. "I don't sugarcoat, my dear."

"He told our sister Violet he's been working odd jobs for a while now," Eve said.

"Since the accident," Annie said. "But he shouldn't be. When Hank got out of the army, Mr. Rogers at the lumber company was more than willing to give Hank work at the saw mill." Her voice was laced with bitterness. "He refused. With so many young men desperate for work, he threw his chance away!"

"You must realize it would have been the worst thing for his condition, Annie," Helena said.

"Condition?" She glared at her. "I thought you were a plain speaker, my dear."

"Helena believes Hank is suffering from shell shock," Eve said.

"What utter nonsense!" the woman exploded. "All he needs is a steady routine, just like the rest of them."

"He had a steady routine in the army," Helena said.

"Lots of the boys who came back want a little breathing room from the discipline they experienced in the military, ma'am," Oliver said.

"But they settle down," she argued. "Like Hank's friend, George Pugg. Like Wild Bill did." The last she said with a hint of feeling.

"Hank is suffering from war fatigue," Helena insisted. "All the signs are there."

Annie glared at her. "Being ill is a luxury to us, my dear. One must push on."

"Does he contribute to the family finances?" Oliver asked.

"Speak plain, Mr. Clarke," she snapped. "I don't like fancy words."

"He helps pay the bills?" Oliver corrected.

"Not exactly," she said. "But he sometimes puts money in the piggy bank. 'For Ellie's operation,' he says."

"She needs an operation?" Helena perked up.

"Mr. and Mrs. Anthony, my neighbors over there," Annie gestured toward the windows where Oliver stood, "have a friend who's a surgeon. He looked at Ellie's leg, and he thinks there might be something he can do to help her walk. But the surgeon is in New York and costs a pretty penny."

"So he's trying to raise money for it," Eve said.

"Look, Mr. Clarke," Annie leaned forward, "I don't make excuses for my grandson. He does things I disapprove of. But he cares about his sister."

"By 'things,' you mean drinking and playing cards." Oliver studied her.

"That's not illegal, is it?" she challenged.

"A friendly game of poker isn't illegal," he agreed. "But poker tables are illegal in the speakeasies."

"Speakeasies!"

"Hank seems familiar with some of them in this area."

"Yes." Annie stared ahead. "Yes, he had that sort of drowned dog look. I should have known." She stiffened. "But he never comes home drunk. He knows I would never stand for that."

"He just stinks of bad whiskey sometimes," Helena guessed.

The woman stared at her and suddenly laughed. The laugh was so unexpected, it startled Eve. But it brought to the woman's face a lightness that showed, when her life was less burdensome, she was once a pretty woman.

"My sister can be a little too plain-speaking sometimes," Eve said. Helena shot her a look.

Annie patted Helena's arm. "Under different circumstances, we might have gotten along, my dear."

"You don't seem very concerned he's heading down an immoral path," Oliver mumbled.

"He must live his own life just like the rest of us, Mr. Clark."

As a sheet of sunlight hit the rug, showing its frayed edges, she added in a softer tone, "And he must suffer the consequences of his actions just like the rest of us."

"Even when he's in danger of bleeding to death from a bad wound to the arm?" Helena challenged.

The woman stared at her. "What are you talking about?"

"We found Hank at the Veterans Hospital in Moody," Oliver said. "That's what Helena is talking about, if I'm not mistaken." He gave her a nod.

The woman was silent for a moment. Eve could see the cracks in her rugged face soften for a moment, as if she were thinking of Hank as a child who had scraped his knee on the playground. "Is he all right?"

"He's fine now," said Eve. "The doctor bandaged him up."

"I'm glad." This came out with a genuine sadness. "Whatever he's done, I don't want him hurt."

"George Pugg told us Wild Bill had a couple of knives he took with him on hauls," Oliver said. "A trench knife with spikes and a pocketknife. Did you notice anything like that when he came to dinner?"

"It would hardly be something he would bring to a dinner party, Mr. Clarke," said the woman.

"I thought maybe he brought them to show Ellie," said the district attorney. "Ex-servicemen sometimes like to show off their relics from the war."

The woman shuddered. "I don't think even Hank would have approved of that, as eager as he was to go to war."

"He didn't bring home any weapons from his army service?" Oliver asked.

"Certainly not!" she said. "Oh, a few trifles, but none of them could hurt anybody."

"But he did buy a gun after the war?" Oliver eyed her. "A Colt Pocket Pistol?"

She shrugged. "I don't know anything about guns, Mr. Clarke."

"But there was a gun in the house?" he persevered.

She pressed her hands together. "Hank insisted on it. For protection, he said." In a harder tone, she added, "I told him Ellie and I got along just fine without a gun while he was at war."

"Do you know where he kept it in the house?"

She jerked her head toward the corner nearest to the fireplace, indicating the secretary desk. It was the kind of heavy, ornate thing with lots of drawers that people bought for a centerpiece of their living rooms in the last century.

"You permit me?" He rose.

"If you wish," she said. "But it isn't loaded. I made Hank promise that, for Ellie's sake."

"Ellie is old enough to know not to fuss with a gun," Helena lectured.

"I didn't say she wasn't!" Annie snapped.

Oliver inspected the desk. He came back with a box in each hand.

"These the bullets for the gun?" He shook a small box at Annie.

"Yes, I think so." She blinked.

"I'll need to take this as evidence." He put it in his pocket.

"Evidence?" She stared at him. Then her face became gray as she leaned her head back. "I remember now. The paper said Hank shot Wild Bill, didn't it?"

"Hank already confessed he owned a gun," said Oliver. "We need to match the bullet we found in Wild Bill with these."

"Didn't Hank give you the pistol?" Annie asked.

"He says he threw it in the garbage cans outside," Oliver said.

"Ridiculous!" Annie scoffed. "Hank would never do a thing like that. Why, a child could find it and — " She swallowed. "Anyway, why do you need it if Hank confessed?"

Oliver gave a lopsided smile. "You would be surprised how

many cases I saw in San Francisco where a confession wasn't enough."

"You mean the judge might not believe Hank?" The woman stared.

"Would that be such a bad thing?" Eve asked.

"Well, naturally not," said the woman. "But it just sounds crazy to me."

"If Hank wasn't likely to throw the gun away," said Oliver, "have you any idea what he might have done with it?"

At the woman's silence, Eve pressed her hand. "Children often have places where they go to be alone or play. Where they feel safe."

Annie chuckled. "This house isn't very big, Eve. There isn't anywhere he could hide." Her voice trailed off as her face grew wrinkled with distraction.

"Outside the house, then?" Helena suggested.

"There was a place up in Rosser Woods where his father used to take him hunting for quail when we didn't have enough money for meat."

"Where in the woods?" Oliver took out his pad and pencil.

"Wherever they hunt for quail," said the woman warily. "I don't know about those things either, Mr. Clarke. I only know about birthing and laundry and taking care of children." She rose. "Speaking of which, I have some laundry I need to get to Mrs. Fernly, and I want to check on Mrs. Solaris. So, if you don't mind —"

"We're not quite finished yet, Mrs. Convoy." Oliver held up the second box, flatter and bigger than the first. "Do these cigars belong to Hank?"

She was quiet for a moment. "They were my son's."

"I'm afraid we'll need to confiscate these too." In a softer tone, he added, "We'll return them when we're through."

"For Heaven's sake, why?"

"We found cigar stubs and ash in the alleyway," he said. "We need to match them with these."

"That's absurd!" the woman exploded. "Hank probably offered Wild Bill a cigar after dinner, and they went out in the alleyway to smoke it. He knows I don't approve of smoking inside the house."

"That's what he told the police," Eve said with a nod.

"Then what's the point of taking them if you already know?" The woman glared at him.

"We need corroborating evidence, ma'am," he explained patiently.

The woman's face relaxed. "I don't have much left of my son, you see."

"We'll return the box with exactly the number of cigars it has now." The district attorney opened it and counted them out. "There are twelve here."

She held on to the back of the chair. "I'm sorry. I wasn't thinking. I know you'll be careful with them." She looked steadily at him. "You'll be careful with my grandson too, won't you, Mr. Clarke? Remember he came to you and confessed."

He took her hand. "I've already promised him that I'll do what I can to see he gets proper legal representation."

"Does he need it?" she asked.

"Does he need it!" Helena exclaimed, but Eve pressed her sister's arm.

"Well, ma'am, he's entitled to a lawyer no matter what the circumstances," Oliver said. Eve could see he was a little stunned.

"You mean anyone accused of a crime needs a lawyer even if he's confessed?" She blinked. "I don't know how these things work, Mr. Clarke."

"Certainly they do," he said. "Especially under these circumstances."

"These circumstances?"

"The injury," Helena said, a little impatient. "Wild Bill attacked him, and he killed him in self-defense."

"Yes, of course," she murmured. "Mr. Clarke, I'd like to see Hank." Eve suddenly noticed she had bright, almost innocent blue eyes. The unevenness of the strict lines on her face with the eyes struck her at that moment.

"I'll arrange it," Oliver promised.

"Thank you," Annie said. "And don't you worry about a lawyer, Mr. Clarke. If Hank needs one, I'll find a way to get him one."

"I'll speak to a lawyer I know who works for the Moody Legal Aid Society," he promised. "He's a good man."

"I thank you for your help." At the door, she held on to his arm. "Mr. Clarke, please don't call Ellie back from Carson City."

"I'll do everything in my power not to," he promised.

The woman spoke passionately for the first time. "She worships Hank, you see."

"Even after all he's done to her?" Helena asked with an equal amount of dispassion.

"Helena," her sister growled.

"You don't know Ellie," said the woman. "She's not the kind to hold a grudge. She takes things as they come."

"Like you," Eve said with a small smile.

"Yes, I suppose like me," Annie admitted. She appealed to the district attorney again. "If she could stay away until after the trial —"

"I don't know if that would be possible," Oliver said.

"Please don't call her back," begged the woman.

"I'll do my best, ma'am," he mumbled as he tipped his hat to her.

None of them said anything until they got into the car and were driving out of the Marlestra district. Eve felt the agitation gathering around her, making her feel small and tight. She threaded her arm through Helena's as she had when they were growing up. Something about the sturdiness of her younger sister's arm kept her nerves steady.

Once they were back on the tree-lined road into the main part of Gyver, Eve broke the silence. "I think I see why Vi called Annie an iron face."

"I suppose it couldn't have been easy for her," Oliver said. "Raising two grandchildren on her own, then this accident with Ellie."

"She cared more about the cigars than she did about her grandson being arrested," Eve observed.

He glanced at her. "You don't approve, I suppose?"

"Eve has very definite opinions about how children should be raised," Helena said.

"It isn't that," Eve insisted. "But if a child of mine did anything wrong for a good reason, I would do everything in my power to prove it."

"I'm sure Vi will be relieved to hear that," Helena said dryly.

Oliver burst out laughing. "Maybe you'll be the one who will do the wrong deed."

"I wouldn't doubt it," Helena said with a smile. "But you're missing the point, Eve."

"Which is?"

"They didn't get along," she said. "That was very clear. Family members who don't get along don't always rush to one another's side."

"I wouldn't go by her first reaction," Oliver said as he turned into their street. "I've seen it happen often enough. The initial shock of their son or daughter or, as in this case, grandchild, being arrested for a crime doesn't register until they've actually seen them behind bars. Then the police can't get rid of them. They're always coming up with ideas about why their family member is innocent."

"I think it was starting to register," Eve said. "She did ask to see Hank, and she seemed determined to find him a lawyer."

"At least you've made some progress," Helena remarked.

He nodded as he stopped in front of their house. "I'll have MacDonald analyze the bullets we picked up with the one from the body and see if they match."

"And send the sheriff and his men out to Rosser Woods to search for the gun?" Helena suggested.

He nodded. "If we can fit the pieces together with the gun, the bullets, and the cigars, that might lead us closer to the truth."

"The truth," Eve sighed. "You mean self-defense or murder, don't you?"

He was quiet for a moment as the motor of his Dodge let out its coughing grumbles. "Yes."

"It's what Annie said about Ellie's operation, isn't it?" Helena asked.

"The bank might loan a veteran money for a business idea," Oliver said. "Even someone like Hank. But a sister's operation is a whole different thing."

"And if the evidence makes you believe it's murder," Eve said quietly. "You'll take Hank to trial."

"He has to, Eve," Helena insisted. "It's his job."

"We'd better not tell Vi," Eve said. "I don't want her more upset over this than she already is. Children get upset —" Her voice trailed off when she realized Violet was eighteen and no longer a child. "You meant it when you said you wouldn't call Ellie back if you didn't have to, didn't you, Oliver?"

"Not if she can't tell us something we don't already know," he said.

"At least she'll be spared," Eve said with a sigh.

"You can't always spare children, Eve," her sister said softly.

Eve, thinking of the dark shadows that lingered around the sixteen-year-old Helena and four-year-old Violet when their parents died, held back tears.

CHAPTER 15

$\mathcal{A}$ warm rain followed that night with a few cries of thunder and lightning, which woke Eve up. She kept seeing the dead man's face in the shape of the curtains dancing in the open window. A photograph of him that sat on the living room table while they interviewed his mother had been right in her line of vision, and she hadn't been able to keep her eyes off it. The boy in the picture was dressed in overalls holding up a sizable fish with a big grin on his face.

At breakfast, she was still preoccupied with that photo.

"You're a little fuzzy this morning, aren't you?" Helena observed.

"If I told you why, you would think me silly," Eve said with a little laugh.

"Tell us anyway," Violet said.

"I was staring at that photograph of Wild Bill with the fish all the time we were talking to Mrs. Hicks yesterday," she said.

"You mean the one on the table?" Helena nodded. "I saw it."

"What's a photograph have to do with it?" Violet took a few lumps of sugar in her coffee.

"I don't know," Eve admitted. "I just kept thinking of that smile on his face. He looked so proud with that fish in his hand."

"His daddy probably caught it and let him pose with it," Violet said. "That's the kind of person Wild Bill was. According to Hank, anyway."

"Don't speak ill of the dead," Helena said, her eyes on her book.

"I'm not speaking ill," Violet insisted. "I'm speaking the truth."

"Maybe Hank wasn't exactly in a mood to be kind about Wild Bill when he said that," Eve said. "Remember, they had a falling out."

"Hank wouldn't say terrible things about someone unless they were true." Violet's lip went out.

Helena looked up, the glasses making her luminous eyes look smaller. "Don't you say terrible things about Kitty when you've had a falling out?"

"I do not!" Violet set the cup down with a slap. "I never say anything about Kitty that isn't true."

Helena laughed and ruffled her sister's messy hair. "All right, Vi, checkmate on that."

Agnes came in with a frown on her face. "You ought to finish up. Mrs. Hick's been waiting for fifteen minutes."

"Mrs. Hicks is here?" Eve set down the slice of toast she had just buttered.

"In the waiting room," said the housekeeper.

"Well, for pity's sake, why didn't you tell us?" Helena closed her book and folded her glasses.

"You would have bolted down your breakfast, and that ain't healthy," Agnes said with determination. "She's all right with the coffee I gave her."

Eve rose, adjusting her jacket. "That's not fair, Agnes. Mrs. Hicks works for a living."

"Well, who in Sam Hill doesn't?" growled the housekeeper.

"She might be on her way to the steakhouse," Helena agreed.

"Even working people take time off to grieve," Agnes insisted.

Violet jumped up, untying her robe. "I want to go with you."

"What!" Agnes sounded like a horn.

"I'm not talking to you," snapped Violet, looking at her sisters. "I want to help with the funeral arrangements."

"You have a job, dear," Eve reminded her.

"We'll be done by the time my shift starts at the drugstore," Violet said.

"I thought you hated all the gloom and doom." Helena eyed her. "Why the sudden interest?"

"Hank would want to know Wild Bill is being — well taken care of." She shuddered a little.

Eve took her youngest sister by the shoulders. "It's sweet of you, honey. But — well, it might be awkward."

"Awkward? How?" Violet stared at her.

"Everyone in town knows you're Hank's friend." Helena folded her napkin neatly on her chair.

"So are lots of us," Violet said stubbornly. "I don't see your point."

"The point is Hank admitted to killing Wild Bill," Eve said. "We believe him when he said he did it in self-defense, but there are a lot of people in town who aren't sure yet."

"You mean they think Hank killed his friend in cold blood," Violet said. "I'm not a child, Eve. You don't need to shield bad things from me anymore."

"How do you think Mrs. Hicks would feel having someone whom she knows supports Hank's story helping her arrange the funeral for the man he killed?" Helena asked. "Did you ever think of that?"

"Of course I thought of it!" Violet snapped. "You two aren't the only ones who know how to take care of the dead. This is one dead I want to help take care of."

"And it's sweet of you," Eve repeated. "But we have to think of business first, and that means making the bereaved feel comfortable."

"I am thinking of business," Violet said. "I came into a third of it when I turned eighteen, didn't I? I have a right to attend the arrangements meeting if I like."

Her lovely features were set like a wooden doll's, and Eve knew in that mood, it would be nearly impossible to make Violet budge from her position.

"She's right, Eve," said Helena. "We can't legally keep Vi from the business."

"Oh, applesauce, who's talking about legal?" Violet snapped. "I'm not going to sue you if you say no. I just want to help Hank's friend, that's all."

Eve's hesitation disappeared at the anxious look on her sister's face. She looked at Helena, who nodded.

She kissed her cheek. "All right, darling. But please be careful what you say."

"Let us do the talking," Helena agreed.

~~~~~

When Violet was dressed, looking almost plain in a blue linen dress, they went down to the funeral home. Mrs. Hicks was seated in the lobby, holding a cup and saucer. The coffee was still to the brim, and she held the edges of the saucer with both hands as if they had not moved since Agnes handed it to her. She was staring across from her at the glass table against the wall with a vase of dry flowers, a bowl of glass fruit, and a pile of business cards for customers.

Eve's heart went out to the woman. It was clear the full distress of why she was there had hit Mrs. Hicks, as it often did for the loved ones when they entered the doors of the funeral home. She recognized the reality that so many family members managed to keep at bay until they were forced to come face-to-face with the funeral arrangements.

Violet was not oblivious to the woman's bewilderment as she
~~~~~

gently took the cup and saucer from her hands and put them on the glass table.

"Good morning, Mrs. Hicks." Eve's voice always went down a notch when she was in the funeral home facing the bereaved family. It was almost like a switch in her throat. "We're glad you're here. We'll do all we can for you."

The woman rose and pulled her scruffy coat around her shoulders. "I know you will, Eve. Let's just get to it."

"Yes, ma'am." Eve glanced at Helena, whose eyes sent the clear message: *No sentiment here.*

And, indeed, when they reached the arrangement room, which had several chairs and couches and a large table in the middle, Mrs. Hicks chose the table, sitting at the head. She rejected Helena's offer to take her hat and coat and sat fully dressed, her hands folded in front of her, waiting.

"We'll need some information for the obituary." Eve opened the notebook she used during arrangement interviews. "Full name, year born, that sort of thing."

"William Matthew Hicks," said the woman. "Born in 1882."

"And his rank in the army?" inquired Helena.

"He was a sergeant" A faint smile appeared on the woman's face. "He was so happy when he got his stripes." She leaned forward. "And he got the Silver Star besides."

"He was a very brave soldier," Violet said. "Hank told me."

The woman shot her a look but said nothing.

"And after the war?" Eve asked.

"He worked at the trucking company in town for a while," she said. "Jesse Gibbons was glad to give him his old job back when the war was over. Said he was the best truck driver he'd ever had. That was until the accident, of course."

"Yes, of course," Helena murmured.

Mrs. Hicks looked down at her hands. "Bill was just trying to help Hank out but he lost his job over it."

"I'm sorry to hear that." Eve glanced at Violet with a warning.

But her younger sister, as always, went her own way. "Hank feels awfully bad about that, Mrs. Hicks," she said in her light, eager tone. "He told me so himself. He went to Jesse and begged him to take Wild Bill back. He took the blame entirely and promised to do anything to pay him back for the truck."

"It wasn't the truck," said Mrs. Hicks in a hard tone. "A man has to think of his reputation. Bill never had any trouble with him, and he was a good driver."

"He went out on his own after that, didn't he?" Eve asked quickly to get them off the subject.

"He always wanted to," Mrs. Hicks said. "His father owned the truck he used and made a good living with it. Bill said it was good luck to him." She gave a faint smile again. "And it was." She then gave Violet an impenetrable look. "It was only Hank that was bad luck to him."

Eve felt her blood run cold as she steeled herself for her sister's snappy comeback. But to her surprise, Violet remained silent, crossing and uncrossing her legs.

"He was always willing to hold out his hand to anyone who needed help," Mrs. Hicks murmured. "He had a big heart like his father." She leaned forward, pressing her hands on the table. "I want that in the obituary. He was always willing to hold out his hand to anyone for help."

"We'll make sure to put it in there, Mrs. Hicks," Helena promised.

"Would you like us to prepare the chapel for the service?" Eve asked. "We have a lovely chapel here if you'd like to see it."

"We won't charge you a penny for it," Violet chimed in. "And you can have any pastor you like. They've all been here."

Helena raised her eyebrows at her younger sister. Eve knew what she was thinking: They had seldom performed funeral services for the people in the Malestra district. Although they opened their doors to everyone in town, they were aware the working-class people thought their services too costly.

Mrs. Hicks, with her shrewdness, did not miss the implication. She looked dispassionately at Violet. "I appreciate your concern, but I prefer the service be done at our church."

"Of course," Eve said with a smile. "We're happy to make sure everything is arranged."

"Thank you," said the woman. "Most churches in our district don't charge for funeral services either." This last she said with a little amusement as she glanced at Violet, whose face turned red.

Eve's heart went out to her sister whom she knew was only trying to help. She reached under the table and pressed Violet's hand with reassurance.

Helena took over with her more sensible approach and explained about the coffin and tomb and laid out the photographs they kept on hand. Mrs. Hicks, in her no-nonsense way, took exactly two minutes to choose both. Both Eve and Helena were stunned as the woman pointed to the casket that was made from metal with brass handles, carvings of elaborate flutes and leaves, and a satin interior. She also insisted upon a large tombstone of black marble.

"Mrs. Hicks," Eve ventured. "The casket might be rather heavy to carry, and the tombstone — well, we might not be able to have it ready in time, as marble takes longer than stone."

"What you. mean, Eve," said the woman in a crusty tone, "is they're both the most expensive items you sell and meant for the rich people."

"They are costly," mumbled Helena.

"Don't you worry about that," said the woman. "I'll find a way to pay for them. I want my son to have the hero's burial he deserves."

"He can have a hero's burial just as good with wood and stone," Violet said. Eve was surprised at how quickly she had caught on to their explanation of the materials.

"Perhaps some soldiers," said Mrs. Hicks. "But my son was a sergeant with medals."

"Yes, ma'am," Violet murmured. She was rolling her gloves in her lap.

"For the flowers, I'd like poppies," said the woman. "Flanders poppies, of course."

"They might be hard to get," Helena said. "The artificial ones are available, of course, but —"

"What about the California poppy?" Violet interrupted. "We can get those from Ethel Chaney."

"It's not the same," said the woman in a soft voice. "Bill loved the bright red color of the Flanders poppies. He said they were the only living things they found in the fields."

"We'll do our best," Eve promised, though she felt Helena's wary gaze on her.

"And one in his buttonhole," Mrs. Hicks insisted. "Where everyone can see it."

"I assume you mean when they view the body," Helena said. "That means embalming, of course."

"Yes, I suppose so," she said.

"You're taking all of this very well, Mrs. Hicks," Eve commended.

"I buried my husband, Eve," she said. "Now I have to bury my son. It's my duty." Her throat caught, and she looked down at her purse as if wanting to open it to take out a handkerchief. "I didn't think I would have to bury them both before their time. But such is God's will."

There was a tense silence for a few minutes. Violet slipped her handkerchief out of her purse and laid it on the table in front of Mrs. Hicks. The woman took it, dabbing at her eyes without looking at anyone.

CHAPTER 16

*E*ve stole a glance at Violet and saw her younger sister had turned a little pale. She gently pushed the pitcher of water and an empty glass toward her, but Violet turned away from them.

"We'll get the death certificate so the body can be released," Helena continued in her official way. "Then we can order the headstone and coffin and the rest of it."

"We'll need clothes to dress Wild Bill," Eve said.

"I've already thought of that," said Mrs. Hicks. "I'd like him buried in his uniform, hat and all. He looked mighty handsome in it." She reached into her purse and took out a box. "And I'd like this pinned on him."

Eve stared down at the round coin hanging from a rainbow-colored sash with a lion in the center. It was simply engraved with Wild Bill's name and the date.

"The medal he received from the Legion of Valor," she murmured.

"You found it?" Violet sounded almost breathless.

Mrs. Hicks gave her a stony look. "The police did."

"Where?" Eve asked, then bit her lip. "I'm sorry. That's none of our business."

"Mr. Clarke and the sheriff were at my home this morning," said the woman. "They found it buried in the backyard."

"Then they must have found the money too," Violet said.

"They found no money," Mrs. Hicks said in a quiet voice.

"But it must be buried there too!" Violet insisted. "Didn't they dig through everything?"

The woman grimaced. "They were very thorough."

"That's odd," Eve said. "Finding one but not the other."

Violet's tone rose a little shrilly. "He must have spent the money, that's all."

"My son did not spend two hundred dollars." Mrs. Hicks glared at her. "He was saving that money for me!"

"But you must admit," Helena began, "if the medal was found but not the money, it's logical —"

"I don't care if it's logical!" the woman snarled. "There's a reason why the medal was there but the money wasn't."

"And that is?" Helena challenged.

"The medal isn't valuable." The woman's lip tightened. "Not to someone who would kill to get money!"

"In other words, you believe Hank stole the two hundred dollars?" Violet jumped up. "Oh, you're wrong! Hank's not a thief."

Mrs. Hicks looked at her steadily. "Most people wouldn't have said he was a killer either. Until now."

"You told us you thought it was all a terrible accident when we visited you," Helena said.

"I've had time to think since then," she said. "I've had time to see."

"But you can't believe Hank would —"

The woman glared at Violet. "And why not? What's a human life to a man who's been in the trenches, always with his gun cocked, always on the watch, always ready to do violence? Bill told me all about it—oh, he told me what it was like." Her eyes narrowed. "What makes you think Hank was any different from all the rest? Because he's your friend?" She said the last with a mocking tone.

Violet stared at her, and Eve was alarmed at her breathless silence. Her younger sister let out a cry, covering her face with both hands, and ran out of the room.

No one spoke for a few minutes. Helena rustled some papers and began collecting the photographs.

"I must apologize for my sister's behavior." Eve felt sick to her stomach. "But you were very hard on her, Mrs. Hicks."

"The man admitted to killing my son," said the woman, her voice pained.

"That doesn't give you the right to — " Helena bit back the rest of her retort.

"You're right, Helena. I shouldn't have said that." She rose. "Is there anything else you need from me?"

"If you can give us the uniform and whatever you'd like to go in the coffin with Wild Bill, we'll see that it goes with him," Eve said.

"I'll send my assistant around to your house this afternoon for them," Helena added.

As they led her through the lobby, Eve's eye caught the open chapel door. Violet sat at one of the front pews, her head bent.

The deep lines in the woman's face softened. "You've been very kind. Everyone thinks I ought to have gone to Chester for the arrangements, but I wanted the sort of funeral my son should have for his contribution to this country. I know you'll make sure he gets it."

"We'll do everything we can," Eve said.

"And please tell Violet I'm sorry for my outburst," she said. "I'm not the sort of woman who lets her emotions get away from her like that."

After they had closed the door, Helena declared, "I wish she had gone to Chester!"

"Perhaps it's better she came to us," Eve sighed.

"I've a feeling it's going to come out one way or another that Wild Bill wasn't as beloved as she thinks he was," Helena remarked.

"Have we ever worked with a grieving mother who didn't think her boy wasn't precious?" Eve put her arm around her sister's shoulders.

"I suppose you're right." Helena was silent for a moment. She nodded toward the chapel.

They entered silently and sat down beside their sister. Eve saw she had one of the Bibles in her hand, though it was closed.

"I've always loved this place," Violet lamented in a soft tone. "It's so quiet with the velvet curtains and the false windows." She peered at Eve. "Dad didn't like those windows, did he?"

"No, he didn't, honey." Eve felt a pinch in her heart as she saw Violet's eyes were smeared with makeup from the tears.

"I think it makes it homier, don't you?" Violet asked.

"I think so," Eve said with a little smile.

"Please don't scold me, Eve." Violet looked desperate.

She hugged her younger sister. "I wasn't going to, honey."

Helena took out her handkerchief. "You'd better wipe that goo out of your eyes before you go to the drugstore."

"I don't care what she says, or what the police think," Violet said fiercely. "Hank didn't steal money from anyone, and he would never kill unless he had to."

"We believe that, darling," Eve assured her.

"They'll probably find the money somewhere else," Helena said. "Even if Wild Bill didn't trust banks, he might have made an exception for two hundred dollars. That's an awful lot of money."

"It's just as Hank said it was," Violet insisted.

"The way I see it, one of two things happened." Helena bent her head in an awkward way, as she always did when she was theorizing. "Either Hank is telling the truth about why he killed Wild Bill —"

"Of course he's telling the truth!" Violet shrieked.

"— or he killed him because he *thought* he had to defend himself from an attack," her sister finished.

"What do you mean?" Eve stared at her.

"I've been reading up on crime and war fatigue," said her sister. "If Hank was having a hallucination that his life was in danger, that could work in his favor. He wouldn't be responsible for shooting Wild Bill."

"But he didn't *think* he was being attacked," Violet snapped. "He *was* attacked. He has a cut on his arm to prove it."

"I'm not saying he wasn't attacked," Helena argued. "I'm only looking at it from the legal perspective."

Violet jumped up. "And I'm looking at it from the friend's perspective!"

"Either way, he gets acquitted," her older sister challenged. "That's what's important, isn't it?"

Violet's shoulders sagged. "Maybe you're right, Helena. I don't know, I'm so confused!" She covered her face with her hands.

Eve gave her sister a quick hug. "Come on, honey. I'll drive you down to the drugstore."

"You needn't bother." Violet wiped the last of the makeup off her face. "I can walk."

"She has to go downtown anyway to get the death certificate and the obituary to Abe," Helena said.

"He'll pump you for details about the funeral arrangements." Violet sniffed.

"I'm sure he will," Eve said as they climbed the stairs to the house.

"He knows we spoke to Annie too." Helena took her younger sister's arm. "Don't tell him anything, Eve."

Violet dressed in her work uniform and reapplied her

makeup. As Eve started the car, her younger sister asked, "What *did* Annie say to you when you visited her, Eve?"

"Not much," Eve said. "Just that she was out after dinner and came home to get Ellie on the milk train to Carson City."

"I mean, what did she say about Hank?"

"Not much," Eve repeated, turning onto Oak Street.

"Oh, don't be such a clam!" Her sister sniffed. "Was she very upset?"

"A little," Eve said. "Toward the end."

"And in the beginning?"

"She didn't seem surprised when we told her Hank was in jail," Eve admitted.

Violet sighed. "They've never gotten along, especially after Hank's father died. Hank said she thought the sun rose and set on his smile."

"Like Mrs. Hicks and her Bill," Eve said with a grimace.

"Oh, Wild Bill wasn't so great," Violet said. "Even Hank didn't think so. Not after the war, that is."

"Oh?"

"How do you think Hank got into those poker games?" her sister challenged. "Wild Bill introduced him to Dale Gifford."

"Who's Dale Gifford?"

"A gambler and a bookie," said Violet. "Hank thinks Wild Bill got some kind of payment for bringing in new clients." She looked out the window. "Poor Hank. As if he didn't have enough trouble after he came back from the war. And then the accident had to happen."

"Ellie isn't bitter about it," Eve pointed out as she stopped to let Hugh and Carrie Hickey cross the street, both of whom waved as they headed for the post office they ran in town. "Annie told us that herself."

"She isn't, but Annie is," said Violet. "Hank said she wanted Ellie to grow up to be a fine lady. You know Ellie's very good with the violin. Or was." The last was said in a softer tone.

"Annie told us." Eve stopped in front of the Rooty Toot Drugstore. "You'll come home for dinner?"

"If Kitty doesn't have other plans," said Violet.

"You know, Annie does care for her grandson." Eve pressed her sister's hand. "She asked Oliver to let her see him."

"I hope she won't lecture him," said her sister as she got out. "Old people do that all the time, don't they?"

Eve made a face at her as she laughed and closed the car door.

CHAPTER 17

The next morning Helena sent her assistant, Charlie, to the Hicks house. He came back with a worn suitcase containing Wild Bill's uniform. The khaki wool jacket with the brass buttons and pants looked almost as if they had just come out of the factory, and the cowhide shoes were scrubbed to perfection. Even the gaiters had been washed until they showed not a speck of mud or dirt.

"It sort of reminds you of a mother getting her son off for his first day of school, doesn't it?" Violet ventured. She had woken up early to help with the preparation of the body.

"Mrs. Hicks wants her son buried like a war hero," Eve reminded her.

"War hero!" Helena grimaced. "He was a sergeant, not General Pershing." She nodded at the insignia with the three chevrons on the shoulders of the uniform.

"Every soldier who came back alive was a hero, as far as I'm concerned," Eve said steadily. "And we're going to see to it that Wild Bill is treated like one, no matter what the circumstances."

"Hear, hear!" Violet raised her hands.

"I don't know that it's a good idea for you to be there with the ladies, honey," Eve said slowly as they laid out the clothes on one of the tables in the morgue, smoothing out every wrinkle.

"Why shouldn't I be?"

"Because they gossip," said Helena simply. "And their gossip is sometimes apt to get nasty."

"I can handle Old Clem," Violet said. "Better than either of you can."

"That's what I'm afraid of," Eve said dryly. "We can't afford to intimidate the ladies. They do a good service."

"Oh, applesauce," Violet smirked, "they love coming here and getting all the dope on the dead bodies. Especially this one, since the corpse expired under questionable circumstances." She sputtered out the last sentence in such a haughty tone that Helena laughed.

"There's nothing questionable about it," Eve said. "Hank admitted he killed Wild Bill. There's no mystery here."

"That's what they want to talk about," Violet insisted.

A little later, the morgue filled with the community ladies who volunteered to dress and arrange the bodies for burial. Eve saw her sister was right. Mrs. Clementine Beaton, the head of Gyver society and the local gossip mongers, immediately came to the point.

"Now, I know he won a medal —" she began.

"Clarence ought to have won that medal," Mrs. Close interjected. "He was in the trenches too."

Mrs. Dalton, Clarence's mother, unbuttoning the uniform jacket, looked a little embarrassed.

"So was Pedro," Mrs. Loy growled.

"Only for the last four months, dear," Mrs. Close said with a sticky smile.

Mrs. Loy growled again and shook out the army pants.

"As I was saying," Mrs. Beaton shot a glance at Mrs. Close, "I know he won a medal, but some of those ex-soldiers simply have no sense of the future."

"Would you have sense of the future if your head was in danger of being blown off every second for months?" Violet asked.

"Eve, I don't think Violet should be here," said Mrs. Beaton in a stoic tone. "She was too close to the deceased."

"I don't give my sisters orders, Mrs. Beaton," Eve said in a sharp tone. "They're free to do what they like."

"What can you expect from those sorts of people anyway?" Mrs. Loy sighed. "It was only a matter of time before one of them in the Mold District went crazy."

"Hank is not crazy!" Violet snarled.

"That's not what Jack Shane told me." The woman, who had Mexican blood, showed her gumption by giving Violet as much snarl as she had gotten.

"I don't know that I would believe everything Jack says, dear," said Mrs. Beaton. "But it's true that most of the trouble we've been having with those veterans this past year comes from that part of town."

"It's been hard for all of them," Eve said with a sigh.

"They have options," Mrs. Close insisted. "They can go back to their previous employer or get themselves a land grant to farm."

"Not everyone has a generous employer who will take them back or the desire to be a farmer," Helena argued.

"Exactly why they turn to crime," the woman said.

"I've heard all sorts of terrible stories," Mrs. Hill said in a whispery tone, her eyes wide.

"We all have, Edith." Mrs. Beaton patted her on the shoulder. "The sheriff promised me he would see to it that everything calmed down with this terrible tragedy of brother murdering brother."

"Hank didn't murder Wild Bill," Violet insisted. "He was attacked, and he had to defend himself."

"So *he* says." Mrs. Close eyed her.

"*He* says it because it's true!"

Eve glanced at Helena, as they both knew their sister's temper was more unchecked than it needed to be.

"Come help me with the makeup, Vi." Helena took her sister by the shoulders and led her to the far corner of the mortuary where she had a desk and filing cabinet.

"You have me all wrong, my dear," said Mrs. Beaton, a touch of sugar in her manner. "I feel for these young men who came back from the war."

"Those who have no family millions to cushion their fall from grace, you mean," Violet snarled as her sister sat her down.

"Vi!" Eve was alarmed as the woman's face went tight.

"Money wouldn't have broken Hank Convoy's fall from grace after that accident," Mrs. Loy said with equal heat. "That poor sister of his!"

Violet was on her feet, clutching the jar of makeup in both hands. "That's not fair, Mrs. Loy. Hank will never forgive himself for that."

"I should think not," said the woman.

"Now, now." Mrs. Dalton patted Violet on the shoulder in sympathy.

"You're very kind, Mrs. Dalton," the young woman said softly.

"Vi, I think you should go to work now," Eve said in a steady tone. "I'm sure Sudie will be glad to see you come in early."

Her sister glared at her. "Not until I've put on the makeup."

"Oh, do let her stay," Mrs. Hill begged. "Violet always makes them look so lively."

Violet threw her an appreciative glance. Eve was relieved to see her temper subside.

"I suppose he got the money somehow," Mrs. Hill murmured as she carefully laced the left shoe on Wild Bill's foot.

"The papers said the police didn't find all that money at his home," Mrs. Close said. "I don't suppose people like him could get a bank account."

"Why not?" asked Helena.

"Well, dear, banks don't just give accounts to anyone."

"If the money wasn't at his home, there must be a reason," Mrs. Beaton said.

"And you think that reason is Hank stole it?" Violet looked at her sharply.

"My, Violet, but you seem to be getting everything all twisted and turned today," the woman snapped. "I assure you that was *not* what I meant. I was simply remarking upon the fact. It seems odd they wouldn't find it there."

"Do you keep two hundred dollars lying about, Mrs. Beaton?" Helena questioned in an almost innocent tone. Violet stifled a giggle.

"It isn't a question of whether it was lying about or not," the woman objected. "The money is gone, and everyone knew Hank needed money."

"I wasn't aware you knew anything about the Malestra people," Helena said dryly.

"I've been helping Eleanora Feather with her work at the American Legion," said Mrs. Beaton. "Now that this Veterans Bureau is going into action, those men will need our aid."

"What has that to do with Hank?" Violet asked as she carefully applied the makeup to Wild Bill's face.

"We know all the men's stories," said the woman. "He came in last week asking for help to get a loan. His sister needs an operation, you know."

"We know," said Helena.

"If Hank did take the money," Mrs. Dalton said in a cautious tone. "I don't know that I blame him. I think I would have done the same thing if I were in his shoes."

"It's a good thing that poor girl is out of the way now," said Mrs. Beaton, shaking her head. "She's suffered enough, poor soul."

"How did you know she wasn't in town?" Eve stared at her.

The woman gave a sly smile. "I told you, my dear, we know everything about those boys."

Mrs. Hill looked like a startled cat. "Oh, but, Clementine, it was Tim who saw them."

"Saw them?" Helena echoed.

"Annie and Ellie," said the woman. "So early in the morning too! It wasn't even three a.m."

"I didn't think Tim knew there was an hour in the morning earlier than ten," Violet said with a snort. Eve gave her a sharp look.

"Annie was seeing her off on the milk train to Carson City," Helena said. "Or didn't the papers say that too?"

"They said Ellie was out of town the night it happened," Mrs. Close related. "I commend Annie for doing that. No use exposing the girl to such goings-on."

"But at such an hour!" Mrs. Hill pressed her hands to her face. "No wonder she was so agitated."

"Was she?" Eve asked.

"Tim said she was nearly jumping out of her skin," said the woman. "Flitting back an forth, back and forth."

"She ought to have waited for the six o'clock train at least," Mrs. Loy said.

"The milk train doesn't cost as much as the morning train," Mrs. Beaton said with authority. "That sort of thing is important to the Malestra people."

"If you had to scrimp and save all your life, it would be important to you too," Violet said.

"I don't see you scrimping and saving, young lady," the woman snapped. "You ought to be grateful your sister provided you with everything you need."

"I am grateful," Violet said in a soft tone. Eve felt a lump in her throat and turned to the medal she was now scrubbing with pumice powder and a cloth before pinning it on Wild Bill.

"Tim said she was so rushed that she didn't even stay to see the train off," Mrs. Hill lamented. "She left her there on the plat-form and went to the telegraph office."

"Telegraph office! At three in the morning?" Mrs. Loy sniffed.

"Heavens, I hope there wasn't a family emergency," Mrs. Dalton blinked.

"Well, of course there was a family emergency, Pearl," Mrs. Beaton said. "Her grandson shot his best friend!"

"She was probably telegraphing the aunt in Carson City," Helena observed as she began to put the things that hadn't been used back in the suitcase.

"Annie is a little too curt in her manner," Mrs. Close said. "Mrs. Earle — my cook, you know, wonderful woman with the souffles and pies — gives her laundry to do now and then, and she says she does a fine job with the starch, but she doesn't much care for her."

"She ought to have seen her granddaughter safely on the train," Mrs. Hill said firmly. "Tim said he didn't like her being left alone on that platform at that time of night, with her not seeing and all. He said he kept his eye on her until she got on the train."

"That was nice of him," Eve murmured absently.

"Maybe Annie sent her to Carson City to get the operation," Mrs. Close offered as she wiped her hands on the towel in the corner. "If they have the money now —"

"You mean because Hank stole Wild Bill's money?" Violet flared. "Hank wouldn't even swipe a cookie off the plate at Gohl's Bakery!"

"Just as you say, my dear," Mrs. Beaton muttered.

Violet closed the jar of makeup with a determined twist. Eve had the feeling she would have been happy to throw it at the woman's head.

The next morning, the grayish-green light to the sky reminded Eve of Wild Bill's uniform. She sat at breakfast with Helena, the morning paper in her lap with the bold headline WILD BILL FUNERAL TODAY! Helena was reading one of the new medical books she asked Dot at the Gyver Public Library to order for her, but Eve had a feeling, in spite of the squinting eyes behind the glasses, she was merely skimming the words, as she turned the pages faster than usual.

"We have to get to the church early." Eve's voice sounded like an echo.

"Vi asked us to wait for her," said her sister.

"I don't know that she should come." Eve peered at her sister's face. "Especially after what happened with Mrs. Hicks."

Helena took off her glasses. "You can't stop her, Eve."

"Oh, I know she has a right to attend just like anyone else," said Eve. "But that doesn't make it a good idea."

"What's not a good idea?" Violet entered the room, dressed in black, carrying a hat with a veil.

"Aren't you overdoing it a little?" Helena nodded at the hat.

"This is for Hank's sake," Violet said. "Wild Bill was his friend, and he can't be there, so —"

"So you want to act like the grieving widow?" Helena sounded almost amused. "The man wasn't married, you know."

Violet looked hurt. "I'm acting like a grieving friend. Just because he and Hank had a fight doesn't mean I can't show respect"

Eve cleared her throat. "I don't think you should come to the funeral, Vi."

"Because I got upset with Mrs. Hicks?" Violet stared down at the plate of food she had served herself as if it were mud. Agnes, who, in spite of her bickering with the youngest Grave sister, petted her shoulders.

"It was unprofessional of you," Helena pointed out.

"Oh, rats!" Violet snapped. "I'm not a mortician like you are."

"You were representing the family business at the time —"

"Helena, dear, please." Eve's voice was quiet. "I'm not talking about that. But the whole thing is going to be upsetting enough to her. We don't want to add to it."

Violet stiffened. "What makes you think I want to add to it? I don't intend to even mention Hank's name at the funeral."

"I don't think it will do any harm for Vi to attend." Helena closed her book and dug into the eggs and sausage. "She knows how to behave at funerals, Eve."

"Of course I do," Violet said. "I've been attending them since I was three."

"That wasn't fair of Papa," Eve said. "I told him so at the time."

"Ain't nice, dressing a little girl in black to attend a stranger's funeral," Agnes agreed as she set the plate of toast on the table. "He oughtn't have done it."

"It wasn't a stranger," Violet threw out. "It was for Mrs. Curtis who used to bring us homemade taffy."

"Now, don't you go sassing me, missy!" the woman barked.

"Agnes, I think the coffee's burning," Helena said. "I can smell it from here."

"Land sakes!" The woman hurried out and bumped into Felix as he came into the dining room.

All three of the sisters stared at him. It was a rarity to see Felix show up at breakfast, as his night shift meant he had off hours and usually didn't appear until much later in the day. Not only was he fully awake, but he was dressed in a dark suit and wore a black armband.

He bent down and kissed his wife's cheek, then took his usual seat at the table.

"You want to go?" Violet ventured in a soft tone.

"I'm part of this family too, aren't I?" He poured himself a glass of juice.

"Agnes, bring Felix his breakfast," Helena said as the woman stood staring with her mouth open. "And stop looking like a fish!"

Felix grinned at the housekeeper. "It's all right, Agnes. I'm of sound mind and body."

"Never said you weren't," Agnes mumbled as she retreated to the kitchen.

"It's not that we're not grateful," Eve said as kindly as she could. "We're just surprised."

"You've never shown an interest in coming before," Helena said.

"Maybe I have more compassion than you think." He glared at her. Helena looked down at her lap. He patted her hand. "I'm sorry, my love. A man is dead under unnatural circumstances. That's a terrible thing."

"Libby Cinder died of unnatural circumstances too, but you slept in when we had the funeral," Violet remarked, sipping her coffee.

"Stop it, Vi," Eve said. "Felix is right. He's part of this family, and he doesn't have to explain why he wants to come."

"Thank you, dear sister-in-law." He bowed. "You always were the no-questions-asked kind of person."

"Don't tease Eve," Helena said sharply.

"But I wasn't, my love," he said. "I meant every word." He plunked three slices of toast in his plate. "I feel for those boys who came back. I always have. Especially when their lives are cut short, on the battlefield or off."

"You feel sorry for Wild Bill?" Helena stared at him.

"Not sorry," he corrected. "Compassionate. That's what we're talking about, remember?"

"His life was cut short," Eve agreed.

"I could care less how it happened," Felix continued. "That's for the police, and the police only —" he glanced at his wife, "— to solve. But the man deserves more than he got."

"Does that mean you'll be attending every funeral we hold for a war veteran?" Helena eyed him.

"He was a friend of your sister's," he said. "I know Vi's broken up about it." He stared into the half-empty plate. "And in spite of what you all think of me, I don't abandon family in their time of need."

Violet's eyes had grown affectionate. "You can be a stinker, God knows, Felix, but sometimes you're a good egg."

"Thank you, my pet." He bowed. "I know in your flapper way, that's a compliment."

"We might need your help carrying the coffin." Helena folded her glasses.

He chuckled. "Always the practical one, aren't you, my love?"

"We're grateful you're coming, Felix," Eve said kindly.

After breakfast, they all headed to the garage, opening the door that led into the mortuary and the back of the hearse to get it ready. When they reached the mortuary, they were met with a crowd of young men in khaki uniforms with two breast pockets and two hip pockets.

"For crying out loud!" Violet stared around the room. "It's the whole platoon!"

"No, miss," said one of the men nearby. "Just the automatic rifle section." He chuckled.

George Pugg addressed Eve, "I hope you don't mind. Your housekeeper let us in."

"These are the men who served with Wild Bill?" Eve felt her heart ache.

"All but one," he said softly. "He's in jail, remember?"

"I'm not likely to forget," she mumbled, thinking of the community women the day before.

"What are they all doing here?" Violet asked.

"Paying their respects, of course," Helena said as Felix went to speak to the men.

Charlie, who had arrived in his ill-fitting suit, his boyish face glistening with sweat, leaned forward. "They want to be pallbearers, Mrs. Wright."

"I gathered that, Charles." She glanced at them. "Not all twelve of them, I hope."

"Only as many as you need," George Pugg said.

"Does Mrs. Hicks know about this?" asked Eve.

"Well, no," he admitted. "But she asked me to see to it that all the boys who served under Wild Bill were at the funeral. They would have come anyway." His voice broke a little. "He was a mighty fine sergeant."

"I know he was," Eve said.

"We'll only need six," Helena said. "Eight at the most."

"You mean seven." Charlie stepped in. "With me and maybe even six if Mr. Wright wants to help carry the coffin." He glanced at the man, who had already ingratiated himself into the tight-knit group with his easygoing ways.

"If you don't mind, I'd rather we do it," George said in a firm tone. "He was our leader in battle. To the army, he was just a regular soldier. But he was more than that to us."

"I think we'd better let the men do it, Charles," Helena said.

"All right, Mrs. Wright," said the young man, but Eve could see he was disappointed. His assistant position kept him mostly in the shadows of their work, and it was only at the funerals that he was visible to the public.

"Now don't sulk, Charlie," Violet scolded, taking his arm. "You can come with us."

"Gee, Miss Grave, that's fine." His face became even shinier.

CHAPTER 18

They moved Wild Bill out of the metal box with the blocks of ice and put him in the ornate coffin Mrs. Hicks had chosen. It was a massive thing because of the cushioned velvet lining inside, and Eve was grateful there were so many men to help carry it into the hearse.

"I don't know how many of your men we can fit —" Eve began.

"Don't worry about that, Eve," said George. "We brought our own transportation. Just tell us where to go."

She gave him the address of the church Mrs. Hicks frequented in the Malestra district, and he gave out orders to the young men as if they were still in service.

"Where's Felix?" Eve asked as she settled into the front seat with Helena at the wheel and Violet and Charlie in the back.

"He wanted to go with them," Helena said as she started the car.

"I'm glad he's coming." Violet sighed.

"Mr. Wright has a sense of family duty," Charlie agreed.

"Family duty didn't stop Hank from going to war," Eve murmured.

"That was different," Helena insisted. "Annie can take care of herself and her granddaughter just fine. Felix's family depended on him for their bread."

"You sound like those old scandalmongers," Violet grumbled. "The way they got their digs into Hank yesterday —"

"Well, what did you expect?" Helena swerved a little to avoid a rock in the road. She drove, as usual, just a little too fast. "That's what they came for."

"I thought they came to do their duty to the community," Eve said dryly.

"They kill two birds with one stone," Charlie said with a grin. "Duty and gossip."

"Well, they don't know anything," Violet said. "But I'll bet it's all over town now that Hank killed Wild Bill for his money."

"They were right about one thing," Eve said. "It's better that Ellie is out of town. I don't know that she could have stood seeing her brother in jail."

"Just because Ellie is handicapped doesn't mean she's not mentally stable," Helena remarked. "On the contrary. Someone who could take losing the use of a leg and eyes as she seems to must have a lot of endurance."

"So odd —" Eve lamented.

"Nothing odd about it," her sister said. "There are people who take such things in stride while others don't. It all depends on one's temperament."

"I wasn't talking about that," Eve said.

"Then what were you talking about?" Violet asked.

"The way Mrs. Hill described Annie," she said. "And Annie hurrying to send a telegram like that."

"It's just as Helena said," Violet insisted. "She had to let the aunt know Ellie was coming, right? You said yourself Annie decided at the last minute to send Ellie on the milk train. Someone had to be at the station to meet her so early."

"That's true," Eve admitted. The street outside the window became a gray line.

"Don't let those gossiping birds bother you, Miss Grave," Charlie said. "They just talk."

"If Hank would have been one of them, like Ivan Beaton or Bill Close, they would have sung a different tune," Violet snarled. "They would believe he killed Wild Bill out of self-defense."

"If Hank had been another Ivan Beaton or Bill Close," said Helena, "the idea of killing for money wouldn't even be on anybody's mind."

"If someone isn't rich, they automatically assume they would steal from someone else," Charlie agree with a sniff.

"What an astute observation, Owl Eyes," Violet said with a smile. "You're using your head for once." She tweaked his wire-rimmed glasses so they slipped down his nose, and Charlie grinned like a clown.

The veterans and Felix were already at the church when they arrived. The pastor descended the stairs of the small building that had a plain structure with a modest cross placed in the corner of a small plot of grass.

He greeted them with an equally plain, mild manner. "I'm Reverend Josiah Phelps." He shook each of their hands, smiling congenially. "Let me know if there is anything I can do to help."

"That's kind of you, Reverend," Eve said with a smile.

He shook his head. "Terrible business."

"Did you know Wild Bill — William Hicks?" Eve asked.

The man chuckled. "Everyone called him Wild Bill, Miss Grace. Of course, he wasn't really as wild as they say."

"He wasn't a saint either, was he, Reverend?" Violet looked at him squarely.

"Violet!"

"Well, it's the truth, isn't it?" Her sister pouted.

"Only God knows what the truth is, child," said the pastor. "Neither you nor I nor anyone can make that distinction."

"No, Reverend," Violet said meekly.

"But one can look at one's deeds in life," the man continued. "Wild Bill's deeds weren't always of the holiest kind."

"But he turned his life around when he came back from the war, didn't he?" Helena asked.

"That he did, Mrs. Wright." The man smiled. "He came to church regularly and joined the adult Bible study class once a week." He shook his head. "Tragic that his life should be taken from him so young."

"He might have died in the war," Helena reminded him.

"He might have," said Reverend Phelps. "But he's in God's hands now."

"And Hank?" Violet asked. "You know he confessed to killing Wild Bill?"

"Mrs. Hicks told me," he said. "That adds to the tragedy." He smiled at her. "I've known Hank Convoy since he was a boy, although one could hardly say he was a regular churchgoer. I judge him no more than I judge Wild Bill or anyone else."

Violet bowed her head. "Thank you."

"We ought to get going," Helena prompted. "We don't want to neglect our duty."

The sisters and Charlie set about arranging the flowers, checking the prayer books and making sure the seating was set. Felix and some of the ex-soldiers helped carry the coffin to the pulpit. Others arranged the eulogies with Reverend Phelps. By the time Mrs. Hicks arrived, the church was in order.

Eve's heart crumbled at the woman who seemed twice as crumbled as the one she saw the first time. She wore a simple black dress and a hat with the veil pulled over her head. She clutched the handbag on her wrist as if it were a comforting toy and shuffled rather than walked.

Reverend Phelps greeted her with warmth and delicacy, but she didn't seem to hear him. She dropped into one of the pews and, holding on to the back of the pew in front of her, looked around the church, her eyes staring like a child. Then, she suddenly burst into tears, covering her face with her gloved hands.

Violet immediately rushed to her and offered words of comfort, an instinct in her that surfaced as a child when she observed the mourners at services. Eve's pride swelled at her sister's unabashed compassion. It was clear Mrs. Hicks appreciated it as well, as she smiled at the girl, patting her head.

The woman recovered and approached Eve and Helena with Violet's arm through hers. "Thank you. This is exactly what I wanted."

Not long afterward, the mourners began to arrive. They were people Eve had only seen in town, and some she did not know at all.

Jesse Gibbons, owner of the Gyver Trucking Company, came in a dark brown suit with the shirt buttoned to the neck. He was a small, stout man with a commanding way.

"He worked for me, you know," he said in an offhand way to Eve and Helena. "Best truck driver I ever had. I guess I should have seen it coming."

"What do you mean?" Helena asked.

"That business with Hank," he said. "I had no choice but to let Wild Bill go. I didn't want to, but the reputation of my company was at stake." He added quickly, "It was business. Wild Bill understood that. I even offered to get him a job somewhere else, but he wanted to strike out on his own."

"What has that to do with his death?" Violet asked.

"Well, Miss Grave, Wild Bill wouldn't speak to Hank after that," he said. "Can't say I blame him."

"A man losing a job over another man's irresponsible behavior is no joke," Felix agreed. "Not for ex-servicemen."

"Oh, it ain't only that," said Jesse. "It was what happened to that little girl. Number one rule of truck driving is, don't hurt anyone, not even yourself. Wild Bill took that seriously. He said any man who even ran over a rabbit with his truck wasn't fit to live."

"So you think they hated each other?" Eve asked quietly.

"You never know what these ex-servicemen will do," he said. "War teaches them to kill first and ask questions later."

George Pugg, who had been standing nearby, gave Jesse a wary look but said in his cheerful tone, "Find you a place, Mr. Gibbons?"

"Oh, certainly, son, certainly." The man cleared his throat as if suddenly realizing George was in uniform.

"Self-serving man," Helena remarked as they watched him go. "I'm sure he's telling everyone he could have prevented Wild Bill's death if he had played peacemaker between them."

"Maybe he could have, if he'd given Hank a job," Violet snarled. "Hank told me he went to him three times before the accident and asked him, and Jesse wouldn't give. He said he wasn't responsible enough."

"Well, my pet, judging from what happened afterward, maybe he was right," Felix said with a small chuckle. Violet glared at him.

Eve was surprised when she saw Annie Convoy coming up the stairs. The woman was in a dark gray dress, and her face looked composed. She watched as the woman approached Mrs. Hicks, who stood with some of the veterans.

Eve glanced at Helena, who said, "She has a right to be here like anybody else."

Mrs. Hicks, however, clearly bore no grudge against Annie, as she took her hand and her face softened at Annie's obvious remorse. Annie raised her handkerchief to her face several times as they spoke together.

"It looks like Mrs. Hicks is comforting Annie rather than the other way around," Violet observed.

"They both lost a son they loved dearly," Eve said.

"You mean they both lost a son they worshiped," Helena corrected.

"Losing a son is losing a son, my love," Felix said sharply. "A mother feels it all the same."

Helena peered at her husband, her face humbled. "You're right, Felix. Maybe I do take too much of a step back on these things."

He patted her hand. "One can't fight one's nature."

Oliver came up the church steps. Something about his warm-heartedness and sturdiness made the feeling of uncertainty Eve had felt since she entered the church disappear.

He motioned her to a corner of the church. "Is the sheriff here yet?"

"I haven't seen him." She studied his face. "Is there something wrong?"

"I hope there won't be," he said. "There's something you should know, Eve."

But just as she looked at him with alarm, the church organ began to play, and everyone looked toward the pulpit.

As there were no more pews or chairs left vacant, the sisters, along with Charlie, Felix, and Oliver, stood against the back wall. Reverend Phelps conducted a brief but powerful memorial in his mild-mannered tone. It was unlike the more grandstanding Reverend Ballard or Reverend Miles, who often conducted the Grave Funeral Home services. His voice was like a calming breeze flowing over the church. Then he stepped aside, and about half of the veterans who had served under Wild Bill read their memorials. Their crisp uniforms made barely a crackle as they read, the emotion clear in their voices as they told of their experiences under Wild Bill's command.

"Funny how someone can be totally different in one place than in another," Eve heard Violet whisper to Charlie.

Oliver leaned close to Eve. "They had a lot of respect for him, didn't they?"

"I can see now why his mother wanted him to have a hero's funeral," Eve said.

"We all have good and bad in us, Eve," said Oliver. "Even people who commit a crime."

"You mean Hank, don't you?" she asked

"I wasn't specifically referring to him."

"Hank isn't a criminal," she reminded him.

"I didn't say he was," said Oliver. "I said he committed a crime."

"Isn't it the same thing in the eyes of the law?" she challenged.

"Not always."

George Pugg spoke in such a loud and clear tone that it almost echoed through the entire church. As he recited his eulogy, Eve heard the creaking of the church doors. She glanced over her shoulder. Sheriff Warner and Deputy Elwood came in, and her breath stopped, as standing between them, in handcuffs, was Hank.

Just as Violet stepped toward him, Eve grabbed her arm. "Not now, honey."

"But he's my friend!"

"He's also the one who killed the man they're burying," Helena hissed as she took Violet's other arm. "Do you want to cause a disturbance?"

Violet succumbed, but her eyes remained on her friend as George went on with his memorial speech.

"That's what I was going to tell you," Oliver whispered to Eve. "He wanted to be here." He added in an awkward tone, "He begged me. They were friends once, after all."

Eve covered his hand. "Your sympathy is a strength, Oliver. Don't be ashamed of it."

Reverend Phelps ended the service and invited people to view Wild Bill in the coffin to pay their last respects. Mrs. Hicks, to Eve's relief, remained sitting in the front row, her head bent into her handkerchief with Rachel Pugg on one side and Annie Convoy on the other, both speaking soft words to her.

She turned to Oliver to ask if he could get Hank away before Mrs. Hicks spotted him, but he had disappeared. She saw him in the corner of the church. Hank and the sheriff were speaking in what looked like sharp terms with the sheriff shaking his head vigorously. Oliver was speaking to both of them in turn.

"What do you suppose is going on there?" Helena asked. Violet, in spite of always being jumpy about viewing the bodies at the funerals, had gone into the line with Felix.

"I can only imagine," said Eve.

"So can I," said Helena. "The foolish boy wants to view the body."

Eve stared at her. "Surely, you can't think he would do that!"

"Why not?" Helena asked. "He's not a cold-blooded killer, Eve. He feels guilt and remorse for what he did. That ought to work in his favor when he goes to trial."

"I don't know that he will," Eve said.

"He has to." Her sister took her arm. "It's the law."

"Maybe there won't be enough evidence to bring him to trial," Eve said stubbornly.

"Nonsense," Helena said. "The police will find evidence one way or the other."

"One way or the other," Eve murmured.

Whatever argument the lawmen were having ceased as Oliver, who clearly had the last word, cut his hands in the air as if ending the discussion. They stayed in the corner while the mourners took their turns. No one seemed to notice them, as they were far enough away from the door to be unobtrusive. But Eve knew Reverend Phelps saw them, as his face was wrinkled with concern.

Violet returned, and Felix wandered out with George and the other veterans. Eve saw her younger sister had been crying, as a handkerchief she recognized as belonging to Felix was in her hand with a few smears of makeup.

"Everybody said he looks peaceful," Violet offered, giving Helena a gracious smile. "You always make them look at peace."

"It's my job, dear." Helena put her arm around her sister. "I took extra care with Wild Bill."

"That was nice of you." Violet leaned her head against her sister's shoulder. "Did they take Hank away?"

"Not yet," Eve said.

"Poor Hank," she said, sniffing. "He would have wanted to be up there with the rest of the veterans giving his own eulogy."

"It wouldn't exactly have been appropriate," Helena said.

"He should be able to mourn his friend," Violet insisted.

"Only Mrs. Hicks has the right to make that decision," her sister argued. "It's her son's funeral."

"I don't think she's seen Hank yet." Eve glanced at the front pews. "Oh, why doesn't Oliver get him out of here before she does?"

"Why shouldn't he let Hank offer his condolences?" Violet insisted.

"Because Hank killed her son," Helena hissed. "These aren't normal circumstances, Vi."

"Weren't you the one who was just telling me that Hank felt guilt and remorse for what he did?" Eve asked. "Don't you think he wants to show that guilt and remorse to the one person who really cared about Wild Bill?"

"Not everything is clear-cut, Helena," Violet said. "Not even in your medical journals."

Helena smiled. "I can't deny that."

The church was now empty except for the reverend and Mrs. Hicks. George had taken his wife out, but Annie remained at her side. She and Reverend Phelps guided Mrs. Hicks to the podium. Eve's stomach tightened as the woman bent over her son's body.

But Mrs. Hicks was no hysterical mother. She held her dignity, her face drawn but with a tenderness in her eyes.

She reached a shaking hand to smooth down the medal pinned on his uniform. She pressed her hands together as if in prayer, looking down at him in silence. Then, she gave a deep sigh, and the reverend closed the coffin lid.

"Wait!" Hank's voice released a distress cry through the church.

With a nod from Oliver, Sheriff Warner and Deputy Elwood grabbed each hand and pulled Hank toward the exit. But he broke away from their grasp and ran down the aisle.

"Hank!" Violet rushed toward him, but Helena stopped her.

Oliver got to Hank first and grabbed both his arms, pinning them in back of him. "Not so fast, son."

Let me go!" The young man's voice rang out in the hollow church. Eve felt ill and Helena steadied her younger sister, who sobbed in her handkerchief.

Mrs. Hicks remained unusually controlled. "Take him back to jail where he belongs, Mr. Clarke. He won't see my son."

The sheriff and deputy took charge of Hank. Eve noticed Sheriff Warner throwing a self-satisfied look at Oliver that said, *What'd I tell you?*

"I'm sorry, ma'am," Oliver said in a shaky voice. "I shouldn't have allowed him here."

"No," she said. "You shouldn't have."

"Please, Mrs. Hicks." Hank's entire body was trembling. "I know what I did was wrong —"

"It was more than wrong." She gave him a steel look. "Killing is a sin, and you'll answer for it."

The young man's voice broke. "I didn't mean to!"

"You killed my son," she said with finality.

"Go away, Hank," hissed his grandmother. "You're not wanted here."

"Please let me see him." Hank was sobbing now. "I want to tell him goodbye."

"You said your goodbye at the point of a gun." Sheriff Warner yanked him back. "Now, come on!"

"Easy, Sheriff," Oliver snarled.

"Reverend!" Hank looked at the man. "Tell her I mean no harm! Tell her I just want to say goodbye to my friend."

Reverend Phelps went to him and laid a hand on his arm. "Please, son. Let Wild Bill's soul be laid to rest. I'll help you unburden yours, but not here and not now." Eve admired the delicacy of his manner.

"Unburden his soul!" Mrs. Hicks snarled. "The devil has his soul!"

"Hank's not a devil!" Violet shrieked.

"Honey, honey," Eve said softly. Her sister collapsed into Helena's arms.

Hank stared at the closed coffin. It was as if all the strength went out of him, and he sank against the sheriff's and deputy's arms. The lawmen had to hold him up as they led him out of the church.

CHAPTER 19

$\mathcal{H}$ampton Cemetery was at the edge of the Malestra District just before the road turned out of Gyver. It had been a while since the Grave Funeral Home had buried someone there, and the first time Violet attended a funeral at that cemetery. Eve noticed how her younger sister's eyes wandered as she walked with Kitty, who had come with her grandmother to pay their respects. Graves were squeezed one next to the other, and gray headstones were chipped and faded, some of them not even standing upright anymore. But the black oak trees offered a comforting shade against the summer sun.

Oliver's profile showed more distress than she would have imagined from a lawman used to attending funerals. She slipped away from Helena and Felix and went to his side.

"What happened back there was all my fault," he whispered.

"You couldn't have known what Hank would do," Eve soothed.

"That's the point," he said. "I should have known. A lawman is supposed to be two steps ahead of the perpetrator."

"Human beings are unpredictable."

"What was I thinking?" Oliver lamented. "Allowing a killer to come to his victim's funeral. I'm the fool. I felt sorry for the boy."

Eve gazed at him. "No one with a compassionate heart is a fool, Oliver."

He looked at her, silent for a moment. His face softened as he tucked her hand in his arm. "I needed to hear that. Thank you, Eve."

She blinked, tears filling her eyes.

The service ended, and people herded out of the cemetery. Violet came up to her holding Kitty's arm. "I think I'll go to the drugstore now, if you don't mind, Eve."

"Of course I don't mind." She cupped her face with her hands.

"I just couldn't face the repast after —"

"She shouldn't have gotten mad at Hank like that," Kitty grumbled. "We were all friends of Wild Bill's."

"He wasn't no friend of yours," Sudie said sharply. "Woman has a right to decide who sees her son's body and who doesn't." She smiled at Eve's worried face, patting her arm. "Don't worry, dear. I'll take good care of her."

"It's better she went," Helena agreed as she watched them filter out with the crowd. "Vi's never been good with funeral receptions."

"Neither am I, I'm afraid," Felix said as he gently took his wife's hand out of the crook of his arm. "I have to be getting back too."

"Take the car." Helena took out the keys. "Eve and I can get a ride back from Oliver."

"I'll put gas in it too," said her husband. "I noticed we're at a quarter tank."

She handed him the keys and suddenly pressed his hand. "Thank you for coming, Felix. I mean it."

There was a silent moment between them, and Felix gave her a quick kiss on the forehead before he bounded out of the cemetery.

"I was surprised to see him here," Oliver said in a low tone.

"We don't always know how his mind works," Eve said. "Sometimes he can be very kind."

Oliver drove them the short distance to Mrs. Hicks' house. Although the sisters had offered to hold the reception at the funeral home where the space was bigger, Mrs. Hicks insisted her son would have wanted their friends and neighbors to comfort her in his own home.

The woman had taken pains to make the living room look less dark and shabby than when they had interviewed her. The darker furnishings were covered with brightly colored afghans and pillows, and the half-broken table with the knickknacks was gone. Four women dressed in mourning were handling the beverages and sandwiches. Agnes stood in the corner with a cross look on her face.

"Those some new ladies you hired, Agnes?" Eve asked.

"They ain't from me," said Agnes. "They're the neighbors. Wanted my ladies to clear out, saying they'd do everything. I knew you'd want me to stay, so I did."

Eve barely hid her smile. "I'm sorry about that, Agnes. Mrs. Hicks has a rather decisive mind."

"Mourning mothers aren't always rational," Helena agreed.

"It's a waste, that's what it is!" Agnes growled. "We got to pay the other ones anyway for showing up."

"That's all right," Eve assured. "We'll let Mrs. Hicks have her way."

"The customer ain't always right," Agnes mumbled as she shuffled to the table with the food and drinks.

"She's pretty territorial about these receptions, isn't she?" Oliver chuckled.

"Just like she is of our house," Helena said. "Agnes thinks it was only an accident of birth that she was born a Bishop and not a Grave."

He laughed, then quickly suppressed it as Mrs. Hicks approached them with Annie at her side.

The woman gave Eve and Helena a wan smile. "Thank you for arranging the funeral."

Eve's breath let out. "I'm glad we could do something, Mrs. Hicks."

One of the neighborly women led in Sheriff Warner and Deputy Elwood, her face pinched to show her distaste for the lawmen.

"Everything all right?" Oliver inquired.

The sheriff grimaced. "I told you it was a bad idea to let the boy come."

"You should have listened, Mr. Clarke." Mrs. Hicks turned a forceful eye on him. "How dare you allow that criminal to come to my son's funeral!"

"It was poor judgment at the very least," Annie agreed.

Sheriff Warner looked almost pompous. Deputy Elwood glanced down at his feet.

Eve's stomach stirred. "It was self-defense, Mrs. Hicks."

"Was it, Eve?" the woman challenged. "Or is that what your sister wants you to believe?"

"It's what we believe," Helena said.

"I realize now I should have asked your permission," Oliver began.

"A funeral is public unless we're told otherwise," Helena said sharply. "We weren't told otherwise."

"I'm not talking about the public," the woman said. "I'm talking about the man who killed my son!"

"Meg, don't upset yourself," Annie soothed. "The deed has been done."

"You're taking this rather calmly, Annie," Eve remarked. "Considering it was your grandson who was thrown out of the church."

"Hank must answer for his own sins," she said in a quiet voice.

"And he will." Mrs. Hicks turned to Oliver. "Mr. Clarke, charge Hank with murder and theft."

"Eh?" The sheriff was alert.

"You didn't find the two hundred dollars Bill won in the house, did you?" she asked.

"That doesn't mean it was stolen, Mrs. Hicks," said the district attorney. "Or that Hank stole it even if it is missing."

"Hank stole it," she insisted. "He's the only one who could have."

"Now, wait a minute!" Annie said. "I admit my grandson committed a grave sin, Meg. But I don't believe he stole any money."

"He's the only one who could have," the woman repeated.

"What makes you so sure?" Helena asked.

"I was putting Bill's things back in order this morning, and I remembered the key," she said.

"Key?" Oliver asked.

"I told you Bill didn't believe in banks," she said. "When he came back from the war, he told me Hank suggested a better way of keeping his money where no one could get at it."

"Buried in the forest?" Sheriff Warner asked.

She stared at him. "Whatever gave you that idea?"

"Nothing, ma'am." The sheriff glanced at Oliver, and Eve knew he was referring to their search for the gun in Rosser Woods.

"Hank said there's a man he knows in Brenas," said Mrs. Hicks. "Sparks, I think his name is. He owns a large vault in the building where he runs his business. He lets ex-servicemen rent safe deposit boxes for much cheaper than the banks."

"Sparks," Oliver mumbled. "What business is he in?"

"Bill didn't say exactly," the woman admitted. "But he teased me once about how he might be able to get me a good price on a vacuum cleaner from this man."

"Electrical appliances wholesaler, maybe." Sheriff Warner

glanced at Oliver. "There's a Sparks & Company Appliances in Brenas."

"Yes, of course!" Annie stared. "Fred Sparks was a friend of my son's."

"That must be the man." Mrs. Hicks' eyes lit up. "He showed me the key once and said if — if anything ever happened to him —" Her voice broke a little. "If anything ever happened to him, I was to take the key to Mr. Sparks, and he would let me into the vault."

"Well, well," Sheriff Warner mumbled.

"I wish you had told us this before, Mrs. Hicks," said Oliver in a tight voice.

"It's not just the money, Mr. Clarke," said the woman. "Bill had some valuables. He didn't have much, but his father left him a gold pocket watch, some pearl cuff links, and a pearl tie pin. He used to take them in his pockets whenever he went out. He didn't trust them at home." She looked straight at Annie. "Bill was wearing one of those coats when he came to dinner that night."

"Yes, he had a coat," Annie said softly.

Sheriff Warner eyed the district attorney. "We searched all of Wild Bill's coat pockets, Mr. Clarke, remember? They were clean."

"My God!" Annie's hands flew to her face. "He took everything."

"Now, wait a minute." Oliver held up his hands. "Your grandson may have put his valuables along with the money in Mr. Sparks' vault. If you'll give us the key, we can take a look."

"I don't have the key."

He stared at her. "But Wild Bill must have left everything to you in his will."

Her lip stiffened. "My son did not expect to die so soon, Mr. Clarke. He made no will."

"You mean you don't know where the key is?" Sheriff Warner asked.

"No one knows where it is," she said sharply. "Hank probably threw it away somewhere after he stole it from my son's coat pocket along with the rest of his things."

Eve realized Annie was holding on to the back of a chair as if trying to steady herself. She quickly guided the woman into it.

"I'm sorry, Annie," Mrs. Hicks said. "You've been good to me. But my son's soul won't rest until he has justice."

"Yes, of course," Annie murmured.

"For the sake of argument, let's say the key was in Wild Bill's coat pocket when Hank killed him," Helena said, and Eve's grip tightened on her arm. But when her sister was formulating a hypothesis, she tended to bypass all signals of propriety. "And let's say Hank took it. How would he know what it was for?"

"He told Bill about Mr. Sparks, didn't he?" the woman snapped. "He would know what the keys looked like. He probably has a box there himself."

"Hank doesn't have two bits to his name, Mrs. Hicks." Annie, recovered, rose and stood very tall. "Any money he has left over from — any money he has, he gives me."

"He wanted you to have it for the household," Eve said.

"He was trying to fulfill his duty," Helena added.

The woman glared at her. "You know nothing of Hank's duty!"

"He knew about the vault," Mrs. Hicks insisted. "He could guess, couldn't he?"

Oliver pressed her arm. "Thank you for telling us all this, ma'am. We'll certainly follow up on it."

"You'll charge Hank with murder and theft?"

"Theft is going to be the least of his problems if he's charged with murder," Sheriff Warner smirked.

"Sheriff!" Eve glared at him. "Perhaps you'll remember Annie is Hank's grandmother."

But the woman looked as if she hadn't been listening. Her

mouth was twisted to show the delicate lines at the corners, and she had balled the handkerchief in her hands.

~~~~~

They left soon afterward, Eve giving Agnes careful instructions on dealing with the dishes once the reception was over. She felt she was babbling half the time, as her mind was on what Mrs. Hicks had just told them, and it was only Agnes' expression of confusion that made her realize she had spoken gibberish that made her correct herself.

As Oliver headed in the direction of town, Eve asked, "I suppose this clinches things, as Violet would say?"

"Clinches things?" Oliver asked.

"In your mind and in Sheriff Warner's mind," she said. "I saw the look on his face when we left."

"Eve means you believe Hank stole the missing valuables," Helena intervened. "Which is not the most important point."

"And what is the most important point?" Oliver asked.

"If Hank did indeed take the valuables and the key — which I still think is yet to be proved — did he kill Wild Bill to get them?"

"When we answer that question, this case will be closed," said the district attorney. "What Mrs. Hicks told us answers one question for me, at least."

"What question?" Eve asked.

"Maybe Hank knew Wild Bill would come with all his valuables on him, including the key to his safe deposit box, and he wanted to get at them."

"By killing him?" Eve asked.

"He asked for the money, and Wild Bill refused," Helena said. "If he has shell shock, he would have seen Wild Bill as his enemy rather than his friend. Shell shock victims usually only see things two ways — with them or against them. And it's usually against them."

"I don't believe it!" Eve declared. "You saw how stricken Hank was at the church. You saw him beg to say goodbye to his friend."
~~~~~

"Hank is a desperate man," Oliver said. "His grandmother told us he was frantic trying to get money for Ellie's operation."

"She didn't say he was frantic," Helena corrected. "She said he was putting money in the piggy bank."

He grinned. "Always fine-tuning, aren't you, Helena?"

She blushed a little. "I know the value of facts, Oliver. In science, in medicine, *and* in the law."

"He could still have been desperate," said the district attorney.

"Desperate enough to kill his best friend for money?" Eve shook her head.

"Guilt drives people to extreme measures, Eve," he said gently as he stopped the car in front of their house. "This boy already carries a lot of guilt."

"Are you going to charge him like Mrs. Hicks wants?" Eve looked steadily at Oliver.

The man stared out the front window, his hands gripping the steering wheel. "I don't know yet."

"A guilty man doesn't kill," Eve snarled as she slammed the car door.

Oliver lingered at the curve for a moment, then drove off.

"That wasn't fair, Eve," said Helena. "He has to think of every perspective."

Eve looked down the road he had driven, now silent and empty. She grabbed her sister's hand. "We can't tell Vi about what Mrs. Hicks said, Helena."

"She'll read about it in the papers," Helena remarked. "If Oliver formally charges Hank, that's public record. Jack Shane is probably camped out at the courthouse now waiting for news."

"He wasn't at the funeral," Eve pointed out.

"No, but Abe was." Helena grimaced. "I saw him talking to some of the neighborhood ladies."

"Then the story will probably be in the *Gyver Bee* this evening." Eve's heart sank.

"Not necessarily." Helena pulled the funeral home key out of her pocket. "He wasn't anywhere near us when Mrs. Hicks dropped her bomb — I looked — and it's not a given she'll tell the neighbors about her suspicions. She doesn't seem the type to share her business with others."

"I still say we shouldn't tell Vi," Eve insisted as they shook out their coats and hats, hanging them on the rack. "You saw how upset she was at the funeral. Give it at least a few days if the papers don't say anything."

Helena studied her. "You can't keep her sheltered from cruelty, Eve. She's not a child anymore."

"So she keeps reminding me," Eve said ruefully. "And so do you, for that matter."

"I don't say we should shove it in her face," said her younger sister. "But if Vi asks me how the reception went after she left, I won't lie to her."

"Errors of omissions aren't lies," Eve said.

"They are to me." The stubborn streak that had belonged to their mother appeared in the angles of her face.

Eve smiled a little, pressing her sister's cheek. "All right, dear. I know when I'm licked, as Vi would say."

"It's not a question of being licked," Helena argued as they headed to the office. "I don't believe in whitewashing, that's all."

"It's not whitewashing when you're trying to protect someone you love from getting hurt." Eve's voice echoed in the quiet room as she plunked down at her desk, staring into the distance.

The angles in Helena's face softened. She put her arm around her sister's shoulders. "Don't worry, Eve. The police will get access to the safety deposit box, and they'll probably find the valuables and the money there, and that will be that."

"That won't be that for Hank," Eve insisted. "Mrs. Hicks will keep pushing. And the sheriff is dying to make a case for murder."

"If it was a shell-shock episode, Hank won't be responsible for his actions," Helena assured her. "His lawyer will make that clear. Oliver is getting him a good one, remember?"

"We can't wait for that now, with Mrs. Hicks on the warpath." Eve gripped her sister's shoulders. "We made Vi a promise, remember?"

"To prove Hank killed Wild Bill out of self-defense," Helena said quietly. "I remember."

"The police can pursue their path," Eve said. "We'll pursue ours."

Helena stared at her. "What do you mean?"

"I mean the two Sherlockas are going to go on their own hunt." Eve's voice was determined.

"Oh, for pity's sake, Eve," her sister scoffed. "We're grown women, not kids."

"Grown women whose younger sister's friend is in trouble," Eve snapped. "She asked us to help, and we can't let her down."

Helena sat down at her desk. "You know I never would. All right. What do you want us to do?"

"I'll let you know when I know," Eve said.

Helena snorted and picked up the phone.

CHAPTER 20

The next morning Agnes greeted Eve and Helena at the foot of the stairs as they came down to breakfast. In a loud whisper, she said, "She's got the itch in her. Came down before I even got the table set. And she's all dressed!"

Eve glanced at her sister as they went into the dining room. Violet was indeed sitting at the table in a blue dress, her face made up, her hands folded in front of her as if waiting to be served.

"You're up early, dear," Eve said as they settled themselves.

"A copacetic observation," Violet said dryly.

"Don't you sass your sister, missy!" Agnes snarled.

"Copacetic means excellent," Violet protested. "It's a perfectly respectable word."

"Now maybe you'll give us a copacetic reason why," Helena said.

"I'm going with you to investigate," said her sister in a cheerful tone.

Eve and Helena exchanged looks. Eve handed her the bacon platter. "Investigate what?"

"Don't be a dumbbell, Eve," her sister said.

"I wish you'd stop using those insults, Vi." Eve sighed.

"Don't even want to talk right at the table," Agnes mumbled as she slapped the coffee pot in front of Violet, making the dark liquid slosh out of the spout.

"All right, dear Agnes," Violet said. "I'll make a deal with you. I'll talk like an old person if you don't burn my hand with that coffee."

"Hmmm!" Agnes retreated.

"I know all about you and Helena playing Sherlocka," said Violet. "I saw it on your faces yesterday at dinner. The police don't care anymore what Hank says. They're going to try and prove he killed Wild Bill and stole his money and his things." At her sisters' silence, she added, "I know you told Agnes to throw away the paper last night, but we get the paper in the drugstore too."

"Abe didn't waste any time," Helena remarked.

"Did you think he would?" Violet asked. "Especially since Oliver told him himself!"

"I don't believe it." Eve grasped the edge of the table.

"You won't believe anything about Oliver that doesn't point to him being an angel," Violet snapped. "But he told Jack they were looking into the possibility that money and valuables belonging to Wild Bill might relate to the killing."

"That doesn't sound like Oliver," Helena objected. "I wouldn't put it past Jack to put words in his mouth."

"It doesn't matter if he did," Violet said. "Everyone thinks the same thing now. That's why we've got to show he's telling the truth."

"Helena and I will do all we can," Eve promised. "But I don't think you should get involved, honey."

"I want to help," Violet said.

"Of course you do," Helena said. "But you're not exactly an objective observer, and that might botch things up."

"Botch things up!"

"People who are personally involved in something like this see things only in their way," Helena said. "Even if the truth points in another direction."

"Oh, applesauce, don't be ridiculous!" Violet slapped her hand down on the table. The coffee cup jumped, and Agnes gave her a cold stare. "I know I acted like a sap yesterday, but that's all over. I'm as logical and rational as you are and as compassionate as Eve."

"We never said you weren't," Eve said gently.

"Vi, we're going after the truth, one way or the other." Helena looked hard at her sister. "Wherever the truth takes us."

"Fair enough," Violet said. "Now, where do we begin?"

"I don't know," Eve admitted. "I thought about it all night, and I just don't know."

"We could speak with Mr. Sparks in Brenas," Helena suggested. "Though I doubt he would give us any information, since we're not the police. It's not like with Libby, where Oliver called us in." She gave Violet a meaningful look. "Oliver himself told you to stay out of it, remember?"

"Then we won't see Mr. Sparks," said her younger sister. "That's his headache, anyway. I think we should see Hank."

"He's already told his story," said Eve.

"He's told his story to the police," said Violet. "Not to us."

"What makes you think he'll tell us something different than what he told them?" Helena challenged.

"Because Hank isn't the kind to spill all the beans to anyone but a friend," her sister said. "It's not the same, hearing about things secondhand. And you just said people see things in a certain way." She looked smugly at her older sister. "Don't you think the police and the district attorney are capable of doing the same thing?"

Helena did not hold back a smile. She always seemed to enjoy it when Violet outwitted her, even when they were girls playing chess and Violet would call "Checkmate!"

"I don't think Sheriff Warner will let us see him," Eve said. "He's a bear when it comes to the jail."

"Then we'll ask Oliver for permission," said her youngest sister.

"Ain't got no call to go to the jail," Agnes growled as she collected the empty platters.

"You never know, Agnes," Violet teased. "I might end up behind bars one day just for the experience."

"If you ain't the most beguiling child —"

"I'm not a child!"

"If I hear about you spending even an hour in jail, even for wildcatting, I'll — I'll —" Agnes took a deep breath. "I'll brain that gum-smacking friend of yours and her fellow!" With this roar, she retreated to the kitchen, leaving the sisters laughing.

"You shouldn't tease her like that," Helena said. "You know how she is about all of us."

"We're not going down there to question Hank." Violet leaned back with a grin. "We're bringing a friend some madeleines."

"Some what?" Helena frowned. "Talk sense, Vi."

"You're both very uncouth," she said. "Those veterans come into the drugstore all the time and talk about the French pastries they ate during the war. That's Hank's favorite."

"And where are we going to find these madeleines?" her sister challenged.

"At the bakery, silly," she said. "Haven't you ever seen those shell-shaped little cakes in the window?"

"Really, Vi." Eve sniffed.

"Well, if some of them had to die, at least they died with the taste of sugar in their mouths." Helena shrugged.

"Now you're being gruesome," Eve snapped.

"Well, what about it?" Violet looked at her sisters. "Do we go down to the courthouse or not? But you have to promise me you'll let me ask Hank the questions. I swear, I can get to the bottom of this theft nonsense."

Eve looked at Helena. "What do you think, dear?"

"It might not be a bad idea," said Helena. "Vi knows Hank better than we do."

They stopped off at Kohl's Bakery first. Eve was glad to see that Karl Kohl, the Kohls' son, was tending the counter alone, though she felt uneasy watching Violet flirt and giggle with him. But she had to admit her younger sister could charm people easily when she wanted to, as she managed to get Karl to give them a dozen madeleines even though he admitted his parents preferred to save them for later in the day.

They went into the courthouse, and Ralph Landry, the elevator boy, greeted them with a tip of his hat, holding the elevator doors open.

He looked down at the bakery box. "Gee, that smells good!"

"Then go to Kohls and get some, stupid," Violet snapped.

"Vi, really," Eve growled.

"Oh, he's just a kid," Violet said.

"A kid who's only four years younger than you are," Helena reminded her in a dry tone. She opened the box Violet held with both hands and slid one of the madeleines wrapped carefully in parchment paper, handing it to him. "Just don't spoil your lunch."

"Thank you, Mrs. Wright." The boy looked pleased. "I'll take it home to the kids. They ain't had cake for — well, for a while." He blushed.

"No, no." Helena shook a finger at him. "This is just for you, Ralph."

"Thank you, ma'am," he repeated, tipping his hat to her.

The sisters reached the third floor, and Ralph opened the elevator doors for them. Ellen was standing there, looking fashionable in a green dress with beads around the collar that hit just below the knee. Her head was bent toward a pouch-style handbag, and she was sliding some folded bills into it. She began stepping into the elevator, her attention still on arranging her purse, so she didn't see them. Ralph, who was holding the doors open, whistled.

The woman jumped, and the purse, still open, fell to the floor. A few things scattered around.

"You clumsy ox!" she snapped.

"Sorry, ma'am." He bent down to retrieve the items. "There are ladies here, and I didn't want you tripping on their shoes when they stepped out."

"Oh, hello." She greeted the sisters with a note of haughtiness. "I didn't see you. I'm sorry I lost my temper."

"It's Ralph you should be apologizing to," Violet said in a steely tone. "He's the one you insulted."

"Oh, no, ma'am." Ralph snapped the purse closed and handed it to Ellen.

"Violet is quite right, Ralph," she said. "I apologize. It was very rude of me."

"That's all right." He stepped aside to let the sisters out of the elevator.

Ellen watched each one in turn. "My, how you all look so different from one another. One wouldn't imagine you were sisters."

"Looks aren't what make a family," Eve mumbled.

"That's a lovely dress, Violet," the woman remarked. "I've always said a young lady ought to start thinking about her wardrobe early in life. My mother used to say, 'the wardrobe makes the lady.'"

"*Our* mother always said, 'A woman gets farther on in life if she has a brain or two in her head,'" Violet said smugly.

Eve exchanged a glance with Helena, and they both hid their smiles, knowing their mother never said such a thing in her life, though she always encouraged her daughters to develop their minds.

"Yes, indeed," said Ellen. "Here to see Oliver? I hope you're not going to give him that." She eyed the bakery box.

"As a matter of fact, we aren't," Helena said.

"I'm glad to hear it," said the woman. "Oliver is reducing, you know. The people in this town seem to enjoy stuffing him with homemade cakes and sweets. There isn't a day when he doesn't bring home something."

"We all appreciate everything Oliver does for the county, Ellen," Eve said.

"And he appreciates all you did to help him with that poor Miss Cinder," said the woman. "He's told me about it often enough. Well, I have my shopping to do. Ta-ta!"

"Ta-ta!" Violet sneered after the elevator doors closed. "She's a high-hatter if I ever saw one!"

"She would love to be a regular invitee to Mrs. Beaton's soirée," Helena agreed.

"Sudie says she overheard her the other day talking about buying a house in Brenas," said her younger sister.

"You mean they want to leave Gyver?" Eve's breath caught for a moment.

"Brenas is part of Gyver county too," Helena reminded her. "There's no reason they shouldn't move to Brenas if they want to."

"Not *they*, Helena, dear," said Violet in a breezy tone as they walked down the hall. "*Her*. That whole place is dripping with privilege, and Ellen is dying to get into it."

"Don't be cruel, Vi," Helena said.

"Well, it's true."

"Oliver wouldn't leave Gyver," Eve said. "He likes it here."

"A man will do many things he doesn't like for his wife," Helena murmured.

"Only if she makes it hell for him not to," Violet said.

They were met by Gladys, Oliver's secretary.

"Haven't seen you in a while, Violet," Gladys said with a smile.

"We need to talk to Oliver." Violet set the box down on Gladys' desk. "Can you watch this for us?"

"Sure can," she said.

"And don't you lay a finger on it, Lee," Violet scolded the clerk whose eyes had been watching them. "If I hear you even opened it, I'll cut off your hand!"

"Aw, shucks," the young man said.

"They're for Hank," she said.

"The veteran who's in jail?"

"The veteran who's in jail was our school chum," Violet said in a sharp tone.

The young man grumbled but said nothing.

Gladys buzzed the district attorney's office. Oliver came out with a big grin on his face.

"Well, well, the Grave sisters," he said. "You see, Gladys, I told you the ladies can't keep away from me." He winked at her.

"Aw, cheese it," Violet said. "We're here on business."

"What business could you have with the district attorney?" Lee sniffed.

She hit him lightly on the shoulder with her handbag, and Oliver laughed heartily as he ushered the sisters into his office.

"Vi, stop being so obnoxious," Helena ordered.

Her sister leaned over the desk, looking the district attorney in the eye. "Do you really believe Hank stole the money and the gold stuff, Oliver?"

"What is this, an interrogation?" Oliver asked, amused.

"Why not?" she said. "Maybe it's time someone gave you a taste of your own medicine."

"Oliver doesn't interrogate anyone," Eve protested. "He only questions."

"It's good I have one Grave sister on my side," Oliver said warmly. "All right, youngster. I'll answer your question. I'm looking into the matter."

"That's no answer," Helena pointed out.

"And it's good I have one Grave sister keeping me honest." He bowed to her. "As the district attorney, I can't have opinions about it one way or the other. I can only investigate the claim Mrs. Hicks made and prove or disprove it."

"Does that include telling the newspapers about it?" Eve eyed him.

"Jack misquoted me," Oliver said. "I warned him I might prosecute him for defamation if he ever tried to claim I said something I didn't."

"What good would that do?" Violet sat at the edge of his desk. "The word will already be out."

"I'm sorry if it upset you," he said in a gentle tone. "We spent the entire morning looking into it."

"And what have you found so far?" Helena asked.

"The gun, for one," he said. "Todd Hilton tipped us off he and Frank Cray go quail hunting in the northern part of the forest every fall."

"Did your ballistics expert confirm that?" Helena asked.

"He did indeed," said Oliver. "Glenn compared the bullet to the gun, and it fit like a glove." He leaned back. "That closes the mystery of the missing gun."

"Did you tell Hank?" Violet asked.

The district attorney nodded. "Hank admitted he now remembers hiding the gun there. But he denied going through Wild Bill's coat pockets. He claims he wasn't even thinking about the money or anything else after he realized Wild Bill was dead."

"Of course he wasn't!" Violet snarled.

"He insisted we go to his house and search his room if we didn't believe him," Oliver said.

"And you did?" Eve asked.

"We had to, Eve," he said. "We have to be thorough."

"Did you find anything?"

He shook his head. "Nothing. Mrs. Convoy let us search the entire house."

"Not to be cynical," Helena said, "but if he challenged you to search the house, he knew you wouldn't find the key or the jewelry."

"He knew because he didn't take them," Violet insisted.

"That wasn't exactly what I meant," said her older sister in a dry tone.

"You and Sheriff Warner are in the same frame of mind," Oliver said. "He thought it would be a waste of time to talk to Mr. Sparks and insisted the valuables and the money couldn't be in the safe deposit box because it was 'too easy.'"

"Did you prove him wrong?" Eve leaned forward.

Oliver pushed some papers around on his desk. "We went to Brenas and spoke with everyone there. Mr. Sparks has a very informal establishment."

"What do you mean?" Helena asked.

"He has a vault with safe deposit boxes for rent all right," he said. "But no formal system of tracking who goes in and out." He grimaced. "He assured us he would put one in place right away now that he realizes how important it is."

"Did Wild Bill have a box there?" asked Eve.

Oliver nodded. "Mr. Sparks, fortunately, remembered him well. He talked to Wild Bill himself the moment he heard Hank sent him. He gave him what he calls one of his 'prime little tombs.'" Here, the district attorney smirked. "Gold-plated door and everything. He even saw him put the money and the valuables inside."

"I thought Mrs. Hicks said Wild Bill always carried that jewelry on him when he went out," Helena said.

Oliver smiled a little. "It seems Mrs. Hicks didn't know everything about her son."

"Are the jewelry and money in the box now?" Violet asked, her eyes bright.

"Now it's empty," he said. "But Mr. Sparks has an explanation for that. Wild Bill came in about three or four days before the dinner with Hank and took all the valuables Mrs. Hicks told us about — the gold watch, the cuff links, and tie pin — and put them in his coat pockets."

"How odd," Eve murmured.

"Maybe he was going to wear the cuff links and tie pin to the dinner," Violet offered.

"Formal wear for dinner with a friend?" Helena scoffed. "Not likely, Vi."

"Mr. Sparks told us further that while he was chatting with Wild Bill, he got a look inside that box," said Oliver. "There was nothing in it but the jewelry."

"You mean the money was gone?" Eve stared.

Oliver grinned. "Mr. Sparks assured me there was no way anyone could have broken into the vault and stolen it," he said. "And Wild Bill wasn't alarmed when he opened it, which means he knew about it." He threaded his hands together. "Mr. Sparks had a theory about that too."

"It seems the man is trying to do the work of the police," Helena remarked.

"Like some sisters I could name." Oliver chuckled. She looked a little sheepish. "He'd heard Wild Bill was gambling."

"We knew that already," Violet pointed out. "Hank told us."

"Mr. Sparks thinks he incurred some heavy losses lately," said Oliver. "That's why he was taking the jewelry."

"You mean he was going to pawn it?" Eve asked.

"That's the theory," said Oliver. "It's very possible he was planning on going to the pawn shop after the dinner on Wednesday night. There's a shop on Dean Street."

"Then Hank didn't take them," Violet said. "Or the money. That's right, isn't it, Oliver?"

"We know now he didn't take the money," Oliver admitted. "I had a man come into my office about an hour ago by the name of Dale Gifford."

"Gifford!" Violet's eyes were wide.

"You know him?" Oliver glanced at her.

"Only by reputation," she said. "I hear things at the drugstore."

The older sisters exchanged a look, as they both guessed where Violet had "heard things." There had been rumors for a while that Sudie's male companion, Paul Friske, had connections with some underworld activity in some of the more unsavory neighboring towns and even owned a speakeasy in a barn somewhere.

"Mr. Gifford owns the Bay Roadhouse outside of town," Oliver continued. "But we know about him and he knows about us. Mr. Gifford saw the story in last evening's paper. He came forward claiming he knew both Hank and Wild Bill. He said Wild Bill had been getting into poker games pretty steadily since he got back from the war and accumulated a lot of debts. He told us about a week before he was killed, Wild Bill paid off those debts."

"How much were they?" Eve asked.

He closed a folder he had been looking in. "Two hundred and twelve dollars."

"Why, that's the entire prize money!" Violet's jaw dropped. "And he told Hank he was saving it for his mother's old age."

"Lucky for us, Gyver Bank & Trust keeps records," Oliver said. "I'm going over there now to check the serial numbers on the bills we seized from Gifford." He rose. "If they match, I'm ready to assume Wild Bill used his prize money to pay off his debts."

"And Hank is free!" Violet squealed.

"Not quite yet, youngster," he said.

"Hank still could have killed Wild Bill intentionally," Helena pointed out.

"Oh, applesauce, that's ridiculous," Violet snarled.

"There's still the matter of the watch and jewelry," Oliver said. "Sheriff Warner is having his men check the pawn shops in the area."

"Maybe Wild Bill lost it in a card game," Eve offered.

Oliver shook his head. "We asked Mr. Gifford about that. He

said Wild Bill hadn't been near the card tables after he paid his debts."

"They won't find anything in the pawn shops," Violet insisted. "Hank didn't take the jewelry."

"Maybe they won't," Oliver said quietly. "But as your sister pointed out, that doesn't mean Hank's motive for killing Wild Bill is what he says it is."

"Oliver, you can't believe Hank would deliberately shoot Wild Bill," Eve said. "Not after this."

"It's not as simple as that, Eve," he said. "Both Mr. Sparks and Mr. Gifford told us Wild Bill was worried about Hank."

"Naturally," said Violet. "They were probably on the way to making up."

"This isn't a school girl squabble, Vi," Helena said. "This was serious."

"I didn't say it wasn't!"

"I didn't mean he was worried about his well-being," Oliver remarked. "He told Mr. Sparks he thought Hank was 'a loose cannon.'"

"Wild Bill would know shell shock when he saw it," Helena insisted.

"Mr. Gifford went further," said the district attorney. "He insisted Wild Bill said several times he feared for his life. He said Hank blamed him for what happened to Ellie and had been going around the gambling circles saying he would 'have it out with Wild Bill' one of these days."

"Baloney!" Violet growled.

"Baloney or not, we have to take it seriously," said Oliver.

"So now the motive is rage rather than money," Helena said. "A man like Wild Bill doesn't fear for his life for nothing."

"You and your textbook conclusions!" Violet snarled. "Hank's been telling the police from the beginning why he killed Wild Bill. He didn't murder him. He was attacked, and he was defending himself."

"That has yet to be proven," her older sister insisted.

"Does Mrs. Hicks know about the money?" Eve asked.

"I just called to tell her," he said.

"Then she can't be angry at Hank anymore," Violet pointed out.

"I wouldn't say she was ever angry," said Eve. "It was more her grief talking."

"She certainly sounded angry when she threw Hank out of the church," her younger sister grumbled.

"That's because you haven't had the direct experience with grief that Eve and I have," Helena said.

"Oh, applesauce, I know anger when I see it," Violet said.

"She must have taken it hard." Eve looked at Oliver.

"Shattered all her illusions about her heroic son," Helena said in a nasty tone.

"Don't be mean, Helena," Violet snapped.

He stared at the far corner of his desk. "She won't believe it, of course. She still wants me to prosecute Hank for murder and theft."

"We'll make her see Hank's telling the truth," Violet said stubbornly.

He leaned toward her. "'I hope by 'we,' you mean me and the police."

"Of course I do," Violet said quickly. "What other 'we' is there?"

He cast a wary eye across the couch where all three sisters sat side by side. Then, he picked up his coat. "Well, now that I have three ladies trapped in my office, I have an excuse not to have lunch alone. Join me at Browly's for steak and eggs?"

Before Eve could open her mouth, Violet said, "We can't. We're going to visit Hank."

He raised an eyebrow at her. "I thought I told you to stay out of it."

"Relax, Oliver." Violet said. "This is a social call."

"Nobody gets social in a jail."

"Well, I do." She flung the door open. "Take a look at that box on Gladys' desk."

Gladys was shooing Ron Wayne, the assistant district attorney, away from the white bakery box.

"Not a very healthy lunch," Oliver remarked.

"We're bringing dessert," Violet said roughly. "Oliver, you have to give us a note so we can see Hank. That brute sheriff probably won't let us in."

"He is a stickler for family members and lawyers only," Eve agreed.

"I'm as good as family," Violet insisted. "We've been friends since high school. I'm much nicer to him than Annie, and she got to see him."

Oliver leaned against the desk. "And all you want is bring him dessert, eh?"

"Truly." She held up her hand as if to swear.

"It takes all three of you to carry that little box?" He eyed Helena first and then Eve.

Eve felt uneasy, but Helena glanced at her as if to say: *Keep up the façade* .

"It can't do any harm, can it, Oliver?" she asked.

"You tell me," he said. "I'm not forgetting you three broke the rules with the Libby Cinder case, asking questions all over the place without my knowledge."

"And solved the case for you," Violet reminded him. "But we just want to see Hank. Please." She regarded him with her eyes like two lamps lit with innocence.

He looked from one to the other and sighed, picking up the box. "All right. I'll take you down myself."

Violet planted a kiss on his cheek and scurried ahead to the elevator

CHAPTER 21

Both the sheriff and the deputy sheriff were out when they reached the police station. Three assistant deputies lounged around, as the rest had gone to lunch.

"Joe, I want you to let the Grave sisters see Hank Convoy," said Oliver.

"Whatever for?" Joe blinked.

"Now, don't ask questions, Joey." Violet gave him a sweet look.

"Hank had lunch yet?" asked Oliver.

"We brought him a tray, but he wouldn't take it," said Assistant Deputy Bobby McKay. "That stew is my ma's recipe too." He looked personally insulted.

"Well, maybe these ladies can coax him to eat this." He set the bakery box down on the counter. "Don't bother checking it. I've already done that." Eve looked at him gratefully. "I'm giving them permission to see Hank, okay?"

"Sure, Mr. Clarke," said Joe. "The sheriff wouldn't object to that."

"He couldn't," said Assistant Deputy Tom Ford with a grin. "Ain't no use going against the district attorney." Joe gave him a dirty look and bent over his sandwich.

"Oh, and Joe," Oliver leaned forward, "make sure the ladies are accompanied by one of the men here."

"That isn't necessary," Violet said quickly.

"Oh, but it is," Oliver emphasized. "We can't let ladies visit a man behind bars without an escort."

Violet's voice rang out, "Of all the —"

"He's only looking out for your best interest, Violet," said Joe. "Hank's a dangerous criminal, you know."

Eve pressed her younger sister's hand when she saw her about to burst out in protest. "I'm sure Hank would never hurt a friend, and we're friends of his. Remember, Oliver?" She gave him a pointed look.

"He killed his best friend, didn't he?" Bobby mumbled.

"Just make sure someone's there to keep an eye on things, eh?" Oliver winked and grinning at the sisters, breezed out of the station.

"Oliver certainly bilked us, didn't he?" Helena mumbled.

"Not on your life," Violet hissed. Then, in the honey-toned voice she had used before, she cooed, "It's nice of you to let us see Hank, Joey." She took his arm.

"It's nothing." The young man grinned as they headed down the hall. "Say, isn't there a dance this Saturday?"

"Sure there is," Violet said. "I counted on you taking me. You wouldn't let me go alone, would you, Joey, dear?" A pout hung on her face.

Helena rolled her eyes at Eve.

"She doesn't give two hoots about Joe," Eve whispered to her sister.

"Vi's more devious than you think, Eve," her sister returned.

"I'll be glad to take you," the young man said as they entered one of the rooms. "I ought to take you to the interrogation room, but this is our lounge. It's cozier."

"That's sweet of you, Joey." Violet straightened the collar of his shirt. "Now, there's no need for you to stay. Hank's a good friend of ours, you know."

"How good a friend?" The young man's eyes narrowed.

"Oh, don't be a goof," Violet said. "You don't want Hank to feel like he's being watched, do you?"

"It would be the worst thing," Helena said quickly. "Look, Joe, I have medical training, remember? Don't you think I know how to keep someone calm?"

"I suppose that's true," Joe admitted.

"I'll tell you what, Joey." Violet put her hands on his chest. "You be a good boy and keep the door open and just go back to your lunch. If we need you, we'll call you right away."

Eve could see the young man was wavering. "If Mr. Clarke found out I left you alone with him —"

"He won't find out," Eve said. "We certainly won't tell him and I'm sure Hank wouldn't."

"He said to keep an eye on things, didn't he?" Helena said. "If we keep the door open, you're keeping an eye on things."

"You got something there, Mrs. Wright." The young man's eyes wandered toward the front desk where his lunch sat half eaten.

"Please, Joey?" Violet looked up at him.

"Well —" The young man patted her arm. "I suppose it's all right, seeing as Mrs. Wright is a doctor and all. You wait here while I get him."

The moment he left the room, Violet burst out, "Well, if that wasn't the dirtiest trick Oliver tried to pull on us!"

"You can't blame him," Helena said. "Your 'social call' act didn't fool him one bit."

"It fooled Joe all right," Violet said with a self-satisfied nod. "At least we can talk to Hank alone. Hank wouldn't have told us anything if a policeman was here."

Clanging sounded from outside, and Joe came in leading Hank. Eve heart sank to see the young man with the defeated look on his face, staring down at the handcuffs. His sandy hair hung over his face, and the sad angle of his features was apparent.

"Hank!" Violet screeched, running to him and throwing her arms around his neck.

He was bewildered at first, but when she let go, it was as if his mind suddenly comprehended. With a big grin, the features lost their sadness. "Hello, Vi. What are you doing here?"

"We've come to see you, silly," she said. Then, she glanced back at Joe. "Okay, Joey?"

The young officer said emphatically, "I'll be right outside if you need me."

"We'll be sure to call." Helena rushed him out of the room and closed the door.

"You remember my sisters, don't you, Hank?" Violet asked.

"Sure I do." He smiled at them. "Mrs. Bishop made the best pink lemonade on the block."

"She hasn't made it in a long time," Eve said.

"Maybe when you get out, you can come over and we'll give you some," Violet said. "And sugar cookies with icing on top. I remember how you like them soft in the middle —" Her voice suddenly lost its animation, and she broke down with a loud sob.

Helena shoved a handkerchief at her. "Do you want Joe to come in here?"

"Don't cry, Vi." The look of sadness came back into his face. "Please don't cry!"

"I'm sorry." Violet wiped her eyes. "I just can't believe it, that's all. And that Joe putting those handcuffs on you!" She glared down at them.

He smiled a little. "That's not so bad. And they've all been nice to me here, even Sheriff Warner." He stared at the floor. "I must have been crazy!"

"You weren't crazy," Eve said gently. "Wild Bill attacked you, and you had to defend yourself."

"I'm glad someone believes me," he said. "They told me this

morning Mrs. Hicks thinks I killed Wild Bill for his prize money and his watch and jewelry. I swear I didn't!"

"Of course you didn't," Violet said in a steady tone. "Oliver's already proved it."

"You mean they know I didn't take the money?" He looked hopeful.

"Dale Gifford told Oliver that Wild Bill paid him two hundred and ten dollars for his debts a week before he was killed," Helena supplied.

"Two hundred and ten dollars!" Hank let out a whistle. "I didn't know Wild Bill owed that much."

"Oliver has to check that the serial numbers on the bills Mr. Gifford gave him match those the bank gave the Legion of Valor," Eve said.

"So you see, you'll be free soon." Violet smiled.

"You forget the police are checking on the watch and jewelry," her sister reminded her.

"I didn't take any watch and jewelry!" Hank's voice echoed in the room. Violet motioned toward the door, and he lowered his tone. "I wouldn't do that to Wild Bill. He told me they were his father's."

"Suppose someone else took them?" Eve suggested. "Maybe someone wandered into the alleyway after you were gone and stole them."

"Sure, that's what happened!" Violet's eyes shone. "Some bum or hobo. The police will find him and it will all be over." She pressed Hank's hand.

Helena was quiet for a moment. "You're forgetting the threats, Vi."

"What threats?"

"Both Mr. Sparks and Mr. Gifford said Wild Bill feared for his life," Eve reminded her.

"Why?" Hank blinked.

"Oh, they said Wild Bill told them you were 'a loose cannon,'" Violet sniffed. "Ridiculous!"

"Maybe I am," Hank said softly. "Maybe Granny's right to think I'll never amount to anything."

"Applesauce!" Violet growled.

Helena laid her hand on his arm. "All you need is a little help, Hank. Once you're out, we'll see that you get it."

He gave her and Eve a sweet smile. "You've always been nice to me, both of you."

Tears welled in the corners of Eve's eyes.

Helena leaned forward. "How's the wound?"

"It doesn't hurt anymore," he said. "I don't even take pills for it."

"May I see it?" she asked.

He stretched his arm out on the only table in the room. Helena brought the blanket lying on the couch and laid it carefully underneath. Then, she slowly unwrapped the bandage. Eve clenched her teeth a little as she exposed the healing gash. But the wound wasn't as bad as she thought it would be.

Violet, licking her lips, demanded, "Well?"

"Well what?"

"Is there anything to show it wasn't self-inflicted?" her sister prompted. "That's what you're looking for, right?"

Hank grinned. "It's uncanny how you three sisters can read one another's mind." In a softer tone, he added, "Ellie and I are like that."

"There isn't anything to show it was or it wasn't." Helena began to wrap the bandage around Hank's arm again.

"What the devil does that mean?" her sister snapped.

"No need to swear, dear," Eve chided.

"It's not easy to tell with a knife wound how it was inflicted," said Helena. "If I could see the knife and the angle of the blood, it might help."

"I can't understand why the police can't find it," Hank

lamented, straightening his sleeve. "I didn't touch it when I — I left it right where it was."

"And where was it?" Eve asked.

"I don't know," he said. "In Wild Bill's hand, I guess."

"If someone stole the watch and jewelry, why wouldn't he steal the knife too?" Violet asked.

"And drag the body behind the garbage cans?" Helena's forehead wrinkled. "That seems like far too much work for anyone to do just for a knife and a few trinkets."

"The tramp may have thought there was a lot more than just a few trinkets if he found the key and realized it belonged to a safe deposit box," Violet challenged.

"A safe deposit box kept in an appliance company in Brenas?" Helena snorted. "That would be nothing short of a miracle."

"That's what I need right now." Hank shook his head. "A miracle."

"Don't say that, Hank," Violet cooed.

"But it's true," he said. "Ever since my dad died, I've made a mess of my life. I should have listened to Granny. I should have stayed at the lumber company instead of fooling around, thinking I could do better."

"You would have withered and died in that saw mill," Violet insisted.

"But I would have brought home a paycheck every week," he argued. "That's all Granny ever wanted me to do. Take my position as the man of the house, like Dad did." He sighed. "Well, at least Ellie isn't around to see all this. I'm glad Granny sent her to Carson City."

"Just in the nick of time," Helena remarked.

"Come on, Hank, eat your madeleines." Violet pushed the box toward him. "They're getting all soggy."

Eve stared at the white cardboard that already had some grease spots on the side from where the cakes had brushed against it. The glare of the lights seemed as bad as the interrogation room, but the furnishings, though old, were comfortable. Her sister's words swung like an echo with the string lamp above her. *In the nick of time, in the nick of time...*

"Hank, are you sure no one was around when you and Wild Bill went out to the alleyway that night?" Eve asked.

He shook his head. "I don't think so. My head is still a little muddled about things."

"So there could have been someone but you don't remember?" Violet pressed.

"The police already checked with the neighbors," Helena reminded her.

"There may have been someone on the street," she argued. "It wasn't that late at night."

"The neighbors would have said so," Helena insisted.

"Maybe not," Hank said in a rueful tone. "They're nice people, but when it comes to the police, they 'keep themselves to themselves,' as they say in the storybooks." He added, "I don't blame them really."

"Well, then, maybe they'll talk to us," Violet said.

"We have no authority —" her sister began.

"All the more reason," Violet snapped. "Look, if we tell them we're trying to help Hank, they might give us something we can take to Oliver. Maybe they saw Wild Bill attack Hank. That would be enough, wouldn't it?"

"I think we should ask Oliver's permission to speak with them," Eve said.

"Oh, applesauce!" Violet sniffed. "We're going as concerned friends of their neighbors. They've known Hank since he was a kid."

"That's true," Hank admitted.

"If they knew something, maybe they would tell us," Eve said. "What do you think, Helena, dear?"

"If Vi wants to, I guess it can't hurt, as long as we tell them we have Hank's permission to talk to them on his behalf." Helena looked at the young man.

For the first time, a ray of hope appeared on his face. "Tell them I asked you to speak with them. They'll help."

"Splendid!" Violet jumped up. "We'll go right away. And you, eat your madeleines!" she scolded.

"Do you really think they'll tell you anything?" Hank asked.

"We can only try." Eve rested her hand on his shoulder. "Don't despair."

He smiled at her. "I can't tell you how much I appreciate all your help. People are saying you're a good bunch of detectives."

"We're not detectives," Helena protested. "We're just trying to help."

"We'll make them talk!" Violet declared so loudly that Joe poked his head through the door. "It's all right, Joey, we're done now. And you!" She glanced at Hank and threw the box open. "Eat!"

The young man grinned and began to dig into the madeleines.

CHAPTER 22

*E*ve convinced Helena to let her drive since the roads into the Malestra district were rough and patchy and required more careful driving. She parked the car on Dean Street, which was now quiet in the wake of the lunch hour, the workers in the warehouses that dotted the street having gone back to their jobs.

"Why here?" Violet asked as she shook her skirt out.

"I thought we would see the Kramers first," said Eve. "They're right behind the Convoys and closest to the alleyway."

"If anyone saw Hank and Wild Bill, they're the most likely witnesses," Helena agreed.

"For crying out loud, don't call them witnesses in front of them," Violet snapped. "That will clam them up for good."

"I wasn't going to," Helena retorted. "I do have some common sense, Vi."

Violet grinned and linked her arm with her sister's. "Only when you're out of that snail-ridden shack you call a laboratory, darling."

Both John and Leslie Kramer were at home with John on his

way out with his coat and hat. But he immediately took them off when he heard why the sisters were there.

"Glad you're working on behalf of Hank and not the police." He showed the sisters into the tiny living room. "That boy's as innocent of murder as a newborn babe."

"Then you don't believe Hank murdered Wild Bill?" Violet asked.

"We sure don't," said Leslie. "We've known Hank since he was a boy. He and our son Jeff were good friends."

"You could help us a great deal," Eve said. "We're looking for anything you might remember about that night."

"Even if it seems insignificant," Violet chimed in.

"I don't know what we could tell you that we haven't already told the police," John said.

"Did you see Wild Bill at the Convoys that night?" Eve asked.

"Your back windows and theirs are pretty close," Helena offered. "Maybe you had your windows open or they did?"

"As a matter of fact, we did," Leslie said. "It was an awfully hot night."

"Sure was," John agreed. "We had all the windows in the house open."

"And the Convoys?" Eve asked.

"Well, the curtains were closed, but they had their windows open, I believe."

"How do you know?" asked Violet.

"We heard them talking," said Leslie. "The family aren't loud talkers as a rule, but when you have all the windows open—"

"So you heard Wild Bill's voice?" Helena asked. "How do you know it was his?"

"Oh, he's visited them plenty of times," said John. "When you live close to people for years, you get to know whose voice belongs to the house and whose doesn't."

"Did you hear what they were saying?" Violet leaned forward. "Oh, I don't mean eavesdropping —" She blushed a little.

John grinned. "I don't think there's anyone around who doesn't eavesdrop on their neighbor once in a while. Can't help yourself."

"No, you can't," Eve admitted.

"I didn't hear much," Leslie said. "We had the phonograph playing. Did you, dear?" She looked at her husband.

He shook his head. "Just heard the voices, that's all."

"How did Wild Bill sound?" Eve asked. "I mean, did he sound happy or mad or — afraid?"

They both were silent for a few moments. "I really can't say, Eve," said John. "I didn't notice anything in particular about him."

"Neither did I," Leslie said. "I'm sure if there was something, we would have noticed it."

Helena glanced through a narrow doorway beyond the living room. "Is that the kitchen?"

Leslie rose. "How terrible of me. I didn't even offer you anything."

"Please don't bother," Eve said quickly.

"I only asked because it seems like the room closest to the alleyway," Helena said in an apologetic tone. "May we see it?"

"Certainly," said Leslie.

The kitchen was tiny but cozy with the barest essentials like a sink, cabinets, and a small kitchen table. Eve noted there was one tiny window that faced Dean Street and a solid white door.

"Does that lead to the alleyway?" Helena nodded toward it.

"Sure does." John opened the door. The exit to the alleyway was similar to the Convoys' with two steps and a small patch of grass and mud on either side. Eve saw the garbage cans were a little distance down the alley in the other direction of Dean Street.

"Did you happen to have the back door open that night too?" Violet asked. "Sometimes Agnes opens ours to let in the breeze."

John chuckled. "Not in this neighborhood, honey."

She blushed again and leaned against the sink.

"Did you see or hear anything coming from the alleyway?" Helena asked.

"Funny you should ask that," he said. "I was doing the dishes that night, and I sure noticed the scent of a Cuban cigar."

"Cuban cigar?" Eve asked.

He grinned. "Best kind of cigar you can get this side of the river. Hank's father used to smoke 'em on special occasions."

"Yes, they were smoking that night," Eve murmured. "Hank and Wild Bill."

"I was tempted to go outside to say hello," the man continued. "See if I could wrangle one out of them. But Leslie was calling me for some gin rummy, and I wanted to finish the dishes."

"Anything else you remember, Mr. Kramer?" Helena asked.

"There was that sound, wasn't there, dear?" Leslie asked.

"Sound?"

"Just as I was finishing, Leslie came in to see what's what," said John. "And we heard it. Sort of like a champagne cork popping."

Eve's breath caught. "Could it have been the sound of a gun?"

"Could have been." John shrugged. "Not a very big one, though."

"And you didn't go out to the alleyway to investigate?" Violet asked, clearly disappointed.

"Cars backfire all the time in this neighborhood," he said, a little annoyed. "If you lived here, you'd know people don't think twice about a noise now and then."

"I'm sorry," Violet said. "I didn't think about that."

He patted her head like a puppy. "Don't think twice about it, honey."

"Is there anything else you can tell us?" Eve asked.

Both Kramers thought for a moment, then shook their heads.

"You've been a great help." Eve smiled as the couple led them to the front door.

"Your father was a decent man, Eve," said John. "Always treated everyone the same." In a softer tone, he added, "We were truly sorry when we heard about him and your mother getting sick all of a sudden like that."

Eve nodded, feeling her throat tighten.

"John, dear, you've got to run," Leslie reminded him. "I'll see the Grave sisters out."

"One more question before you leave, John," Eve said. "Did either of you notice anyone around that night you've never seen before?"

John shook his head. "Can't say I did." He kissed Leslie on the cheek and waving at the sisters, started down the street.

All three sisters looked at Leslie, who was staring out the open doorway. "Your question made me remember something."

"You saw someone?" Violet perked up. "A tramp, maybe?"

"Not exactly," said the woman. "But as I was making sure the doors was locked for the night, I noticed a taxi sitting across the street."

"About what time was this?" Helena asked.

"I or John usually check the doors around ten or so," she said. "We like knowing they're locked before we go to bed so we don't have to worry about it."

"Is it usual to see taxis that time of night?" Eve asked.

"Not around here," she said with a small laugh. "I suppose that's why it caught my attention."

"What did it look like?"

"Oh, just a regular taxi cab, you know," said the woman. "It had Huff & Mullins on the door."

"Huff & Mullins Taxi Service," Helena said with a nod.

"But no tramp?" Violet's face fell.

The woman smiled. "We keep a pretty close neighborhood watch around here. Someone like that wouldn't be around here for long."

Eve pressed her hand. "Thank you for answering us honestly, Leslie."

When they were out on the street again, Violet pounced. "The taxi driver must have seen what happened!"

"Then why hasn't he come forward and told the police?" Eve challenged.

"Nobody likes to get mixed up with them," Violet said. "Not people in the Mold District."

"Don't hold out too much hope, Vi," Helena cautioned. "This is a dark street at night."

"It can't hurt to ask Josephine and Amelia if they had a cab out that night," Eve said. "But I think we ought to finish here first. The Kramers gave us some good information, and the others might also."

"Where to next?" Helena asked. "The Blakes or the Anthonys?"

"What do you think, dear?" Eve asked.

"I say the Blakes," Violet said. "They're right next to the Convoys."

"They're also farther away from the alley," Helena pointed out.

"Well, so are the Anthonys." She glanced at the house next to the Kramers.

"I didn't say it wasn't a good idea," Helena said.

"All right, then." Eve started up Dean Street. "Let's go through Yew Street."

"It's much faster to get to the Blakes through the alleyway."

Eve was silent for a moment.

Violet answered for her, "Eve doesn't want to go through the alley because of me. Because it was the crime scene."

"Oh, for pity's sake!" Helena said gruffly. "What nonsense!"

"I'm not a baby, Eve," said Violet in her usual exasperated tone. "I think we ought to see the crime scene anyway. We only know what Oliver told us."

"It's not even a crime scene anymore," Helena pointed out. "They've cleared the barriers and the police."

Eve sighed. "I suppose I'm just being silly."

The alleyway was now empty of any hint that something had

been amiss only days before. Eve could not keep her eyes away from the garbage cans when they passed, relieved to see they were in a tidy corner against the building, and any sign of blood on the street was gone.

"The police certainly did a thorough job cleaning up," Violet observed.

"A gruesome way of putting it," Eve said.

"Darling, we've been seeing gruesome things since we were born," her younger sister reminded her.

"There's nothing gruesome about someone who has died," Helena insisted. "We're all going to experience it one day."

"Must you put it like that?" Eve shuddered.

They reached Wadding and passed the Convoy house. Eve couldn't resist peering at the front windows, but the curtains were closed, and she couldn't see a thing.

Henry and Selma Blake, an older couple, were at home and received them with a cordial but less friendly manner than the Kramers.

"Can't think what interest you would have in this nasty business, Miss Grave," Henry said to Eve. Even though everyone in town was informal, Henry still held on to his Victorian manners.

"Hank is a friend of mine," Violet answered. "We're trying to prove he killed Wild Bill out of self-defense."

"That ain't your business," Henry insisted. "That's the police's job."

"They're trying to help, Henry," Selma insisted. "Why shouldn't they?"

"Because women ain't got no business sticking their noses into the law!" he declared.

Eve glanced at Helena, seeing by the look on her face that she wanted to respond, but she kept silent. Violet frowned but followed her sister's example.

"Oh, stop being a ninny," his wife smiled at the sisters. "Hank's a nice boy. How can we help?"

"You told the police you saw Wild Bill at the doorway of the Convoy's house that night," Eve began.

"We just saw him for a minute," Selma said.

"Did you notice anything unusual about him?" Helena asked.

"Unusual?"

"Was he carrying something?" Violet inquired. "Anything in his hands?"

"What a silly question!" Henry sniffed.

"It's not silly," Violet snapped. "People bring things with them when they come to dinner all the time, like flowers or a cake."

"I never brought anything to anyone in my life," Henry said.

"I'm not surprised," Helena mumbled.

"I didn't see him carrying anything," said Selma. "But Wild Bill was at the Convoys so often, he was like one of the family."

"Had his coat pockets stuffed to the gills," Henry remarked. "Like all those ex-servicemen." He chuckled. "Habit, I guess, since they have to haul everything with them on the battlefield."

"You couldn't see what was in the pockets?" asked Violet. "Wild Bill didn't open his coat to pull something out, for example?"

"Now, why you so interested in what Wild Bill had in his pockets?" Henry scoffed.

Helena pressed her sister's wrist as if anticipating her sharp response. "What was Wild Bill's attitude toward Hank when he met him at the door?"

"We told the police that," Selma reminded her.

"They were friendly," Henry said.

"How do you know?"

"Eh?" He squinted at her.

"How do you know they were friendly?" Helena asked. "Did they greet one another heartily, did they shake hands, what?"

Henry scratched his head. "Well, no, as a matter of fact."

"Did they smile at one another?" Helena persisted.

"No," Selma answered. "I don't remember they did much of anything."

"Why wouldn't they be friendly?" Henry asked.

"Why wouldn't they be friendly indeed," Helena mumbled.

"Did you see or hear anything that struck you as out of the ordinary that night?" Eve asked.

"Like what do you mean?" Henry squinted.

"For instance, did you hear a popping noise coming from the alleyway?" she asked.

"What tomfoolery is this?" he snarled.

Violet had clearly had enough. Leaning close to the man, she shouted in his ear, "Did you or didn't you?"

Her boldness paid off. The man lost a little of his tyranny and said in a normal tone of voice, "No."

"Our hearing hasn't been so good in the last years," Selma said.

"Don't talk nonsense!" her husband growled.

"It really hasn't, Henry," she said. "Why, we don't even hear the garbage truck in the mornings anymore."

"What about strangers in the neighborhood?" Violet asked. "Have you seen anyone?"

Selma blinked. "People pass through here all the time."

"I mean someone nasty-looking, like a hobo," said Violet.

This seemed to bring Henry to his wit's end. He rose, looking at her furiously. "Now what in tarnation do you want to ask a stupid question like that for?"

"Oh, go lay an egg!" Violet snarled. "Come on, let's get out of here."

"Thank you, Selma." Eve pressed her hand. "We appreciate your taking the time to talk to us."

"Women getting mixed up with —" Henry sneered.

He was cut off by Violet, who held up her purse in an almost menacing way and shouted, "Mixed up with what?"

"Nothing," he mumbled.

CHAPTER 23

"Phew! What a pill!" Violet remarked after they emerged into the sunshine.

"I'm sure we know what he thinks of the nineteenth amendment," Helena said dryly.

"They were no help," Violet grumbled.

"We shouldn't have expected they would be." Helena took her younger sister's arm. "The house is far enough away from the alley that even if their hearing was fine, they probably wouldn't have noticed anything."

"Or thought it was coming from farther away," Eve agreed. "I really don't think we should bother the Anthonys if the Blakes couldn't tell us anything."

"One doesn't inform the other," Helena argued. "The Anthonys aren't hard of hearing, and they may have heard or seen something."

"At the very least, they probably can confirm the taxi was sitting outside that night," Violet chimed in. "I think we should speak to them."

Eve smiled. "All right, honey. You're the head Sherlocka on this thing."

Violet saluted her.

They passed Annie's house again. The curtains were still drawn. Two boys and a girl of about eight or nine were playing ball in the alleyway not far from the garbage cans. Something about their playing near where Wild Bill's body had been comforted Eve.

"Throw the ball, Dick!" the girl shouted. "And don't be a sissy about it!"

"You practically fell over the last time." This came from a blond boy who looked a little older than the other two.

"Did not!"

"Your dress was all dirty, Ruthie," said the one called Dick.

"It was not!"

"Hey, Ruthie." Violet grabbed the girl by the arm. "Were you playing here on Wednesday night?"

"Vi!" Eve felt her hands grow cold.

"They might have seen or heard something," her sister defended.

"You mean the night that man got killed?" asked the older boy. All three children surrounded them.

"That's the night," said Violet.

"Nah, we were playing in the other alley." The boy pointed to Dean Street. "Worst luck."

"Did you hear anything?" Violet stooped a little. "Like a cork popping?"

"I heard it," said Dick.

"Oh, don't believe him, he's always telling lies." Ruthie waved her hand at him.

"No, I'm not!" the boy said. "I was just about to throw the ball when I heard it."

"Did you see anyone running away?" Violet persisted.

"I saw someone," said the older boy. "He looked scared."

"How could you tell he was scared?" Helena asked. "The street must have been dark."

"Wasn't that dark," the boy insisted. "A car had its lights on."

"What kind of car?" Helena asked.

The boy shrugged. "Just a car."

"If I'da seen it, I would've known what kind," Dick said with pride. "I'm an expert on cars."

"Oh, nuts." The older boy stuck his tongue out at him.

"Could it have been a taxi?" Violet asked.

"I couldn't tell," he said. "But it was standing outside that house." He pointed to the Anthony house. "Right across the street."

"Do you know the people in this neighborhood?" Violet asked.

The children nodded in turn.

"Do you know Hank Convoy?" she asked. "He lives in this house right here." She indicated the back door that belonged to the Convoy house.

"Oh, sure, we know him," said Dick.

"Ellie sometimes plays with us," said Ruthie. "She can't do nothing much 'cause she's blind and walks funny, but she's real nice."

"Was her brother the man running in the street?" Violet persisted.

The older boy shrugged. "Could've been."

"One more question," Violet said. "Have you seen a bum hanging around here lately?"

"Heck, no," Dick said. "We'd've run him out with sticks if we had."

Violet laughed. "Thanks, kiddos." She dispensed coins to each of them. They yelled with glee and ran out of the alley.

"Now you've spoiled their dinner," Helena said, amused. "They'll go straight for the candy store down the street."

"Oh, applesauce, we got what we wanted to know," said Violet as they began to walk toward Dean Street. "They saw the taxi too."

"The boy didn't say it was the taxi," Helena reminded her. "He wasn't an expert on cars, remember?"

"Leslie said it's unusual for cars to be parked outside on the street that time of night," Violet insisted. "It had to have been the same car. Oh, damn!"

"Vi, don't curse," Eve said.

"Well, my heel's caught in this muck," her sister grumbled.

They had reached a part along the houses with a little grass and wildflowers. Violet's heel was dug into one of the muddy patches.

"You shouldn't be wearing those shoes," Helena remarked. "Here." She pulled a handkerchief from her purse. "Lift your leg up, and I'll clean it off."

As her sisters busied themselves, Eve examined the grass. It was a poor attempt at some kind of greenery, though she saw that someone had tried to make it into something more. A few flowers were planted near the border of the houses, but they bent away from the sun, and their petals had dried a long time ago. She noticed the footprints of children in the mud and dirt.

"At least the kids enjoy it," she remarked.

"Enjoy what?" Helena glanced at her.

"The grass," she said. "Or what there is of it. I wonder whose is whose." She bent down. "These are the smallest so they must be Ruthie's."

Helena, shaking out the handkerchief before folding it neatly with the clean side out, glanced down. "The boy who's not an expert on cars looked like he had long feet, and he was wearing shoes with the toe pointed a little."

"Fancy you noticing that." Violet shook out her high-heeled pump before putting it back on.

"Then these must belong to him," said Eve.

"That means these belong to Dick." Helena pointed to a third set of footprints that were wider than Ruthie's but shorter than the other boy's."

"How do you know?" Eve eyed her.

"A matter of deduction, my dear Watsonette." Helena grinned.

"I think you're both loony," Violet snorted.

"I wonder to whom these belong." Eve pointed to footprints that were a little farther back, nearer to the Convoy front door.

Helena bent down. "They're bigger than the others."

"Maybe they have a friend who comes here to play sometimes." Violet took out a compact and a tube of lipstick.

"There's something very odd about these prints." Helena took out the magnifying glass she always carried with her and bent down to examine them so her face was almost hidden.

Violet giggled. "You look like an anteater."

"The print from the left foot has a definite mark," her sister said.

"Maybe the child was standing there for a time watching the others play," Eve suggested.

"They might be Ellie's," Violet offered. "The kids said she played with them sometimes."

"Which of her feet was injured in the accident, Vi?" Helena said. "Did Hank tell you?"

Her sister shrank back a little. "I would never ask him a question like that!"

"I'm talking about hearsay," her sister snapped. "People are gossiping all the time at the drugstore."

"Why don't you ask Old Clem?" Violet sniffed. "She'd tell you in a red-hot minute."

Helena straightened out. "At any rate, they were probably made fresh today."

"I don't know," Eve said. "This is a pretty isolated corner of the alleyway."

"Who cares?" Violet yawned. "We'd better get going. I have to get to work soon."

They made it to the Anthony house. The yellow curtains on the windows made it look almost dainty, though quite opaque.

Sarah Anthony opened the door for them. She was a tall, slim woman with a wide smile.

"You were in the alley a moment ago, weren't you?" She brought in a tray of iced tea and glasses.

"How did you know?" Eve asked.

She smiled. "I heard your voices. My, but it's nice when sisters are together."

"Yes, it is." Eve threw an affectionate glance at both her younger siblings. Helena gave a sheepish grin while Violet suppressed a snort.

"We're talking to all the neighbors, Sarah," Helena said. "We want to help get Hank out of this."

"Poor young man." She sighed. "Ellie knows how troubled he's been, what with the war, and then everything that happened."

"You know Ellie?" Violet asked.

"We're good friends," said the woman. "Annie asked me to watch her when she was a child while she was away with her midwife or laundry calls. Since the accident, Ellie's been helping me with my embroidery projects." She chuckled. "I give her half of what I earn when I sell them." Then, in a more serious tone, she said, "Ellie doesn't blame Hank for anything, you know."

"She's a brave girl," Eve said.

Helena, she could see, was anxious to get down to the business at hand, and Violet glanced at her watch.

"We're asking people if they remember seeing or hearing anything unusual the night Wild Bill was killed," she said.

"Yes, the police asked us that," Sarah said.

"But people seem to be remembering things they didn't when the police spoke to them," Helena said.

Sarah sighed. "We don't like the police around here."

"I gathered that," she said dryly.

"I do recall Frank telling me he heard running outside in the street when he was closing the shutters for the night," she said.

"Dean Street?" Violet asked.

The woman nodded. "He poked his head outside the door but didn't see anyone."

"Nevertheless, he heard someone running?" asked Helena.

"It sounded like that," she said.

"It must have been Hank," Violet murmured. In a louder tone, she asked, "When was this?"

"Around ten, I should think," she said. "That's when we usually close the shutters for the night."

"Did you see anyone?" Violet asked. "I mean, anyone roaming around the neighborhood that shouldn't be here?"

"You mean like a hobo?" Sarah asked. "We don't see people like that often."

"And when you do, the children run them out," Helena guessed, smiling a little.

Eve could see Violet was disappointed that her theory of the thieving derelict was now completely shot down. "Did you see a car parked on the street that night, Sarah? Leslie Kramer said she saw a taxi sitting outside."

Sarah blinked. "Not that I recall, but I wasn't paying particular attention to that part of the house that night. I was more preoccupied with the dinner and dishes."

"Do you think Frank did?" Helena asked.

"I can ask him when he gets home," she offered.

Eve leaned forward. "Did Ellie say anything to you about Wild Bill's visit?"

The woman smiled. "She was excited about it. Hank had some kind of argument with him and hadn't spoken to him for a long time. She felt bad because she thought it had to do with her and the accident."

"Hank feels just awful about that, Sarah," Violet said.

"Oh, I know that," she said.

"You spoke to Hank?" she asked.

"Well, no, not really," she said. "But Ellie told me." She suddenly rose. "Would you like to see some pictures of Ellie?

Frank got a Kodak last year, and he's delighted with any excuse to use it."

Eve saw Violet's nose wrinkle a little at the maternal pride in the woman's voice.

"If you'd like to show us," Eve said politely.

When the woman went into the bedroom, Violet hissed at her, "Really, Eve!"

"We have to humor her, Vi," Eve whispered. "She's helping us, remember?"

"I don't see any harm in looking at them for a few minutes," Helena agreed.

"Oh, nuts!" Violet sniffed.

Sarah came back in with an album. The three sisters sat side by side on the couch as Eve opened the booklet in her lap. The photographs were a little blurred in the beginning, but it was clear Frank had become more confident in his photography skills as the year went on. Later pictures were steadier and clearer.

"She's a lovely child." Eve studied the round face with almond eyes and deep smile.

"Were these taken before or after her accident?" Helena asked.

"After," said the woman. "She's very photogenic, isn't she?"

"She's a doll," Violet declared, her compassion overriding her youthful impatience. "Hank always speaks of her as an angel."

"Well, I wouldn't say that." The woman chuckled. "But she helps me a lot, and the children in the neighborhood like to play with her."

"They told us," said Eve.

"She can throw a ball right into your arms," Sarah said.

"Really?" Violet stared at her.

"Frank explained it to me once," she said. "It has something to do with her heightened awareness of space. She knows what distance someone is standing and what direction by the sounds they make with their feet and voice."

"Remarkable." Eve breathed.

She looked at Helena for affirmation. Her sister had taken out her magnifying glass and her head bent to one photo showing Ellie sitting on the stoop of what looked like the Convoy back door with an expression of watchfulness.

"My sister likes to examine things up close," she said apologetically.

Helena straightened. "Do you know anything about Ellie's injury, Sarah?"

"I don't know all the fancy names," admitted Sarah. "But as I understood it, her left leg was broken and didn't heal properly. So they had to reconnect it somehow." Violet flinched. "Oh, it doesn't sound very pleasant, I know, but she gets along. One leg is shorter than the other only by a little bit."

"Her shoes." Helena pointed to the photo. "They're specially made for her, aren't they?"

"Yes," she said. "Annie had to send for them from a cobbler in Boston. Oh, they're not so pretty, but they're sturdy."

"Are they her only pair?" Helena asked.

"As a matter of fact, no, they're not," Sarah said. "She also has a pair of Mary Jane's. When we found out Annie couldn't afford to have a nice pair for her, we all chipped in and sent her the money — anonymously — so she could get them from the Boston cobbler."

"We?" Violet asked.

"Those of us in the neighborhood," she said. "We take care of one another in times of need. A man gets injured in the mill, we take care of the house while the wife attends to her husband. A family's Christmas cupboard is bare, we fill it. That's how we are."

"What a lovely gesture," Eve murmured.

"We even persuaded the Blakes to contribute," Sarah said with a laugh. "It wasn't easy!"

"I'll bet, with that old stick-in-the-mud," Violet said ruefully.

Helena put her magnifying glass back in her purse. "I would

much rather have shoes that last through the winter than pretty, petty things." Violet glared at her.

Eve rose. "Thank you for showing us the photos and for your help, Sarah."

"I don't think I helped much," the woman said. "I have a feeling you were fishing for something in particular."

"Fishing!" Violet snorted as they climbed into the car. "We were fishing all right. And got skunked!"

"Because your tramp turned out to be a ghost?" Helena asked with a grin. "That was a far-fetched idea anyway."

"All right, I'll admit it was," Violet said. "And what about your idea of the footprints?"

"That's a hypothesis half proven," Helena said.

"Is that why you were so interested in Ellie's shoes?" Eve eyed her. "You formed a hypothesis?"

"What we saw just now in the alleyway tipped me off," said her sister. "The left footprint was much deeper in the mud than the right. Ellie's left shoe probably has a higher lift than the right because it's shorter. Higher means heavier so when she walks, she sort of dips into it because it's heavier."

"But those prints were too far away from where Wild Bill was killed," Violet protested.

"Those prints were," Helena said. "But Ellie probably spends a lot of time in the alleyway."

"What do you mean?"

"Hank said Ellie was in the house all evening after Annie left for the Solaris house," said Helena. "What if she wasn't? What if she heard the scuffle between Hank and Wild Bill from inside the house — with her heightened sense of hearing — and came outside? And Hank, in his confused state, didn't see her?"

Violet's eyes shone bright. "You really think she did?"

"It's a hypothesis, Vi," said her sister. "The question is, how can we prove it?"

"What about George Parks?" Eve offered. "He took photos of

the crime scene that night. If Ellie's prints were anywhere, the photos might show it."

"I didn't think of that." Helena pressed her sister's hand.

"To think after all this time, we have a witness!" Violet breathed.

"We *might* have a witness," Helena corrected. "All this has yet to be proven, remember."

"We may even have two witnesses," Eve said. "We know there was a taxi waiting here that night. Maybe the driver with Mullins & Huff saw the attack on Hank."

"From across the street?" Helena got out of the car and walked to the place across from the Kramers' house, looking in the direction of the alleyway. "It's too far away to see in the dark."

"He had his headlights on," Eve argued. "It's worth a try."

Violet settled against the seat. "I say we go to the taxi service first and then accost George."

"The only place you're going is work," Helena insisted. "It's a quarter to two."

"But we have a new lead," Violet protested. "You can't go without me."

"We can and we will," Eve said firmly as she started the car. "You've got to attend to your responsibilities, Vi. You keep insisting you're not a child anymore."

"Hank is my responsibility too," Violet said.

"We'll attend to Hank," promised Helena.

This did not satisfy their sister, and she stared out the window sulking all the way downtown.

CHAPTER 24

After they dropped Violet off at the drugstore, somewhat appeased by their promise to update her when they were finished, they parked the car in a lot next to the bank where the Mullins & Huff Taxi Services kept their vehicles. They could see Amelia Mullins in the small office, pecking away at an adding machine, and a young woman at the desk on the typewriter. A few men with caps pulled over their eyes were lounging around waiting for calls.

Amelia was a tall, plain woman with the face of an ostrich who spoke in a soft grated tone. She looked up when Eve and Helena came in. "Afternoon," she said with a nod. "Don't tell me that tin can of yours finally broke down." She raised an eye at the Ford Model T.

"It has another year or so on it at least," Helena insisted.

The woman chuckled. "You ought to at least get one of the new models with an electric starter."

"It's not our car we've come to talk to you about, Amelia," said Eve. "Was there a call for one of your cabs out to Dean Street the night Wild Bill Hicks was killed?"

"Helping the police again, are you?" She eyed them.

"Unofficially," Helena said.

The woman laughed. "About time the police around here got a woman's help." She leaned all the way back in her chair. "Jo and I were just talking about that this morning, as a matter of fact."

"Then there was a call," Eve said.

"Sure there was, but how did you know?"

"The neighbors told us," said Helena. "We'd like to talk to the driver who went out on that call."

"Why, Jo did," she said. "I can't think why it's important since Hank already said he did it."

"It might be and it might not" said Helena evasively. "We won't know until we talk to Josephine."

"She's in the back," she said. "Ten fifty-seven had some problems with the brakes so she's tending to it."

"Why not let Rapp's Garage take care of it?" Eve asked.

The woman cackled with laughter. "I wouldn't trust Horace with a toy car! There ain't nothing Jo can't do when she gets her hands on a vehicle." She winked. "You have any problems with that tin can of yours, you bring it 'round here, and Jo'll fix it up."

"Thanks, Amelia." Helena smiled.

They went out the second door of the office that led straight into the garage. The two cabs belonging to the two drivers in the office were parked there, as well as a third one in the corner. A pair of well-covered legs were sticking out of the car, but when Helena called, the figure slid out from underneath. Josephine Huff had a mannish style to her but her features were sweet and her voice surprisingly silky.

"Yep, I was out on Dean Street that night," she answered Helena's question.

"Then why didn't you tell the police?" Eve asked.

"No cause to." She wiped her grease-stained hands. "Hank said he did it."

"The police still need your statement, Jo," Helena said.

She shrugged. "Well, honey, to tell the truth, it wouldn't have been good for business."

"Why?" Helena asked. "You had nothing to do with any of this. You were just out doing your job."

"Exactly." She leaned against the car. "We sometimes have to keep secrets, if you know what I mean."

"I'm afraid we don't," Eve said.

She grinned. "Let me put it this way. A businessman has a paramour on the side. He's not exactly going to take his car to drive her to Carson City for a good time 'cause his wife might look at the gas gauge in the morning. See?"

Eve blushed, and Helena mumbled, "Oh, for pity's sake."

"We're not interested in what you were doing there, or who you were picking up," Eve said. "We just want to know if you heard or saw anything."

"I heard a gunshot."

"You mean something that sounded like a car backfiring." Eve nodded. "The neighbors heard it too."

"I mean a gun, honey," she said. "I know how a backfiring car sounds better than most people."

"What time was that?"

"Well, the clock on the dashboard read ten-fifteen," she said.

Helena glanced at her sister. "That fits. And did you see anything?"

"Only Hank running out of the alleyway," she said.

"Nothing in the alleyway?"

The woman shook her head. "I was parked too far ahead of the warehouse across the street, so my view wasn't of the alleyway." She sighed. "Now I wish I'd parked a little closer. I heard Hank's saying it was self-defense."

"How do you know the person running out of the alley was Hank?" Eve asked.

"Saw him clearly for a second under the headlights," she said.

"I had them on full blast." She shuddered. "I get a little antsy waiting on a dark street in the Mold District."

"How did he look to you?" asked Helena.

"Poor kid." She shook her head. "He was dazed all right. Just reeling around. I thought he was drunk at first, holding his arm up like that."

"Like what?"

"Like a bird with a broken wing," she said. "Saw a handkerchief wrapped around it too."

"Was there any blood?" Helena asked.

"Honey, I couldn't tell on that dark street." She shrugged. "It did look pretty dirty, though."

"Anything else?"

"I think he had something in his hand." Josephine cocked her head. "Something small and black."

"The gun!" Eve looked at Helena.

Josephine snapped her fingers. "That's what it was! It must have been. I thought it looked funny, him carrying it like that."

"Like what?"

"Like it was a handle he was holding on to," said the woman. "Lurching around like he was."

"An instinct," Helena said. "When we're unsteady, we grab hold of whatever we can."

"Thanks, Jo." Eve pressed her arm. "You've given us a lot."

As they started back toward the office, the woman suddenly called out, "I don't know if it means anything, but when my client came out of the warehouse, I had to turn around and I went past the alleyway."

Both sisters turned around.

"Well, I can't be sure, mind you," she said. "I saw it through the rearview mirror as I went into the driveway of the house across the way to turn around, so it was to my back." She shook out the rag she had used to wipe her hands. "But the alley didn't look completely empty."

"Naturally not," said Helena. "There was a dead body in it."

"No, I don't mean that," she said. "Like someone was there."

"Someone?" Helena asked. "Did you see the face?"

"I didn't exactly see them," said Josephine. "My back lights shone into the alleyway for a minute, and I saw a door opening." She then added, "I had the window of the cab open, and as we passed, I heard the faint voice of a woman."

"Could it have been a girl?" Eve asked.

"Maybe." She shrugged. "I couldn't hear it that well."

"Jo." Helena's voice was steely. "We might need you to repeat that to the police."

"I'll do what you think is best," said the woman. "I guess I should have gone to them in the first place, eh?"

"Yes, you should have," said Helena, her tone kinder. "But it's understandable why you didn't."

"You were right, Helena!" Eve was almost gleeful as they got back to their car. "Ellie was in the alleyway that night!"

"Now don't go jumping to conclusions, Eve," her sister insisted. "Not until we talk to George. Let's leave the car here and walk."

They trudged down a side street and came upon an old brick building where the Gyver Clothing Emporium was housed on the ground floor. They waved at Louise Woods, who was standing outside the doorway, fanning herself with a paper fan.

"Is George in his studio?" Eve asked.

"I think so," she said. "I heard him trampling around up there." She glanced above her.

George lived in a small apartment above the clothing store. They knocked on the door, and at the "come in!" call, they went in. Eve winced at the messy apartment with things scattered all over the place, the sink in the kitchen piled high with dirty dishes and spilled food.

"The confirmed bachelor," Helena said dryly. "George! For pity's sake, clean this place!"

George emerged from the closet he used as a studio. "If I'd known I was going to get such charming company, I would have." He grinned. "How d'you do?"

"We would do better if we didn't have to look at those dishes." Eve rolled up her sleeves. "I'm assuming you have some soap handy?"

"You don't have to do that, Eve," he said.

"She may as well," said Helena. "We've got a favor to ask of you, so it's an exchange."

"Don't tell me you need my services for a funeral," he said with a laugh.

"No, a crime scene."

"Oh, the Wild Bill case." He crossed his arms. "I was wondering whether Oliver was going to involve you two in that."

"We've involved ourselves." Helena pushed aside a stack of photography magazines from the corner of the couch and sat down. "We're working for Hank."

"What's there to work on?" George shrugged. "He killed Wild Bill, and he admitted it."

"He killed him out of self-defense," Eve said over the sound of the running water.

"So he says," George said.

"So we're here to prove," Helena replied in a harsh tone. "We want to see those photographs you took of the crime scene the next morning."

He stuck one hand in his pocket and brushed at the top of the bureau he was leaning against with the other. "Who says I took photographs?"

"Oliver did," she said. "You're the official crime scene photographer in this county, remember?" She eyed him.

"They're with the police," he said. "That's evidence, remember?"

She leaned forward. "I also remember how excited you were

down by the river taking photographs of the Libby Cinder crime scene."

"So?"

"So, I'll bet you made your own copies of those photographs for your collection," she said. Eve turned to her in surprise but knew better than to interfere.

"What are you getting at, Helena?" He lifted his chin in defiance.

"You know what I'm getting at," she said. "The photographs may be with the police, but you have your own set."

"Who says I do?"

"I say it." She glanced at him.

"All right, maybe I do have a copy," he admitted.

"Do you think Oliver would take kindly to knowing you keep your own set of crime scene photos?"

"It's not against the law," he grumbled.

"It's against ethics," she declared.

"So is seeing them without permission from the district attorney," he retorted.

"Then we'll both keep quiet," Helena said.

"We're trying to help Hank." Eve wiped her hands on a semi-clean towel.

He grinned. "I wasn't going to balk, Eve. I just don't like being threatened." He glared at Helena.

"You know Helena didn't mean it." Eve patted the young man's shoulder.

"I know," he said with a laugh as he headed for his closet studio. "I'll get them for you." Over his shoulder, he threw at Helena, "I could name a few naughty things you did, like swipe frogs and mice from the science lab to do experiments at home!"

Eve burst out laughing as he closed the closet door. "You did do that."

Helena grinned. "He was starting to get a little too big for his britches since Oliver made him the official crime scene photographer."

George came out with an envelope and, clearing the coffee table with one swoop of his arm, lined up the pictures. "I can help if you tell me what you're looking for."

"Footprints," Helena said shortly as she took out the magnifying glass.

"What good would that do?" George asked. "We know who was there."

"There may have been someone else the police overlooked," Eve said.

His eyes widened with excitement. "You mean someone who knows Hank is telling the truth?"

"That's what we're trying to determine." Helena bent her head. "George, did you take any pictures of the side opposite the garbage cans?"

"Sure I did." He pushed a few forward. "I took pictures of every inch of that alley from end to end."

"Good work," Eve commended.

The young man blushed. "I know my job, Eve."

Helena held up a photograph. "Was this one taken outside the back door of the Convoy house?"

"That one and these other two." He pointed to the pictures. "You can see that patch of dirt on the steps is a little sandy. I guess that's where Hank and Wild Bill just sort of threw the dirt away with their feet when they came down."

"Probably," Helena agreed. "Eve, look at this." She gave her sister the magnifying glass. "That's a part of the grass and flowers we saw on the left of the Convoy back door."

"When did you see it?" George asked.

"We went there this morning." Eve held the picture close against the magnifying glass. "There are footprints there."

"Probably some kids playing." George shrugged. "I saw a bunch of kids' footprints father down the alley."

"But these are special footprints," Helena said. "See how the groove in the heel of the left foot sinks down farther into the mud than the right?"

"You think those were Ellie's shoes?" Eve asked.

"Ellie!" George stared. "You mean Hank's kid sister?"

"Don't you go yapping your mouth at Oliver or the police about this," Helena snapped. "We're going on a hypothesis right now."

"I'm no stool pigeon," he sniffed.

Eve felt the rather prickly cushion against her back as her eyes fell on a photo of the alleyway that showed from some distance a tall, lanky man lying on the ground. She thought of how Wild Bill looked after Helena's work, the jagged hair smoothed down, the face shaven and almost handsome, the limbs set in silent surrender to his fate in the coffin.

Wild Bill was buried in his uniform with his medal, but not with all the things he treasured. Wild Bill, who had been worried about Ellie traveling alone on the train in spite of his gruffness and his unclean reputation. That train in the early morning twilight, Ellie waving a hand in the direction of the platform, thinking her grandmother was waving back when she was not there...

"We might have to tell the police about them," Helena was saying in a slightly irritated tone to George. "They may need to have the print enlarged to get a better view of the footprints."

"Oliver might sack me as the official crime photographer," George sulked.

Helena smiled as she rose. "I'll tell you what, George. We'll tell him we asked to see the negatives. Oliver would expect you to save those, wouldn't he? We won't get you in trouble. Will we, Eve?"

"No trouble," Eve said in a misty tone as she stood, a little wobbly.

Her sister caught her arm. "You all right, Eve?"

"I think so." She pressed her head. "I have a bit of a headache."

"Well, we haven't eaten since breakfast," Helena pointed out. "Suppose we go to the drugstore and get a bite? Vi's expecting us to update her anyway."

"Yes, all right," Eve said.

As they made their way slowly down the stairs with her sister still holding her arm, Eve thought she heard a train whistle in the distance.

CHAPTER 25

The drugstore was empty except for a group of five teenagers who had stopped by for ice cream sodas before heading home. Violet waved her sisters down and burst out from behind the counter with Kitty's disapproving mouth puckered after her.

"Well?" Violet asked.

"Well what?" Helena steered Eve toward a corner table. To Sudie, who had followed them, she said, "Bring us two tuna sandwiches and lemonades, will you? And a glass of water and an aspirin tablet."

"I'm all right," Eve insisted. She did feel somewhat recovered. "It was just the mess in that studio."

"No wonder two women already turned down George's marriage proposals," Helena snorted.

"Sudie, bring three sandwiches and lemonades." Violet took off the white smock she wore when she worked. Kitty glared at her. "I haven't had lunch either."

"All those chocolate malteds you sneak behind the counter should be sufficient nourishment," Helena chuckled.

"I do not sneak chocolate malteds behind the counter." Her

239

sister was indignant. "Bad for my figure." She smoothed down the high-waisted dress.

"You ought to get back to work, Vi," Helena said. "Kitty looks positively murderous."

"Then you and Eve will just have to be the Sherlockas who put her in jail," Violet said.

"Death is no joke!" Eve burst out. "No matter how it happens, or who witnesses it."

Violet stared at her. "What's eating you?"

"Here, Eve, drink this down." Helena placed the glass of water and the aspirin pill in her hand.

"She okay?" Sudie looked at Eve with concern.

"Just a headache," Helena assured her.

"I'll get the food right away, honey," the woman promised.

"You're a peach, Sudie." Violet hugged her.

"I don't think Kitty thinks so just now," Helena said dryly.

"Oh, she's just crabby because I won't let her go to the new Valentino picture with Joe Reid," Sudie said. "He's getting too boozed up lately, so I told her to stay away from him for a while."

"Good thinking," said Eve.

"Well, what did you find out?" Violet asked.

Helena filled her in on what Josephine had told them and their findings with George's photographs.

Violet said nothing as Sudie put the food down on the table. But when she was gone, Violet leaned back, saying in a troubled voice, "So Ellie was there that night."

"She might have come outside because she heard the quarrel and the shot," said Helena.

"Well, then why didn't Annie say so?" Violet snarled.

"Hold on, Vi," said her sister. "Ellie might not have heard the most important part — Wild Bill threatening Hank."

"She might not have known," Eve said quietly, picking at the sandwich. "Yes, that must be it. She was telling the truth."

"What are you talking about?" Helena asked.

"Annie told us she never went near the alleyway when she came home at two-thirty to take Ellie to the milk train," Eve said. "Remember, honey?"

"I remember." Helena nodded.

"Are you saying she's lying?" Violet asked. "Maybe she saw something!"

"I don't think she was lying about that," Helena said. "It's too easy to check when she left the Solaris house after the baby was born."

Eve's stomach strengthened a little, and she was able to take a few bites. As her courage returned, she said, "Suppose a young girl heard or saw something frightening. What do you think she would do?"

"Scream her head off," Violet answered. "That's what I would do."

"I don't mean she was threatened," said Eve. "Just if she saw or heard something, like someone walking around outside her window."

"Call someone, I suppose," Helena said.

"Exactly," Eve said. "She would tell someone she trusted."

"Oh, come on," Violet snorted. "Ellie's fifteen, not five."

"And how many times did you run to my room insisting someone was trying to get into the house when you were that age?" Helena challenged. Violet made a face at her.

"I can't get what Mrs. Hill told us out of my mind about Annie's behavior that night," Eve said. "Her suddenly changing her mind about when Ellie was going to see her aunt, for instance. Did Annie strike you as the sort of person to make last-minute decisions like that?"

"I wouldn't have thought so," Helena admitted. "But then, a midwife sometimes has to act quickly to avoid complications with the mother and child, doesn't she?"

"But she's sort of a doctor's helper," Violet pointed out. "Doctors are always procedural, aren't they?"

"All good doctors," Helena said in an amused tone. "There are some not-so-good doctors who go by faith or intuition."

"And what about Annie being so rushed and agitated that she didn't even stay to see Ellie off on the train?" As Eve spoke, her conviction grew. "And her concern about Oliver calling Ellie back from Carson City?"

"That was natural," Helena argued. "She knows how close Ellie and Hank are, and she didn't want her upset."

"Exactly," said Eve. "They're close, aren't they?"

"Just what are you driving at, Eve?" Violet asked.

"If Ellie heard something, or she was out in the alleyway, and she was scared, she would have told her grandmother the minute she got home, wouldn't she?"

"She might have," Helena said.

"That would explain the rush to get Ellie out of town," said her older sister.

"Well, she wouldn't want her involved," Helena said.

"I know what you're trying to get at." Violet's cheeks changed from the ruby shade of her rouge to fleshy pink. "She didn't want Ellie to tell what she knew."

"Calm down, honey." Helena put her arm around her.

"We have to do something!" Her sister took out her handkerchief and wiped her tearing eyes.

"We will do something." Eve pressed her hand. "We'll go see Louis Durham."

"Why him?" Helena glanced at her.

"Annie said he took care of Ellie on the train," she said. "He might be able to tell us something about her."

"Like what?" asked Violet.

"I don't know!" Eve snapped. "Maybe Ellie confided in him. Maybe he knows to whom Annie sent the telegram and why she was so agitated."

"I didn't get the impression he was that good a friend," Helena said.

"Annie said he was a friend of her son's," Eve pointed out. "I suspect Annie thinks quite highly of anyone in whom her son found favor."

"I think Eve's right," Violet said. "We ought to go down to the train station and see Louis."

"*We* go down to the train station. *You* don't." Helena gathered the torn paper and cups. "You have work to do, remember?"

"This is infinitely more important," Violet insisted. When Sudie came to the table, she said, "Sudie, I have to go with my sisters. We're hot on the trail."

"Oh, for pity's sake," Helena mumbled.

"Something about Hank?" The woman looked eager.

"That's right." Violet put her arm around her. "I'll come in to work on Sunday to make it up."

"Kitty will have a conniption," said Sudie. "She likes being here alone on Sundays so she can gab with your pals over free ice cream sodas."

"It'll be good for her, then," Violet said. "I'll crack the whip on her." This was followed by a gesture of swinging a whip back and forth.

Sudie laughed and gave her a hug. "All right, doll, go. It's dead as a doornail here with all the kids gone to the pep rally in Neovale."

Violet squealed and took off the white coat, hanging it on the rack behind the counter. Kitty snarled at her.

The train station was bustling with the evening trains coming and going. But they found Louis Durham had just returned on the Carson City train and could spare them a little time before the train pulled out again.

He was a lively man with the worn look of someone who had been working all his life, though never defeated by the hard work. He was eager to speak with the sisters when he discovered Violet was a friend of Hank's.

"Boy's mind is twisted up from the war," Louis insisted in a booming tone as they sat in the shack the staff used for their break. "I've seen lots of young men that way. I praise the Lord my son Jack came back with only a broken leg. Lots of boys got it much worse, body and soul." He shook his head.

"Then you don't believe Hank intended to kill Wild Bill?" Eve asked.

"No, miss," he said. "I've known Hank since he was a boy. Taught him how to throw a curveball. Couldn't even kill a fly when it got in his way."

"You knew Hank's father?" Helena asked.

"Yes, ma'am," he said. "He was a good man. Shame he died like that." He sighed. "It hasn't been easy for Annie taking care of two kids just when she ought to be enjoying her old age. That didn't give her the right to treat Hank like she did, though."

"How did she treat him?" Violet put her chin in her hand.

"I hate to say it this way, but like a criminal," said Louis. "After Ellie had her accident — poor child — Annie just sort of gave up on Hank, I guess. Didn't much care for him, if you know what I mean." He added quickly, "Oh, she gave him shelter and food and all that, but I mean in the heart. Looking after a child's not only about the things you can see."

"No, it isn't," Eve said softly, thinking of how she had to take care of her own sisters after their parents died.

"Thing is, Annie wasn't just giving up." He took out a pipe and, with a nod from the sisters, lit it. "It was like something was festering inside her. Like when you see the wind hit the ground, and the dust swirls around, you know the storm is coming."

"How poetic." Violet sighed.

He laughed. "Oh, I used to get a verse in now and then when I was young."

"But she took good care of Ellie," Eve said.

"Ellie's kind of her only hope now," he said. "The way she sees it, that is."

"Annie told us Ellie was so excited to visit her aunt, she let her go a week earlier than she'd planned," Helena said.

"Well, well." The man leaned back. "That explains it, then."

"Explains what?"

"Her showing up at the station like that," he said. "And for the milk train yet!"

"She didn't check with the station to see if you would be here that night?" Eve guessed.

"No, and it's lucky I agreed to change shifts with another guy for that morning," he said. "I don't usually work the milk train anymore. My bones aren't agreeable to waking up at two o'clock in the morning in my old age." He chuckled.

"When was Ellie supposed to go to Carson City?" asked Violet.

"This Thursday," he said.

"And not on the milk train," Helena concluded.

"No, ma'am. Annie didn't want her traveling at that hour all by herself," he said. "We settled on the afternoon train."

"Was it like Annie to do something like that?" asked Eve.

"I'm not sure I know what you mean, miss."

"You've known her for a long time," she said. "Have you ever known her to be the kind of woman to change her mind on a whim like she did with Ellie's trip to Carson City?"

"Well, no, miss," he said. "I can't say I have. Annie's the type who keeps steady to her mind once it's made up." He added with a grin, "Like most of you women."

Violet sniffed at this rather unflattering portrait of their sex but said nothing.

"Somebody saw Annie here that night," Eve said.

"Early morning," Helena corrected her.

"Early morning," her sister said. "They said Annie seemed, well, agitated and nervous."

"Well, miss, who wouldn't be at that hour?" he asked. "I guess Ellie traveling alone made her nervous too, although I kept telling her that I'd be watching her and gave her a seat close to where I stay during the train ride, so I'd be right there if she needed anything. And it didn't help they came ten minutes before the train pulled out." Here, he gave them an even look. "I wish people would stop catching trains at the last minute. Makes it harder on us porters."

"I imagine," Helena said.

"What about Ellie?" Violet asked. "Was she nervous too?"

"Well, now." He chewed on his pipe.

"Oh, you must remember." Violet pressed his arm. "You were responsible for her during the trip, after all."

"I don't know as I'd call it nervous," he said.

"She was excited?" Eve offered.

"Not that either," he said. "Oh, she wanted to go, sure, but she was reluctant, I guess."

"Strange, considering Annie told us she was full of chatter about the trip to her aunt's that night at dinner," Helena said.

"I guess Carson City was like going to New York for Ellie. Of course, it's nothing but a three-horse town," he added ruefully. "Gyver's just as good, even if it isn't as big."

"Was there anything you noticed about Ellie's behavior that struck you?" Helena asked. "Anything you can put your finger on?"

He squinted. "I felt like she wanted to talk to me a few times — tell me something — and then the bell rang, and I had to tend to a passenger. When I'd come back, it had gone out of her."

"I wish she'd told it!" Violet sighed.

"It was probably just something about the train." He smiled. "It was Ellie's first train trip, you know."

Helena leaned forward. "Louis, I'm going to ask you a very important question, though it might seem odd to you. Did you notice Ellie's shoes?"

"Shoes?" He stared at her.

"Yes, what were her shoes like?"

"Well, sort of old-fashioned boots with the laces up to the ankle," he said. "Black leather. Kind of plain, but I expect a girl doesn't need fancy things at that age. She did have a nicer pair of Mary Janes, though. I saw them when I helped her unpack."

"You helped a young woman unpack her things? Naughty, naughty." Violet shook a teasing finger at him, and he blushed.

"Oh, stop it, Vi," Helena snapped. "Did you notice the sole on the left shoe? Was it higher than the right?"

He thought for a moment. "Well, yes, ma'am, now that you mention it. I did notice that. Made her sort of lean in when she walked. But she's a good walker," he defended. "Didn't slow me down a bit when I got her off the train and delivered her to her aunt."

"Of course not," Helena said, and Eve could see she was filing away the description of the shoes in her mind. Then, she suddenly blurted out, "Were the shoes clean?"

"Eh?" He blinked.

"Were the shoes Ellie was wearing clean?" she repeated.

"Sure were," he said. "Annie isn't the type to let her grandkids go dirty, you know."

"I didn't mean that," Helena said. "I mean did it look like they were just cleaned and polished?"

"I'd say so," he said. "Lots of people do that, you know. They get all spruced up for a train ride. They want to look good for the people who meet them at the station." He chuckled.

Eve noted Violet looking at her sister as if she were a peacock that had suddenly walked into the drugstore and ordered a malted milk.

"We were also told that Annie sent a telegram from the station," Eve said. "Somebody saw her go into the telegraph office."

"Yes, and that was odd," he said.

"Why was that odd?" Violet asked. "Lots of people send telegrams from the station, don't they?"

"Not Annie," he said. "She once said telegrams were a waste of money when the mail service can get a letter out in a couple of days."

"Well, maybe she was afraid her daughter wouldn't get the letter in time to meet Ellie at the train station," Eve offered. "It was a last-minute decision."

"Sure that's true," said Louis. "Jack — he works at the telegram office in the Carson City station — told me he went himself to Paula's house not thirty minutes before the train reached Carson City to tell her Ellie was coming. I guess I just didn't figure it was because Annie sent a telegram."

A train whistle shrieked, filling the air with its piercing sound. Louis put his pipe in his coat pocket. "Afraid I have to leave you ladies now. That's the signal my train is leaving soon."

"The Carson City train?" Eve asked. He nodded. "Will you be seeing your son when you get to the station?"

"Jack and I don't mix when we're both on duty," he said. "But sometimes, if I'm taking the last train out at night, I'll walk to his house, get some supper, and stay the night." He sighed. "Not much to come home to now that my wife is dead."

"I'm sorry." Eve laid her hand on his arm.

"Oh, it's not so bad," he said. "Jack's got a lively two-year-old, and I get to see my grandson." He grinned and waved at them as he made his way back to the tracks.

CHAPTER 26

When he was gone, Eve took Helena's arm. "Well, dear, what now?"

"I think we ought to tell Oliver what we know," Helena said. "Let him and the police take over from here."

"I think we've got to talk to Ellie now." Violet hooked her arm on Helena's.

Helena's gait wasn't as quick as her sister's. "That's Oliver's job, not ours."

"You said we don't have enough evidence right now to convince him Ellie was a witness," Violet pointed out. "Clean shoes, a quick getaway —"

"Don't talk like the motion pictures," Helena interrupted.

"Oh, applesauce!" Her sister sniffed.

"I don't think Ellie will talk to Oliver," Eve said.

"Of course she won't," said Violet as they went up the stairs of the station platform. "Annie probably told her if she didn't keep her mouth shut, Hank would hang. The battle-axe!"

"She had her reasons, Vi," Helena said.

"Reason or not, if Ellie saw something, we need to know about it and so do the police," her younger sister objected.

"So we just buy a ticket to Carson City and break down Paula's door demanding to see Ellie?" Helena eyed her.

"Of course not," said Eve. "We knock on the door like ladies and say we're friends of Hank's and we want to talk to his sister."

Helena laughed. "I suppose she couldn't refuse us with that."

"Ellie could save Hank from getting hanged." Violet's voice was unsteady. "You realize that's what it amounts to, don't you?"

"Don't be dramatic," her older sister snapped. "And keep your voice down!"

"All the more reason for us to see Ellie," Eve pointed out. "We can explain to her that if she did witness anything, it will help Hank if she comes forward."

"She'll want to help her brother," Violet said. "They're crazy about each other."

"I hate to remind both of you, but she's still a minor," Helena argued.

"We're coming to her as friends, dear," said Eve. "Not investigators."

"I doubt Annie will see it that way," Helena mumbled. But as they reached the ticket window, she said, "Three second-class tickets to Carson City, Al."

"None left," said Al Raymond, the stationmaster, a crusty, middle-aged man who chewed tobacco. "Can't expect to get good seats fifteen minutes before the train leaves, Mrs. Wright."

"All right, then, third class," she said.

"Third class!" Violet sniffed.

"Kind of full on the evening train," he remarked.

"That doesn't bother us," Helena said.

The man grinned and issued her the tickets. "Seeing as you're always in the company of the stiffs, I guess it wouldn't."

There was a small space on the bench, and Eve sat Violet down while she and Helena remained standing in spite of Violet's protests. "You need to rest your feet from those heels," Helena pointed out.

"Oh, they don't hurt," her sister insisted. "I'm used to them."

"Considering how many pairs you've bought with your salary so far, I don't doubt it," said her sister dryly.

"Well, what do you expect me to do with the money, save it for a rainy day?" Her sister sniffed. "Speaking of shoes, what was all that about Ellie's?"

"Obvious, my dear Watsonette," Eve said with a grin. "She wanted to see whether the mud from the alleyway was stuck on Ellie's shoes when she left, since it was so last-minute. That would have proved she was there that night."

"Not quite, Watsonette," Helena said with a wider grin. "I asked to get the answer I got."

"Talk sense," Violet said.

"I always talk sense," her sister snapped. "I expected the shoes to be clean and shiny. Because if Ellie hadn't been in the alleyway that night and gotten her shoes dirty, they wouldn't have had to be cleaned."

"You mean Annie cleaned them," Eve said slowly.

"It's just a guess," her sister cautioned. "But I'm beginning to believe you were right when you said Annie was lying to us about not going near the alleyway that night."

"If she was capable of cleaning Ellie's shoes to hide the fact that she was there, she was capable of dragging a body behind the garbage cans," Eve said.

"And you accuse me of thinking too much like the motion pictures," Violet grumbled.

"Hank said he never touched the body," Eve insisted. "Someone must have hidden it behind the garbage cans. Annie's a pretty strong woman for her height and weight."

"Midwives have to be," Helena said.

"But it's ghoulish!" Violet shuddered. "Oh, pardon me." The rather large woman sitting next to her drew away.

"We don't know the whys behind it yet, Vi," said Eve. "That's for Oliver to find out. But we have to get a look at that telegram."

"You mean the one Annie sent?" Helena asked with a shrug. "What good would that do?"

"If she said anything to her daughter about why Ellie was coming earlier than planned, it might tip off the police that she knows more than she's told," Eve said.

"True," Helena admitted, "Except that telegrams might be privileged information."

"Who says?" Violet demanded.

"I don't know who says," Helena retorted. "But would you want someone walking into the telegraph office and demanding to see a telegram you sent?"

"If it could get a friend acquitted of murder, I would!" Violet said.

"Well, I think we should go to the telegraph office when we get to Carson City and talk to Jack Durham," Eve said. "He might let us see it once he learns why we want it. Hank was a friend of his, after all."

"There's more than just legalities here, Eve," Helena argued. "You might cost that young man his job if —" She stopped. "Well, good evening, Dan."

Daniel Frazer, the Moody district attorney, tipped his hat to all three sisters. "Evening, ladies." His good-natured face regarded them with curiosity as his sandy hair blew in the wind. "I noticed you arguing back there, and I thought I'd break it up."

"We weren't arguing," Violet insisted. "We were having a discussion."

"It seemed a little more heated than that." He grinned. "I'm glad to see you're staying out of trouble."

"Trouble?" Violet blinked.

"I've been in on this Hank Convoy case from the beginning," he said. "Oliver told me you've been trying to get involved."

"We're just trying to help a friend," Violet defended.

"I realize you were of some use to him during the Libby Cinder case," Dan began.

"Some use!" Helena glared at him.

"We cracked the case wide open for him." Violet sniffed.

"Vi, really," Eve said.

"But it's dangerous to get involved in police work if you're not the police," Dan continued. "Police and lawyers are trained to handle clues and evidence and criminals. The general public only knows what they read in the detective novels, or what they see in the motion pictures, most of it inaccurate."

Violet crossed her arms. "Are you finished being a wet blanket?"

"Dan is only trying to be kind, Vi," Eve said.

"But I suppose I was lecturing." Daniel took out a cigarette. "I'm sorry. What are you three up to this evening?"

"We were just talking about where we'd go when we got to Carson City," Violet said in a breezy tone. "My sisters are buying me a new dress for the fall."

Eve and Helena exchanged looks but said nothing.

Daniel eyed her. "Kind of far to go for a dress, isn't it?"

"Oh, I get tired of the old-fashioned duds around here." Violet waved a gloved hand.

Just then, the train pulled into the station, and people began to rise and stretch.

"If you give me your tickets, I'll help you find your car," he offered.

"That won't be necessary," Helena said stiffly.

He laughed. "You wouldn't even let me carry your books when we were in college."

"Why should I?" she countered. "We're not courting."

"No," he said softly, "We're not."

"We're on the third-class car anyway," Eve said. "We couldn't get anything else at the last minute."

"It just so happens I'm traveling on the third-class car myself," he said.

The car was, as the stationmaster had predicted, full but not crowded. They found two empty seats near a young man, and Daniel persuaded him to give up his for Violet. The young man did this gladly, and Violet rewarded him with a coquettish smile.

They chatted about the town news, and the subject quickly fell on the Wild Bill murder case.

"Hank had to kill Wild Bill," Violet insisted. "He attacked him with a knife. He had to defend himself, didn't he?"

"It has yet to be proven," Daniel reminded her, his good-natured lightness gone. "I hate to say it, but the evidence isn't pointing in that direction."

"Oh, evidence!" Violet snarled.

"Yes, evidence," Daniel said. "It's all we have to go on."

"I know the police need proof." Leaning back with her arms crossed, Violet mumbled, "And we'll get it."

Eve couldn't tell by Daniel's glance out the window if he heard her or not. "If those poor boys coming back from the service had gotten all they needed, maybe we wouldn't be seeing so much crime," she said quickly.

"Don't blame the veterans, Eve," Helena insisted.

"It's this Prohibition more than anything else," Daniel agreed.

"You were in the war, weren't you, Dan?" Violet asked. "You saw what it was like."

"I didn't see the trenches," he said ruefully. "A law degree made me ripe for JAGD."

"What's that?" she asked.

"Judge Advocate's General Department," he said. "I was no more than a glorified legal clerk. The army didn't think much of a first lieutenant with the ink barely dry on his law degree."

"You're a fine lawyer, Dan," Helena insisted.

He bowed. "And you're a fine doctor, Helena."

"Helena thinks Hank was suffering from war fatigue when he shot that gun," Eve chimed in.

Her sister nodded. "Even if Oliver goes ahead with this idea that Hank murdered Wild Bill —" a growl came from Violet, "—

his lawyer shouldn't have much trouble proving he was irrational when he did it."

"You think so?" Daniel eyed her. "You know establishing a medical condition has to precede a crime. Has Hank been diagnosed?"

"Not yet," she admitted. "But they can get doctors for that."

"Just in time to avoid a murder conviction, eh?"

"Don't be an ornery ass, Dan," she snapped.

He laughed. "Did you think I've changed since college?" His tone became serious again. "His lawyer is going to have a hard time proving Hank didn't know what he was doing then, even if he shows he's suffering from shell shock now."

"Lucky for Hank you're not the Gyver County D.A.!" Violet growled.

"If I were, I would behave just like Oliver," he insisted. "Maintain my compassion but do my duty."

"Just as you do as a lawyer," Helena agreed. "And as a lawyer, I'd like to put a question to you."

"I'll answer a legal question." He grinned.

"Eve and I were discussing telegrams and the law."

"Oh?"

"I think telegrams are privileged information and can't be divulged even in a court of law, and Eve thinks they can," Helena said carefully.

"Odd topic of conversation between sisters," he remarked.

"We saw the telegraph office at the station, and it gave us the idea," Violet chimed in.

"A very interesting question, really," he said. "We're talking about shielding certain information — usually incriminating information — between certain people as private and confidential when we're talking about privilege."

"We know that," Violet said impatiently. "Are telegrams privileged or aren't they?"

"That's not an easy question to answer, Violet," he said. "The telegraph operators certainly would like them to be. Some even tried in court."

"But they failed?" Helena guessed.

"Well, yes, they did," he said. "There was a case in Maine in the 1870s where the court ruled that telegrams were another form of communication, and their mode of communication was irrelevant. Verbal messages are, after all, admissible in court."

"But aren't letters considered privileged?" Helena half turned in her seat.

"It's not the same, Helena," he argued. "Letters are meant to be private between two individuals. Telegrams, on the other hand, are publicly created and transmitted by an operator. The West Virginia Supreme Court argued in 1874 that putting telegrams in the realm of privileged communication would put too many limitations on court case evidence."

"So a telegraph operator who refused to produce a telegram because of privilege could be arrested and jailed?" asked Violet.

"He could indeed," said Daniel. "Of course, it would depend on the case and the circumstances." He eyed her. "Don't tell me you have some ideas about telegrams being produced if Hank Convoy goes to trial."

"There isn't going to be a trial," Violet said firmly.

"There still has to be a trial no matter what happens," Daniel argued. "Hank admitted to committing a crime."

"Oliver will see Hank is telling the truth, and that will be that."

"That will be that, eh?" Daniel asked with a grin.

She made a face at him and turned to the window.

~~~~~

Not long afterward, the train reached the Carson City station. It was much larger than the one in Gyver and more bustling with tracks running in several directions for trains to Virginia City and Reno. Daniel helped the sisters carefully down the car steps.

"I'd be happy to share my cab with you." He nodded toward
~~~~~

the row of cabs parked not far from the station. "My client is downtown as well."

"That's kind of you, but —" Eve glanced at Helena.

"I'd rather walk," Violet said. "I haven't been to Carson City since I was a kid."

He looked amused. "The downtown is a ways from here. It's going to be awful hard with those shoes." He glanced down at her heels.

"You'd be surprised how well I can do with these pumps," she insisted. "Well, so long, Danny!" She took each sister's arm and steered them in the opposite direction of the taxis.

"Vi, that was rude," Eve scolded. "He's such a nice young man."

"Oh, applesauce, I'll make it up to him later," her younger sister said. "We have more important things to think about, like finding the telegraph office."

"I concur I was wrong about that," Helena admitted. "That doesn't mean he'll let us see Annie's telegram, though. He might not even have a copy of it anymore."

"He'll remember it," Eve insisted. "His father accompanied Ellie all the way to Carson City, and they know the family."

The telegraph office did not consist of much more than an L-shaped desk pushed into the corner of a very small office. A young man in shirt sleeves sat with various forms and papers scattered about. The telegraph was in front of him, and he was tapping at the key as he looked down at the form. Eve motioned for silence as they waited until the young man had transmitted the message. When he was done, he turned his chair to the sisters.

"May I help you?" he asked in a cordial tone.

"Are you Jack Durham?" Eve asked.

"Yes, ma'am," he said.

"We're from Gyver," Helena said. "We were chatting with your father a while ago."

His face softened. "You know Dad?"

"We know him through Hank Convoy," Violet said. "Hank's a friend of mine."

The young man shook his head. "Poor fellow with this Wild Bill business."

"Then you know about it?" Eve asked.

"Sure I do," he said. "It's all bunk what the papers say. Hank would never deliberately kill anyone. Unless he had to, of course. We all had to in the war."

"You'll help us, then!" Violet planted herself on the edge of the desk.

"How can I help?" he asked.

"Annie sent a telegram to this office that night," Eve said. "We'd like to see it, if you still have it."

"Well, ma'am —"

"Miss," she said firmly.

"Well, miss, I don't know as I can do that," he said. "You see, that was confidential —"

"But it isn't," Violet interrupted. "We spoke to a very reliable lawyer, and he told us telegrams aren't privileged."

Rather than answer, the young man looked past her. "Yes, sir, how can I help you?"

"I'd like to send a telegram — Well, hello." Daniel greeted the sisters. "We just seem to meet in all the right places, don't we?"

"You're following us!" Violet growled.

"Not at all," he said. "As a matter of fact, I was checking my papers for my client meeting and realized I'd forgotten something. I was going to telegraph my office."

"Dan." Helena took his arm. "Didn't you just tell us telegrams aren't privileged information?"

He glanced at each sister in turn. Then, he laid his jacket and briefcase on a small chair in the corner. "Not if they might be related to a criminal investigation."

"You're a lawyer?" The young man stared.

"I'm the district attorney for Moody County," he said. "These ladies are right. There's no law prohibiting telegraph operators from showing telegram communications for judicial purposes. You run this station, don't you, Mr. —"

"Durham," the young man said. "Yes, sir."

"You keep copies of telegrams for a certain amount of time for your records?"

"Yes," he answered slowly.

"I assume we're looking for a telegram sent by Mrs. Annie Convoy on August eighteenth?" He glanced at the sisters.

"Early morning of August eighteenth," Helena corrected.

"All right, then. I believe it would be expedient for you to show it to us."

"Yes, sir!" The young man had steadied his nerves. "August eighteenth, you say?" He rummaged through a stack of forms with different looping handwriting in one of the cubby holes of the desk.

"You knew all the time what we were after, didn't you?" Helena eyed him.

Daniel laughed. "You know I was always good at putting two and two together in school, even when you insisted they made five and not four."

"I suppose we were rather obvious," Eve said with a blush.

"Oliver would never forgive me if I let you three get yourselves into trouble," Daniel said.

"Who says we're getting ourselves into trouble?" Violet said stiffly. "We know what we're doing."

Jack handed them a wrinkled page. "Ink's kind of smeared by now, but I can read it to you if you like."

"That won't be necessary," Helena said as she took out her magnifying glass. "I think I can read it fine." She read aloud, "Ellie coming 3 a.m. train. Hank in trouble. Ellie upset. Keep silent. Hide newspapers. Annie.'"

"'Hank in trouble!" Violet said. "Annie *did* know about Wild

Bill in the alleyway. And Ellie *did* see something. This proves it!" She snatched the telegram from her sister's hand.

"Hold on, now," Daniel said. "What's this all about?"

"Annie told us she didn't know about what Hank did that night," Eve related. "At around two a.m. the morning Wild Bill's body was found, she came home to take Ellie to catch the milk train to Carson City, but she swore she didn't go near the alleyway."

"She put on a good act," Helena remarked. "I really thought she only knew about the crime when she read the papers later that morning."

"What a phony!" Violet snarled. "She ought to be arrested!"

"If she was covering up a crime, she will be," Daniel said. "Mr. Durham, I'm taking this telegram to the Gyver County D.A. He'll decide what to do with it."

"Yes, sir," said Jack meekly. The sound of the telegraph clicked, and he turned to his work.

They left the telegraph office and stood outside on the now quiet platform.

"When he's finished, I'll wire Oliver to come down here with the sheriff to get Ellie Convoy," said Daniel. "I think they'll want to talk to her now."

"No, wait!" Eve grabbed his arm. "Let us talk to her first."

He raised an eyebrow at each sister in turn. "I know you helped Oliver find Libby Cinder's killer, but this should be in the hands of the proper authorities."

"Who will get nothing out of Ellie," Eve said roughly. "That girl won't talk, Daniel."

"Annie must have done a good job of scaring the hell out of her," Violet declared. Eve winced at the brash language.

"Once Oliver explains to her —"

"He can explain his head off," Violet snapped. "Hank told me Ellie's been shy since her accident. He's the only one she really opens up to. She's no chatterbox."

"Ellie is fifteen, Dan," Helena intervened. "Don't we need permission to talk to her?"

"We're coming as friends, dear," Eve reminded her. "Daniel's a friend of ours who just happens to know the law."

"We're all friends," Violet insisted. Suddenly, her youthful pep left her for a moment, and she looked ten years older. "Please, Danny. That poor kid's been through enough, and Hank wouldn't want her to face the kind of questioning Sheriff Warner would do. If we can get her to come back with us of her own free will, she won't have to."

The Moody district attorney looked from one sister to the other. "On one condition. You let me come with you to make sure you're asking the right questions. And," he held up a finger, "if Ellie refuses to come back with you to Gyver, we call Oliver and the sheriff to come and get her."

"Deal!" Violet grinned.

"What about your client?" Helena asked a little dryly.

"I called him already from the public booth and told him I'd be late on account of those papers," said Dan.

"And you called your office to send them down at the same time," Helena concluded.

He grinned. "When you were so persistent about telegrams and the law and then refused my offer of the cab, I figured you were heading for the telegraph office here. Forgive me for being nosy?"

He appealed to them like a dog begging for a bone, and all three sisters laughed.

CHAPTER 27

They received instructions from the station master about where Paula Convoy, Ellie's aunt, lived based on the address on the telegram and took a taxi to a quiet area that faced the Sierra Nevada mountains. Houses dotted the dry brush landscape, and the sun was glaring down at them as if keeping a close watch.

The cab pulled up to a medium-sized white house with yellow trim and a little greener in the garden than they had seen so far.

"Lovely place," Eve remarked.

"We ought to tell him to wait." Helena nodded at the taxi driver. "I don't think we can walk back to town if we have to."

"Wide spaces out here," Daniel agreed.

The front door was already open with a woman standing in the doorway. The defined lines of her face and her watchful eyes matched Annie's, though this woman was taller and lankier.

"She's not going to be easy to sway," Helena said in a low tone. "I'm sure Annie has her on her guard."

"For the wrong reasons," Eve agreed.

The woman came forward with something like cordiality. "You're from Gyver, aren't you?"

Violet stepped forward. "I'm Violet Grave, Miss Convoy. These are my sisters Eve and Helena, and this is Mr. Daniel Frazer." The woman nodded at each of them in turn. "Hank told me all about you. He's very fond of you."

This softened the woman's features. "How is Hank?"

"He's fine," Violet assured her, taking her hand.

"They've got him —" She lowered her voice. "He's in jail, isn't he?"

"He's not arrested, Miss Convoy," Daniel said. "That is, he hasn't been formally charged yet."

She blinked. "Hank's a good boy."

"A good boy who did a bad thing," Daniel said gently.

"Please!" She threw a glance toward the back of the house. "You know Ellie is staying with me?" They nodded. "She doesn't know anything about Hank. I've been keeping the papers from her."

"But you've been reading them yourself," Helena observed. "Or has Annie been writing you?"

"Mother's never been one for writing," the woman lamented.

"She wrote this." Daniel showed her the telegram. "Miss Convoy, we've come to talk to Ellie."

"Oh, no!" The woman's arms immediately clamped the doorframe as if forbidding them to enter. "You can't do that."

"Please, Miss Convoy," Violet begged. "We think she might have seen something."

"Ellie can't see, Miss Grave," said the woman in a jagged tone.

"I meant she heard something," Violet corrected. "She might know something that could help Hank."

"What could she know?" The woman's voice trailed off.

"Miss Convoy." Helena put her arm around her younger sister. "We think Ellie was in the alleyway when Wild Bill was killed. She may be able to prove he attacked Hank, and Hank had to kill him out of self-defense."

"I know the papers say that's what Hank's been saying, but I didn't think the police believed it." The woman pressed her hands together.

With a frank look, Violet asked, "Do you believe it, Miss Convoy?"

"Call me Paula," the woman said. "If you're asking me if I think my nephew is a liar, I know he's not."

"Then you must let us see Ellie," Eve said.

"Ellie knows something is wrong," the woman lamented. "I've tried to shield her because that's what Mama wanted. I even stopped taking her into town so she wouldn't hear the gossip."

"Don't you think she wants to help Hank?" Violet asked. "Annie scared her to death just like she scared you to death! Do you think that's fair to Hank?"

A breeze blew past, bringing a blast of hot air. "You're right, Violet. It's not fair to Hank, and it's not fair to Ellie. She would want to help if she can." She looked at Daniel with frightened eyes. "Please be gentle with her."

"I'm a lawyer, ma'am," he said as he took off his hat. "It's my business to know how to put questions to witnesses."

"Witness?" the woman murmured. "Yes, I suppose Ellie might be a witness. I suppose so."

Miss Convoy led them through to the back yard. The scent of marigolds waffled in the air, lending a pleasant summer breeze to the early evening. Ellie was in the corner of the yard with a basket in her lap and a paper bag open beside her, preparing snap peas for cooking. Her long, deft fingers carefully felt for the edges of each bean, expertly snapping off the stems and leaves before depositing the refuse in the paper bag and putting the bean inside the basket again.

"My neighbor just brought us a bagful of beans," Paula explained. "Ellie insisted on helping."

"I don't like to be idle," the girl said in a tone very different from her grandmother's abrasive voice.

"Like your grandmother," Eve said with a smile.

"Granny's always doing something," Ellie agreed.

She looked to Eve to be tall for her age with a pleasant face that had more of Hank's round features than her grandmother's harsher ones. Her blond hair was tied back with a ribbon, and her eyes, looking wide and frozen, were the same sea blue as Hank's.

Miss Convoy noticed Eve watching and said in a kind voice, "She and Hank look more like their mother than my brother."

"Let me talk to her, Dan," Violet whispered.

The man nodded. Violet seated herself next to the girl. "Remember me, Ellie? I'm Violet Grave, Hank's friend from school."

"Of course," said Ellie. "You're the one who helped Hank pick the cameo he bought me for my last birthday."

"That's right," Violet said. "I'm here with my sisters, Helena and Eve."

"I remember you," said Ellie. "There was a girl once who got killed in the saw mill a few years ago where Papa was working." She spoke in a self-possessed tone.

"Mary King," Eve remembered.

"Papa asked your father if he would bury her because the Kings had no money," said Ellie. "He tried to pay your father, but your father wouldn't take it. He was so kind."

"Yes, he was," Helena said softly.

Daniel leaned forward. "Ellie, I'm Daniel Frazer, the Moody County district attorney. We've come to talk to you about your brother, Hank — well, he's not in a good way right now."

"You mean he's in trouble." Ellie's face tightened.

"He's been arrested, honey." Paula put her arm around her niece's shoulders.

The girl took this with only a hint of alarm. "It's because of Wild Bill, isn't it?"

"What about Wild Bill?" Violet pressed her hand.

"They had a scuffle."

"I'm afraid it's a little more serious than that," Daniel said. "Wild Bill has been killed, Ellie."

There was silence for a moment. Ellie held a long bean in her hands, grasping each edge. "Hank did it, didn't he?"

"Yes," said Helena. "He confessed he shot Wild Bill."

"Shot?" The girl was quiet for a moment. "Shot." Her voice became ragged. "That's what it was, wasn't it?" Suddenly, she cried out, "Granny should have let me stay!"

"You didn't want to come to Carson City?" Eve asked.

"Not that night," she said.

"You mean early morning," Helena said gently.

"I told Granny —" Here, she swallowed.

"Ellie, if you know something about what happened that night between your brother and Wild Bill, you must tell us." Daniel took her hands.

"Granny said Hank would get in trouble if I told." Her voice became more agitated. "But he got in trouble anyway, didn't he?"

"Hank told the police Wild Bill attacked him with a knife," said Eve. "He defended himself."

"Oh, but it was just like that!" Ellie shrieked. The basket fell from her lap, spilling the beans on the grass.

"Now, calm down, honey," Paula said.

"Granny said they would find Wild Bill in the alley, and they would blame Hank," Ellie said. "That's why it was better to send me away and keep quiet about — about what I heard."

"Heard from where?" asked Daniel

"From the open window in my room," she said. "It was a hot night, so I had it open all the way."

"Does your window face the alley?" Eve asked.

The girl nodded.

Daniel sat beside her and said in a gentle voice, "Ellie, tell us what you witnessed. Start from the beginning, and tell us slowly. No need to rush."

"I'll tell everything," she promised. She paused for a moment, and her hand reached out a little.

Her aunt seemed to know what she wanted and took it. "Go ahead, dear."

"Granny left to go help Mrs. Solaris with her baby," she said. "We — that is, me, Hank, and Wild Bill — stayed talking for a little bit. Wild Bill was telling us about some of the people he had met the week before driving a haul of peaches and melons to Sacramento."

"Annie told us you were about to play the violin when she had to leave," Eve said.

"I lost my nerve," Ellie admitted. "I haven't played in a long time, and with a guest there — but Granny was so insistent."

"I can imagine she was," Helena said.

"It was nicer just talking." Ellie smiled. "But then, Hank told Wild Bill he had some of Papa's good cigars, but they had to smoke in the alley, as Granny didn't allow smoking in the house."

"Why didn't you go with them?" Violet asked.

"I don't like the smell of cigars." Ellie was quiet for a moment. "When you lose your eyesight, your other senses become a lot stronger. The doctor told me that."

"You mean smells are magnified," Helena said. "So are sounds, tastes, and touches."

The girl smiled. "You're a doctor, aren't you?"

"I studied medicine," Helena said quietly. "Please go on, Ellie."

"Hank and Wild Bill went out to the alley, and I went upstairs to read," she said.

"But can you read—" Violet began, then covered her mouth with her gloved hand.

Ellie turned toward her. "I learned to read braille last year."

"Oh, naturally," Violet said. "Silly me."

Eve had never seen her sister so embarrassed and gave her a compassionate look.

"Did you hear your brother and Wild Bill talking in the alley?" Daniel asked.

"Yes, sir," she said. "As I told you, my window was open, and it faces the alley. I couldn't hear everything — they were further down so the smoke wouldn't be anywhere near Granny's house, or she'd have a fit — but I heard their voices and most of what they said."

"Were they fighting?" asked Violet.

"Oh, no," said Ellie. "They were talking real friendly to each other. Laughing about times they had during the war with some of the French girls." She blushed slightly.

"This was early in the evening, I take it?" Daniel asked.

"Not really early," Ellie said. "The clock downstairs rang nine when they went outside."

"Were they only talking about old times?" Helena asked.

"Well, no," she said. "Hank told Wild Bill about what Dr. Murphy said. He's a doctor in New York who Sara Anthony — she's our neighbor — knows. He has some operation he's done on people like me to make them walk better."

"That's what Hank told the police," Violet said, looking meaningfully at Daniel.

"He told Wild Bill about some truck he wanted to buy and fix up so he could work again," said Ellie.

"What did Wild Bill say?" Helena asked.

"Nothing," said Ellie. "It was just Hank talking."

"Then what happened?" Eve asked.

"Hank asked Wild Bill for money," she said. "A hundred and twenty dollars."

"Did he say what for?" Daniel asked.

"He wanted it for me!" The cry rang through the quiet air. "This is all my fault!" She hid her face in her hands.

"Ellie, Ellie," Paula murmured. "Of course it wasn't your fault, honey."

"I don't think it was for the operation," Helena said. "Train tickets from here to New York would have cost around one hundred dollars each, and the operation itself would probably have cost a hundred —"

"Oh, stop talking like an accountant!" Violet snapped.

"It was probably for the truck," Daniel said. "I'm guessing he wanted to work for the money."

Ellie stared. "I never thought of that!"

"I'm sorry if my sister upset you." Violet glared at Helena.

"I'm not upset," Ellie insisted. "I just hadn't thought of it in that way. He would have worked like a dog just so I could walk better. Now I'm going to do the same to make sure the police let him out of jail." Her tone was determined and strong.

CHAPTER 28

After Paula made and served iced tea to everyone, Ellie continued her story.

"Wild Bill got sort of mad," she said. "He said he put that money where no one would get at it, and it was for his mother in her old age."

"He paid off gambling debts with it a week before," Violet grumbled.

"Oh! You mean he didn't have the money when Hank asked him for it?" Ellie asked.

"A shame he didn't just tell Hank that," Daniel said. "How did Hank take Wild Bill's refusal?"

"You don't know Hank, Mr. Frazer," said Ellie. "He never asked for money from anyone in his life. He was ashamed."

"How do you know?" asked Helena.

"I could hear it in his voice," Ellie said. "The way he told Wild Bill he'd get him another cigar just to show there were no hard feelings."

"So that's when Hank went back into the house," Helena guessed.

"Yes," Ellie said. "I heard him come in, so I went downstairs. I asked him if everything was all right. He said everything was fine, and I ought to be getting ready for bed, as it was almost nine-thirty." She gave a small smile. "Granny insists I go to bed at nine. It takes me some time to get ready."

"Was there anything strange about his tone or his manner?" asked Daniel. "The police are trying to get a line on what happened between them. Hank doesn't seem to remember much."

"How did you know that?" Helena eyed him.

"I told you Oliver has been keeping me updated," he reminded her.

"No, but I heard a lot of noise as I was going up the stairs," she said. "Like Hank was rummaging through the drawer."

"Weren't the cigars there?" Eve asked.

"Yes, but it was more than that," she said. "He opened another drawer and took out something heavy."

"Heavy?" Helena asked.

"It sounded like it," the girl said. "Oh, I don't mean dragging heavy, but something he needed to keep careful hold of. Yes, he was very careful with it."

Helena glanced at her sisters. "It must have been the gun."

"Oh! Do you think it was?" Ellie shivered.

Paula squeezed her shoulders. "Don't be afraid, honey."

"He kept the gun downstairs, didn't he?" asked Helena. "Annie told us."

"Yes," she said. "He wanted to be able to grab it if he had to use it." She suddenly covered her face. "Oh, God!"

"Can you go on, Ellie?" Daniel asked kindly.

"I'm all right," she insisted, the strong and assured tone returning. "It just all makes sense now."

"What does?" Violet asked.

"I got upstairs and started to get ready for bed. But I heard their voices again. Something about Hank's — it scared me." She looked troubled as she leaned against her aunt's shoulder. "I decided to go outside. I thought I could stop them, you see."

"You went out the back door and stood in the gravel," Helena guessed.

"That's right." The girl looked in her direction. "How did you know?"

"We saw your footprints in the photographs the crime scene photographer took that night," she said.

"Crime scene!" Ellie looked alarmed. "Oh, but they were farther down the alley."

"The entire alley is the crime scene," said Violet. "They found Wild Bill hidden behind the trash cans."

"You mean he was there when —" The girl turned pale and shaking.

"We don't know," Eve said in a soothing tone. "Please go on, dear."

"I was going to call out to them when I heard Hank say, 'I'll pay you back a dollar at a time if I have to, but I need that money. And you're going to give it to me.'" She shivered again. "It didn't sound like Hank at all."

"Shell shock changes a man," Helena said with sympathy.

"Wild Bill said, 'At ease, soldier. I'll give you what you want. Now, how about that cigar, eh?'"

"But he didn't have it to give," Eve sighed.

"He was probably trying to calm Hank down by agreeing," Helena said. "A wise strategy, as far as it goes."

"Why didn't Wild Bill just tell Hank he spent it already?" Violet asked.

"He probably figured Hank wouldn't believe him," Daniel said. "Not in the state he was in. Remember, they fought in the war together. They knew one another well." He turned to Ellie. "Then what happened, Ellie?"

"I think Hank started to cry," said Ellie. "He kept saying, 'Why do you make me do it? Why do you make me say those things?' Then Wild Bill said, 'Give me the cigar, Hank.'"

"Then what happened?"

"Hank was sobbing and digging into his pockets," Ellie said. "I heard that. Then, Wild Bill said, 'I'll kill you now!' It was so frightening!"

"I'm sure it was," Eve said softly.

"You don't understand," said the girl. "He was speaking in such a nice voice, and then he was suddenly screaming like a banshee."

"So there's no doubt it was Wild Bill's voice?" Violet asked.

"I heard him clearly," said Ellie. "Then there were some noises, and Wild Bill shouted, 'Remember how I taught you to knife a German right in the back?' Hank gave a yell."

"That must have been when he lifted his arm to defend himself from the stabbing, and Wild Bill cut his arm," Helena surmised.

"You see?" Violet glowered. "I've said all along that Hank was telling the truth."

Daniel raised his hand to signal her to be quiet. "Tell us the rest of it, Ellie."

"I heard a popping sound," Ellie said. "I thought it was a car or something. But it was Hank's gun, wasn't it? Wasn't it?" She looked around wildly.

"Yes, dear, it was," Eve said in a quiet voice. "What did you do then?"

"I shouted, 'Hank!' I don't think he heard me. He didn't answer."

"He probably didn't register it," Helena said. "He said he was in a daze after the shot."

"There was quiet," said Ellie. "It was so eerie. Then I heard quick steps, like someone was running, but it was away from me, not toward me."

"Hank running to Dean Street," Daniel agreed. "It all fits."

"Of course it fits," Violet said. "I told you Hank was telling the truth."

"What happened after that, Ellie?" Eve asked.

"I went inside," she said. "I was shaking all over. I just sat down on the couch and waited until Granny came home. I waited a long time."

"How do you know?" asked Daniel.

"It was after two in the morning before she came," said Ellie. "I heard the chimes on the clock."

"And what happened then, dear?" Eve asked.

"I told her," she said. "I told her everything. She said I was to go upstairs and pack because I was going on the milk train to see Aunt Paula, and we only had a half hour before the train left. She said —" she gasped, "she said not to tell anyone, not even Aunt Paula, what happened. She said if I did, Hank would be arrested." She grasped her aunt's shoulder. "Aunt Paula, why didn't she want me to tell? Didn't she know it would save Hank?"

"I don't know, honey," Paula said in a soft tone. "I suppose she didn't think the police would believe you."

"But I was there!" Ellie insisted. "I can't see, but I heard everything."

"My God," Paula breathed. "Mother, Mother." She spoke as if it were a prayer.

Daniel grasped her hand. "Ellie, would you repeat your story to the Gyver district attorney?"

"Of course I will." Ellie rose. "I'll go pack right now."

He looked at Paula. "Miss Convoy, I think you should come with Ellie."

"Yes," said the woman. "It's the only thing to do."

Daniel rose and looked at his pocket watch. "I'm afraid I must leave you all. My secretary has probably been waiting at the train station for at least a half hour wondering where I am."

"If you wait a few moments, we can all drive in," Paula said.

He shook his head. "That's kind of you, but I asked the taxi to wait." With a rueful smile, he added, "Remind me to always have you in my camp in the future, Grave sisters."

"You never can tell," Helena said with a smile.

By the time they got to the station, they had to take the late train, which was empty, since most of the people went on the earlier train. They sat in the parlor car which they had almost to themselves. Violet and Helena engaged Ellie in a game of cards when she produced her special pack. Eve and Paula sat a few seats away.

"It's been difficult for her, hasn't it?" Eve remarked, watching the girl. "And yet, she seems so cheerful."

"Ellie's like Joe and Mama," said Paula as she knitted. "She accepts that life isn't easy, and you have to take what comes."

"But not Hank," Eve guessed.

Paula smiled a little. "No, not Hank. He's a fighter like his mother." She stared out the window for a few minutes, then turned to Eve. "You mustn't judge Hank too harshly. He hasn't had it easy either."

"I don't judge him," Eve promised. "He was always kind to us, and my sister thinks the world of him."

"It was just Mama put a huge burden on his shoulders," said the woman. "She oughtn't to have done that."

"You mean when his father died?" Eve asked.

Paula nodded. "Mama worshipped Joe. He was a good man, my brother. But he was the sort of man who didn't like change, if you know what I mean. Mama depended on him to be the man of the family when my father died."

"And she depended on Hank to be the man of the family when his father died," Eve murmured.

"Hank was only seventeen," Paula defended. "Mama made him quit school — his last year too — and take a job at the lumber mill."

"But it wasn't for him," Eve said.

Paula gave her a rueful smile. "Hank likes to be out in the open air. Not in a factory breathing in sawdust all day."

"The worst thing for him," Eve agreed, thinking of what Helena had said when they spoke to Annie.

"He quit after six months," the woman went on. "Then he just sort of roamed around taking odd jobs. Mama never said a word. She didn't have to. She has a way with her expression and her manner that's like an ax falling on your back every time you're with her."

"Silent condemnation," Eve said with a nod.

"Hank's really a sensitive boy," said Paula. "Ellie, she takes things as they come. But Hank, he fights against them. Inside, that is."

"But he didn't fight with his grandmother," Eve said.

Paula shrugged. "Mama never gave him anything to fight against. She was just silent."

"Is that when he joined the army?" asked Eve.

The woman nodded. "Not long after his eighteenth birthday. He did it without telling anyone. I suppose he had the right since he was an adult."

"But Annie didn't approve," Eve guessed.

"Hank said she went around with a wooden face," said Paula. "That's how Mama gets when she's furious. No words. Just the wooden face."

"Poor Hank." Eve shivered.

"I think he was relieved to go," said Paula.

"Your mother called it 'escaping his responsibilities,'" Eve said softly.

"That's not true!" Paula protested.

Eve pressed her hand. "I never thought it was, Paula."

"He was trying to find a way to grow up," the woman said. "His way, that is, not Mama's way."

"But he didn't find his way," Eve guessed.

"It was the war," Paula said. "It confused him so much, like so many of the young men."

"So he just went back to odd jobs," Eve said.

"But he started drinking and gambling too." Paula sighed. "It was like some demon had gotten hold of him and was shaking him, telling him to live, live, live. That's what he told me."

"So many of the young men are like that," Eve murmured. "Horror and shell shock."

"Mama thought he would come back from the war as the man she wanted him to be." Paula went back to her knitting but the needles clicked now in an agitated way. "I remember we were waiting at the train station for Hank's train to come in, and she said to me, 'He'll be what his father was now. They grow up in the army.'"

"They didn't get along, did they?" Eve asked.

"Oh, they never fought. I told you Mama refuses to fight. To fight you have to have an adversary. But Mama won't do that." The woman's eyes were crusty. "She won't scream. She won't accuse. She won't even speak. She'll just look at you with those cold, hostile eyes of hers."

"But Hank learned how to fight in the war," Eve said. The scenery outside the window was one blurred line. "A soldier can see his enemy, even if it's only a bunch of khaki uniforms running toward him."

"Or at least he knows what he's fighting," Paula agreed. "Maybe not why, but what."

"It must have been difficult for him," Eve said.

"I blame Mama for that," she said. "If she had screamed or pointed a finger, just once, and had it out with him, I think he would have given up the bootleg liquor and the cards. He would have been sober when he —" She swallowed.

"When he was driving Wild Bill's truck the night he injured Ellie," Eve said quietly.

"He didn't mean it." Paula's voice broke. "He'd been driving all weekend up and down from Sacramento to San Francisco and back to Gyver and then all over again. He drank to stay awake, he told me once. He came back the night there was a blackout for hours."

"I remember," Eve said. "The whole town was dark."

"He didn't see her waiting for him in the alley," she said. "He nearly ran over her. She ran hard into the wall of the warehouse across the street, stumbling against some concrete blocks that were there. She hit her head, and her leg got crushed."

"Poor thing." Eve's throat felt dry.

"And Mama never forgave him," said Paula. "I thought for sure she'd have it out with him then."

"But she kept silent," Eve murmured. "Always silent, the storm brewing within."

"Don't be too hard on her, Eve." Paula covered her hand. "She's had a hard life. All her dreams were pinned on Ellie being a concert violinist."

"And then they shattered like a row of china dolls." Eve watched as the blurred line of scenery once more became separated into sky and ground.

CHAPTER 29

By the time the train reached the station in Gyver, it was eight o'clock. Ellie was jumpy, hopping a little in place and pressing her hands together even though it was a warm night. The air surrounded them at a standstill with a slight pale color from the steam of the train.

Helena pulled Eve aside. "Ellie doesn't want to go home just now, Eve."

"Not go home?" Her sister stared at her. "You mean to her grandmother?"

"Can you blame her?" Helena asked. "The poor kid is confused right now. And maybe a little angry."

Paula approached them while Violet took Ellie to the news-stand that was still open, loading her arms with candy and magazines in her generous way. "Is there a hotel in town?"

"There's the Gyver Hotel," Helena said.

"You needn't go to any hotel," Eve said firmly. "We have plenty of room at our house."

"Oh, I couldn't think of it."

"Of course you'll stay with us!" Violet, joining them with Ellie, was indignant. "Ellie and I are friends now. I'd never let friends stay in a hotel while they were in town."

"You're so nice, Vi." The girl pressed her cheek to Violet's shoulder.

"We should tell Oliver," Helena said in a quiet voice to Eve. "I don't think this can wait."

"Tomorrow morning will be soon enough," Eve said.

"No, I want to tell Mr. Clarke everything," Ellie said. "If we tell him tonight, do you think Hank could come home tomorrow?"

"I'm sure Oliver will do all he can," Eve promised, taking her arm. "But you're tired, dear. It's been a long day."

"I'm not tired," the girl insisted. "I've been so worried about things not being right. I want to go to the district attorney and tell him everything."

"It's late, honey," Paula reminded her.

"Not so late," Ellie insisted.

"I'm sure Oliver will be up," Helena said. "And so will his wife." She said the last under her breath.

The lights of the Clarke house were on in the living room when they came. For once, the Clarke maid did not answer the door. It was Ellen Clarke herself who answered.

"Well, what's all this?" She glanced from face to face, her eyes lingering on Ellie.

"We're here to talk to Oliver." Violet, with her usual forthrightness, pushed past her. "Oliver!"

"Don't shout so," the woman snapped. "My maid has a headache, and she's gone to bed."

"Is that why the lady of the house is answering the door?" Violet eyed her.

"Vi, hush," Eve said. "We really do need to talk to him, Ellen. This is Ellie, Hank Convoy's sister, and his aunt, Paula. Ellie has something she needs to tell Oliver."

"Please, Mrs. Clarke." Ellie tilted her head a little, clutching at the small handbag she carried. "It's very important."

Eve gave the woman credit. For all her sniffing over proprieties and her love of social standing, Ellen also had a sharp perception. She took Ellie's arm. "Of course, my dear. Come right in."

The sisters and Paula followed. Paula eagerly looked around the house with its refined colors and elegant furnishings. Eve could only imagine Paula had rarely been in such a large house.

Oliver was settled on the couch, pipe in hand, but he jumped up when they came in. "Well, well, what a surprise!"

"We're sorry to bother you," Eve said.

"It's not the first time," Ellen said under her breath.

"This is Ellie Convoy, Oliver." Helena put her hand on the girl's shoulder. "And this is Paula Convoy, Ellie's aunt."

"I see." He immediately seated the two strangers. "Come from Carson City, eh?"

"We all just got off the train," Violet put in.

"Been visiting, I see." He glanced at his wife. "Ellen, I think we can get these ladies a quick bite, don't you? Some sandwiches and coffee, maybe?"

"Mrs. Finestone is off today, and Jennifer's gone to bed with a headache, Oliver." Ellen gave him a nasty look.

"Please don't bother," Eve said. "Agnes will make us something when we get home. The Convoys are staying with us."

"I see." He sat down, lighting his pipe. "I assume you have something important to tell me, Ellie."

"Yes, sir," said the girl. "Hank's telling you the truth. He killed Wild Bill because Wild Bill was going to kill him!"

"Calm down, youngster," he said in a kind voice. "Tell me everything from the beginning, and let's see what we can make of it, eh?"

Ellie told her story in the same meticulous detail she had told it to the Grave sisters and Daniel Frazer. She sounded more assured, as if bringing the evidence closer to where Hank was being held was a comfort to her. Eve noted there was no flaw in her retelling. Every detail she had mentioned to them was now turned over to Oliver in exactly the same way.

"You see now he shouldn't be in jail," Paula said when her niece finished. "He ought to be home."

"If he wants to go home," Ellie added in a soft tone.

"You appreciate we'll need an official statement tomorrow," Oliver said. "We'll still have to charge Hank, and he'll go to trial." Then, in a kinder tone, he added, "But I think with the evidence we have, the jury will come to a quick decision to acquit him."

"Then Hank won't get out of jail yet." Ellie's face fell.

He patted her hand. "I don't think he'll be there much longer, Ellie. We'll move as quickly as we can."

"I told you all along Hank was telling the truth." Violet crossed her arms and grinned triumphantly. "You should have believed me."

"Oliver can't carry out justice based on what he believes or doesn't believe," Helena chided her. "The police must have evidence."

"We still have the missing valuables to contend with," Oliver reminded her.

"And the missing knife," Helena chimed in.

"Some drunk robbed him," Violet insisted.

"None of the neighbors saw anyone," Eve reminded her.

"I don't care!" Violet snapped. "There could still have been some hobo running around who happened to be at the wrong place at the wrong time."

"Well, we'll continue to look into that," said Oliver, rising. "You all go home and get some sleep. Paula, you and Ellie come to my office in the morning, and I promise you we'll get all of this sorted out as quickly as we can."

"Thank you, Mr. Clarke." Ellie held out her hands, and he grasped them for a few moments in silence as if overwhelmed by her gratitude.

Eve felt a heaviness persist in her chest She let the others leave first and then caught Helena's hand. "Take them home, Helena," she said quietly. "I have to talk to Oliver."

"About what we found out earlier today?" Her sister eyed her.

"Just take them home," she said. "And you and Vi make sandwiches or something so Agnes doesn't have to get up."

"Agnes is probably already up," Helena said with a chuckle. "And she'd bite our heads off if she heard we allowed guests to eat a cold dinner."

Eve closed the door and turned to the Clarkes. "I've got to talk to you, Oliver."

"Now?" Ellen asked.

"Ellen, sweet, why don't you go up to bed?" Oliver gave her a tender kiss. "I'll be up in a few minutes."

"Don't keep him too long," Ellen said. "We *did* have an appointment tomorrow morning in Brenas, but I suppose we don't now, do we?" She gave him a piercing look as she went up the stairs.

Eve noted the guilty look on his face, and when they got back to the living room, he produced a bottle of whisky from the cabinet and held it up. "Pre-Prohibition," he promised.

She shook her head, feeling the last thing she needed was liquor. "I'm sorry we spoiled your plans to go to Brenas tomorrow," she mumbled.

"They weren't my plans," he growled. Then, his face became more businesslike as he poured himself a short drink. "If it helps Hank get out of this mess, it's well worth it."

"You're a funny sort of a district attorney," she mused.

He gave her one of his boyish grins. "I always seem reluctant to believe the cut-and-dried evidence like Sheriff Warner does, don't I?" He sat down beside her. "But here we have a confession. Hank shot Wild Bill. End of story."

"Except that's not the end of the story," Eve reminded him. "The question this time wasn't who did it but why they did it."

"Self-defense." He nodded. "All right, you've proved it."

"But the unanswered questions?" she asked. "The missing pearl tie pin and cuff links? The diamond pocket watch? The safe deposit box key? The knife?"

"We'll locate those things," he insisted. "But they're irrelevant now."

"Not to Mrs. Hicks," Eve said softly.

"They'll turn up," he assured her.

"Oliver, don't you find it very odd that the key is missing?" she asked. "The valuables we could believe were stolen by some derelict who happened to pass through the alleyway that night, though I don't believe that for a minute, and I don't think you do either."

He nodded. "If someone was in that alley after Hank abandoned it, we would have heard about it from the neighbors."

"But the key?" she asked. "And the knife? What use would a hobo have for those things?"

He studied her with hooded eyes. "Just what are you getting at, Eve?"

"Hank insists he never touched Wild Bill after he fired the gun," said Eve. "I believe him. What's more, I think I know who did."

She proceeded to tell him all she and her sisters had discovered from the Convoy neighbors, Josephine Huff, Louis Durham, and Jack Durham. She also related to him the intense conversation she had with Paula on the train.

He sat listening, holding the whiskey glass cupped in his hand. It was empty now, and the ice he put in it had melted into a pool of slightly pale water. His features were set with a sternness that one found in a lawyer or lawman picking out the important details of a confession.

When she was finished, he said, "Do you realize what you're suggesting, Eve?"

"I do," she said quietly. She reached into her purse and pulled out the wrinkled copy of the telegram. "Here's what

Annie sent her daughter that night. You can see for yourself, Oliver."

He read it slowly as the minutes stretched. Then he set the empty glass down on the table. He walked around in a small circle, his hands in his pockets. "It's incredible!" he murmured. "I could understand a grandmother hiding the body of the man her grandson killed. She wanted to shield him, sure. But the rest of it —"

"She didn't hide Wild Bill's body to shield Hank," Eve insisted. "She hid it to make it look as if Hank were trying to shield it."

"Good God!" His face was aghast.

"Oliver, what are you going to do?" She peered at him.

He stood for a moment, looking down at his feet. Then, he pulled her up off the couch. "We've got to find out if it's the truth or not, Eve. To close this case, if nothing else."

"But Hank!" Eve said. "If he knew — and Ellie —"

"It's better they knew the truth than live a lie," he said harshly. "If there's one thing I've learned about life and crime, it's the innocent can't stay innocent indefinitely."

"No, that's true," she admitted. "They can't." She slipped her arms into the coat Oliver held up for her. "Will — can she be arrested? For concealing evidence or whatever it is?"

He opened the door and gazed into the darkness. "I don't know yet."

She felt his dilemma and pressed his hand.

~~~~~

It took a long time for Annie to answer the door. There was no light on the front porch, so Oliver had to light a match to see the doorbell. Under the milky glow of the flickering flame, Eve saw the curtains were still as tightly drawn as they were that morning when she and her sisters went to the Blakes'. She also noted the morning and evening papers were tossed aside on the porch as if no one had touched them since the paper boy threw them there.
~~~~~

"Oliver." She was suddenly alarmed. "Maybe Annie is sick."

"Maybe she's out on a call," he said. "If she doesn't answer, I'll tell the sheriff to contact Dr. Lloyd to see if she's with him."

"And if she isn't?"

His face set. "Then I'll tell Sheriff Warner to send some of his men to scour the city for her."

But the threats weren't necessary, as Annie answered the door after a few more rings. Eve was struck by her appearance. She looked ten years older with a gray pallor on her face, heavily lit by the hall light, and lines in places Eve had not seen before. Her eyes regarded them with a rat-like gaze. "It's late, Mr. Clarke," she said shortly.

"This is important, Mrs. Convoy," he said. "We need to come in."

"In the morning," the woman said in a decided tone and proceeded to close the door.

But Oliver's hand shot out to stop it. "We're coming in." His tone was uncompromising.

The woman backed away and allowed him to open the door all the way. Annie led them to the living room, her step suddenly uncertain and her back a little stooped. Eve saw right away that all the curtains and windows were closed in the house, and the faint scent of mustiness crept into the air. She immediately opened both windows in the living room and parted the curtains. The light August breeze which, for once, was not heavy with heat, blew into the house, clearing the staleness.

"I gather this is about Hank," she said.

"No, ma'am," said Oliver. "This is about Ellie."

"Ellie?" She was more alert. "What about Ellie? Is she hurt? Has she been in some — accident?" The last word dropped like a wooden peg on the floor.

"She's back in Gyver," said Eve. "She and Paula are staying with us."

"Back in Gyver!" The woman stared at her. Suddenly, she

regained some of her old vigor as she glared at Oliver. "This is your doing, isn't it, Mr. Clarke? How dare you call my granddaughter back to town without my consent!"

"He didn't," Eve answered. "Ellie came back on her own."

The woman's face wrinkled as she sat back. "I don't understand."

"I think you do." Oliver looked hard at her. "Ellie's just told me about what she heard and observed the night your grandson killed Wild Bill."

The only sound for a moment were the crickets outside, their late-night song cutting through the house. Annie slouched a little in the chair but only said, "I see."

"We see a few things too." Oliver took the crinkled telegram out of his pocket and laid it on the table. "The telegrapher in Carson City gave us this."

She stared down at it.

"You lied to us, Mrs. Convoy," said Oliver. "You told us you didn't go near the alleyway when you came home from the Solaris house."

"What makes you think I did?" she asked.

"'Hank in trouble. Keep silent. Hide newspapers.'" He repeated each line with more vigor.

Annie held his gaze for a moment. Then she stared ahead. "All right, Mr. Clarke. You win. I did go into the alleyway that night."

"You hid Wild Bill's body behind the garbage cans," Eve said.

"Of course I did!" the woman snapped. "Wouldn't you if you found out that untamed sister of yours had killed a man?"

Eve flinched a little but held tight to the edge of the chair. "I might. Only you didn't."

"Just what do you mean by that?" Annie demanded.

"You didn't hide the body so the police wouldn't find it," Oliver said. "You hid it so the police would think Hank didn't want them to find it."

"That's absurd!"

"Ellie told us she waited up for you to come home," the district attorney said. "You got home at around two-thirty in the morning, just like you told us. Except things didn't go exactly as you told us after that."

"And how did things go?" she challenged. "Tell me, Mr. Clarke."

"Ellie told you what she'd heard and witnessed," he continued. "You told her to go upstairs and then you went out to the alley. You saw Wild Bill lying on the ground. You then went inside and got Ellie packed and out of the house to the train station."

"I wasn't going to let my granddaughter be mixed up in a crime!" Annie thundered.

"But you would let Hank hang for a crime he didn't really commit," Eve said softly.

"If you have accusations to make against me, Eve, I'd be very careful," the woman warned. "There is such a thing as slander."

"This isn't slander, Mrs. Convoy," Oliver said. "It's setting someone up for a crime. The crime of murder!"

Annie's lined face lost its tightness and the stoop became more pronounced. "Won't you please let me go to bed now?"

"Not until we sort all of this out," the district attorney demanded. "Hank was telling the truth when he said Wild Bill came at him with a knife and the intent to kill. He shot him out of self-defense."

"Then he'll be let go, and that will be that," said the woman.

"But that isn't that, Annie," Eve said. "He has to come back here. He has to live with his grandmother's resentment and rage, and the knowledge that she tried to get him hanged."

"You're being a little dramatic, Eve, aren't you?" The woman grimaced.

"Is she, Mrs. Convoy?" Oliver looked hard at her. "The police are out to catch criminals, and we're grateful for any help from the public. But we don't like frame-ups!"

"Why would I do anything like that to my own grandson?" she challenged.

"Because you hated him," Eve said simply. "You wanted him to be the provider for you and Ellie like his father had. But he was only a boy." She broke into a sob. "A boy of seventeen! You should have been taking care of him, not him taking care of you!"

"What do you know about it?" Annie shouted. "What do you know about what I lost when I lost my Joe or the sacrifices I made for him and the promises he made to me?"

"It wasn't for Hank to fulfill those promises," Oliver said.

The woman gasped, staring at him. In a defeated tone, she said, "No. Maybe it wasn't."

"Mrs. Convoy." He sat down beside her and took her hand. "Don't you owe it to both your grandchildren to tell the truth now?"

She was silent for a long time. The crickets began their song again, this time in a more somber pitch that sounded like a dirge to Eve.

Annie turned to Oliver. "What do you want to know, Mr. Clarke?"

"We know you hid the body behind the garbage cans," said Oliver. "We want to know what you did with the knife and the valuables and the key. And why you took them in the first place."

"It was all so clear to me," the woman lamented.

Eve pressed the woman's arm. "What was clear, Annie?"

"Hank wasn't a good boy," she said. "He could have been something. Mr. Rogers wanted him at the mill. He said Joe always told him how good Hank was with his hands. He could have been a saw filer at the mill. He could have put his sister through music school. Ellie was a fine violin player, you know." She looked at Eve with a small, vague smile.

"She told us," Eve said.

"But he refused to settle down.," the woman said. "And then

the drinking and gambling. And the accident." Her voice grew vicious. "He ruined Ellie's life, and he ruined mine!"

"And you saw fit to try and ruin his," Oliver said in a final tone.

"No!" She looked at him. "No, Mr. Clarke, not ruin. Seek justice, for me and for Ellie."

"Justice is not hanging a man who didn't commit a crime," Oliver growled.

"He did commit a crime!" she shrieked. "He committed the crime of neglecting the women in his family. For that, there is no justice."

"But framing him for murder was the next best thing." Eve's hands were shaking and she hid them behind her.

"I knew once Ellie told her story that the police would see it was self-defense," she said. "But we all have to pay for our sins in this world, Eve."

"So you took the things from Wild Bill to make it look like Hank killed him for money," Oliver concluded.

"I didn't plan it that way," she admitted. "I was only going to hide the body once Ellie left. I rushed back here before anyone found him and dragged Wild Bill behind those garbage cans. But then I saw he was wearing his coat. I had to move his arms to get the knife out of his hand." She shuddered. "I thought if the police found it, then it would prove Hank was really attacked."

"Go on, Mrs. Convoy," Oliver commanded. "We want to hear the rest of it."

"That's when I noticed how the pockets were bulging out of his coat," she said. "It didn't look right to me. We don't have much, but we do have some silver and I thought — I know now it was crazy. Wild Bill wasn't a thief."

"But you thought you could make your grandson look like one when you discovered the valuables and the safe deposit box key," Eve said.

"I was a fool!" She buried her head in her hands.

"Yes, Mrs. Convoy, you were," Oliver said. "Where are those things now? The valuables and the knife?"

"I buried them." Her voice came out muffled.

"Buried them!" Eve stared at the billowing curtains.

Annie uncovered her face. "I went back to the Solaris house. I knew Mary's husband had already left for his shift at the mill. She and the kids were asleep, and Dr. Lloyd had gone. I went into their backyard and buried everything."

Oliver pressed her shoulder. "You get some rest now, Mrs. Convoy. I'll send the sheriff here in the morning, and we'll go to the Solaris house and dig those things up."

"Is it necessary?" She looked at him. "You don't need the knife now, do you?"

"We'll need it to close the case," he said. "And those things of Wild Bill's belong to his mother now. Don't you think she ought to have them?"

"Yes." The woman's lip quivered. "Every mother ought to have what's left of her son." She studied Oliver. "I suppose I'll be arrested now for tampering with evidence and obstructing justice, and whatever else you can find."

"That will be up to the judge," Oliver said in a harsh tone.

"And my grandchildren?" Her voice broke. "They'll have to know everything, won't they?"

"They have a right, don't they, Annie?" Eve asked.

Annie looked at her. The lines broke for the first time, and the softened face looked almost like a child's. "Do you think they'll hate me, Eve?"

"That's for them to decide," she said.

CHAPTER 30

It was a week later. The heat had broken a little with cloudy skies, but there was no rain. Hampton Cemetery looked less grim to Eve than the first time she saw it. There was a little color in the trees, and someone had placed flowers on several graves in the row where Wild Bill was buried. The roses they bought that morning from Chaney's Florist added their own light scent over the graveyard.

"Mrs. Hicks certainly did indulge, didn't she?" Paula remarked as she studied the tombstone.

"She insisted on black marble," Helena said.

Ellie moved her hands slowly over the gravestone's etched writing. "He was a nice man," she murmured. "He promised to show me card tricks one day. He never got the chance." Her voice caught, and she buried her face in her aunt's shoulder.

"Jimmy Gallager can teach you card tricks," Violet promised, putting her arm around her. "He used to do magic tricks for the kids in the neighborhood."

"And take pennies from them," Helena snorted.

"He did not!" Violet protested. "He never took pennies from kids who couldn't afford it."

"Don't tell me you're starting to get sweet on him," her sister teased.

"Oh, dry up!" Violet said.

The gate creaked, and Eve glanced over her shoulder. Oliver came in grasping Hank's arm. She felt relief wash over her. The trial against Hank, as he predicted, was speedy and clear-cut, and Hank was released that morning.

Hank stumbled forward and, ran to his sister, sweeping her up with a tight embrace. She laughed and ruffled his hair.

Oliver grinned as he stood beside her. "We got our quick acquittal all right."

"And Annie?" Helena glanced at him.

"We're not prosecuting her for the frame-up," he said. "She led us to where she hid the knife and the valuables. They were all there."

"Could Hank sue her in civil court if he wanted?" Helena questioned.

"He ought to!" Violet said.

"Don't be so vindictive, Vi," Eve chided.

"Well, she could have gotten him hung."

"But she didn't," Oliver reminded her. "He could have taken her to court for malicious prosecution. Joe Curry even suggested it. But Hank said he just wants to put all this behind him, for Ellie's sake."

"I think that's very wise," Eve said with a nod.

"Blood is thicker than water?" Her youngest sister eyed her.

She put her arm around her. "And don't you forget it, missy, as Agnes would say."

Oliver let out a roar.

They moved down the path while the Convoy family paid their respects to Wild Bill. Eve was glad to see Hank seemed calmer and more assured.

"You're all right now, aren't you, Hank?" she asked as they slowly walked out of the cemetery.

"I will be," he said. "Mr. Curry's going to help me get medical aid so I can see a doctor."

"They can really help," Helena chimed in.

"He said it ought to be easy with my war record and the statement Mr. Clarke wrote," he said. "Funny how all the awful things that happened are actually going to help me now."

"There's a good veterans hospital in Reno," Paula offered.

"The one in Moody's very good too," Helena defended.

"Aunt Paula's invited us to live with her," Ellie said. "We're not going to stay with Granny." Her tone was hard.

"Honey, you mustn't blame her," Eve said softly.

"She did a bad thing, Eve," Ellie said. "I don't know if I can ever forgive her."

"I have," Hank said quietly.

"It will be hard for her, living on her own," Eve murmured.

"She's decided to live with my cousin in Southern California," Paula said. "They just had another baby, and they need someone to take care of the children while they both work."

"Best thing for her," Oliver agreed.

"She's not a bad person, really," Hank insisted. "She's always had a set of rules she lives by. Sometimes, she can't see past those rules."

"She'll be living by someone else's rules from now on," Paula remarked. "Perhaps that's God's punishment for the self-righteous."

Violet managed to coax her sisters into allowing her to take the car so she could help Ellie and Hank pack their things and take all three of the Convoys to the train station before her shift began at the drugstore.

As Oliver opened the car door for them, he gave them an easy smile. "I had a conversation with Dan this morning. He told me how you roped him into helping you get Ellie back to town."

"We didn't rope him into anything," Helena said. "Dan is a lawyer, just like you are, and he saw his duty."

"It wasn't his case, Helena," Eve objected. "He was doing it to help us."

"I'm grateful to him and to both of you. Again." Oliver shut the door on the driver's side.

"If you must know, we made Vi a promise," said Helena. "She wrangled it out of us."

"A promise?"

"To prove Hank killed Wild Bill in self-defense," Eve said. "Vi can be as persuasive as a lion standing over you with a club when she wants to be."

He burst out laughing as he started the car.

~~~~~

Author's Note

Hi awesome reader!

Thank you for reading *The Missing Witness*! I hope you enjoyed this second installment of the Grave Sisters Mysteries.

We think of the nineteen twenties as a time for fun and ease. It's not called the Roaring Twenties for nothing. We think of jazz music, flappers with bobbed hair and short skirts, and bootleg liquor. We think of the good times people had partying through the night, driving recklessly in motor cars (just beginning to become a staple of modern life at the time) and drinking lots and lots of champagne.

But there's a side we don't often hear about and that's the young soldiers who were still reeling from the effects of World War I (at least in the early part of the nineteen twenties). Keep in mind that the memory of the war wasn't all that remote for many people in
~~~~~

1921 when this book is set. The scars (physical, psychological, and social) still remained on the veterans and the people who loved and supported them.

That's the feeling I wanted to bring forth in this book. I've always been more interested in the aftermath of war than the war itself. To me, history begins with the people and the common people at that. I like to know how people lived and behaved and felt during different eras in history and when those eras lurk in the shadows of war, it's even more fascinating. I also love to learn about the resilience and strength of societies that endured more troubling times than we have. I hope you found the story of Hank, Wild Bill, and others here as interesting as I did.

Where can you find the Grave Sisters next? Keep in mind that Gyver isn't the only community that is dealing with crime. The town of Moody right across the river also has its share of crimes. You met Daniel Frazer, the young district attorney of Moody county, in this book (and in Book 1, *The Case of the Washed-Up Corpse*; if you haven't read that book yet, you can pick up a copy of it here: https://tammayauthor.com/the-case-of-the-washed-up-corpse-grave-sisters-mysteries-book-1). You might recall that Daniel is no stranger to the sisters. He knows Helena quite well, in fact, as they went to school in Pasadena together. You'll hear more about that and about the escapade their old college chums got themselves into — which includes murder— in *A Weekend Getaway Murder*, which you can find here: https://tammayauthor.com/a-weekend-getaway-murder-grave-sisters-mysteries-book-3. While this book is still in pre-first draft mode, turn the page for more about this book, including a sneak peak at the cover and a few highlights on what to expect!

. . .

Happy reading!
Tam

Here's the book description:

Violet's friend claims self-defense - but is it murder?

In small towns like Gyver, WWI veterans don't have it easy. In a nation just emerging from an economic depression, jobs are few and far between. Disability and shell shock are real, and battle fatigue is taking its toll on their bodies and souls.

Three years after the end of the war, Violet Grave's friend, Hank Convoy, is one of these vets struggling to survive. With a grandmother and a disabled sister to support, he takes whatever odd jobs he can get. But like Violet, he's a product of Jazz Age youth culture, so most of what he earns goes toward cards and bootleg liquor.

To add to his troubles, he's arrested on suspicion of murdering an army buddy found in the alleyway near his house.

Violet begs her older sisters, Eve and Helena, to help prove Hank killed out of self-defense and not cold-blooded murder.

Will the sisters solve this confusing case based on cigar ash, a missing revolver, and some missing jewelry? And what about the witness who left the marks of a strange pair of shoes in the dirt the night it happened?

What to expect in this book:
    • You'll get to know Daniel Frazer, the Moody County D.A., a lot better than in the first two books of the series.
    • You'll meet a couple of new people in town, including a forensics expert trained in fingerprinting and a lady lawyer.
    • Oliver, the Gyver County D.A., will take more of a backseat in the story, as he's following his own case and dealing with a rather obnoxious father-in-law!

Get a copy of *A Weekend Getaway Murder* on preorder <u>here</u> https://tammayauthor.com/a-weekend-getaway-murder-grave-sisters-mysteries-book-3 Still need to create website book link.
    Did you know I also have another series featuring a sassy and sensitive female sleuth who helps the local police solve

crimes? The setting for this series predates the Grave Sisters Mysteries by about twenty years but it's a lot of fun! Read onward to see how you can get a free book to start off this series!

Hatfield and Jackson immediately took their positions as lawmen. Jackson used the Abberton's phone to summon Deputy Assistant Edison and other deputy assistants while Hatfield calmed people down and requested everyone stay where they were. Adele joined the Abbertons, leaving Lady Augusta in Nin's care.

Mr. Abberton was holding back Freddie McCarthy, who looked more curious than distressed. "I think she only fainted."

"Take her upstairs," Sheriff Hatfield ordered.

"I'll find Dr. Rhodes," Adele said.

Finding Dr. Rhodes, whom she had seen earlier devouring the *hor d'oeuvres*, proved easier said than done. She finally located him sifting through an abandoned bucket of champagne bottles.

"Doctor, there's been an accident," she began.

"I can see that." He continued searching the bottles. "That man said there was an 1862 here somewhere —"

"An accident in need of a doctor's assistance," she said.

"Smelling salts revive one from fainting spells, as I'm sure even you know, Miss Gossling."

"It may be more serious than a fainting spell," she insisted.

He looked at her with mock amusement. "Are you claiming you have medical expertise now as well as police detection?"

"I know when a woman needs help, doctor," she said.

He went back to searching the champagne bottles. "I'm sure a phone call to Mr. Sanders will do the trick."

Adele lost her temper. "Why should I waste time calling your assistant when you're already here? This may be a party, Dr. Rhodes, but you are still obliged to fulfill the duty of your profession, just as the sheriff and my brother are fulfilling theirs."

The man gave her a sniveling look, but went into the hall and came back with his doctor's bag. "You see, Miss Gossling, I am always fulfilling the duty of my profession, even for swooning females."

She managed to hold her tongue as she led him upstairs.

They found Mis McCarthy in her room still unconscious. Around her were the Abbertons, Sheriff Hatfield and Jackson. Freddie McCarthy kept tiptoeing toward the bed, peering at his sister.

Jackson took Adele's side as the doctor examined the young woman. "Your friend took Lady Augusta home," he said. "We thought it best." He took her hand. "You ought to go home too, Del. I'm sure Tomas is standing at the open doorway, rubbing his hands, and fretting like a mother hen."

"I think I ought to stay." Adele glanced at Mrs. Abberton. She had expected the woman to be calm, as she imagined she had seen many young ladies faint and looked upon it as little more than a social embarrassment. But Mrs. Abberton was staring down at the girl, her eyes wide and her lips parted. Adele put her arm around the woman's shoulders, guiding her into a chair.

The doctor closed his bag. "You've once again misjudged your powers of observation, Miss Gossling." He cast a stony eye toward her. "Miss McCarthy is merely in a swoon." He looked at Mr. Abberton. "You've spirits of ammonia in the house, I take it?"

"Freddie." Mr. Abberton summoned the boy. "Go and get the bottle marked SPIRITS OF AMONIA out of the cabinet in my study. Here's the key."

"I don't mind." The boy scurried away.

"What caused it, doctor?" asked Mr. Abberton.

Dr. Rhodes threw up his hands. "Who knows what excuses young ladies find for their fainting spells? A tight corset, perhaps."

"That seems likely." The man nodded. "Miss McCarthy is most conscientious about her appearance." He glanced at his wife as if to confirm this. Mrs. Abberton, still startled, nodded.

"Or perhaps she was trying to gain attention." The doctor rose. "It's not uncommon in ladies her age."

"It may not be uncommon," Adele said in an icy tone. "But neither is it necessary for the guest of honor at a large party to feign a swoon to gain attention. If anything, I should think she would have avoided it in order not to draw more attention to herself."

The doctor handed Mr. Abberton a box. "Here's a sedative as well. When she decides she's had enough of this game, you may allow her to take one." He gave a sweeping nod to the room. "I bid you all good night and trust you won't need my services again this evening. Or, shall I say, this morning?"

"You might at least say Happy New Year," Adele mumbled.

He gave her a sour look as he left the room.

Freddie came in with a small bottle. He handed it to Mr. Abberton and retreated to the corner next to Adele. "Why do doctors have to be so awful?" he whispered.

"Not all of them are awful," Adele promised. "Dr. Rhodes is an exception."

"I wouldn't worry, son." Jackson patted him on the back.

"I'm not worried," said the boy cheerfully. "I want to see how long before Eleanor wakes up. Once she went into a faint for five hours!"

Mr. Abberton held the bottle out to his wife. "You ought to do it, Hester. She might be more comforted to wake up to a woman's face."

Mrs. Abberton's hands gripped the arms of her chair. Adele stepped forward. "I'll do it, sir, if you'll permit me."

"My sister worked alongside nurses and doctors in San Francisco's settlement houses," Jackson added. "She knows what she's doing."

The man glanced at his wife, then handed Adele the bottle.

She couldn't help but think Freddie was right, as she barely had time to open the bottle when the girl's eyes flew open. Unlike other women Adele had seen coming out of a swoon, Miss McCarthy's gaze was clear and focused. "Why, what a lot of people!"

"You fainted, dear," Mr. Coldwell said.

"Did I?" Her hand flew to her head, as if checking that the pins and combs were still in place.

"You're all right, aren't you?" Mrs. Abberton spoke softly. "You're really all right?"

"Of course I'm all right." The girl was indignant.

"You gave us all a bit of a fright," the sheriff said.

Miss McCarthy sat up. "I didn't mean to. It was so close in that room."

"Yes," said Mrs. Abberton. "Yes, that was it. That must have been it."

"Freddie, run and tell Mrs. Wells to make a strong cup of coffee and bring it here," said Mr. Abberton. "As quickly as you can."

"Coffee!" Miss McCarthy laughed. "Heavens, no! I haven't had my first taste of champagne yet." She flung her hand out to her brother. "Bring me a bottle of champagne, my good man."

"I don't mind," he said.

Before he could saunter out the door, Mrs. Abberton jumped up. "I'll get it."

"I really think we ought to get coffee," Mr. Abberton mumbled.

"She wants champagne," Mrs. Abberton was almost stern. "It's a celebration, after all!" She practically fled from the room.

Adele followed her and caught her arm. She spoke in a soft tone. "Mrs. Abberton, why did Miss McCarthy faint?"

"She just told you, didn't she?" The woman gave a shrill laugh. "Albert said we ought to open some windows, but it was such a windy night, I —"

"It wasn't the windows," said Adele. "Or the corset."

"Of course it was!" The woman examined some bottles on the floor. "I never could read these labels."

"You were staring at Miss McCarthy as if something more was wrong."

"What an imagination you have, dear," the woman said.

"Miss McCarthy had her hands on her throat when she fell," Adele continued. "You were looking at her throat."

"Nonsense," the woman hissed.

"I noticed she wasn't wearing her ruby necklace," Adele declared.

Mrs. Abberton tore through a row of bottles lying on a table.

One rolled onto the floor with a crack and the bubbly drink spilled across the marble. She sunk into one of the chairs. "You've always been very observant, Miss Gossling."

"You saw it too."

"Just before the lights went out," she said. "But Eleanor is one of those girls who gets easily flustered with her jewelry. She says it weighs her down."

"If that's true, why were you so alarmed?" Adele asked.

"I wasn't," the woman insisted. "She has a locked box for that necklace. Albert tried to persuade her to put it in our safe, but she refused."

"That's rather unusual," Adele said.

"Eleanor's a lovely girl, but rather flighty," the woman said in a harsh tone. "I expect Celestine spoils her."

"If the necklace is missing, there might be a theft involved," Adele suggested.

Jewelry goes missing all the time. But does that mean theft? And why is Mrs. Abberton so nervous?

How can you get your hands on a copy of *The Missing Ruby Necklace*, not available in any bookstore? Simple. Go to this link: https://landing.mailerlite.com/webforms/landing/ l2u0c3. What else will you get when you get this novella? How about fun facts about women in history and true crime classic mysteries, which are just as fascinating, if not more so, as contemporary true crimes?

ABOUT THE AUTHOR

Writing has been Tam's voice since the age of fourteen. She writes stories set in the past featuring sassy, sensitive women characters. Readers experience in her books women struggling to carve out an identity for themselves during eras when their options were limited. Her stories are set mostly around the Bay Area because she adores sourdough bread, Ghirardelli chocolate, and San Francisco history.

Tam is the author of the Adele Gossling Mysteries, which takes place in the early 20th century and features suffragist and epistolary expert Adele Gossling, whose talent for solving crimes doesn't sit well with her small town's conventional ideas about women. Tam also has a new series, the Grave Sisters Mysteries, about three sisters who own a funeral home and help the county D.A. solve crimes in a 1920s small California town.

Tam also writes historical fiction about women breaking loose from the social and psychological expectations of their time. She has a 4-book series set in the 1890s, the Waxwood Series, and a post-World War II short story collection, *Lessons From My Mother's Life*.

Although Tam left her heart in San Francisco, she lives in the Midwest because it's cheaper. When she's not writing, she's devouring everything classic (books, films, art, music), concocting yummy plant-based dishes, and exploring her new riverside town.

Tam May can be reached at:
   WEBSITE: http://tammayauthor.com/
   EMAIL: tammay70@tammayauthor.com
   FACEBOOK: https://www.facebook.com/tammayauthor
   INSTAGRAM: https://www.instagram.com/tammayauthor/
   PINTEREST: https://www.pinterest.com/tammayauthor/

www.ingramcontent.com/pod-product-compliance
Lightning Source LLC
Chambersburg PA
CBHW031325210726

48287CB00005B/1703